THE QUEST FOR GLORY

The Captured Girl: Book Two

By

Tom Reppert

Copyright © 2024 Tom Reppert
All rights reserved

ISBN: 979-8-9851639-4-0

Helen's Son's Publishing
Sagle, ID

PART ONE
THE BIG DIE-UP

CHAPTER ONE

Lone Tree, Montana Territory, March 18, 1887

As the twenty men and one woman rode hard up the valley hell-bent on catching cow thieves, they passed through a nightmare landscape. The rotting carcasses of cattle lay scattered on the mud and wet grass and patches of snow left from the worst winter anyone could remember. The smell of death hung thick in the air. During the endless blizzards and minus fifty-degree temperatures, the poor beasts had packed up on the banks of frozen streams straining for water they couldn't get to, wandered into coulees searching for warmth that wasn't there, and often just froze to death where they stood.

The thaw had finally begun earlier this month, revealing countless thousands of dead steers. Maybe millions, young Billy Baker thought. People said bodies lay on the open range all the way to Miles City and beyond.

As they rode in a bunched-up pack, the horses' hooves pounding on the mud sounded like hollow thunder. The riders wore bandanas over their faces to ease the stench, but for Billy it did little good. The smell still got inside him, filled his chest, clogged his throat. For the rest of his life, he didn't think he'd ever get that stench out of him. He knew damn sure he'd never get the sight of all these dead steers out of his mind. More than once this day, he feared he'd spill the contents of his stomach.

Last year, fresh out of a Philadelphia dental college and harboring dreams of Billy the Kid, wild Indians, and trail drives, he'd come west to be a cowboy. Now, he wished he'd never left Pennsylvania. The chase party had been formed in Lone Tree just a few hours before when Texas Jack Carlyle, a hand at the Bar T, rushed into town to report he'd seen several men driving steers north out of the valley. He was sure they were stolen cows. Ranchers meeting at the Grange Hall formed the party and rode out after them. The idea of chasing bandits excited Billy, so he'd gone with them.

Approaching a ridgeline, the woman leading held a hand up, slowing the party to an easy trot. The sun had fallen behind the Absaroka Mountains, and twilight was upon them. With a distinct chill in the air, he pulled out his plaid coat from his bedroll, worked it on, and wondered if she was giving up, then doubted it. Not her.

Billy's boss Clive Dunford, the second son of the Earl of Wexham and supposed personal friend of the Prince of Wales, clucked his horse up beside her. His knee length black boots were spattered with mud. His long barreled French hunting rifle lay across his saddle horn, his fingers holding tightly to it. A thick lock of black hair stuck to his forehead like it had been painted on. He didn't take to orders coming from anyone let alone a woman. Surely not this one. Not Morgan Raines.

Those two hated each other, having fallen out a year ago over his nibs' contract with the government to provide five hundred cows to the Cheyenne Indian Reservation on the Tongue River. After the money was paid, less than a hundred of said cows showed up. The agent couldn't get the money back since Dunford swore to a district judge he'd brought five hundred head to the delivery point. The authorities should look to the agent himself for the discrepancy.

People in the valley were split on the matter, but the Raines woman wasn't. Right in Lone Tree's Delmonico Steak House while Dunford was eating lunch with his wife, the woman called him a thief to his face and dumped a bucket of cow manure and blood on his fancy new suit. His wife toppled over her chair scrambling out of the way. As the Raines woman strode from the establishment, Dunford had screamed obscenities at her. People talked about it for weeks.

Apparently, her actions had not truly surprised anyone. Billy couldn't understand her fury though till he remembered she'd lived with those same Cheyenne Indians herself and as some said was still more Indian than white.

The worst bone of contention between them was the death of Dunford's son Louis later that same night in a fire at the Englishman's house, which he blamed on the woman. Had it not been for Morgan Raines's actions, Dunford would have been at home to save him. It changed his nibs. He'd been a friendly sort, everyone's pal, but now he was a cold fish taken with sudden bursts of temper. Baker preferred the earlier rendition of the man but suspected this one was truer to his nature.

The dentist turned cowboy listened in as Dunford spoke to her now, "We are too close to the trees, madam. You must see that. Your brigands could be hiding there. A fair shot might bring down several of us. It is the essence of good sense to move our party farther away."

Mrs. Raines sat her horse silently for so long that his nibs began to twist in his English saddle. Then she turned to him and said evenly, "Those *brigands* are several miles away. Besides, four men ambushing twenty is not exactly a smart play. But if you're scared, your highness, you're welcome to ride off on your own."

Dunford's back stiffened. About to reply, he shook his head in disgust and jerked his reins so violently his horse squealed. He moved back beside Billy. No one liked a man who treated horse flesh like that. Young Billy wondered if all English lords were like him.

In the mud, the tracks of the cow thieves were easy enough to follow. Even he could do it though he'd only been in the West a year. But the woman said there were thirty head of cattle or there abouts, and just four men. With all the hoof prints jumbled together, he didn't know how she could determine that, but everyone accepted it as gospel.

At the ridgeline, she ordered them to halt. "We'll be here for a while," she said.

A few of the men dismounted and rolled cigarettes. Some nibbled on hard tack. Others sat in their saddles and waited. They followed her orders without reservation.

The woman rode a tough little roan mustang, which pretty much described her, small and tough. Also, she was pretty and not too old, Billy thought, late twenties, maybe thirty. She wore a hat with a flat crown. Her auburn hair fell from it in a single ponytail. Above her bandana, her eyes were steel grey like the twilight sky.

Mrs. Raines had a half-breed son named Seamus, just fifteen, who was now out tracking the rustlers by himself. His own mother sending him to do such a dangerous thing. It was said she'd given him birth while living with the Cheyenne. Quite the story and he knew it well enough. Known as *The Captured Girl*, she'd been famous once. When he was a boy, Billy had even read dime novels about her. Morgan O'Connor was her name then. They said she'd killed more than twenty men, white and Indian alike.

While twilight held, Morgan studied the landscape for movement, expecting her son back soon. Seamus had been out ahead of them for an hour now. She had little worry about him on his own. He was nearly as good a tracker as she and capable with a gun. Her focus was on the pursuit. Cattle thieves, rustlers, she hated them. You spend years of sweat, on the cattle, most of the time barely breaking even, and these outlaws come along and in one go, steal what's yours. It puts your families at risk. Her jaw clenched. She wished she could shoot them all.

Uncle Frank Templeton came up beside her, the bandana down about his neck revealing his square face with his thick gray mustache and stubble of beard. He had a weary look about him. She supposed they all did. These were not good times. Though everyone called him

Uncle Frank, he was the actual uncle of her brother Conor's wife Dora, and she was the only family Frank had left. Their ranches now operated as one.

"You worried about Seamus?" he asked.

"Yes, but not in this work. He's equal to it. With him, I'm more worried about other things than this."

"He's at that age, Morgan," he said. "He's just trying to figure out who he is. Being a breed makes it harder. Hell, I haven't figured it out yet and I'm not a breed."

The hint of a smile showed in the crinkle of her eyes. "Well, he doesn't seem to need my help anymore."

Uncle Frank leaned forward, resting his hands on his pommel. "He will. Don't worry, he will. He'll be fine. He's a good lad."

She gave a curt nod. A quarter of a mile off, she saw maybe two hundred dead cows along a barbed wire fence as if some giant hand had strewn them there. In the desperate cold, they'd wandered up to it and bunched against the fence. Nowhere else to go, they died. The odor was strong here. She pinched her nose then gave up.

Following her gaze, Uncle Frank lifted his bandana. After a minute, he said with a catch in his voice, "This die-up will finish most of the ranchers."

There'd been such a demand for beef that the years of '83, '84, and '85 had been remarkable for cattlemen. Everyone made money. Nobody, including her, could see an end to it.

Many others, rich New Yorkers, wealthy British, and even a Frenchman or two threw in speculating on the cattle boom. They bought land and brought in cows by the hundreds of thousands and set them out on the open range. Too many for the grass, and now she had fears her family wouldn't survive the bust, the Die-up. She had led them to this folly. That settled like scalding water in her bones. The boom was over. That much was clear. Everybody was trying to keep afloat. And the damn rustlers were picking at their bones.

Morgan knew he was actually asking her a question. Were she and her husband Will finished and therefore Uncle Frank as well?

She didn't answer him because she didn't know. Right now, Will and Conor were out trying to find what herd they had left after the killing winter. Already, they knew it would not be many.

A grin suddenly flashed on Uncle Frank's face. "We had some good times though while it lasted, didn't we, Morgan?"

Morgan thought about it. Yes, they'd had good times indeed. The first image that lodged in her head was Conor's wedding. That was a day. He'd struggled in white society after his time with the Cheyenne. Younger than her when captured, he'd lived with them longer. One of the few people he found he could talk to was Dora Templeton. Last year just after his twenty-third birthday, they married on the Templeton Ranch, and Uncle Frank threw one hell of a shivaree for them afterward in town.

Glancing at him, she drew down her bandana and grinned. "We sure as hell did, and we will again."

They laughed, and the other cowboys must have thought them mad.

The day of Conor's wedding had dawned cold but with a cloudless sky that was breathless in its heady enormity. He and Dora had held off till after the fall roundup, and then Dora broke her leg tumbling off a ladder in her barn. Morgan had long known the girl was a bit on the clumsy side. Still on crutches into November, she wanted the deed done so the wedding was scheduled for the next week. Morgan's gift to them was a Bible with the date marked inside the flap. *Conor O'Connor and Dora Templeton wedding, November 11, 1886.*

Just before eleven that morning in the Templeton ranch house, she took Dora still on her crutches upstairs to get her into the wedding gown. It was a beige, taffeta dress that her Uncle Frank had ordered all the way from Marshal Fields in Chicago. She was a rawboned girl bigger than most, blond haired, and always ready to put in a hard day's work. Her hands trembled so much she couldn't hook or button anything. The guest gathering outside could be heard, noisy and raucous as if it were a roping contest.

"Calm down, Dora," Morgan told her. "You said this is what you wanted since the day Conor came home. Now, you have it. Conor loves you. I can tell you if you didn't marry him, he'd never marry."

The girl fell silent for several seconds as Morgan finished buttoning the front. "Morgan," she said tentatively, "do you think he ever scalped anyone?"

Shocked, Morgan stepped back. "Goodness, you worried he's going to scalp you in your sleep?"

"No, no, I'm not worried about that. I just always wondered. After all, he lived with the Indians longer than even you, and you… you're…." She didn't finish, looking down at her white shoes. What was the girl about to say? That Morgan went about killing people?

She didn't answer, and after a moment, Dora muttered, "I do love him so."

At noon, ready to get married, the bride made her way downstairs. Morgan saw her eleven-year-old daughter Glory waiting for them at the bottom and felt a sudden surge of warmth. Growing like a cornstalk, she already stood two inches over five feet, tall and lanky like her father who was halfway past six feet. The girl's reddish auburn hair fluttered as the freckles across her nose bunched with her distressed expression. "Oh, my Lord, Dora," she exclaimed. "Hurry! Get out of that ugly old thing and put on your wedding dress. The preacher's waiting."

Nearly in tears, Dora's face crumpled in horror. Glory broke into a wide grin that usually dazzled people, but Morgan snapped, "Young lady, you apologize. Look what you've done."

Glory sighed but grabbed Dora's hand. "Aunt Dora, I was just funning. Don't you know that? Why, you're the prettiest thing I've ever seen."

Straightening up and smoothing her dress, Dora said sharply, "Yes, yes, very funny, Glory. You had me going."

Morgan scowled as she walked past her daughter. "Get to your place."

With the day so sunny, the ceremony happened outside as planned. Conor and Dora stood on the porch in front of the preacher with two hundred or so neighbors, cowboys, and towns people in attendance. Uncle Frank beamed with delight. Seamus, Morgan's oldest boy, was best man and Glory one of the bridesmaids. Morgan was proud of her children, looking smart in their Sunday best.

She took her place beside her husband Will. She seldom cried, but for this she did. Six years of her life had been spent attempting to find Conor among the Cheyenne, and now here he was being married on the Templeton's front porch. As she sobbed, Will slid his one arm around her.

Afterward, as the throng cheered, Conor carried Dora over the threshold into the house. Then, everyone rushed to town for the shivaree.

That evening saw reel after reel danced, whiskey and beer flow, and only a few fights. While Seamus stayed on, nervous about sparking Alice Olson, a nearby rancher's daughter, Morgan left the Grange Hall at ten with Glory, riding in the back of a hay-strewn wagon. As instructed, Teddy Pike, one of her cowhands, drove. A hunter's moon hovered amid a brilliant starfield, and the air was so fresh Morgan could taste pine and cedar on it.

Before they got out of town, Pike began to sing *Beautiful Dreamer*, and Glory clapped excitedly. The cowboy was famous throughout Montana Territory for his singing voice and his good nature. Everyone liked Teddy Pike. His squeaky laugh was infectious, and he had a sociable way about him. Glory had a girlish infatuation with him and told him they'd get married someday. He winked at Morgan, placed his hand over his heart, and said earnestly to the girl, "I look forward to that day, Miss Raines."

Pike serenaded them all the way home.

That was the last good day. The next day, it began snowing.

Memories of last November's snowfall led Morgan down a path of stark images. Blizzards one after another, endless fields of white, temperatures so low that an early calf dropped out of its mother's womb froze to death before it hit the snow. It all bottomed out in the tragedy facing her now, facing all of them. The end of their way of life. If that happened, her family might break apart, and that she could not abide. Whatever came to pass, her Bow String Ranch had to survive.

Morgan's thoughts returned to the present. In the last of the twilight, she caught the movement of a rider coming out of the trees a hundred yards away. A couple men drew their rifles.

"Hold up," Morgan told them. "That's my son."

It was spoken pleasantly enough, but no one missed the warning in it.

Seamus drew up in front of his mother. Though half white, the boy looked Indian with long black hair, his bandana folded and tied about his forehead to hold it in place. His strange eyes always startled people. They were different colors, one pale gray and the other a brown so dark it resembled carbon. That one gray eye seemed to be Morgan's only contribution to his appearance. Otherwise, he was all Spotted Horse, her first husband.

He did wear his stepfather's old cavalry jacket, though, but the coppery skin gave his half-breed status away. As was often the case, he didn't seem to fit in either the white or the Cheyenne worlds, but he did fit in Morgan's. He knew he was loved, and he'd once told her that was enough for him. These days though, it didn't always seem to be. More and more lately, he'd become sullen and withdrawn.

Dunford and the cowboys gathered around them.

"They're in the trees three miles ahead," the boy said. "They're settled. They even got themselves a fire going. The cattle are blocked off in a small coulee near the camp."

"Then we have them," Dunford announced, drawing his pistol, and looking at them all. "Why are we waiting? We must attack now. Surprise is the thing."

Frank snorted. "This ain't Piccadilly, guv. We don't need no parades." He turned to Morgan. "How you figure we go at them?"

"You, me, and Seamus will take them," Morgan said. "I'll fire a single shot, and then the rest of you come up."

They didn't like that plan. They shifted about, exchanging glances among themselves.

She stared hard at them. "I know you boys can handle yourselves., but too many of us will give them warning. People could get killed that don't have to. If there's killing to be done, we'll do it."

Mollified, several nodded, then with a sick look, Seamus said, "Ma, Teddy Pike is one of them."

CHAPTER TWO

Lone Tree, Montana Territory, March 18, 1887

Cold coming with the dark, Morgan pulled on her sheepskin coat and set her horse out at an easy walk, Seamus by her side. The other men, even Dunford, fell in behind by twos. She'd been saddened to learn Teddy Pike was among the thieves. She liked Teddy and had kept him on over the winter as a line rider though there was not much for him to do for the cattle. Stealing from her was a betrayal, and it couldn't be countenanced. He'd pay a hard price for it. Her feelings for him made it harder to do what was right, but it would not stop her. Teddy chose his path.

A half hour later, they reached a small creek running fast in the spring runoff. The glow of the outlaws' campfire could be seen through the set of trees a quarter of a mile up into the foothills. Leaving the other men with Carlisle, Morgan hiked on foot alongside the creek with Frank and Seamus. The rush of water masked the older man's heavy footsteps. When they closed to thirty yards, they knelt just outside the firelight.

The night was silent but for the muttering of the outlaws' voices and the stamp of their horses tied to a nearby alder tree. She saw four men by the fire, two of them curled in blankets and two sitting on their saddles, passing a bottle back and forth. One of these was Teddy Pike.

"No guard," she whispered barely above a sigh of wind.

Frank shook his head. "Damn brazen."

"Damn stupid," Seamus mouthed.

The man sitting with Pike had on a bright red shirt and a yellow bandana like he was just fresh from the east. He sported several days growth of beard and long, shaggy brown hair. Morgan had never met the man but knew of him, Diamond Joe Sweet, a gambler and known thief. His hat hung on the saddle pommel beside him along with his holster and pistol. After a quick swallow of rye, he handed the bottle to Pike, who took a long pull and belched loudly.

"Damn, Pike you got no manners at all," Sweet said in mock disbelief, taking back the bottle as it glinted odd patterns of light from the fire.

"Sure, I do. I'm collecting them for some day when I'm in the right company."

"Why, I'm affronted by that," Sweet said as if angry, then chuckled. "I'm saving my manners for some pretty piece of calico. Be plenty of fluff we get these damn cows sold."

Seamus exchanged a glance with Morgan. The boy had ridden herd with Pike on many occasions and drank his first beer in town at Rosa's with him. His look asked the question about somehow getting the cowboy out of this. She gave no hint of her thoughts, which was the answer he understood. They would not be letting him go.

In the warmth of the campfire, Teddy Pike was feeling drunk, and he was in a good mood. After that bitter winter in which he nearly froze his pickle solid every time he'd relieved himself, he wanted to strike out for warmer territory, like maybe hell itself. Now, he'd have just enough money to do it. He had a brother in California and thought he might go there.

"I'm headed for Miles City," Pike told Sweet the easy lie. "Lay low for a while."

"Not too low," Sweet replied. "There's money to be made. Lot of strays on the range, those that didn't die up, free for the taking. We can make ourselves rich."

"Don't want to push my luck."

Sweet leaned forward and pointed a finger at Pike. "We push it far as I say. Tomorrow, we get started before dawn. I want to be out of this valley before these *farmers* get onto us."

That was the worst word to call a rancher, and he could imagine how Mrs. Raines would react to it. You were either a rancher or a farmer, and in these parts, they were not farmers.

Pike held up the bottle and looked at it. "Fine by me, but I ain't going to be too spry in the morning I drink anymore of this swill."

"You can get yourself spry when we get this here herd sold," Sweet replied.

Pike nodded but didn't tell him this would be his one and only time rustling. He'd made sure none of the cows belonged to the Raines's Bow String Ranch, so he didn't feel he'd stepped too far onto the outlaw trail. Now, he'd be gone out of the territory as soon as he got his cut.

Suddenly, Sweet gave a sharp squeak, and both men jumped. A woman stood not five feet away as if a magician put her there. Auburn hair fell in a ponytail from under a wide-brimmed hat, fierce grey eyes fixed on them. Her rifle muzzle was not exactly aimed their way but still poised to shoot.

Pike moaned because he knew who it was. Mrs. Raines. Her reputation was that she could shoot all four of them before they could spit and wouldn't blink an eye doing it. He'd seen her bring down an elk from three hundred yards. And this was no three hundred yards. He'd have to be at his affable best to talk himself out of this one.

The other man held up one hand. "Whoa there, Missy. We ain't got no cash if you stopped by to rob us. We're just poor cowboys with a tiny little herd and a bunch more cowboys off there in the woods night-hawking them. Sit yourself down a spell." He smiled without humor. "We sure don't mind visitors."

"Shut up. Do not move," she said.

Her voice froze Sweet in place, one hand in the air, the other by his saddle. An instant later, he brought up his pistol. Morgan fired and blew out a chunk of meat, bone, and blood from his forearm. His gun went flying.

"The bitch shot me!" he screamed. "The bitch shot me!"

The other two men in blankets rose up startled. One, a man with white hair, grabbed for his carbine, but Seamus clubbed him with the barrel of his pistol. "Easy, old timer," the boy said. "I don't want to shoot you."

The old man grimaced, rubbing his head, and stared hard at Seamus. "Damn, Injun. I thought we killed all you."

Just then a wild commotion came from the trees and a few seconds later, the other men crashed through on horseback, their pistols out, then pulled up, seeing the outlaws taken.

Dismounting, Carlisle joined Morgan at the fire. "Dunford's gone, ma'am. His nibs said he was going to surprise attack the outlaws, and if any man had any bravery, they'd come along. None did. So, with just him and the boy, he foregoed his surprise attack and just rode off cursing us and you with some not so generous words."

"He's of no consequence," she said. "Right now, we have work to do."

"Yes, ma'am, I'd say we do."

Teddy called out, rushing his words together, "Ma'am, ma'am, Mrs. Raines, it's sure good you came along when you did cause this here isn't what it seems like."

"It's exactly what it seems like, Teddy," Morgan replied not unkindly.

Instantly, he shifted his attention to the men now dismounting their horses. "Boys, it's good to see you all. I'm in desperate straits here and need rescuing from these thieves. I think they stole the cattle back over there in the trees, and I was…"

"Shut up, Pike" the white-haired man said. "You're making me sick. You was in it from the get go."

"We know the right of it, Teddy," Carlisle said. "You done got yourself into this pickle on your own."

Carrying torches, two men returned from where the cattle grazed in a small coulee not twenty yards away. One of them said, "Best we can tell there are three brands, Lazy S, the Box C, and the Pitchfork."

Not her brand, Morgan thought, but next time it would be. No law but their own could handle the rustling problem. A couple years back Granville Stuart ran his vigilantes that people called the Stranglers. Carlisle had been one of them. They hung twenty or thirty men, but it didn't make much of a dint in the rustling problem. Every spring, men stole cattle, crippling the ranchers' ability to operate, and not a peace officer anywhere to be found.

"I'm getting the law on you, on all you bastards," Sweet screeched. "The sheriff up in Livingston's a friend of mine. You think you can turn me into the law, and I'm just going to sit quiet?" His face contorted in pain, and he held his arm tighter. "Damn, this hurts."

Carlisle leaned down toward him. "Don't worry, Pard. It ain't going to be hurting much longer."

"Get it done," Morgan said to Carlisle. She nodded toward a nearby Ponderosa Pine. "That ought to do it. Bring their horses over. Tie their hands."

"All of them?" Seamus asked. His voice sounded hard as the other men, but Morgan detected a small hitch in it. Pike was his friend.

"All of them," she replied.

The four men wailed and argued for a while, Teddy most of all, pleading for his life, but finally he gave up as hopelessness settled in.

Using the ropes from the thieves' saddles, Carlisle tied the nooses just right, explaining as he went how a bad noose wrongly placed could take an hour strangling a man. He'd seen that once and never wanted to see it again. He said to the thieves, "I promise you boys, it'll be quick."

Hands tied behind their backs, the four men had been propped onto their horses, nooses about their necks. Two of them were breathing so hard they sounded like blacksmith bellows. Sweet though, ignoring the pain, straightened his back.

Teddy sat upright as well. "Boys, you need not feel bad about me," he said. "I got myself in this predicament. You're just doing what needs doing." He gazed down at Morgan. "It's been a pleasure knowing you, ma'am." He chuckled. "Current situation notwithstanding. I'm sorry I let you down. Seamus, you've been a good pard. Next time you hoist a beer in Rosa's think of me." He gave a madhouse cackle. "At least, it will be warm where I'm going."

"For God's sake, can we get on with it?" Sweet shouted.

Morgan nodded and the men behind the horses slapped their rumps, and they shot away. Within seconds, all four men were swinging from the limb, dead. Carlisle had done his job well.

CHAPTER THREE

Lone Tree, Montana Territory, March 18, 1887

A mile off from Morgan Raines's vigilantes, Dunford split from Baker without a word, the young man heading south for Lone Tree and he north for Livingston. Anger still seethed within the Englishman as he pushed his horse hard. Earlier that bloody fool Baker had forgotten to relay an important message from Ben Mason, the Livingston banker, till just after the woman had gone off to catch the thieves herself.

Nervously, the boy had held out the telegram, saying in his whiny voice, "I'm sorry, sir. With all the excitement, I clean forgot. It came just before noon. It's from Mr. Mason."

Dunford snatched it from him. "Bloody hell, Baker, it's night. How am I supposed to read it?"

"It says, *Most urgent. Auditor here. Must meet at once.*"

That quickened Dunford's heart. He wadded the telegram and stuck it in his pocket. The team of auditors wasn't due for weeks but apparently, they were here now. That meant things had finally fallen apart. Ben Mason, the president of the Livingston Bank and Trust, had surely flown the country by now with his wife, leaving Dunford to face the wrath of their many victims. The two men had emptied the bank vaults with fraudulent loans, outright thievery, and false schemes that took in bankers, merchants, and ranchers as far away as Miles City. Mason could no longer mask the deception; the bank would fail. The doors would not open on Monday, and as soon as the auditor caught one look at the books, there'd be hell to pay.

These people would hang him, and that Raines woman would hold the rope. When Dunford was but six years old, his father brought him to London to watch the infamous Catherine Wilson hanged outside Newgate prison. They'd been among thousands who'd packed into Old Bailey Street as the noose was placed around her neck. As the life was being choked out of her, excitement spilled through his little body. He saw his own thrill reflected on other people's faces, including his father's. He was sorry he had to miss the hanging of the cow thieves, but he had no desire for himself to face the Newgate drop and become *the man with a wry mouth and pissing pair of breeches*. And because of the message from Baker, that was what would happen if he didn't now flee this infernal country.

The night was filled with stars that cast enough light for him to see ahead. Though he had a three-hour ride through dangerous country, he was not concerned. The land he knew well enough, and he feared no attack from beast or human alike. His ability with a pistol and rifle was well known. He'd dispatched two men in tavern duels that had given him a measure of fame. For some reason, though, he was dubbed the Authentic English Bob, though his name was not even Robert. Who could explain the American mind?

When his horse began to labor, Dunford eased up on him. He couldn't risk not reaching home, and he had far to go yet. As he rode, his mind inevitably drifted to his father, the honorable Earl of Wexham. The two hated each other. Then when he was seventeen, their relationship finally broke apart.. He'd just returned to Wexham from Mother Clap's bawdy house in London where he'd been staying for the last two weeks. His father was incensed. Clive had been expelled from Harrow for stealing. He had talked his way out of many petty crimes before but not this one. His hand had literally been caught in the pocket of the headmaster's waistcoat. The school had produced poets and prime ministers and now in Clive Dunford, a common footpad. It had brought unbearable shame onto the family.

This had been too much for the earl. He exiled his son from the family altogether and cut him off from any allowance. He would no longer pay for a son who was a wastrel, a gambler, and a punter. It was time for him to make his own way in the military or the clergy or as a catamite, for all he cared. The money destined for Clive would now be added to that maintaining the earldom and the heir, his older brother Harold.

Neither the military nor the clergy appealed to Dunford and being seventeen indeed made him a target for catamites. This didn't appeal to him either, so he found himself on his own in London, living by his wits, gambling, and carrying out petty dodges. Early on, he learned there was unlimited money to be had if he could just find a way to avail himself of it.

A few months into his exile, starving, living in the attic of a St. Giles brothel, Dunford did the unthinkable. He saved a man's life. When he saw the drunk stumble out of a Covent Garden tavern late one night, a broad-shouldered bulldog of a man, Dunford followed him with unfriendly intent. He formed a simple plan, club him with a cudgel, steal his purse, and flee. But quick as a bear trap, someone else got there first, another assailant who knocked the mark to the cobblestones. They struggled as the thief tried to rifle his victim's pockets. The thief drew a knife, ready to finish his prey. Incensed this usurper was stealing his prize, Dunford rushed in and dropped him with a hard cudgel blow across the head, laying him out unconscious on the cobble stones.

The broad-shouldered man sat up, groaned, and rubbed his head. Dunford was stunned when he saw him draw out a knife and plunge it into the thief's throat. For several seconds, the man thrashed in a macabre dance of death, then was still.

That was when Dunford recognized the bulldog. It was Charlie Acker, the King of Thieves, leader of the notorious Black Alley Gang.

Taking a deep breath, he seized his chance. "Are you hurt, Mr. Acker?"

The crime boss stared up at him. "No, just full up to the knocker with good gin. Who the hell are you, lad?"

Dunford swept his cap off his head and bowed. "Clive Dunford, son of the Earl of Wexham, at your service."

The man glared at him, and Dunford worried he had appeared only a silly boy of no consequence.

"You are, are you?" Acker muttered, rubbing his head again. "Well, I'm Bonnie Prince Charlie."

Dunford extended his hand. "Honor to meet you, milord."

Acker took the hand and let Dunford pull him to his feet.

This meeting turned Dunford's fortunes. During the next few years, they became close friends and compatriots in crime. Dunford worked for him, mostly in the smuggling business while pursuing his own schemes and frauds. He had a knack for the dodge. People trusted him abd Acker backed him. That should have kept him flush, but his profligacies, women and gambling, had him barely breaking even. He had nowhere near with the riches he sought, wealth so great he'd never have another concern paying the next gambling bill.

In the smuggling runs to the Continent, he finally met Acker's partner, none other than than the famous copper Detective Sergeant Henry Hobbs of the Metropolitan Police. The man was sly and ruthless, and always pushing for more.

Dunford met the man the second time during the sordid affair when his sister-in-law was abducted. That was in the summer of 1881. Dunford's brother did something that could not be tolerated. Harold married. The bride was the beauteous Lady Maud Weatherby, daughter of the Marquis of Burnham. A perfect match, the society pages said. To make it worse, soon after the wedding, she was up the pole. Pregnant. This could not be. The child might well be a boy, and he would be two heirs from the earldom.

Dunford contacted Charlie Acker, who willingly took on the task for no money at all. Instead, he wanted future considerations. What that would be he wouldn't say. Dunford wanted the nasty work done so readily agreed. Poor Maud was snatched off the Strand in broad daylight by a gang of blackguards, so said the newspapers. The

Metropolitan Police's investigation, led by Detective Sergeant Hobbs, had no leads as to the kidnappers nor to her whereabouts.

Harold was frantic as was the earl and Maud's father the marquis, and, of course, Clive, who at his father's allowance, returned home to support his brother in this time of need. When DS Hobbs came up to Wexham to discuss the case with Harold and the family, Dunford finally saw the man. He looked more a stevedore than a copper, above average height, sturdy, with a square jaw and a craggy face, and full Prince Albert beard. With the men of the family gathered, he glanced at Clive once, held his gaze a second, then began his questioning. Of course, it was all sham. He knew exactly where Acker was keeping the woman. Hobbs explained the kidnappers would likely hold her for ransom.

It was a horror when the next day her naked body was found floating in the Thames.

The very week of Maud's funeral, Dunford discovered his path to the fabulous wealth he so desired. From the dailies, he became aware of the great cattle boom in America and at first dismissed it. What did he know or care about cows? But the news of it was everywhere. According to the *Fortnightly Review*, the boom was making more Englishmen rich than all the gold mines and diamond mines in the world and with little initial output of cash. Here was his chance. He gathered what money he could muster, including a sizeable loan from Acker again for future consideration, and in the spring of 1882, set off for America.

Since then, Dunford had married a New York wife, had a son, made, stole, and spent many fortunes, but now the jig was up. It was time to save his own hide as the Americans would say. In leaving Montana Territory, he had only one regret. Morgan Raines. His hate burned inside him like coal from the pits of Hell. She had arisen from the rabble with her wheedling pretentions of society, but those were easily shed like a snake's skin the moment she was challenged. Then, she would let loose her gutter ferocity, her true self laid bare for all to see.

The abominable incident in which she'd dumped a bucket of blood and cow shit over him in front of his wife and his friends was not to be borne. It had been the most despicable offense in his life. That act of defilement demanded retribution. Had she been alone, he'd have shot her on the spot and taken the consequences. But her half-breed boy was with her, and he had a rifle, in which it was said, he was expert. A chance gone abegging.

That night at his house, Dunford's rage exploded, turning over furniture, smashing flower vases, and crashing oil lamps to the floor. With this last, his wife had screamed as flames shot up the walls and drapes in the parlor. He tried to stifle them, but it was hopeless. The furniture lit up like kindling, and soon the entire house was ablaze.

Lydia shrieked, "Louis!"

The boy was upstairs asleep. Dunford dashed through the heat and smoke to the stairs, but they were already crumpling. He could not reach his boy. Backing away, he carried his wife outside to safety and watched the fire take his house and his son. He heard the boy screaming for him. He did nothing. He could do nothing.

It was Morgan Raines's fault. All of it. Had it not been for the woman shaming him that day, his son would yet be alive. She had killed the boy as if she'd taken a gun and shot him. In the abyss of his great agony, he swore *like for like, eye for an eye, a life for a life*. Morgan's daughter for his son. Life would not be put right until that girl lay dead at the woman's feet, and she felt the same loss he had this night. Then he would only be satisfied when he saw that woman's head grinning in a glass jar.

Three hours later, Dunford reached Livingston and rode across the railroad tracks into town. Raucous noise spilled out from saloons down at the end of Main Street. As he passed Mason's bank, he could just barely read the sign in the starlight, *Livingston Bank and Trust*. The words underneath were too small to make, out but he knew them: *Your money is safe with us*.

He chuckled. It never was.

He passed through town, heading northeast over the prairie grass, three more miles to his ranch. After the fire, he'd borrowed money to rebuild the house. It had taken several months, but it was once again as it had been before. In the starlight, it looked like an English manor house with its mansard roof and dormer windows. Usually when he saw it after a long day at the racetrack or a two-week hunt with friends, he felt a swell of warmth and pride. Tonight, he felt only dread. He and his wife must return to Livingston by midnight to catch the eastbound train.

He almost cheered when he entered the house and saw his wife Lydia waiting for him, dressed and packed. She was not much to look at but she smart and completely devoted to him. They made the train with minutes to spare. Before leaving, Dunford made sure the station master would remember him. That was essential to his plan. He paid the man ten dollars to deliver the horses and buckboard to the livery and patted him on the back as if they'd been old friends, which they definitely had not. Then he boarded the train moments before it left the station.

Just past eight the following morning, they pulled into Billings where he instructed his wife to go on and wait for him at her father's house New York. Her eyes went wide with surprise, but she only nodded. Lydia was never one to question. He kissed her cheek with affection, grabbed his carpet bag and hunting rifle, stepped off the train.

Within half an hour, he'd bought a horse at the livery stable and provisioned himself at the mercantile. Then, he set out for Lone Tree. He had unfinished business with that vile woman, and he'd see it done before he quit the country.

CHAPTER FOUR

Montana Territory, March 21, 1887

I, Glory Raines, twelve now though everyone forgot my birthday, had an imagination that Lame Deer said flew with the birds. I didn't know whether that was good or bad, and the old bat wouldn't say. My imagination wanted me to live in a make-believe world, but I had too many dead brothers and sisters for that, and besides, ranch life was too hard to dream of princes and knights and heroes sweeping me off my feet.

I was not supposed to know what was going on with our money problems, but I did. That was why they forgot me, I figured, or maybe they just didn't care. The winter that took so many cattle from all us ranchers put every family in a bad way including us. I wasn't stupid. A cattle ranch that didn't have cattle was kind of pointless. What could we sell? The air? The clouds?

On a rainy Monday morning, draped in their slickers, their faces set stern as stone statues, the four men I loved most in the world, Papa, Uncle Conor, Uncle Frank, and Seamus, rode off to do battle with a ruthless foe, the Livingston bankers. Everyone was worried. Mama stood on the porch with Dora, shawls pulled tight around their shoulders, watching them go. That's when Lame Deer pulled the wagon up for me. While Seamus got to ride to Livingston with Papa, I had to go to school, even when it was raining. I didn't think it was fair even though I liked school and did well. Our teacher Miss

Cabbage Face said I could put words together like Mr. P. T. Barnum, whoever that was.

Yet, as I rode in the wagon huddled with Lame Deer against the wind and rain, I was a bit frightened. I knew there was a big hole in all this, something dark and damp and deep into which we all were about to fall.

After the men left, Morgan told herself the ranch would be fine. The winter may have taken much of their herd, but they had a substantial amount of cash in the bank, enough to bring in the new tougher stock Will wanted. Yet, she was still concerned. That was the nature of the cattle business. Disaster was always a day away.

By sundown, the men had not yet returned, and she tried to hide her worry from Glory and Dora, who were fussing around with dinner. Morgan stood at the side window, which had a view of the ridgeline. Just outside in the waning twilight, Lame Deer was taking down washing from the clotheslines, singing a Cheyanne wolf song said to have been learned from wolves themselves in the long ago. This one had a sweet melody that Morgan remembered. It was her favorite. The words of a girl to her suitor. "Put your arms around me. I am not looking."

She watched the old woman folding the clothing into a basket and felt a surge of warmth for her. In this, she had been lucky. She'd had three mothers, all loving, all strong. Her own true mam, who gave her strength and wisdom and life for her, then Owl Woman, who did the same, and finally Lame Deer, who possessed such resilience and unyielding determination. Morgan tried to let the warmth wash away the bad heart that had plagued her all day, but it couldn't.

This was, indeed, a bad day. Sixteen years ago, Big Crow and his Cheyenne war party raided this ranch and slaughtered her family. Outside was Lame Deer's melody, but inside Morgan's head were the gunshots and screams of that day. The bloody images of the slaughter filled up every part of her and the memories she'd held at bay since this morning overwhelmed her.

On the day the Cheyenne raided her family's ranch, fourteen-year-old Morgan O'Connor was hunting with Oscar Fernandez, their old handyman. Handy, he wasn't. Useless more like it. Her reputation as a sharpshooter had already spread through the territory, the little eagle-eyed girl from Lone Tree who could pop out the eye of a squirrel from a hundred yards. Mostly, she shot sage hen, rabbits, and wild turkeys to augment the family larder and to sell in the nearby town. That day she'd brought down a deer.

When the attack came, three Indians had veered off from the war party to chase after her and Oscar. The rest charged screaming toward the ranch. Fernandez died immediately, an arrow to the neck. Morgan sat her horse dumbstruck by panic, unable to move, but her mount Rhiannon had enough sense to race away, carrying her with him. When he too went down, hurling her to the ground, Morgan lay stunned. The three warriors were bearing down on her. Desperate to save her family, she finally shook from her stupor. A cold calm washed over her. She levelled the Winchester and rapidly shot all three.

Springing up, Morgan raced home, despair eating away at her, knowing she'd be too late. Over a slight rise, her ranch house appeared a few hundred yards away. Indians milled in front of her house, firing into it with bows and rifles. She saw two men lying on the ground, one next to the well and the other by the corral. Too far to see detail, she knew she was looking at the bodies of her father and brother Patrick.

Her mother, ten-year-old sister Fi, and eight-year-old brother Conor must still be inside. Finally, several Indians rushed the house, crashing through the door. One flew back out, and a half second later, Morgan heard the sound of the shotgun blast. More Indians swarmed into the house. Her heart was dying.

Her legs having the strength of putty, she fell hard to the ground, gasping for air. Slowly, she crawled out onto a stone ledge where she could make out more clearly the bodies of her father and brother

Patrick, stripped naked, mutilated, and scalped. Seeing them sent waves of nausea through her and she retched up her breakfast.

Moments later, when Conor and Fi were dragged out of the house, Morgan whispered, "Don't struggle. Don't struggle. Let them take you. I will find you."

Conor was lifted up to an Indian on horseback, but Fi still stood in the grip of the oddest man Morgan had ever seen, an Indian so massive across the shoulders that he looked like the side of a house with a head on it. This she would learn later was Big Crow. Amid the crowd of men around her sister, the man drew his club up and swung.

Morgan screamed, "No!"

They hadn't heard her in the cacophony of yelling. When she looked up, Big Crow was lifting Fi's beautiful hair into the air and screeching a war cry. The other Indians closed in around him, whooping over a ten-year-old girl. He leapt on his horse and Conor shifted to him.

She wanted to scream; she wanted to fire the rifle and shoot them all. If she did either, they'd catch her, and Conor would still be lost. As they rode away shrieking their war whoops, she lowered the rifle and raced down to the house, hoping her mother was somehow yet alive. She was, but only for a minute, enough time for to plead with Morgan to bring Conor and Fiona back.

Holding her scalped mother's hand, she promised she would, although Fiona was already dead. But Conor wasn't, and she whispered as her mother died, that she'd never stop till she herself was dead or he was back.

A few moments later, Big Crow's giant frame appeared just inside the doorway with several warriors close behind. In overwhelming panic, Morgan scrambled back against the wall.

Then he came at her.

Someone was speaking to her, and Morgan stifled a scream as the terrible images faded off. She blinked. She was on the porch and the door was open. Somehow, she'd come outside.

"Are you alright, Mama," Glory asked.

"Fiona?" Morgan whispered and blinked again. No, this was not Fiona but Glory. Fiona was gone. Her brilliant life ended by Big Crow all those years ago.

"No, Mama, it's me Glory. Are you alright?" the girl repeated. "You look like the mule kicked you in the head."

Morgan forced a smile. "I'm fine, honey." That's when she realized the men were here, riding down from the ridge. She called to Dora in the kitchen. "They're back."

Her sister-in-law rushed out to the porch, wiping her hands on her apron.

When the men rode in, there was not a smile on their faces, and Morgan understood the news was bad. Will cut off any questions. "We'll all talk tonight."

A few minutes later in their bedroom, his back to her, he gripped a basin on the dresser with his one hand, so tight he was spilling water. Leaning past him, she handed him a cloth. His brow furrowed in a concentration so intense she could see blood vessels on his temple throb. She helped him out of his shirt and let the silence stretch between them. That silence seemed to have physical substance. She didn't want to break it for she sensed breaking it would unleash a whirlwind of trouble.

When Will fumbled to rinse out the cloth, she closed her hand over his and took it. Stepping behind him, she rubbed down the nub of his left arm, his shoulders, and then his back.

Finally, he said, "The Templeton Ranch is done and maybe we are too. The Livingston Bank and Trust failed. Our money is gone. Uncle Frank wanted to shoot the banker at Rothstein Brothers, who held his lien and closed on it, then wanted to shoot himself."

There it was. Morgan gave a slight intake of breath but continued the cloth across his back. He went on to detail the devastation across the territory from Virginia City to Miles City as if everyone else going bust would make it easier for them. Ranches were going under, businesses were boarding up, and too many others lost everything. His telling it came out in short, harsh patches. The worst of it was

Uncle Frank, who used his Bar T as collateral to get loans from the Rothstein Brothers Bank to invest in a slaughtering plant in Billings of all things and then a feedlot way over in Wisconsin, which made no sense at all. They were Dunford's schemes, both baldfaced frauds, Will said, that had taken in many investors.

When Will fell silent, he was like a man only catching his breath. She knew he had not gotten the worst yet. "What else?"

He turned to face Morgan. His next words stunned her. "Ben Mason is dead," he said. "He shot himself right in front of his wife. He and Dunford were tied up in all sorts of shenanigans with the bank. That English bastard is nothing more than a common sharper."

Morgan stepped back, barely able to contain her fury with Dunford. "I should have shot that son of a bitch at Delmonico's."

He glanced over his shoulder at her, his face darkening. "Too late. Dunford's gone back to England. He got away with it all. Sherriff Conklin says he's hardly going to pursue him there, and after all, he says, the Englishman didn't hold a gun to anyone's head and make them put money in Mason's bank or invest in his schemes."

"He's a worthless, tax collecting fool."

"Here's the nub of it, Morgan. Our savings are gone. All of it. Just gone. There'll be no getting any of it back. I'd much rather have faced Crazy Horse again than tell you all this."

She placed her hand on his chest. "You're not to blame. If anyone, it's me. I pushed you and Conor to put the money in the bank."

He wrapped his arm around her. "No, Morgan, we all agreed on the bank. Conor and me both. And you sure as hell didn't bring the winter." He gave a genuine grin. "We're rich, don't you know? We have each other. We have the kids. We can sell the place and start over."

She balked at that. She did not want to sell the place. It was hers and too many of her family were buried here. The answer came as if it had been in her mind all along. She looked up at him. "I don't want to start over someplace else, Will. We've got too much blood and sweat in this ranch." Her voice grew intense. "You said the old ways are done, the open range is dead, that we need more land of our own and new breeds of cattle to survive this country. That costs hard money, which we don't have anymore. But you know I can get it."

With a long sigh, he closed his eyes. She saw that he knew what she meant. Her heart emptied at the thought of it. To earn the money needed, she'd have to leave them for months, maybe even a year or longer, and she dreaded being apart from the people she loved. She would not feel whole without Will, and it would be a Hell of loneliness without her children.

"You don't have to, Morgan. We'll get by."

"I do," she insisted with finality, and he didn't argue. Pulling his face down, she kissed him. "It's the only way. I love you, Will. I'm a lucky woman. And you're right. We are rich."

After supper, Will called a family meeting. They sat around the fireplace where a blaze warmed the room. He began, "As we all know, both ranches are in trouble. The winter took most of our herds and the banks our money. But we're not destitute. We've got enough cash on hand for a bit. We won't starve but we've got to figure out what to do."

Conor and Will went on to discuss the two ranches and what was needed to keep them going, which essentially was money and cattle, neither of which they had in great supply. All the while Uncle Frank remained silent, his face miserable, and his head bowed.

Like a hard winter storm, the realization that she would soon be leaving them laid waste to Morgan's thoughts. She studied each in turn, wanting to memorize facial expressions, a turn of phrase, gestures, all to carry with her like photographs when she left. By the fireplace, her old friend Lame Deer sat in the rocking chair, keeping the fire stoked. She puffed on her corncob pipe, not worried at all. After her life fending off starvation and enemies like the Crow and US army, she did not rattle over white concerns about money.

In one way or another, the Cheyenne woman had been with Morgan for sixteen years. Miraculously, back in the spring of "79, the old woman had shown up in Lone Tree, speaking no English and calling out Morgan's name in her language. That name was Crow Killer. In town to pick up supplies, Uncle Frank came across her surrounded by people, some yelling insults, others trying to help the mad Indian woman who was shouting crazily. He knew with certainty who she was looking for and brought her straight out to the Bow String ranch. On seeing each other, the two women hugged and cried and hugged again.

As it turned out, Lame Deer had walked five hundred miles from Fort Robinson. There she'd escaped with others from a fort prison where Dull knife's entire band was being held. They had just returned from the southern plains where they'd been sent the previous year. They broke out from that reservation and fought their way north only to be thrown into the Fort Robinson stockade. When Dull Knife and all his people refused to return south, the army withheld food and wood to heat the rooms. Lame Deer and more than a hundred Cheyenne broke out of the fort and fled north. Nearly all were killed, wounded or recaptured. Only a few escaped the army's pursuit, among them Lame Deer.

When Morgan was captured by the Cheyenne at fourteen, the old Indian woman became her closest friend and one of her mothers. Now, she was helping to raise Morgan's own children. After so many years at the Bow String Ranch, she wore white people's clothes and used knives and forks at a table like any proper white woman. Morgan knew, though, inside she was still all Cheyenne.

Conor sat on the couch, his arm draped over Dora's shoulder, explaining things to everyone with his usual calm, as if this was nothing more than a small grassfire. His wife was gripping her skirt and trying desperately to maintain a reassuring smile.

Next to them, Seamus stood against the wall by the mantel, his arms folded, shifting his eyes from speaker to speaker with intensity. Morgan felt a swell of pride for her son, both a boy and yet a man. To her, he looked like his father Spotted Horse before a raid, his blood face on.

She had given birth to four children. Two had died. Will, Jr. at age four of pneumonia and Baby Lenora at three months. She just stopped breathing one night and never took another breath. Morgan didn't think there could be any greater pain than losing a child. She wished she could have taken their places in the little cemetery on the hillside above the house. They lay there now with Da, Mam, brother Patrick, and sister Fiona, buried by Uncle Frank years ago. Much of her heart was buried with them.

Sometimes Morgan had trouble remembering their faces, except Fiona. Her face was never lost to her. Never, for she saw it every day in her eleven-year-old daughter Glory. The girl was so much like Fi in looks and spirit, ornery to the bone. With all the trouble, they'd missed giving her a birthday party, but it would come when they'd figured all this out, when they could smile without straining.

Suddenly, the back door slammed shut, and the girl rushed in from feeding the chickens. "You haven't started without me, have you, Pa?"

"Just the prelims, honey. We've been waiting for you for the important parts," he said.

"Good. We can start then," Glory said. When she passed, Morgan reached out for her, then pulled back when the girl strode by, scooped up a stool and sat beside Lame Deer. Placing her elbows on her knees, she gave her full attention to her father.

"There is a way forward," Will said finally and nodded to Morgan.

Morgan walked to the rolltop desk where Will kept the books. From inside, she pulled out the telegram that had come back in early January. "I received this several weeks ago," she said, returning. I get one every year about that time, and I've politely refused the offer within. This year I think I should accept."

She opened the telegram and read aloud:

"To Morgan Raines, née O'Connor, Care of Bow String Ranch, Montana Territory,

Once again, we are preparing a spectacular season of the Wild West and wish for you to join us. This year we travel to London. If you *accept, you must reach New York City by March 31 when we depart for England. Notify Nate Salsbury at the St. Denis Hotel in New York as to your plans. Weekly salary $250.*

Your friend, Bill Cody"

At the salary, Dora gasped, and Uncle Frank looked up.

Morgan set the telegram in her lap. "We've all fought and bled for this ranch too many years to give up. I'm promised more than a thousand a month. It should give us a chance."

Excited, Seamus stepped forward, "I'm coming with you. You tell them I'm Spotted Horse's son, Mama. If they took that old trickster Sitting Bull last year, they'd want the son of Spotted Horse. That should be even more money."

Lame Deer spoke up, "I go." She tapped her pipe ash into the fireplace. "I all time want see England. Talk to white grandmother. Tell her, send no more Englisher man to Lone Tree."

Glory jumped up, her eyes alight. "Well, then, I'm going, too. You can handle the ranch without me, can't you, Pa?"

Everyone laughed, even Uncle Frank.

"No," Morgan said sharply, louder than she intended, and Glory blinked as if slapped.

Morgan didn't like telling her that, for she did want the girl with her but feared she'd be too busy to protect a child as unpredictable as her daughter, especially in London with its slums and vicious underworld as bad as New York's. She could not bear the thought of losing her. She would not allow her to come. She would be safer with her father, Conor, and Dora in a place they all knew.

Seeing the girl's expression of hurt, Morgan almost relented, then repeated, "I'm sorry, Glory. I can't take you with me. You'll have to stay and help with the ranch."

Lifting his long frame from the chair, Will walked over to his daughter, cupped her chin, and said, "Actually, honey, wih all we got going on here now, we will need you badly."

"Yes, Papa," Glory managed to say, her voice choked.

Will turned to Morgan, "It seems you have companions for the long voyage."

Just then, Glory sprang up and ran outside, slamming the back door.

CHAPTER FIVE

Montana Territory, March 22, 1887

At nine when the Rothstein Brothers Bank opened, Morgan and Will joined a crowd of hundreds pushing their way in to see Arthur Rothstein himself. The owner of the only bank left standing in Livingston had made the trip all the way from the main branch in Virginia City to settle the nerves of his depositors.

On this day, most people wanted to withdraw money and the rest to apply for loans. Rothstein did not allow withdrawals of more than ten percent from savings. As for loans, the bank owner was notoriously miserly with passing out money without substantial collateral, and after the winter, few had it. Six heavily armed guards flanked the doors and tellers' cages to keep the unruly crowd under control.

An assistant screened each loan applicant, turning most away. When Will told him he'd come to pay off a mortgage, the one on the Bar T ranch, he and Morgan were moved to the front of the line. He didn't mention he'd be asking for a loan to do that. Within ten minutes, they were led into Rothstein's office.

The banker sat at his desk, studying a property document of the Bar T when they entered. He didn't look up but gestured to the two chairs. In his late thirties, he had a stern countenance with a prominent Adam's apple and wirerimmed spectacles balanced on the tip of his nose.

He set the document aside and glanced up, studying them, a man and wife, owners of the Bow String Ranch. To his knowledge, they had no lien and wanted to pay off an in-law's loan. That was refreshing on this day, money coming in and not out. He assessed the two, typical ranching types, salt of the earth and all that, relatively young, severe expressions. The man was unusually tall with a weathered face, and one arm lost no doubt in a ranch accident.

The woman's smallish stature made them an odd pairing. She was pretty, though he could see her looks were left over from a youth that was gone forever. Cooking, bearing children, vegetable gardens, and milking cows was her lot, then she would die. Her only hope was for someday a rocking chair on the porch. He realized her grey eyes had fixed him with a hard stare, which surprised him, made him uneasy.

He cleared his throat and placed the document on a stack of papers, then looked at Will. "So, you wish to pay off the loan on your in-law's ranch. I must say that's a pleasant surprise. Everyone's asking for money today, and no one has collateral for it. The days of offering a handshake as a guarantee are gone. Let's explore yours. How many head of cattle did you begin the winter with?"

"About ten thousand," Will answered.

"And how many survived the winter?"

Will hesitated. "Maybe three thousand. It's impossible to say how many will make it to the fall. We'll need to feed and revitalize a lot of cows."

The word *revitalize* in such a hard man suggested some education. Perhaps he'd be smart enough to survive the current crisis, or more likely he was a stubborn fool like most of them.

Will went on, "We need money to run both ranches. We must bring in new stock and hire at least fifteen hands. All that will cost."

Rothstein asked, "I assume you've brought your deed?"

"We're not offering the ranch as collateral," Will said.

Abruptly, the banker leaned back in his chair with a loud sigh. His perpetual frown deepened. "Let me understand this. You want me to loan you the money to pay off your in-law's mortgage and without collateral?"

"No, we have other collateral, "Will said.

Rothstein's Adam's apple bobbed. He made money in large part by approving loans that would be repaid at a good profit or the collateral, which would have to be substantial, would be forfeited. He was curious what they might have. He squinted at the rancher. "If your surety is not your ranch, what is it that you intend to offer?"

Will nodded to Morgan who removed a telegram from a pocket and slid it across the desk. Puzzled, the banker picked it up and began reading. After a moment, his eyes lifted to her, then went back to the telegram.

Finally, he set it on the desk. "What could you possibly be doing with Mr. Cody's troupe? Cooking?"

Her gaze remained steady. "I doubt it. Not at two hundred and fifty dollars a week. Likely, he'll want me to shoot things. I'm pretty good at that."

Rothstein sat for a longtime rapping his fingers on his desk, then abruptly went to the door and called in the local bank manager, a pale young man with a poor excuse for a moustache, more fuzz than hair. "Wheeler, do you know these people?"

"Yes, sir," he answered nervously. "Mr. and Mrs. Raines. They are good folks."

"And her, what do you know about her?"

Wheeler's face reddened. He glanced at her shyly then said to Rothstein as if it were obvious. "Well, she's the Captured Girl, sir. Everyone knows her. She's more famous than Billy the Kid. They say she shot Frank Nash in the forehead from four hundred yards in the dead of night, and then…"

"That's enough," Rothstein cut in. "You can go, Wheeler." He came back to his desk and addressed Morgan. "You're not going to claim you did that, are you?"

She replied evenly, "Of course not. It was closer to a hundred yards and not at night but dusk. I did shoot Nash in the forehead though. No man had it coming more."

Staring into her flat gray eyes, Rothstein cleared his throat. "Yes, well, indeed." Then he tapped the telegram with his finger. "You've accepted Mr. Cody's offer?"

"I have. We sent the telegram to New York this morning."

Rothstein took his time lighting a cigar and studied it for a full minute. "All right. I'll approve the loan in full, but you'll have to stay employed by Mr. Cody till the loan is paid off. We'll work out the details and you both can sign the papers before noon. I'll keep the telegram. A sizeable amount each month will go to paying down the debt. Is that acceptable?"

They both nodded, and Will said, "It is."

Before leaving the office, he and Rothstein shook hands on it.

In the early afternoon, they rode back toward the Bow String, Will carrying five hundred dollars and Morgan balancing her rifle across the pommel of her saddle. As much as people talked about civilization having come to the territory and statehood just around the corner, both knew this was still not a country where outlaws had vanished like the Indian threat of past years. Gangs roamed the vastness stealing cattle, holding up stagecoaches and trains, and robbing banks. Travelers were always in peril, and they had too much to lose not to be ready.

Yet, both were in cheerful moods, better than the morning when they'd left home. They'd succeeded with their new bank far more than they thought likely. It would be a long, tough struggle ahead, but now they had a chance. Morgan knew in her heart they'd make it. Will was that good of a rancher, and Conor would never quit on a thing no matter what he faced. They'd work the two ranches as one, but the Templeton Bar T now belonged to Conor and Dora, and the Bow String to Will and Morgan. She just longed for the day when she'd return to her family and have them all together again.

About halfway home, they turned in among the trees along the banks of the Yellowstone to let the horses drink. The afternoon had grown cloudless, the sun burning hot overhead, though the temperatures were likely in the mid-sixties. It would finish the last patches of snow still clinging to the ground.

They dismounted, Morgan still with the rifle.

"I wonder how cold the water is." Will removed his bandana, knelt at the water's edge and washed his face. The river was running fast, a little up from spring runoff.

"Cold I suspect," Morgan replied.

"Not that bad." He stood. "I fancy a swim."

She laughed. "Will, you're mad. We'd probably drown or die of cold."

He smiled. "Getting warm afterward would be worth it." He then gestured ten yards upstream. "There's an eddy. It should be safe enough to splash around in."

"You're serious?"

"I am. My wife is leaving me in a couple days and will be gone for a year, maybe more. I want this time with her to be as memorable as I can make it. Time with no one else but her."

Her free hand on her hip, she cocked her head. "I suppose you'll save me if the current pulls me out."

He shrugged "I thought more like you'd be saving me."

He spread both bedrolls out on the ground and took the rifle from her, setting it against a tree. With his one hand, he began unbuttoning her dress as she fumbled furiously on the buttons of his shirt. Each bit of clothing removed was coupled with caresses. His touch on bare skin shocked her. When all their clothes were shed, they stood naked facing each other. Morgan took his face in her hands, bringing it down, and slowly kissed his eyelids and then his lips.

His arm around her, he felt her strong, slender back, and pulled her body to his. Will groaned loudly as he felt the exquisite pain of great joy, knowing only days were left of it.

They didn't make it into the water. In a quick motion, he drew her down onto the bedrolls and buried his face in her neck, kissing her there, on her shoulders, then up to her mouth. He felt his desire coming fierce. As she pulled him into her, he choked out, "I love you, Morgan. I'll love you till my dying breath."

An hour later, dressed and their bedrolls strapped back on their saddles, about to remount, Morgan took two quick strides toward the river, gazing across to the foothills and the forests a half mile beyond.

"What is it?" Will asked.

She didn't answer at first then said, "I don't know. I saw a flash of something. Maybe someone is up there."

In an instant, she could go from a loving, playful woman to the lethal, watchful one suddenly before him now, and he loved both variations of her. That was how she was raised by her white parents and her Indian ones. He never would dismiss her concerns. She had been right too many times. It was that kind of country, but whatever it was, it was on the other side of the river and up into the foothills.

He remounted his horse. "We better get home. If it is someone, we gave them an eyeful."

That evening as dusk waned and dark clouds rolled into the valley casting all in gloom, Clive Dunford hurried in a crouch up to the ridgeline overlooking the Bow String ranch. It would soon rain, and he wanted this business done before then. Sprawling down on the grass, he set his hunting rifle beside him and observed the ranch house below, some hundred and fifty yards distant. The woman's crippled husband was chopping wood over by the barn with his one arm but no one else was about, the place quiet but for the fall of his axe.

A vegetable garden ran along one side of the house. A clothesline nearby had a couple things still hanging. Perhaps the woman would send her daughter out to retrieve them and make his task easier. Otherwise, he'd have to wait till the man went inside and then approach. He'd shoot the little nit through the window, jump on his horse and race off like the hounds of hell were after him, which they probably would be.

Once away, no one could accuse him of this. After all, his train, the one so many saw him board last Friday, was in New York by now.

When lights came on in the windows, his stomach tightened with anticipation.

As Seamus lit the last oil lamp, Morgan was sitting by the fire, stretching a hank of blue yarn between her outstretched hands while Dora rolled it into a ball. About an hour before, Conor and Uncle Frank had ridden over to the Templeton ranch to stay the night so they could be up early next morning to start repairs on the barn. It had part of the roof missing and would take all of them pitching in to finish before she left for New York and England.

From outside, Morgan heard Will's axe as he attempted to work off his frustration that he had to let her go. No matter how much she tried to convince him otherwise, some part of him felt it was his fault his family was being split asunder. The winter had done them in, not Will, and if anyone had blame it was his nibs, the earl's son, Dunford. He stole every damn penny of theirs out of their bank. Mason, too, but the man was dead, and she could not muster any sympathy for his passing.

Across the room, Glory sat scowling at her, saying nothing, attention drawn nowhere else, as if her fierce stare would change her mind. Her auburn red hair gleamed in the flickering firelight. She'd been sulking since she learned Morgan, Seamus, and Lame Deer were going to England and not her. Morgan thought it best just to ignore her anger and act like nothing was wrong.

She hated leaving her daughter at this age. The girl had little control over her wild impulses, which too often got her into more trouble than she could handle, much like Morgan herself at that age. Morgan's biggest job was that of mother, and she wouldn't be doing it, not for the next year, unable to help her daughter through this period. But she needed to save the ranch to save Glory and the rest of her family.

"I'm sorry to leave you with so much responsibility, Dora, with you know who," Morgan said in a voice loud enough for Glory to hear. She hoped her daughter would find it amusing.

Dora shrugged and patted her belly. "I got my own coming. It'll be good to get some practice in with yours."

"I fear more than you'd ever want." Morgan glanced at her

daughter whose fierce expression was unchanged. "It'll be like trying to rope a twister."

They both chuckled, but Glory did not.

Abruptly, the girl jumped to her feet. "I know you're talking about me. I'm going outside with Papa."

She headed for the door. Morgan called after her. "Take a shawl. It's getting chilly."

Without responding, the girl snatched a wrap off one of the hooks and went out.

Dunford flinched when he saw the figure in the doorway silhouetted against the light. With dusk almost fallen to a moonless, overcast night, he could barely make out the shape, like a moving shadow in the yard. He knew it was female when she pulled a shawl around her shoulders, but it was not Morgan. It was the girl. He watched her walk toward the woodpile. It didn't bother him that she was a child. She was Morgan Raines's child. That woman had caused his son's death. It was only fitting that this girl pay for her mother's sin. Eye for eye. Didn't it say so in the Bible?

He lifted the rifle and aimed down the sights, making himself perfectly still. She abruptly turned and did an odd skipping run to the clothesline and pulled off what looked like a dress. Then, in that hopping gait, she headed toward her father chopping wood. Dunford aimed at her and fired. She went down.

He heard the man scream her name as he raced for her. She scrambled to her feet to run to him. Dunford took aim again.

When Morgan heard the shot, she sprinted for the door, grabbing her rifle propped beside it. As she bolted out into the yard, the second shot cracked loud in the night.

CHAPTER SIX

Montana Territory, March 22, 1887

As the rain began falling, Dunford slid down from the ridgeline, ran into the trees where he'd tied his horse and swung aboard. He rode off at a hard gallop, kicking the beast's flanks.

"I've done it. I've done it," he shouted. He hadn't missed that second shot. The pounding exhilaration made him feel like he could fly. He'd killed the girl, of that he was sure, mortally wounding his great enemy by doing so. Let her live with that misery for a while as he had to do.

In this past year, he'd lost nearly all, but now he knew his fortunes were turning once again. It should be called Dunford's Luck. Like his father, the massive extravagances of his life ate away at his funds, forcing him to devise more schemes to refill the coffers.

From his first moment in the American West, his goal had been to cut out a piece of land in Montana and make it England, and that had cost a small fortune. He'd built his grand manor, imported expensive furniture from Chicago and New York and kept a stable of thoroughbred racehorses. Along with other English transplants, he set up racetracks and bet heavily. His costly hunting parties going after bear, elk, mountain lion, and the rare buffalo had become legendary. He loved playing cards at the Cattlemen's Club, which included not just Englishmen but the region's ranchers. All that drained his wealth, but as he'd told his father years ago, money was to spend, so he lived like Cardinal Wolsey. His life here had been a jubilee. They'd not forget him.

When he guessed he was about four miles from the Bow String ranch, he eased up on his mount. Staying in the foothills, he'd ride all night and make for the train station at Big Timber. There, he'd board the eastbound to New York, pick up Lydia and then across the seas home.

It was time to make his next fortune, and he knew just the man to do it with, his old friend Charlie Acker, king of thieves and murderers.

In the rain and darkness, Morgan could make out two bodies in the yard near the woodpile. Dread buckled her knees, and she nearly went down but ran to them. Will was draped atop Glory, neither moving. She let out a piercing scream and dropped beside them. For the first time in her life, she didn't know what to do. She grabbed her husband. "Will, Will, are you all right?"

He wasn't. Even in the darkness, she could see the hole in his back. Under him, Glory's face was covered in blood. Morgan reached down and touched her daughter's cheek. "Not you, baby. Please God, not you too."

Glory's eyes opened, and she began blinking rapidly. Her lips trembled. Then she shrieked and shrieked again.

Lame Deer was beside her "Lift him."

Seamus and Dora now there turned Will onto his side while Lame Deer and Morgan dragged Glory out from under him. Morgan turned to her husband as the girl sank into the Indian woman's arms and sobbed.

Lame Deer checked her face. "Where you hurt?"

In a small voice, the girl said, "I'm not hurt. It's Papa's blood."

Will awakened, rain pelting his face.

Morgan said "Will, we need to get you inside."

Seamus said, "Papa, can you stand?"

"No, son, I don't think I can."

"Then we'll carry you," Morgan said. "We'll get the doctor here and you'll heal up no matter how long it takes."

His voice sounded brittle. "Yes, ma'am. I'll do that."

When the four adults lifted him, he groaned and passed out. They hurried in and took him into his and Morgan's bedroom. Immediately, Lame Deer sent Seamus for Doc Simon in Lone Tree.

After Morgan quickly removed Will's jacket and shirt, Morgan immediately saw his wounds were mortal. The realization sent her soul into hell. She could not lose Will.

"I'll be fine," Will said. "When the doc gets here, he'll fix me up fine."

"Yes, he'll do just that," she said

Morgan and Lame Deer stripped him down to his union bottoms so they could tend the wounds, one blood-soaked hole in the left side of his back and a bigger, massive one on his stomach. Only one bullet did this, and he was bleeding badly. There was no coming back from it.

Glory stood at her father's bedside the whole time, staring wild-eyed as the wounds were uncovered. Morgan would have spared her, but the girl would not leave the room, and Morgan had no time to deal with it. Besides, this was her father. She had a right to be here.

With towels and ripped sheets Dora brought, Morgan and Lame Deer staunched the flow of blood as best they could, their forearms drenched crimson.

That's when the doctor arrived. Morgan gently told Glory, "Step back, honey. Give the doctor room."

Doc Simon was a young man fresh from the east. Carrying his black bag, he hurried in and immediately began his examination. Despite the intense pain, Will went along with all the probing without a word escaping his clenched teeth. When the examination ended, the doctor remained silent for several seconds.

Weakened, Will asked, "What's the verdict, Doc. Straight out."

Doc Simon spoke louder than needed. "Your body is failing, Mr. Raines. A large bullet entered your back just left of the spinal column.

I suspect it passed through the left kidney, emerging on the right side of the abdomen in the region of the gall bladder. It must have caused the great vessels to hemorrhage, all of which will inevitably cause death."

Glory gave a soft whimper, and Seamus stepped over to his sister. She fell into his arms and cried.

Will nodded. "I thought as much, Doc. How long have I got?"

"An hour, sir. Maybe two, but no more. I'm sorry. I have morphine in my bag. It will make it easier for you."

. "No." Will lifted his stump as if to block him. "I know morphine. It makes you stupid. I want all my senses up until the last."

He reached out and took Morgan's hand. His hand felt like gripping ice and hers had blood over it. She stopped herself from reacting to the touch. He gave a gentle squeeze, then released her.

Will glanced over at his children. "Seamus, Glory, come here."

Glory ran over and buried herself in his one-armed hug. He looked past her up to Seamus. "No man could have a better son. You know you have a tough job ahead."

The boy nodded. That was all that was said between them, all that needed saying.

"Glory," he said softly.

"Yes, Papa." Her lips trembled. "What's my job?"

"Honey, your job is the toughest of all. You're to live a good life for me. I will be there every step of the way. I'll be the warmth from the fireplace in winter and the cooling breeze in summer. I'll be there watching when you marry the lucky man who grabs your heart and when you raise your children. I will forever be watching over you. Never forget that."

Morgan's eyes watered, but she would not shed tears while he was alive.

An hour later, Will died.

The room was crowded by then. Nearly thirty people. The doctor's wife had sent word to Conor and Uncle Frank, who made it before the end along with several cowboys who'd been staying in the Templeton bunk house till they could be hired on. They all knew Will. At his passing, tears filled their eyes.

Morgan wanted to crawl under the covers with him but just sat there gripping his hand, trying to breathe.

Lame Deer put a hand on Will's chest. "He is with God now."

What a strange thing for the Indian woman to say. She'd been to church in town only once to see what it was all about. But Morgan thought about God often. She believed in both the God of her parents and the Cheyenne way of heaven and earth, and oddly, she saw those two as the same, a different illumination of identical things.

Her voice was cold. "Yes, he is with God now. But he is not here."

The cowboys constructed a separate room at the back of the parlor with hung sheets and drapes. Will's body was taken there. The next day, Wilson and Brown mortuary came and put him in a flower strewn coffin for the viewing as hundreds of people arrived to pay their respects. Many brought food and drink. For the cowboys Will worked with, the day was a wild celebration of his life, which Morgan saw as an Irish wake, just what she wanted.

Arthur Rothstein came up to her. "My condolences, Mrs. Raines. I wish I could say Virginia City had less violence, but I can't. It's a terrible thing for a good man to die in such a way."

"Thank you, Mr. Rothstein."

"Do you still intend to travel to England?"

"Of course. Why wouldn't I?" she snapped.

"That's what I assumed. I had to be sure."

To allow those from around the territory to attend, the funeral would be in two days. She wished Sergeant Reardon could make it, but far away in California, he wouldn't hear about it till her letter reached him. The one person who remained by her side throughout the day was her brother Conor, who she'd known nearly all her life. They'd been taken by the Cheyene together.

That night, with Will filling her mind, the tears kept coming, silent tears, loud tears that wracked her body beyond exhaustion. When she did drift off, Will came to her so real she felt the substance of him. She awoke several times, and each time she did, it brought back the crushing pain of his loss. She didn't want the real world; she wanted back into the dream world where her husband was alive.

Then Morgan fell into a long dream that played random images of their life together from the moment she'd come upon him during the Battle of Crazy Woman Creek to their evenings here on the porch after a hard day's work. A life together that was far too short.

Something was tugging on her toe, and she awoke. Lame Deer stood at the foot of the bed.

"What is it?" Morgan muttered.

The Indian woman yanked hard on the toe again. "Take care of your daughter."

Outside, darkness was like the black inside a cave. I was sitting on the ground in my night dress beside the woodpile where Papa was shot. I wasn't sure how I got there. My feet were bare, my knees drawn up with my arms wrapped around them. For a moment, I thought I was caught in a nightmare, and I'd soon wake up. But when icicles curled around my spine, I knew I was indeed in a nightmare but a real one. The sorrow was eating me up inside. I shivered, seeing Papa throw himself over me, the bullet hitting his body, and the splash of his blood on my face. I saw it again and again.

I heard someone screaming and realized it was me but only in my head. I couldn't make it come out of my mouth, even now.

Suddenly, Mama rushed out of the dark, scooped me up and carried me straight back to the house. I cried like a babe in her arms. I'd thought she forgot me.

She took me into my bedroom, and we sat on the bed, her holding me and rocking me. She whispered I'd be alright, though I didn't think I ever would.

I heard her say under her breath, "Damn him." I didn't know who she meant.

My skinny legs dangled down out of my night shirt. I did't want to go to sleep because I'd end up dreaming again about Papa getting shot.

Mama held me and we remained like that for a long time. Finally, I said, "I'm so sorry."

Mama was taken aback. "For what? Glory, you had nothing to do with what happened."

"Papa was protecting me."

Looking like she'd been punched, Mama couldn't speak at first, then said, "Oh, honey, that's what parents do. Everything your father did and everything I do in life is to protect you and Seamus. You'll find that out when you have children. You had no fault in this. Lordy, don't ever think that."

"I see Papa all the time." I couldn't go on. I leaned into her and cried as she held me.

After a moment, she brushed my hair back. "I Know. So do I. I can't promise you those thoughts will go away any time soon, but they will ease over time. They'll find a place in your heart where you can live day to day like Papa wanted you to."

"Please, Mama, don't leave me behind," I begged. "I can't stay here. I can't go near that barn. I want to go with you to England. Please."

Mama's eyes actually went wet with tears. "Of course, you will. We have to go right after we put your father to rest, or we're not going to make it."

Two days later in the small, family cemetery above the ranch house, Captain Will Raines was buried in his military uniform. There he'd rest for eternity beside Morgan's parents, brother Patrick, sister Fiona, their children Will Jr. and Baby Lenora, and someday Morgan herself. At least two hundred people showed up for the funeral, including one surprise visitor, Billy Baker, Dunford's man. Throughout, numb emotionally, she ignored the man, as the minister spoke for more than half an hour and showed no signs of stopping till Morgan stood up and said, "Amen."

Will's coffin was lowered, the hole filled in, and everyone began walking down to the ranch house, Glory crying softly and clinging to her. That's when Billy Baker approached.

Hat in hand, he said, "Ma'am, I'm so sorry. I can't tell you how much…"

"Thank you, Mr. Baker," Morgan cut him off and turned to go. He was not a bad man, quite the opposite, but he was Dunford's man, and Dunford was an out and out bastard.

"Ma'am, there's something I need to tell you," he said.

She turned back to him. "What?" she snapped.

"Ma'am, I was mavericking up in the foothills when I saw you and, er…"

"…and Will."

"Yes, you and your husband returning I suppose from Livingston."

"Get to the point, Mr. Baker."

"About two hours later, I saw Clive Dunford. He was keeping in the trees, careful like, not wanting to be seen. He passed not a hundred feet from me, so I know it was him."

Murder filled her eyes, and Baker stepped back in fear. A hammer pounded in her chest. There could be no doubt. It was Dunford who killed Will. Everyone had said he'd left the country days ago, yet he'd come back. In her mind, she saw his face, so smug, so sure of himself, thinking no doubt once home in England, he'd escaped justice. But she would be there soon, and she would bring justice. There would be a reckoning. Blood for blood.

She startled Baker when she spoke, "Go on."

He turned his hat nervously in his hands. "Well, that's it, Ma'am. That's all of it except everyone thinks he went off on that train with his family. I suppose he did, but he came back. It doesn't take a Philadelphia lawyer to figure out why. I thought you should know."

"And now I do. Thank you, Mr. Baker. I'm in your debt."

When Mrs. Raines walked down the hill, Baker watched her go. He knew she would meet up with Dunford in England and was not sure who would survive the encounter or how many others would fall around them. Mrs. Raines had long proven herself a top shootist with a rifle, but Dunford could handle a rifle as well, and he was a back shooter.

CHAPTER SEVEN

Tilbury Docks, England, March 31, 1887

On his arrival in England, Dunford was surprised to find his mother waiting at Tilbury docks dressed in black. He was exhausted, having travelled for much of the last nine days straight from Montana to this spot. Likely a record of sorts should he publicize it, which he surely would not. He wondered how his mother even knew he was coming and on which ship then remembered he'd sent a cable to the family solicitor Edgar Winterbottom.

He forced a smile. "Did Winterbottom tell you of our..."

She interrupted him. "I have sad news, Clive. Your father and brother have perished at sea. They were sailing the yacht from the Channel Islands when a sudden storm hit." She dabbed at her eyes with a handkerchief. "It is a crushingly sad time for the family."

The news lifted his spirits immediately. *Both of them dead!* It couldn't have been better. For his mother's sake, he fitted an appropriate expression of shock and sadness on his face. Yet certainly, he felt no sorrow. He and his father never got along, and his brother barely recognized his existence. Unfortunately, they had the bad manners to take the yacht down with them.

When the porter addressed him as Milord, the impact hit him. He was now the earl. He owned Wexham Hall and the twenty-thousand-acres in the Midlands. His future was assured.

His mother mistook his silence for sadness. "Yes, my son, it is a great loss."

Abruptly, he gestured toward Lydia. "Mother, this is my wife Lydia."

The dowager stared with disdain. The American woman curtsied and extended her hand, which the older woman ignored, turning back to her son.

Dunford told his wife. "No, no, dearest, you are now the Countess of Wexham. You do not curtsy to Mother or anyone of lesser rank. Rest assured, I shall have someone prepare you for your new role. I'm sure Mother will help."

They found a coach and left for a hotel in London. Having just inherited the earldom, something he'd desired since childhood, Dunford would stay over an extra day to meet with the estate's solicitor. Since his own personal finances were precariously low, he was eager to find out just how much the estate was worth.

The next morning he was shown into the Fleet Street office of the eminent Edgar Winterbottom, a rotund man with grey hair and a bushy walrus mustache. In fact, except for the pale skin, he looked exactly like a great sea lion about to bellow. Whenever Dunford had seen him as a child, he had the urge to toss him a fish. Sitting before him now, that thought almost made him laugh.

From behind his desk, the man lifted his great girth and extended his hand. "Lord Wexham, I'm sorry about your father and brother. It was quite the shock."

"Yes, it was a shock to us all," Dunford managed. "I don't mean to seem rushed, but shall we get on with it? I'm sure you have a busy day ahead as do I."

"As you wish." Winterbottom gestured toward the chair in front of his desk and slid a leather-bound folder across to him. "This is the Wexham estate, milord. Debts and assets alike."

Opening it, Dunford began reading. After just thirty seconds, his jubilant mood crashed like a shot fowl. The debts were enormous, over two hundred thousand pounds and growing daily. The upkeep on the estate was staggering. That alone would gobble up all his own finances in a month or two, then when the estate was seized, he'd be a penniless, landless earl. Within society, he'd be a figure of scorn and laughter. He must sack most of the estate staff and quickly.

He glanced up in frustration. "My god, none of the operations show a profit. None. There's only debt."

"That is the case, milord," Winterbottom said, folding his hands over his huge belly. "Your father, shall I say, was not much interested in the business aspects of his position. He led quite the high life. As you know these great country homes are massive drains on the purse, thousands of pounds each year to maintain. In the end, he mortgaged the entire estate and borrowed and bought on credit extensively, All of which you now owe plus sizeable interest."

Not answering at first, Dunford stared at the documents as if the answer were there.

Winterbottom went on, "The creditors, I'm afraid, are barking at the door, and I cannot keep them at bay much longer. Your once great estate will no longer exist in another two months unless you begin generating enormous income."

So that was it. Dunford couldn't remember a time when he didn't dream of being the great earl of Wexham with a great estate at hand. Now he would be but for just weeks. It was intolerable.

He looked up and replied with a calm he did not feel, "I'm aware of that, Mr. Winterbottom. I assure you I will meet my father's debts and put the estate back on solid footing. The money is at hand. You may tell that to the creditors."

In the documents, he noticed a report on his tenant farmers, thirty of them with some fifteen hundred head of sheep and cows among them, and not a one up to date in rent. Most were years in arrears. He jabbed the sheet of paper. "These tenant farms are a drain on the estate. Why has nothing been done?"

"Perhaps, the late earl felt their fortunes would change and thus his, but then those farms haven't shown a profit since your grandfather's time. There are large families living in each..."

"There's some fifteen hundred head of sheep."

"In aggregate, milord. Not enough for each one to maintain their families and pay the full rent."

Dunford only stared back, rage growing inside him. People living free on his lands without paying. He'd remove them and sell the livestock. That should provide ready cash but not near enough.

As if the lawyer read his mind, he said, "Are you aware that these families have lived on Wexham land since the time of good King Henry?"

"I'm not running charity houses, Mr. Winterbottom," Dunford replied.

One last document caught his attention, a deed to great swathes of land in South Africa and a gold mine. He shoved it across the desk to the solicitor. "What is this?"

Winterbottom picked it up. "Ah, yes, the gold mine. Last year, your father bought it. It's in the Transvaal. Have you heard of the Witwatersrand strike?"

Dunford's eyes lit up. "Of course. News of it even reached America."

"The richest in the world I'm told," Winterbottom said.

Dunford's hopes lifted. "How much money is it generating?"

The solicitor shook his head and slid the deed back across the desk. "None I'm sorry to say. Men are getting rich every day in the Rand, but unfortunately, you are not one of them. Your mine is not paying off. The latest letter from your manager states no gold, and they've been at it more than a year."

With a sharp intake of breath, Dunford slammed the deed down on the other documents. "And how much is this gold mine costing me?"

"More than four thousand pounds a year."

Dunford was shocked. "Four thousand pounds! So much?"

"That's a pittance. Most mining operations are far more expensive. You're paying the manager and several miners using picks and shovels. A limited operation."

Raising his voice, Dunford said, "Close it down. Don't send another penny."

Winterbottom nodded. "As you say. There are no pennies to send anyway. I'll cable the manager to terminate operations. It must go to Durbin, then weeks, maybe months by mail to the Transvaal. Those documents are copies, milord. You may keep them.""

Depressed and angry, Dunford closed the folder, tucked it into his case, and retreated from the office. He felt himself caught in the middle of an American cattle stampede. Suddenly, his position and standing in society, so assured yesterday, would soon crash into a pit more desperate than the Black Hole of Calcutta. He desperately needed to find a way out of this. He would not be an earl with no home, no land, and no money. That would make him the damn laughingstock of the entire country.

In a foul mood, he made his way over to St. Giles Rookery, one of London's worst slums and looked up his old friend Charlie Acker. There, in his youth when he was estranged from his father and destitute, he and Acker had swung the stick, mugging the wealthy gentry who'd come seeking prostitutes. Nowadays, from his office in the Stick and Dove brothel, he ran the lucrative West End underworld. Everything from a string of children purse snatchers to smuggling and prostitution.

A woman was what Dunford was looking for, and Acker provided her, his oldest whore, one he was about to kick to the street. The new earl and the old prostitute went upstairs where he savagely beat her. Then as she lay unconscious on the bed, took her. His tension released, he dropped a single penny on her belly and left. He spent the rest of the day drinking with Acker.

"You seem in a hopeless state, Clive me boy." The crime boss laughed and gave him a slap on the back. "That's not like you, the one always full of ideas. You'll come up with something. You always do. Why else do you think I been backing you all these years?"

The next day, after a seventy-mile train ride, Dunford arrived home for the first time in seven years. As the coach plodded down the long drive toward Wexham Hall, an insufferable despair settled upon him. On either side of the long drive where once stood magnificent gardens, were decayed and rotting plants. In the shade of a cloudy sky, Wexham Hall appeared as gloom itself, the walls dingy and the paint peeling, the windows unwashed, and the front sedges growing wild. Not only were the fifty servants costing him a fortune, they were layabouts.

In a great line they waited in front of the massive oak door, the butler, the housekeeper, the footmen in faded livery, and the house staff. In his grandfather's time, a hundred servants had been employed in the great house, and when he was a child, nearly seventy.

A footman rushed to open the door, and the family stepped out.

"Welcome home, milady," Wilkerson, the butler, said to the dowager countess.

In her black widow's garb, tall and stately, she strode past. "Thank you, Wilkerson."

Then followed the dumpy, new countess.

"Milord, it's good to see you again," Wilkerson said to Dunford.

"What a bloody mess, eh, Wilkerson?" Dunford replied. "You and I will set things right."

"As you say, milord."

When in the vestibule, he said quietly to the butler, "Before the end of the day, I want you to dismiss every single servant but the housekeeper, the cook, one house maid and two footmen. And of course yourself. You are safe. Are my instruction clear, Wilkerson?"

The butler appeared stunned, his face draining of color. "Yes, my lord."

Later, after a simple lunch set on a small table, Dunford followed Wilkerson from room to room and saw further proof of the depth to which his family had fallen. The entrance hall and front parlor had been fitted with decent old furniture, but the other rooms, the music room, billiards room, library, and more were bare as if a West End gang had stripped them, taking everything including the wall settings.

In the library where only a few dusty books remained along with a single worn chair Dunford said, "Thank you, Wilkerson. I've seen enough. That will be all."

The butler left the room, and Dunford sat in the chair, both angry and determined. Of course, he and his father were both profligate, but at least he, Clive, always had the ability to earn fortune after fortune. Didn't Acker say so?

In his lap, he held the folder of documents from Winterbottom's office. After several minutes, he began to consider his problem. This poverty that his dead father and brother dropped on him must not stand, but working long hours here to keep the place afloat did not suit him. He was a born thief, a sharper who could wring money out of a miserly aunt. a man with the charm of the devil and the wit to induce the gullible to part with their most prized possessions. This was how he must save the estate.

Whatever he did, he knew he must do it with a show of wealth, appear the successful lord of a great estate, someone who didn't need money at all. For any plan to work, instead of cutting costs, he would put on the pomp.

He opened the leather folder and took out the deed to the gold mine.

By the time Dunford joined Lydia and his mother in the parlor for tea, a plan to acquire great wealth had formed in his mind. His dark mood had changed to one of ebullience. He saw his wife, though, still frightened by their state of affairs. Certainly not the grandly appointed house she'd expected. With a reassuring smile, he went over to her and kissed her cheek.

"All will be well, my dearest," he told her. "I have it well in hand."

Her temperament shifted drastically, and she produced a genuine smile. That was why he loved her. She had absolute faith in him.

From the other chair, his mother suddenly exclaimed, "Oh, dear." She had been going through the mail that had accumulated over the last few days.

"What is it, Mother?" he asked.

"An invitation from the Duchess of Northampton. I'm invited to tea." She handed it to him. The square of white pasteboard read:

<u>*The Earl and Countess of Wexham*</u>

THE DUKE AND DUCHESS OF NORTHAMPTON
At Becket Castle, April 22, 1887
Carriages   *Tea*
Three o'clock   *Four o'clock*

Dunford stared at the card and saw the stars aligning for him. He vaguely remembered the duke from years ago on one of the few occasions his family had visited Becket Castle. A taciturn, snobbish boy, he'd rather sit in the library reading from his books than playing croquet or tennis with the other lads. Their estate was thirty-five thousand acres on the other side of Wellingborough, no more than eight miles from Wexham Hall. Back then, they were going bankrupt till the grown Edward Becket landed Julia Kruger of New York, daughter of one of the wealthiest men in America. Her father, unlike Lydia's, had gifted Becket a huge endowment that saved their estate.

When he became duke, he invested his wife's money in railroads and construction in London, making over the city itself with great new office buildings and mansions. Now, he was one of the wealthiest men in the kingdom, if not the world, which made him a ripe apple to be plucked. The date of the tea would give Dunford time enough to prepare. Much needed to be done. This would be the greatest confidence game ever attempted.

"As I recall," he said, "the duchess is American."

His mother frowned. "Yes, one of those unctuous New Yorkers. Kruger, I believe was her name before she trapped the duke into her web."

Dunford saw Lydia flinch.

With a long sigh, the dowager added, "I can't possibly attend with your father so recently departed."

Considering what he had in mind and with Becket's rich business friends, this could reap him millions. He actually smiled. "But, Mother, the invitation is not for you," he said. "It is for the Earl and Countess of Wexham. Rest assured, Lydia and I will attend. I do look forward to seeing my old friend the duke again."

PART TWO
THE WILD WEST

CHAPTER EIGHT

New York City, March 31, 1887

The month I turned twelve, I found myself in New York City, passing through on my way to England. Every time I think back on those days, I sink completely into the girl I was, someone immature and damaged. I can't help it. That era in my life is hard to navigate with its treacherous shoals and submerged rocks everywhere, with its famous people and moments of great impact of which I was a part. It was a time characterized by adventures, great sorrow that still has its sharp talons in me, and overall, by love. Yes, love. It took me a longtime to figure that out, but what else would you call it?

That day in New York, as my family and I raced through the city, the place shocked my little girl peepers.

"I swear, New York is a fine city, as big as all get out," I cried in my wonderment. "I've never seen so many tall buildings and them all pressed together like calves after a single teat. There's not enough room for them all."

"Glory, don't lean so far out of the carriage. You'll fall out," Mama said.

"Yes, ma'am." I leaned back but only a little.

I couldn't help it. It was like seeing a giant in a circus. Thousands of people crowded into these streets with wagons and carriages like our own clattering on the cobblestone loud enough to beat the devil. It seemed the whole world was here. The wind blew in cold from the river, but I didn't feel it with all the excitement. Our hired carriage was racing from Grand Central Depot toward the harbor where the steamship *State of Nebraska* was soon to set off for Merrie Olde England. It would carry Buffalo Bill's Wild West show, a bunch of wild animals including buffalo, and me. That was if we made it in time.

So taken was I with it all, at least an hour had gone by without me thinking once on Papa, since when I did, I started crying. Mama cried a lot too, but she pretended not to. It had not been a good week for the Raines family. Apparently, the Englishman Clive Dunford and his banking friends stole all our money and almost put our ranch into the ground. So then Mama, seeing nothing for it, agreed to join Buffalo Bill in England. Then someone murdered my father. He was trying to protect me, and that got him killed. Lame Deer said it was Clive Dunford who did it. If I ever see him, I'll stick him with my knife.

The ache inside gnawed at me and I doubted it would ever go away.Crying again, I wiped my eyes with the back of my hand.

"You better close your mouth, Glory. You'll catch your fill of flies," Seamus said, smiling at his own wit. He hadn't seen my tears.

"Button your lip. You're not funny," I snaped petulantly.

Back then, my looks were all important to me, and it was quite well known that a gaping mouth was not considered pretty. So I closed mine. I was indeed pretty, more so than Mama. Everyone said as pretty as Aunt Julia, who I'd never seen but whom we would be visiting soon. With me so proud of my comeliness, Mama often called me Vainglory instead of just Glory.

Seamus gave a chuckle. He was not always scowling like he did even before Papa died. I thought it was this trip that got him excited, the grand adventure. Last night on the train, he'd asked me an odd thing that I thought had much to do with his weeks of surliness. Did I think of him as a redskin? His gaze was so earnest I knew this meant something to him.

"Of course not," I told him. "Everyone knows you're a gypsy. The

Cheyenne stole you from a circus where you were billed as *The World's Ugliest Baby*. Then they dropped you on Mama's lap." I held up my hand. "God's truth, Seamus."

He stared at me a long moment, then laughed and shook his head. He reached out and ruffled my hair. I hated that and slapped his hand away.

In the change of trains in Chicago, Mama telegraphed the show's manager, a Mr. Nate Salisbury, at the St. Denis Hotel, telling him we were still coming and should arrive on the 31st. She told him that an urgent family matter had held us up in Lone Tree several days. That family matter was the worst thing that ever happened, but she didn't telegraph that.

When our horses clip clopped onto the pier, I was thrilled to see that the *State of Nebraska* still at the dock. It had to be the biggest ship in the world. Longer than a hundred canoes. It could probably hold all Lone Tree. But I thought we still might not make it aboard. There were so many people, so much bustle and confusion that we couldn't move forward. Thousands had crowded onto the pier, waving at those on deck. They couldn't all be family. A band up there was playing *The Girl I Left Behind me*. I had a beautiful singing voice, another of my vanities, and had sung it many times with Teddy Pike, who was now dead.

Mama waved over several porters to take our baggage onto the ship. She carried her rifle, a Winchester 86, in a buckskin jacket, and that was all we brought as we pushed through the crowd. While Seamus held my hand, Lame Deer in the lead was striking people out of the way with her umbrella.

At the gangplank, at least thirty Indians sat in a circle blocking the way, their blankets pulled tight around them against the cold wind. Most were Lakota, but Mama said she recognized a couple Cheyenne, and Lame Deer did too. They were all chanting their death songs, Lakota and Cheyenne alike. In the middle of the pack, a white man was haranguing them in English, pleading with them to board the ship so they could get underway, but they ignored him. He was tall, sporting a full beard, and wore a long topcoat with a fur collar. In the stiff wind, he struggled to keep a bowler hat on his head. A real dandy.

I'd been to the Cheyenne reservation a few times including once when we drove cattle to the agency, but I didn't know any of the Cheyenne here.

Mama stepped up to the white man. "Can I help? I speak Cheyenne and some Lakota. We all do." She indicated Lame Deer. "My friend is Cheyenne."

Surprised, he stared at her. "Who are you?"

"Morgan Raines. Bill Cody hired me for the Wild West show."

His eyebrows rose in recognition. "Ah, you're the Captured Girl. Not very big, are you? No matter. Annie's shorter yet. It's the Wild West, not a show. This is real. You're real, aren't you? So it's the real Wild West and not a show."

Mama nodded. "I'm real."

"You'll make a great addition to the company. Fit you in between the raid on the cabin and the Deadwood stage, eh what." He stuck out his hand, and she shook it. "I'm Nate Salsbury, Cody's partner. I manage the business. Even the little girl?"

"Even the little girl what?" Mama asked.

I was the little girl, but I was nearly tall as Mama.

"She too can speak the Indian lingo?"

"Yes." Mama gestured to the Indians. "What's all this?"

Facing them, he placed his hands on his hips. "We have seventy of their brethren already aboard, but these here refuse to get on the damn ship, pardon my French. I don't know what's wrong with them, and my interpreters are nowhere to be found. Perhaps, drunk already."

Lame Deer was talking with a Cheyenne woman in animated conversation. Salsbury asked Morgan, "What are they saying?"

"It seems they're certain they're going to die when they're out of sight of land. They believe their souls will then wander over the water forever searching for the place of the dead."

"That's crazy," he said.

Mama stiffened. "Is it? Not to them." Her voice was like barbed wire. You didn't want to buck her when she was like that, but then Salsbury didn't know Mama.

"Wonderful," Salsbury grumbled. "Tell them they won't die on the ship."

She ignored him, stepping between a couple Lakota men to meet the Cheyenne man now standing with Lame Deer and the other Indian woman. I knew him. He was a famous warrior named Iron Chest because he wore old Spanish armor on his upper body. He did so during the Indian Wars, and he did so now. I could see dents where bullets had struck the breast plate.

Seamus and I tagged along with Mama in among the Lakota and Cheyenne. I saw the woman had a club foot and then knew who she was too. Since her birth, she'd been called Broken Foot, never escaping that name. In telling me Mama's story, Lame Deer said that when she was captured by Big Crow and taken to his camp, she was treated brutally. Only Broken Foot had been kind to her.

Lame Deer warned me never to mention the name of Big Crow in Mama's presence, she hated him so. I never did. I knew he'd murdered my grandparents, my Uncle Patrick, and Aunt Fiona when she was my age.

Broken Foot's husband Iron Chest smiled widely at seeing Mama. "I remember you, Crow Killer." That's the name Mama was given when she lived with Running Hawk's band. "The People in all the camps remember you. They tell of the battle when Crow Killer brought down many enemy warriors with her spirit rifle. The years have been kind to you. You still look a girl."

Mama laughed sharply, then indicated Seamus and me. "Not a girl anymore. These are my children. This is Glory and Ho'nehe."

I stood a little taller, but he ignored me and stared at Seamus. "You are the son of Spotted Horse."

My brother puffed out his chest and snapped off a nod. Well, whoop-de-do, I thought. My papa was as good as Spotted Horse, but

I never in my life brought that up with Seamus. He saw both men as his fathers so that was good enough.

Mama gestured to the ship and said to the Cheyenne couple, "If we die at sea, Spotted Horse will find us and lead us to Seyan."

I doubted if she really believed that, but maybe truth from the Indian part of her.

Iron Chest and Broken Foot agreed and followed us up the gangway. Glancing back to the dock, I saw the Lakota still sitting there like boulders, unlikely to move or be moved. They were someone else's problem. We got the Cheyenne to come aboard.

CHAPTER NINE

Steamship State of Nebraska, March 31, 1887

When Morgan, Lame Deer and Glory reached their cabin, their trunk and bags were already there. A damp, mildew smell clung to the place. It was small with vanity tables, a single bed where the three of them would sleep, and bright, electric lamps. Never had Glory seen such a thing, and Lame Deer too had been staring at them since they'd boarded and entered the hallways and now here in the cabin.

Glory said, "What will they think of next?"

A few minutes later when Lame Deer went up on deck to look for old friends, Morgan set out in search of Buffalo Bill, Glory along with her. Worried about what he planned for her in the show, she wanted to make clear what she would and wouldn't do.

"I want to sing in the show, Mama," Glory said, excited. "Do you think he'll let me sing. Next to Teddy Pike I was the best singer in the valley."

"Don't get your hopes up," Morgan said. "I don't think it's that kind of show."

They found Bill in the cargo hold standing on the guardrail talking with two other men. A loud discord of animal braying, whinnies, and moans filled the great enclosure.

"Mama, look," Glory said, frowning down into the hold.

"I see, Honey."

Below was an awful chaos of animals. Horses, maybe two hundred, danced about in one steel corral, fifteen to twenty buffalo bawled in another while cattle, mules, and elk were strewn along the hull. With all of them, their eyes bulged with terror and a stink of feces lifted from them.

They approached the three men. Morgan had never met Bill in person. Standing there in his fringed buckskin coat, she thought him someone of notable bearing like a general or two she'd seen. He had greying hair that flowed in long tresses down to his shoulders while on his chin was that famous pointed beard of his, like a goat's. Another man wore a blue uniform, and Morgan realized this must be the ship's captain. The third man was Salsbury.

Instead of talking to the two men, Buffalo Bill was making a speech, which might not have been too bad, but in his hand was a sword which he swung about absently as he spoke. Morgan wondered if he planned to stick one of them. Ducking the sword, Glory ran up and tugged at his coats.

Surprised, he glanced at her. "Now, who's this? A young lass, eh? One of those wild west performers. Can I do something for you, little girl?"

Her daughter didn't like being called a little girl because she wasn't that little anymore. Favoring her father, she was taller than most girls her age. But she gave him her best smile. "I'm Glory Raines, and I can sing pretty as a nightingale."

"Another Jinny Lind, are you?" he said and patted her head as if she were three years old.

Nettled by that, she said, "Yes, and you're going to have to punch some holes in the side of the ship or you're going to have a lot of dead animals before we get to England."

It was impertinent, but Morgan favored the ways of Cheyenne parents, giving their children their heads for the most part. Let them get into trouble and out of it on their own. But suddenly, she realized that would be a bad idea. Glory was angry all the time, mostly at her but really at her father for being killed. And she felt guilty about it because it happened saving her. Morgan knew this to be so for that was how she'd felt all those years ago when her own family was slaughtered, and she survived. It took a long time for that to sort itself out.

Buffalo Bill blinked like he didn't understand. Sheathing his sword, he frowned at Morgan. "Is this one yours, Madam?"

"She is. I'm Morgan Raines, Mr. Cody. I'm here to join your Wild West, but I wanted you to know I'm not a sharpshooter like Annie Oakley."

He glanced at Salsbury, then back to her. "I thought you were."

"I shoot, but I don't have any tricks, and I won't reenact my life for others."

She fixed him with her hard gaze, but he seemed oblivious to it. "Ah, yes, the Captured Girl has arrived," he said, the frown in his eyes gone. "It's a pleasure to finally meet you, Mrs. Raines. We've a wonderful action sequence you're going to love. It tells a story just right, maybe yours, maybe not. The important thing is the audience will dote on it and you. Don't worry, we'll fit the rest of your party into the show in some way I'm sure."

"My boy is the son of Spotted Horse," she said. She wanted Seamus in the show on top wages. They needed the money. But she also wanted it known that he was her son and that at one time Spotted Horse was her husband. She didn't want that to come out later and have trouble with Cody or anyone else. The Cheyenne knew but none of the others did.

Bill pondered this. "Your son. Do tell." He looked to Salsbury. "That puts another shade on the matter. We don't have Sitting Bull with us this season, and we need an Indian the people can hate. Spotted Horse's son just might do the trick."

When Salsbury nodded, Bill turned back to Morgan. "That all right with you, Madam?"

"Depends on the wages."

He waved that away. "We'll get together after we've set off and figure the pay and his part in the show." Bill looked at Glory again, then to the man in uniform. "Captain Braes, can you cut ventilation holes in the side of the ship?"

"Not in the side, sir, no, but I think we can get air down here by cutting them topside."

That settled for the moment, Morgan and Glory went up on deck to look for Lame Deer and found her with Seamus, who was sharing a room with two cowboys. Just then, the engines roared, startling them, and soon the *State of Nebraska* slipped out of the harbor and ploughed through the water as it headed down river.

"I guess Mr. Salsbury got all the Lakota aboard," Glory said, "but I bet they still think they're going to die out there at sea."

Seamus chuckled. "I think you're scared about it too."

"If the ship sinks, I can swim back," Glory said. "You're half Indian and everyone knows Indians can't swim. You'll only make it halfway back."

He laughed. "That's crazy, Glory. Maybe I'll throw you in and see how far you get."

Morgan turned to the rail as Lame Deer scolded the two in Cheyenne for troubling their mother. As the city shoreline went by, a cold breeze came from down river.

Seamus asked, "Mama, when will we see Auntie Julia?"

"We'll see," Morgan answered. "I sent a cablegram to her from Chicago saying we were coming. She knows we're coming."

At mention of her old friend, Morgan's mind drifted back, meandering through their strange relationship, the daughter of one of America's richest robber barons and an Irish girl from Five Points who'd grown up on the western frontier. And now, Julia was an English duchess and Morgan a famous shootist in the Wild West. That defined the saying *strange bedfellows*.

Glory gripped the rail beside her. "I'm downright flabbergasted. You sent a telegram all the way to England? They have wires on the ocean?"

"Well, she didn't send it by carrier pigeon," Seamus said.

"She might already have it. She'll be expecting us," Morgan said.

Wind whipped through Glory's hair as her face took on a look of excitement. "What's she like, Mama? They say she's as beautiful as Helen of Troy, who was the most beautiful woman ever though how would anyone know? Helen of Troy lived a thousand years ago, and there are no photographs of her. Is the duchess pretty as me, Mama?"

Seamus waved dismissively. "Much prettier, Monkey. And she doesn't snort like you."

"Monkeys don't snort, and neither do I. You're just jealous cause you look like a frog."

"You two, stop it," Morgan snapped, and they fell silent. She was angry. That her husband, their father, died that way and her two kids were joking like nothing had happened. She knew that was unfair. It was better they had moments of being normal, but her fury still held.

At that moment, the ship was passing an unfinished, giant statue of a woman holding a torch. Men were working on platforms up and down its height.

Glory pointed at it. "What's that statue?"

Seamus shrugged. "Lady Liberty. I read about it."

Morgan felt a presence behind her and turned. Her face drained of color. The large Indian stood like a massive bull buffalo. His face was face wrinkled now, but his eyes were lifeless and scary as they had been all those years ago. The of them glared at each other for several seconds then Morgan fished in her dress for the pistol she always kept there.

Without any emotion, the Indian turned and walked away. Now, with the gun in her hand, Morgan was trembling from fright or rage. Maybe both.

"Who was that?" Glory asked, alarmed.

Morgan didn't answer, but Seamus did. "Big Crow."

CHAPTER TEN

Earls Court London, April 15, 1887

Morgan Raines
Buffalo Bill's Wild West
Earls Court, West End London

Morgan,

Edward and I are most eager to see you again. We have tickets for the first performance of the Wild West. You and yours then must come to Becket Castle on the weekend of May 20th for a ball, which will include the Prince of Wales, and stay for the spring fair on Saturday. I'm sure Mr. Cody will allow it if I ask.

PS. You're still the world's worst lady's maid.
Duchess of Northampton

A low gray sky hung just above the tentpoles, giving a pall of gloom to all things as Morgan walked through the company's town of white tents. Having just read again, the telegram she'd received that morning, she smiled at that familiar jab in the postscript. It was true. She'd been a terrible lady's maid, but then there wasn't enough money in the world to persuade anyone else to take on Julia Kruger, the dragon of Fifth Avenue.

Through letters over the years, the two women maintained their odd friendship. They'd come to see themselves as the only two of a unique breed, unrelenting women set in their ways despite being hated for those ways and both indifferent to that hate.

"Auntie Julia is coming!" Seamus had exclaimed that morning in their tent when she first read the telegram. He'd known and loved her all those years ago. "She won't even recognize me."

Glory had jumped up announcing she was actually going to meet a real princess.

"A duchess, Oonaha Keso," Seamus corrected, using the Cheyenne nickname *Little Frog*. "She's a duchess, not a princess."

The change in the girl was instant, her hair shaking about in her fury. "I'm twelve. I am not little, and I'm not a frog." She stomped out of the tent, throwing the flap aside violently with Lame Deer hurrying after her.

At Glory's retreating back, Seamus shrugged helplessly. "I didn't mean to…"

"I know," Morgan said. "She's mourning her father. It's the best she can do."

Seamus gave a long sigh. "Yeah, me too."

That was Glory these days, all clatter and fury with long moments of moody silences, and Morgan understood it. She felt the same way but as painful as her grief was, she could deal with it. Glory couldn't.

But she was indeed twelve now. A birthday party was held in the Nebraska's salon as they crossed the Atlantic, but it was a dour affair. No one wanted to be there, least of all Glory, who cried when she was told to make a wish and blow out the candles. Just about everyone was sick from the rough seas including her, Morgan, and Lame Deer. No one could eat the cake except Annie Oakley and her husband Frank Butler, the only two beyond the ship's crew not ill. The stink of vomit filled the salon when they all staggered their way to their rooms.

As she hurried through the encampment toward Annie Oakley's tent, Morgan slipped the telegram back into her pocket. That morning, she, Annie, and Lillian Smith, the company's other sharpshooter, were to practice a showpiece together. Annie had a reputation for relentlessly practicing, and already a brilliant shot, what she wanted to perfect was her act. This one had the three women racing into the arena on horseback where they'd scoop up their pistols off the ground and shoot glass balls out of the air. Morgan had never used a pistol in that way before but felt she could do the riding part easily enough. She doubted, though, she could match the two sharpshooters in picking off glass balls.

In her tent, Annie was sitting at a small camp table cleaning her pistol. She was a pretty woman, not five feet tall, with dark brown hair and piercing brown eyes. Morgan thought her a sweet friendly person except when it came to money then all her sweetness hardened into steely resolve to keep her pennies in her pocket. Many of the company called her Missie. Bill did. Last year, Sitting Bull dubbed her Little Miss Sure Shot. But in private, she preferred Annie, so Morgan stuck with that.

"Ready, Annie?" Morgan called from the tent flap.

Quickly reassembling her pistol, the famous markswoman answered, "Let's do some shooting."

They left the tent, heading toward the corral where the cowboys practiced. That's always where they'd find Lillian flirting with every one of them even though she was married to Joe Kidd, a top rider.

"That girl's always sparking," Annie said, shaking her head disapprovingly. "She ought to take heed of her reputation."

As the Wild West's two performing sharpshooters, Annie's and Lilian's rivalry began almost immediately after Lillian joined the show last year. Quickly, it grew in bitterness. To Morgan, Bill tried to be impartial, but each thought he favored the other.

Morgan knew Annie had grown up dirt poor. Before she was even ten, both her father and stepfather had died, and she'd been forced to support her family with her hunting. No wonder she was so tight with a penny. Lillian's arrival threatened her status as the premier sharpshooter and therefore her earning ability. Then the young girl's lackadaisical approach to rehearsal put the show at risk. Annie couldn't abide that.

As for Lillian, she surely saw it differently. At just sixteen, she took a more than healthy pride in her abilities as a shooter, in fact she thought she was the best in the world. On joining the Wild West, she announced, "Annie Oakley is done for."

Now, as part of the performance with both women, Morgan found herself squarely in the middle. She tried not to take sides, but she did get along better with the older woman than with Lillian, who was much besotted with herself. But then, the girl was young, something that also bothered Annie. After the sixteen-year-old joined the company, Annie, who was twenty-six, started claiming to be twenty.

When they reached the corral, Morgan was surprised to see who Lillian was currently sparking, her son Seamus. And he was sparking her right back. She was a curvaceous, buxom girl and her son was grinning like a circus clown. At something he said, both laughed. Giggled more like it.

This part of her son's life Morgan did not want to interfere with. But Lillian was married. Seamus had been roughed up by Alice Olson, a girl back home who'd dismissed him because of his Cheyenne blood, and now he was vulnerable with the Smith girl. This could easily get him shot. Joe Kidd was no man to trifle with. But then neither was her son.

Lillian saw them first, rolled her eyes and sighed heavily, "Oh, dear, here comes your mother and Nanny Annie." She leaned in, pressing her body against his, whispered something, and giggled again.

Flushing red, Seamus quickly looked at Morgan, then put on his Cheyenne face, showing no emotion. Yet she well understood her son. He was angry, and that anger was directed at his mother. Now, what had she done?

"Lillian, we have the arena for rehearsal. Time's a wasting," Annie said, her tone making it clear she'd brook no opposition.

"Bill calls me California. Can't you, Missie?" the girl replied with the hint of a simper.

Annie turned and walked toward the arena.

Lillian glanced at Seamus, shrugged, and followed.

"I've got work to do," Seamus said to his mother and swung up on his horse.

She grabbed the reins. "Wait. Find Glory and make sure she gets to the mess tent this time. She's in the village with Lame Deer."

The village was the group of tepees the Lakota and Cheyenne had set up.

"Why can't Lame Deer do it?" he asked.

"You know her. She lets that girl do whatever she wants. I need to make sure Glory's with me at this afternoon's rehearsal."

He gave a curt nod and loped his horse toward a trio of cowboys roping steers.

CHAPTER ELEVEN

Earls Court, April 15, 1887

The best coup sticks were made of wood and wrapped in animal hide, then decorated in horsetail hair, strands of glass beads, and eagle feathers. Cheyenne and Lakota warriors used them to touch their enemies in battle. That showed their bravery. If you didn't have a pretty one handy, you could use an arrow or bow.

This morning, I was using a long arrow made of hard oak from Oliver Gatewood. Me and my fellow warriors ran among the city of big white tents that was the Wild West encampment looking to count coup against any stragglers. If I were ever caught, I'd be in trouble with Mama. Before I left our tent earlier, she warned me, "Glory, you stick with Lame Deer till the noon meal. I want you staying clear of trouble, you hear me? No more of this Tomfoolery you've been getting up to. You're not too big to have your backsides tanned."

Everyone seemed to think I had lost my wits and gone wild because of what happened to Papa. Yes, I was angry and sad, both in full measure, but what did that have to do with being a warrior. As for Mama, She'd never taken her hand to me, and I sure didn't want to start. But what she didn't know, she couldn't do anything about.

An hour ago, I'd slipped out of Iron Chest's lodge, escaping Lame Deer's, shall I say, less than watchful care. Right off, I rounded up my little band, three Cheyenne boys and a Lakota girl. That was Gatewood's daughter Shadow Horse. Two of the boys had colorful coup sticks with hair, beads, and feathers while the rest of us made do with arrows. Any unmindful cowboy, vaquero, or Indian was subject to our attack. We rush in fast, strike with our sticks, and race away, giving war whoops and laughing.

We'd already counted coup on two cowboys when we came upon Bill himself. He was just arriving from the fancy hotel where he slept at night. Not in his big old tent. I would dearly love to give him quite a whack since he'd not given me a damn thing to do in the show except being a piece of furniture in some of the acts. No singing, no wild riding like Seamus, no shooting like Mama. Nothing. I thought I could sneak up and whack him on the buttocks, but I preferred to hit him on the ear. Hurt more and he deserved it. But that might get us all sent home.

The old blowhard heard me first though. When he did, mock alarm twisted his face into a tortured grimace. He cried out, "A dastardly attack from the heathen horde. I shall not falter."

He drew his saber and waved it around. Still, no cowards us, we dashed in, me fastest and struck him a hard one. After that, he rushed off laughing. To give him credit, he could have stopped our rampaging with just a word, but he never did.

Even though our hits could sting and maybe bring a welt or two, like Bill, most of our quarry played along. A few, though, grew angry and took a real swat at us. Joe Kidd, a small and wiry cowboy, mean as a desert rattler, was one of them. Fiddling with a lasso, he was moseying along the path toward the corral where the cowboys practice, paying no attention.

We charged in but he dodged aside and snatched Swift Bear by his long braid and began whacking his bottom with vicious blows. Swift Bear yowled from the shame and hurt. I struck Kidd a great whack on his nose, bloodying it. He screamed at me in pain and fury. By my side, Shadow Horse swung her stick as well, shouting her shrill war cry. Then our other two warriors jumped in, swinging their coup sticks hard as they could. Joe Kidd released Swift Bear and fled.

From a safe distance, he shouted, "You kids are a menace. I'm going to have Bill flog the lot of you." Then he hurried off.

We whooped and cheered. We were true warriors. Mama wanted me to be a frilly prairie princess with a husband and lots of children. Actually, I'd always wanted that too. But I like being a warrior too, and someone carried enough meanness and evil in his heart to shoot Papa in the back. So, I knew I had to be more like Mama should I ever run into him.

Only one person we never went after. Mama told me to stay away from Big Crow, and this wasn't her normal hard warning. It had an element of fear attached to it. I knew that long before I was born, he'd killed my grandparents, my Uncle Patrick, and my Aunt Fiona when she was my age. Every bit of life she had to live taken from her. The rest of my band agreed since everyone in camp was afraid of Big Crow.

Yet, I told myself, I wasn't afraid. On this day, counting coup on Big Crow was my secret goal. He would feel my coup stick. This wass something I must do alone. That's what I said to myself. But really,, if I chickened out, I didn't want anyone else to see. With the noon mess approaching, I parted from my friends and approached Big Crow's lodge. He liked to eat and made sure he was always first in line at the mess tent, so I knew he'd be coming out soon.

I'd been waiting only a minute when he stepped out. Seeing me, a scowl darkened his face, which was saying something since his face always seemed to be scowling. Standing above me, he was big, bigger than a mountain. I felt my knees trembling. This had been foolish.

"What do you want, little bug?" he asked in Cheyenne, not too pleasantly.

I wanted to tell him if he was Mama's enemy, he was also mine. In my head, I could hear myself saying it, but the words didn't come out. I was so scared I felt like I was going to pee. After a moment, he laughed, not a funny laugh like Bill's, but a mean laugh, and he started to walk away.

I shouted something I hadn't even planned on. "Why do you hate my mother?"

He stared at me a long time, then said, "She was wasicus. Then she was of the People. Now, she is wasicus again."

I understood his words, white, then Cheyenne, then white again. This angered me. What nonsense. He had no right to tell my mother who she must be. I lifted my chin and addressed him like I was an Indian somebody, "Big Crow, you are also wasicus. You are here in the wasicus camp taking wasicus money."

This was a slap, and he actually flinched. He balled his fist and started toward me, then abruptly stopped, looking behind me. A hand touched my shoulder. It was Lame Deer.

"Go on with you, Old Fool," she said. "Don't let a little girl scare you."

His jaw tightened; a killing rage filled his eyes. This was what Mama saw all those years ago when she was taken by the Cheyenne. After a long moment, he walked away.

I trembled a bit but pretended I was unconcerned, then I spotted Seamus approaching. He was sweating and wiping his forehead with his kerchief.

I ran to him. "Are you going to be a cowboy or Indian at this afternoon's rehearsal?"

"Indian, I think. Come on. Mama wants you in the mess tent."

He started away, and we followed him. A company meeting after lunch was to go over any changes in the program before rehearsal. I was anxious to see if Bill had changed his mind at what I'd be doing, which right now was absolutely nothing. If he hadn't, I had my own plans for the show that will get everyone's attention. Just wait for that one, Mr. Bill Cody.

CHAPTER TWELVE

Becket Castle, Northampton, April 22, 1887

When the footman opened the carriage door for her, Julia Krueger Becket, the Duchess of Northampton, stepped down looking every bit the beautiful, noble lady she'd always wanted to be. Her elderly butler Carlton stood by the giant oak door of her own private castle with two footmen flanking him. She was returning from Manchester, a dreadful city of factories, where she'd spent the last two days smiling so much at her husband's managers that her face muscles were sore. The tea with the county gentry was this afternoon, and she must handle another crises her twelve year old son Toby had stirred up. He had inherited all her selfish traits without her skill to hide them.

"Did you have a pleasant trip, your grace?" Carlton asked with a supercilious nod.

"Thank you, Carlton, I did," she replied, then stepped over to one of the footmen. "William, it's good to have you back. I was so sorry to hear of your mother's passing. Such a terrible thing."

"Thank you, y-your grace," he said with a tremorous hitch in his voice. "The flowers you sent were much appreciated."

She nodded and entered the house. Removing her gloves as she came into the drawing room where her son was haranguing the housekeeper. Neither of them saw her.

Toby stamped his foot. "Mrs. Garrett, I must have my suit redone this minute. It no longer fits. I can't look like a vagabond."

"Milord, not today," the housekeeper replied calmly. "Your mother is about to arrive, and we must prepare for the tea. I cannot spare anyone. I will see it done tomorrow."

Her son was sporting a black eye and his hair was tousled. "You have to do what I say. I'm an earl," he insisted, stomping his foot again. "I wish to wear that suit for the tea. I demand you order it done now."

Julia shut the door hard, but only Toby jumped. Both turned toward her. "Thank you, Mrs. Garrett," she said. "I'll take it from here."

"Yes, your grace,"

When the housekeeper left, Toby said in a pleading voice, "I just wanted her to fix my suit, the blue one. Mama. She should…"

"Come with me, Toby," Julia cut him off. She opened the French doors and strode out onto the flagstone terrace with her son slowly following. She was angry with him, angry with the school for allowing him to be preyed upon by bullies, and angry with Edward for always being away managing his many businesses and leaving these problems to her.

The afternoon sun lit up the crimson of her dress and an angelic glow to her features. It made her appearance a lie for to her knowledge she was never angelic. Never had an angelic thought. She and her son stood at the balustrade overlooking the gardens and the panoramic sweep of grassland beyond. There, cows grazed as if a Gainsborough painting.

Her boy was handsome like his father, curly dark hair, and blue eyes, his handsome face marred by the puffy blackeye. A permanent smirk inhabited his face, her only contribution to his physiognomy. Haughty, that was her son, unrepentantly haughty.

"So, what was it this time, Toby? What did you do?" she asked.

Scrunching his face in wounded innocence, he answered, "Nothing, Mama. I swear. Only what is just and right. I am their earl and someday I'll be their duke. They must show me proper respect and deference. I insist upon it. That is all."

His nose actually went up in a pose of superiority. Had he learned that from her too? Since marrying Edward, she'd been trying to subdue her own worst traits, and her own arrogance was one of them. Not that she cared a whit what people thought about her, but she did care what they thought of her family, of her stewardship of the estate, of her husband Edward.

Toby added, "I shouldn't even have to attend such a school. It's not Eton, Mama."

"You were expelled from Eton. Your father put you in this new school so you could learn to get along with people who, as you say, will someday be your responsibility as their duke. He and I insist you try."

He seemed confused. "But they are there to learn how to get along with *me*."

Leaning down, she tapped the side of his head sharply near the black eye. He winced. She said, "If you were not so high-handed, perhaps you wouldn't get smacked so often."

"Yes, Mama," he said with contrition. He had a little bit of the toady in him. That characteristic was all his own.

Julia had surprised herself by how much she loved each of her children and how much time she spent with them. She gave hugs like candy at Christmas. She'd never thought much about children before she had them, little poppets who'd come so grudgingly out of her body. At first, Edward had found her approach unsettling, the children always about. It was not how he'd been raised or anyone else he knew. It was so lower class, then he rebelled against his own prejudice and went along with it. Now, he understood that after returning from the cutthroat world of business in London, the love of his wife and children proved to be a magical restorative.

When she and Edward first arrived in England more than a decade ago and took up life at Becket Castle, he was gone to London on business so often she'd insisted she herself run the estate. It was unusual, but she'd hardly be the first to do so. A few other women in England ran estates, some even with their husbands still alive.

Despite opposition from Mr. Hastings, the estate's manager, Edward had agreed.

As it turned out, Julia had been more successful than anyone had suspected possible, turning the estate operations into a profit for the first time in decades. She valued money and the work necessary to acquire it. She loved the power and satisfaction it gave her, riding the countryside atop her great steed, playing the lady of the manor to the tenants, the farm hands, and the business manager Old Hastings. She was tough in her dealings, though she hid it behind a winning smile.

Quickly, she learned if she performed some small kindness, people would readily go along with her. So she did. She'd provided gifts to her tenants, sent doctors to tend their sick, even made visits herself. She'd started charities and put on fairs. The people of the shire would do anything for her. Of course, she gave balls and dinners as well for the landed gentry and prominent citizens as far away as London. Quickly, she'd made herself queen of society, admired by all. She wished fat old Mrs. Astor could see her now.

Julia blinked in the bright sun. Not more than a hundred yards away, a man was coming toward the house. Then she saw it was not a man but a boy, Tom Langham. Even at sixteen, he was frightfully big and known as a brawler, all since his father died.

"I've hired Tom Langham to accompany you, even in school," she said. "That's why I was late. I stopped by his farm before coming here."

Toby's face lit up. "He'll be my squire."

"If you must call him that, yes." Julia nodded, remembering that the two of them had played that game as young boys, lord and squire, both with wild imaginations about knights of the Round Table and slaying dragons in battle. Tom's mother had worked at the castle on special occasions when Julia gave a ball or other social events and brought her oldest son along to play with his young friend. They formed an odd pairing, the farmer's lad, five years older, was squire to the knight, the lord's son. Toby's position and the death of Tom's father brought the friendship to an end. Till now. Now, his job would be to protect her son at all times, in all places.

Toby raced down the steps toward him.

Abruptly halting, Tom removed his broad-rimmed farm hat and swept it down in a deep bow. "Lord Exeter," he said addressing Toby by his title. "It's good to see you this fine day."

"And you, Squire Tom." Toby leapt up on his back. "To the stables, good steed, to the stables." And Tom carried him toward the back.

Julia sighed. Poor lad, she thought, from a squire to a horse in a blink. Will her son ever grow up?

Later, in her bedroom with gray-haired Hatch, her lady's maid, she was dressing for the tea, sliding into a bottle green gown. Edward was back from Manchester, in his own room getting ready.

Hatch finished the ties on the back, and Julia stared at herself in the mirror. Nearly perfect but something was missing. She needed just the right touch with her jewelry. This little tea party was mainly for Edward's business friends and their wives, so he wanted her to impress them. She flipped open the sapphire and ruby studded jewelry box.

"Will you wear it today, your grace?" Hatch asked.

Julia knew what she meant by *it*, the Tudor Diamond, a thirty-nine carat, pear shaped blue diamond surrounded by ten smaller gemstones. So the story went, three years ago, Edward bought it from an old French nobleman who'd come into its possession as payment for fighting for the rebels in Belgium's independence more than fifty years before. Into his eighties now, without heirs and penniless, he accepted Edward's generous offer of six hundred thousand pounds.

Reports of the piece's renown soon circulated throughout the country. The Tudor Diamond, it was said, had been owned by Queen Elizabeth herself, but she sold it in Antwerp to fund her navy against the Spanish Armada. Then more than two hundred years later, it came into the French nobleman's treasury, and finally to the Duke and Duchess of Northampton.

It didn't seem to matter that no one had heard this story till three years before. In truth, Edward had made it up to give the jewelry greater value. He had commissioned it from a diamond merchant in Antwerp. The jewelry piece itself was worth more than four hundred thousand, but with this origin story attached to it, the value was priceless. Julia was aware and even proud that Edward sought every advantage he could muster in business and in life. Having a beautiful wife and beautiful things like the Tudor Diamond were telling advantages.

"Not very subtle, is it, Hatch?" Julia replied. "But I think it will do just fine."

The lady's maid drew it from the box and draped the gold chain over Julia's neck. Looking at the duchess in the mirror, she gasped. "Beauty on beauty."

Julia smiled, pleased. "Yes, it will do in a pinch." She smoothed her dress. "Now, shall we go down and dazzle the great commonality as they arrive."

CHAPTER THIRTEEN

Becket Castle, April 22, 1887

Outside on the back lawn of Becket Castle Dunford and his wife Lydia were greeted by the duke and duchess. Lydia curtsied so low, Clive thought she would topple over. It was embarrassing, and he struggled to keep his framed smile in place.

Arising still clinging to the duchess's hand, she stammered to the duchess, "When I was sixteen, your grace, your parents invited my family to tea with several others. You played the piano and sang. It was the most beautiful thing I'd ever heard. I still dream about it. What an artist the world lost when you became royalty."

Dunford stiffened. That was ignorant and an unforgivable breach of etiquette. He thought his plan was being sabotaged by his own wife before it could begin.

But the duke laughed. "We're not quite royalty, Countess, but I suppose I am the villain for taking her away from such pursuits. We shall have to invite you and your husband to a private performance soon."

And the duchess was smiling. She patted Lydia's hand. "It's so kind of you to say, Countess. I look forward to playing for you again someday."

Dunford relaxed. It had actually turned the trick, but he'd have to warn Lydia to keep her gob shut among her betters.

The duchess extended her hand to him, and he shook it lightly.

"So nice to meet you, Earl," she said. "I was so sorry to hear about your father's and brother's passing."

Caught off guard, he hesitated before bringing up the right expression of sorrow. "Thank you, your grace. I think it has affected Mama the worst."

"Of course."

He held the duchess's hand a beat too long. Even knowing of her renowned beauty, he was still awed by seeing it for the first time. The woman was truly stunning, but he doubted it would be a good idea to seduce this duchess and risk the dodge aimed at her husband. Dunford's attention was caught by the jewel at her neck, the famous Tudor Diamond he'd heard so much about. A bit gaudy for a tea party but still as mesmerizing as the the woman herself.

She withdrew her hand from his with a curious regard, then she turned to Lydia. "Why don't you join us for a round of croquet, Countess."

The tea had been well along when Dunford's opportunity came to set his scheme in place. The duchess, Lydia, and a few other men and women were playing croquet while the duke and three of his friends stood smoking cigars by the steps to the terrace. He was well aware of their success in business, their constant air of superiority, and their ability to cheat those beyond their circle.

To Dunford, the duke looked a toff in his close-fit trousers, cravat, and jacket, a handsome man over whom the ladies swooned. Then there was short, portly Edgar Wilson, cartoonish owner of textile factories in Manchester. Beside him stood cadaverous and wheezing George Winthrop, who couldn't keep a bit of spittle from dribbling down his beard. He owned mines in Scotland.

The last of the duke's toadies was Sir John Coppersmith, hero of Roarke's Drift and a Cape Colony big game hunter. The skin of his clean shaven face was bronze from a life in the sun. *Handsome John*, the dailies called him when they described his adventures on the dark continent. He had no business interests with these men to speak of but a friendship with Becket, who employed him in some capacity in

Southern Africa to hunt for his railroad construction crews. All were as well appointed as the duke, but no one would mistake them as toffs. More like monkeys in evening clothes, Dunford thought, even Coppersmith.

When he went over and joined them, they ignored him as if he were not up to snuff, continuing to talk business. The toadies all acquiesced to the duke's opinion.

They were saying something about railroads and Dunford interjected himself, addressing the duke, "I understand, your grace, that you designed the Lilly Langtry locomotive. I dare say it's a singular achievement. I admire it very much."

The four turned to him as if one of the castle dogs had peed on their trousers. With a hint of skepticism, Northampton said, "You do? And what is it about the locomotive you admire?"

Dunford put on an embarrassed half-smile. "Well, not the engineering. I know nothing about engineering. It's the look of the thing, like it came out of the Royal Society of Art."

The duke gave a genuine smile this time. "Exactly. That's very astute and kind of you to say, Earl. Few seem to notice that aspect of it."

Dunford's comment had hit the mark, and he was in.

Wilson flicked cigar ash onto the grass and said to the duke, "I've noticed heavy usage on the Manchester to Liverpool line. Perhaps new rail lines would be a good investment. What say you, your grace?"

They were off talking among themselves again, but Dunford listened as one of the group. After a few minutes, Winthrop said, "I'm considering an investment in American cattle. That has been a treasure trove for years. We should take advantage. It is malfeasance not to do so. Worth, perhaps, a hundred thousand investment each I should think."

The duke studied his cigar a moment. "Since my brief respite in the West, I've kept a distance. But I suppose it might be worth forming an investment company for the purpose."

Dunford saw his opportunity and seized it. "Gentlemen, keep your purses firmly in your pockets. That would be a waste of good money."

The four men stared at him with annoyed expressions.

Dunford took a half-step in and spoke with urgency. "I've just returned from the American West this very month and I can inform you unequivocally the American cattle boom is over. This past winter wiped out the great herds, and many banks failed. Not to put too fine a point on it, when I left, the carcasses of the poor beasts littered the landscape. Perhaps the news has not yet fully reached our shores."

There was an audible intake of breath from Winthrop. "Are you certain?"

"I am, sir."

"That's sad to hear," the duke said. "It seemed perfect country for such an enterprise."

Dunford replied, "And so it was, your grace, till the winter ended it all. I did make quite the fortune there, and thankfully sold my cattle last year before winter" He paused to set up the the main play. "Instead of cattle, I bought a gold mine in the Rand. You have railroads there, your grace, you must have considered it."

He saw their eyes flicker with curiosity. The duke said, "I have, but Cecil Rhodes and his DeBeers outfit seem to have taken all the choice mines."

"Yes, but not all. There are still some plum properties left. I own one."

The portly man Wilson said, "I've been considering such an investment. Is it profitable?"

"Oh, yes," Dunford said. To lie well, he'd learned, was a form of high art. "Better than I ever expected. Better than cattle during the boom years. I haven't even gotten to the main vein yet. My men use just picks and shovels. As you might suspect, that's not quite what's needed to bring in the motherlode." He leaned in and spoke with calm certainty. "I'm told it could be millions, but then I'm taking it slow, step by step. I don't have the financing to bite off the whole portion quite yet."

He'd said enough. He'd set the hook in deep. He was about to excuse himself to rejoin his wife when the duke said, "You were in Montana territory, were you not, Earl?"

Dunford frowned, suspicious of this enquiry. Did he know something he shouldn't. "Yes, your grace."

"Anywhere near a town called Lone Tree?"

"Indeed, I had holdings there," he answered cautiously.

"Then you might know an old friend of mine and my wife's, Morgan Raines."

Dunford stiffened and for a second his mask fell. Both hate and fright showed there, but then were gone and no one seemed to notice. He forced a uneasy smile. "Yes, your grace, I am acquainted with the woman."

"Ah, remarkable, indeed. She is currently in London with the Wild West," the duke said. "My wife is arranging a ball for next month. Mrs. Raines will be there, and I'm sure she'll be delighted to see you. I'll see that you and the countess are among the guests."

Dunford thanked him and excused himself, going over to his wife and the croquet. With effort, he walked steadily, his mind rushing through this. She was here in England. Was that just a coincidence? She could not possibly know about his involvement in her daughter's end. She could not. After a moment, he decided this may in fact be a good turn. When he saw the Raines woman at the ball, he would pour on the sympathies, how sad the cruel vagaries of life, so terrible that her spawn should have died so young. Inundated with such good will, she'll come to hate the mention of her daughter.

CHAPTER FOURTEEN

London, May 2, 1887,

A week before opening day, Mama was rehearsing all the time on her three showpieces, the emigrant train, the three sharpshooters killing glass balls, and the Indian attack on the cabin. Me, I had nothing to do but sit in Mama's wagon in the first piece, not singing a lick.

Bill could be a tyrant and made the company toil from morning well into the evening. Nothing seemed to be working though. The full rehearsals were chaos with a lot of riding and shooting but it made no sense. All the work didn't bother Mama. She stayed locked into her roles like she thought she was Sarah Bernhardt. I barely saw her, which meant Lame Deer was to watch out for me. I barely saw her either. I was pretty much on my own. So that was how I got me a dog.

My small band of renegades had snuck away from Earls Court for London proper and terrorized some local citizens with our coup sticks. Seeing them run off like we were real Indians made us all laugh hysterically. After we escaped an angry mob with two bobbies and made it back to camp, it turned out a little mongrel dog had followed us, primarily me. Apparently, he knew a source of food when he saw one. I took to feeding it scraps from the mess tent, so of course then, he stuck around me like a bee to honey.

When Mama saw me hugging the filthy thing, she reacted like we were under attack. "Glory!" she shouted, "get away from that mangy dog. You'll get fleas or worse."

Shocked by her voice, I jumped back. "It's my dog, Mama. I'm calling him Archie because his bark has a British accent."

"He looks like he's nobody's dog but his own," she said. When she stepped toward him, he snarled. She swung her boot at him, but he jumped aside and scurried behind me.

"No, Mama!" I screamed. "Archie's my dog. I want to keep him. Please."

I could tell she didn't like the snarling, flea-infested mutt, but after much thought, she allowed it. He would be something to occupy my time, she told me, instead of running around with my gang of miscreants. "You must give it a bath then," she added. "Use the lye soaps, and when he's clean, and I mean truly clean because I will check him, then you come right back here for your bath. It'll be lye soap for you as well. If he gets into trouble, you get into trouble. And the dog goes."

I jumped with delight. "Thanks, Mama, I will."

Once the dog was clean, he turned out to have a shiny gold coat of fur. I put a blue ribbon on him, which Seamus thought made him look ridiculous. He wanted to tie the ribbon to his tail so he would always be chasing it. I wouldn't let him. But everyone else, including Lame Deer, thought he was cute. I'd taken to sleeping on a cot like Seamus, and the little sneak, Archie not Seamus, stole into the tent at night and slept with me.

The next day, the dog became the fifth member of our band of raiders.

Rehearsals were not getting any better. Horsemen attacking the wrong people, people not showing up for a scene, Annie and Lillian feuding so much they stopped practicing together.

The company had a command performance before the Prince of Wales, and it was a disaster. Nothing went right. No one seemed to know where they were supposed to go and more than one rider collided with another. Yet the prince and his entourage were delighted.

He asked Bill if he might meet the three women sharpshooters. They were brought up to him, and Bill introduced Mama, Annie, and Lillian, all curtsying before royalty as we all were taught. Then he made the rift between Annie and Lillian deeper by asking Bill which of the three was the best shot. Among them, this question was worse than asking who was the prettiest.

He said, "Lillian, I suppose. All three can shoot, your highness, but she won the California championship."

That was stretching the blanket some, I thought. Lillian called herself the Champion of California, but there was no record anywhere of her ever winning a shooting contest there or anywhere. Annie bristled. She had made her reputation winning shooting contests. Her glare could have lit Bill's beard on fire. Lillian grinned widely, showing all her large teeth, and nodded to Annie with a smug grin.

The prince turned to Mama. "Do you agree, Miss O'Connor, or do you claim the honor?"

"I know better, your highness," she replied. "Lillian is good, but Annie is the best I've ever seen."

"Then where does that leave you?" the prince pressed, enjoying himself. "Third best?"

"Perhaps I am. But I'm the best when someone is shooting back."

He blinked, then grinned. "I bet you are."

The night before the opening performance, Annie and her husband Frank invited their closest friends out for a meal to celebrate before the disaster that the next day would be. Mama, Seamus, Lame Deer, Iron Chest with his Spanish breastplate, and me came along with Mr. Gatewood, his Lakota wife Walks Along Woman, and their daughter Shadow Horse, my chief lieutenant in our warrior band. This generosity was surprising since Annie usually kept her money so tight in her fist it would take a crowbar to pry it loose. Good old Annie though. Instead of a fancy restaurant, she took us to a cheap Chop House that was as much saloon as eatery and ordered the basic sixpenny plates for everyone.

As we ate, I noticed something odd about Lame Deer and puzzled over it. Then, it came to me. Her hair was completely gray. That had happened so gradually that seeing her daily it didn't take. She was a tough, small woman, but my God, she was old. She had memories as a child of the time before the fur trappers when the first white man came to Cheyenne country. Back in the wooly mammoth days, I'd once kidded her. She'd snorted and said, "Before then."

She realized I was staring at her and shook her head with mock disappointment. I smiled and went back to my food.

After most of the meal was eaten, Mr. Gatewood began telling a story about how he came by the mini ball he kept around his neck in a buckskin pouch.

"There we was just north of the Picketwire when Injuns hit us. Cheyenne they was. A hard fight, lasted two days. Three against a thousand. It was touch and go, touch and go."

He stroked his bushy, white beard, considering his next words. Everyone including the nearby diners and beer drinkers listened with rapt attention. Though his false teeth slid every so often, he didn't skip a word.

"We drove off assault after assault. Then by nightfall of the second night, they was gone. I guess they'd had enough. We poked our heads above our barricade and saw not hide nor hair of them. I can surely tell you though, they were three of the toughest buggers I ever come across."

Everyone laughed, including the chop house patrons, and strangest of all, the great warrior Iron Chest had this high-pitched cackle. Mr. Gatewood stood and bowed. When he sat down, I pulled at his buckskin jacket. "But how did you get that mini ball?"

He took it out of its little pouch and held it up for everyone to study and we did like it was the Tudor Diamond. "You see," he said, "this here Injun had an old blunderbuss. Don't ask me where he got it for I don't know. Getting near the time we drove them off, he come right up to me and fired. That gun exploded this giant plume of smoke. The mini ball hit me in the mouth, knocked out a bunch of my teeth, and bloodied me up some."

As if to illustrate the point, his false teeth fell out onto the table. He scooped them up, set them back in, and went on without a by your leave. "But the ball keeps going, you see, right up my nose and gets stuck in my skull. I had one powerful headache, but I lived. It done give me headaches for a lot of years like the top of my head was coming off. Near drive me crazy."

"Did you go to a doctor to take it out?" I asked, taken in by the story.

"I did, Miss Glory. According to the docs, it was way too risky to cut on," he replied. "Then ten years on, I was up near Cripple Creek eating dinner one night with some pards when those hot Mexican beans made me sneeze. That mini ball shot right out my nose and landed on the plate. And here it is." He dropped the little ball onto his plate with a clank.

After a moment of silence, everyone laughed again, and the Londoners applauded.

At that moment, an officious man wearing a neat suit and a pinch-lipped expression weaved his way through the tables toward us. With him were four beefy toughs who looked like they expected and wanted a brawl. In great distress, our group's waiter trailed them.

Red in the face, the officious man stormed up to our table. "I am Malcolm Fernsby, the manager here. There has been a terrible mistake. This establishment does not, nor will it ever serve people of the dark-skinned races." His wave of the hand took in Seamus, Lame Deer, Iron Chest, Walks Along Woman, and Shadow Horse. "I served in the Natal during the recent Zulu rebellion, and I'll not have fakirs sitting in my establishment. The rest of you may remain to finish your meals. However...." Slowly, one at a time, he punched his finger in the air in the direction of the Cheyenne, Lakota, and Seamus. "You, you, you, you, and you must leave immediately."

When no one moved, the manager nodded to his men. Once they began forward, Mama was the first to step into their path, blocking the way. I knew she would be. They had threatened Seamus. One of the men smirked, so she drew the gun she kept hidden in her dress at all times, aimed it at his face, and cocked back the hammer. The smirk disappeared. Fear swam in his eyes and he blinked rapidly. I heard the loud cock of several guns around me as each of the men and Annie stood, aiming their pistols at the four men.

Mr. Gatewood said to the man facing Mama. "Don't be embarrassed, son. That look of hers would pucker a bear's ass." He turned to the manager. "I believe I'll sit here and finish my meal with my friends. All of them. That okay with you, Mr. Manager?"

The man's mouth moved but he didn't respond.

Mr. Gatewood addressed the chop house audience more than the manager. "We are from the Wild West, and wild we are. We're going to finish our meal and drink at our leisure." His voice rose theatrically." I am Orville Gatewood, the famous scout, and I done got fifty scalps on my belt. This here is my wife Walks Along Woman, and that's her friend Lame Deer. They are tough as saddle leather and tougher than you."

The manager rolled on the balls of his feet, about to speak, then gave up the idea.

Mr. Gatewood went on, "The Indian with the iron shirt is the great Cheyenne Chief Iron Chest. Nothing he likes better than white people's scalps. This is Morgan O'Connor, the famous Captured Girl. She done put more bad men in the ground than Admiral Nelson, but then his he put into the sea. That there is her son Wolf of the Cheyenne, son of the great Spotted Horse. Now that Indian had men wetting themselves at mention of his name, and Wolf is a chip off the old block."

Like a Master of Ceremonies, he turned to the Butlers. "Unless you're an ignorant bumpkin, these two you know. The pretty one is Little Miss Sure Shot, Annie Oakley herself, and the not so pretty one is her happy husband, Frank Butler. Buffalo Bill's going to be mighty disappointed iffen you folks don't come tomorrow to see us, the wildest, most rootin tootin show you'll ever see. He might have to send his Indians out raiding Old London Town if you don't."

He holstered his gun to genial laughter and sat down as Mama and the others did the same. The manager hesitated only a second more, then cocked his head to his men and retreated.

Nearly half an hour later, after Mr. Gatewood had nursed a beer to its dregs, Annie settled up the bill with the manager, haggling the price down to a few pennies, then we left.

Though it was night, streetlamps illuminated the the several blocks back to Earls Court. People were still out, and some looked like nefarious customers to me, but no one bothered us. The men all carried their guns in holsters belted conspicuously around their waists, something never seen in London. With the next day's opening performance seemingly settling into everyone's thoughts, no one spoke much except for me and Shadow Horse. We chattered excitedly but in low, secretive tones.

Shadow Horse said, "I know you're planning something for tomorrow's show. What is it? Tell me, please."

I shrugged. "Maybe I am, maybe I'm not."

Shadow Horse grabbed my arm. "Let me be a part of it."

I didn't want to get her in trouble. "It's best I do it alone. Just have my horse nearby. It will be the last showpiece, the raid on the cabin. I promise it will shake them up good."

She grinned then we both laughed.

CHAPTER FIFTEEN

Earls Court London, May 9, 1887

>The Illustrated Sporting and Dramatic News
>*Opening Day of Buffalo Bill's Wild West*
>*A Grand Affair*
>*By Chester Bosworth*

On a sublimely sunny day in Earls Court, everybody who is anybody and innumerable nobodies crowded into the vast arena to see the Yankeeries and the Buffalo Billeriees of the Wild West. To rousing tunes from the "cowboy" band, thousands upon thousands of eager attendees claimed their positions on the tiered wooden benches, each of them grinning ear to ear like grateful fruit sellers who sold rotten apples to unsuspecting customers.

The American prairie and snowcapped Rocky Mountains greeted them, painted upon a towering forty-foot canvas that stretched a quarter mile across the arena. A forlorn log cabin, a patch of shrubbery, and an animal pen were set upon the field. A few minutes before the show, uniformed ushers led great personages of society and wealth to their box seats, a show unto themselves in their regal day dresses and frock coats. Among them tread the large party of the Duke and Duchess of Northampton, that gentle lady of renowned beauty and character...

As Julia took her seat in the box, she admitted to herself she too was feeling the excitement of the moment. There seemed something akin to unbounded energy spreading throughout the arena. People chattered like magpies, shouting back and forth. Indeed, these westerners, these Buffalo Billeriees, as they were being called, had captured the imagination of her adopted country.

As a gentle breeze stirred up dust, she dabbed a kerchief to her eyes against it, looking close to crying, though she was nowhere near it. Like Morgan, she was not one for tears. What a strange relationship the two had despite oceans and years of separation.

They'd been enemies, then allies, then friends. They knew that darkness dwelled within each other's souls, and still they accepted one another. Few people had liked either one. Simply put, Morgan had saved her life and the lives of her family. All Julia had, she owed to her friend, and she could never repay that. Now, as if conjured out of one of her dime novels, Morgan was about to appear in this great arena.

Edward sat beside her, along with young Cousin Isobel, a poor relative from Norwich saddled upon them by the girl's mother. Isobel was so shy and quiet Julia had suspected her dull-witted at first, even though she constantly read great tomes about astronomy and other sciences. At seventeen, the whiff of desperation hung about her. This was her second season "coming out." Last year was a failure. Not the hint of a proposal of marriage. If a girl wasn't engaged within six months after her first coming out, she would most assuredly go through a second. If no prospect presented himself this year, the ominous future of the old maid loomed before her.

Being homely, her chances of finding a husband were slim. She had a small, ugly gap between her front teeth, and at the most inappropriate times, such as when she was nervous, she tended to whistle her S's and soft C's. But when she smiled, despite her gap teeth, she could be thought of as passably tolerant. She seldom smiled though.

Julia's three young daughters were shepherded into the box by their nanny, Mrs. Schneider, a fussy German, while Tom Langham accompanied Toby. The farm lad was still uncomfortable in his costly finery, quivering as if ants crawled inside them. Today, Toby was more excited about attending the Wild West than she'd ever seen him about anything. Since disembarking from the South Kensington station with the throngs coming this way, he'd been ceaselessly commenting on everything from people's attire, alternately drab or pretentious, to the cowboys and Indians soon to be on display, making himself out to be something of an expert.

Edward had warned him to behave. He did so only when he found the new American treat called popcorn, which he purchased on entering the arena and readily devoured.

"Why are they making us wait?" Toby called out, bouncing on his seat. "We are here. They can begin. Is your friend coming out first, Mama? Did she do all those things it says in the program? Shoot up all those people?"

More frantic, he suddenly pointed down into the arena where a space existed between tall plants, separating the painted canvas from the grandstand. People and horses could be seen milling about. "Look, there they are. I see them behind the painting. Come out. Come out!"

"Calm yourself, Toby," Julia said. "You're not riff raff. You're an earl. Behave like it."

Abruptly, Julia jumped when a large, rotund fellow at a podium thirty yards away spoke in a voice so loud it could tumble cities. An outdoor voice to be sure. "Ladies and gentlemen, I'm Frank Richmond, and I'm the orator for the Wild West. My pleasant task here is to explain this Grand Processional Review of Groups and Individual characters, to introduce the wonders of the plains, the peculiarities of buckjumpers, the skill of the men with the lasso and rifle, the marvelous horsemanship of the Wild West's children and much, much more."

Backstage, the commotion of more than a hundred riders around me fell off when Bill shouted, "Line it up."

I watched the cowboys in red sashes and chaps, vaqueros in their silk shirts and fancy sombreros, Cheyenne and Lakota in full battle regalia, war paint, and war bonnets as they moved by twos and threes into place. Mama and several other women sat their horses nearby, the creak of saddle leather and the jangling of bells on the horses sent a thrill of anticipation through me. I rode with the pack of children riders, including Shadow Horse, who kept grinning at me as if I were going to sprout wings and fly.

In her saddle, she leaned toward me and whispered, "Are you actually doing it, Glory?"

"Samuel's goat!" I whisper-shouted. "Steady on, Shadow." Then I grinned. "Yes, soon."

"Get ready London," Orville Gatewood proclaimed, leaning forward on his horse and peeking out through an opening at the packed grandstand. His voice rose loud. "Boys, it's as busy out there as a whorehouse on nickel night."

Laughter rolled through everyone, including me and the other young ones while several men whooped in reply.

Mama tried to frown but failed. "Mr. Gatewood, the children, sir."

He took his hat off and placed it over his heart. "I'm truly sorry, ma'am."

Then Mama gave me a hard look. Now why did she do that? She couldn't know what I was planning. I knew she had no particular worry about me or any of us riding out in the first mad charge that would open the show. We were all born on horseback. So it must have been one of her general, all-purpose scowls.

With the thunderous voice of Frank Richmond rising again from the grandstands, everyone settled into place.

"Ladies and gentlemen," I heard the man bellow. "Buffalo Bill and Nate Salsbury proudly present the one and only, genuine and authentic, unique and original Wild West!"

Buffalo Bill shouted, "Curtain up."

When the band in the arena blasted a martial tune, all us riders surged out into the arena.

At the sudden appearance of the wild horsemen, Julia's pulse raced. So loud were they, the horses' hooves pounded inside her chest. As the riders swept by the grandstand, Toby screamed with delight, Cousin Isabel released a frightened squeak, and everyone leaned forward in their seats breathlessly. Shockingly, none of the women rode sidesaddle but astride. Julia couldn't see Morgan, but a young girl with hair reddish auburn and golden in the sunlight raced to the front, her legs pumping at the horse's flanks. The crowd cheered her on as if it were the Derby. Somehow, Julia knew this was Morgan's daughter and cheered, her voice joining the wild din.

Buffalo Bill rode out last. The horde circled about and halted, stretching across the arena in front of the great canvas painting and faced the audience in silence. The entire crowd of more than thirty thousand grew quiet. Then one of the Indians screeched a blood-chilling war cry, and the entire mass charged directly at the grandstand, yelling and whooping. Around Julia, people gasped and screamed.

Not twenty feet from the stands, the riders pulled up abruptly, and Buffalo Bill rode out in front. Sweeping off his hat, both he and his horse bowed. The audience roared its approval, and spotting Morgan among them, Julia found herself heartily clapping.

Then the show began.

After the delightfully clever gunwork of Miss Annie Oakley, Julia finally saw Morgan in a scenario. She was driving the lead wagon of the emigrant train into the arena, the girl with the flaming auburn hair beside her. A dozen or more wagons with settler types at the reins followed.

Julia pointed at her. "Toby, that's her on the lead wagon."

The performance was interesting enough, an attack by the Indians, a rescue by Buffalo Bill and his troopers, lots of gunfire, and at the end, the rescuers dancing a Virginia Reel with the emigrants.

Toby folded his arms and said, disappointed. "All she did was drive a coach and dance, Mama. I can do that."

"Hold your horses, son. There's more to come."

After two other acts, more did come. Next, the program had Annie Oakley, Lillian Smith, and Morgan O'Connor set to perform an exhibition of shooting.

Miss Oakley's assistant placed three pistols out in the middle of the arena and retreated to work the target machine. A short silence fell. Then suddenly, the three women burst into the arena, riding at a breakneck pace, Morgan shrieked a chilling Indian war cry, and easily the best rider of the three, sprinted quickly ahead. The pigeons and glass balls were already being hurled skyward.

Morgan leaned down from the saddle so far the audience screamed as if she were falling, but instead she scooped up her gun, whirled the horse about, and brought down every pigeon, every glass ball before they hit the ground. The other two women leapt from their horses, picked up their guns, and began firing at a new batch of targets.

Once Morgan was on the ground, the three women stood side by side and with excellent teamwork lit up the arena.

Breathless, feeling a sense of enormous pride she could not explain, Julia announced loudly, "I don't think a single glass ball survived the encounter. What do you thibnk about Morgan now, Toby?"

Toby was applauding wildly.

The Illustrated Sporting and Dramatic News:
Opening Day of Buffalo Bill's Wild West
A Grand Affair
By Chester Bosworth

...By the time of the show's last act, the attack on the log cabin, one might admit to trembling perturbations of the mind after so many scenes of excitement and feats of daring, but this last one brought the heart to a stop. This poor writer has never seen anything of the like.

Tragedy loomed darkly over the entire sequence of events. Two unforeseen and terrible mishaps caused the misfortune. Here, in this act, Miss Morgan O'Connor, the one known as the Captured Girl for her years living with the aboriginal tribes of the Far West, must withstand another attack by the redmen, holding them off with her rifle till Buffalo Bill and the troopers once again ride to the rescue. A rousing feast to the eyes and ears it promised to be. A frightful and alarming interlude it became.

As expected, the Indians struck, screaming their blood chilling cries and driving a herd of buffalo before them. They circled the cabin in wide arcs as Miss O'Connor stood on the porch firing her rifle at them. Nearby, in the animal pen where a score of long-horned cows was held within, the beasts, panicked by the great clamor, broke through their containment. Quickly, they were caught up in the wild melee of Indian ponies and buffalo racing about the cabin.

Thereupon, the young girl with the flashing hair who sped to the front in the show's opening charge appeared from behind the shrubbery and attempted to make her way through the swirling tumult of Indians, horses, and cattle to join Miss O'Connor. Carrying a rifle, she made several efforts but backed off each time when no break opened. Being off to the side and hidden by the riders as the girl was, Miss O'Connor did not see her, nor did it seem any of the attackers did, focused as they were on the dwelling. Surely, this was foolish for someone so young to be attempting something so dangerous, yet clearly, she had pluck. Finally, a bit of gap opened, and into the breach she went, a mad dash for the cabin.

That was when the second mishap occurred. All the while, a small dog had been observed by the shrub from which the girl had come, barking again and again but unheard in the din. Abruptly, it pursued into the breach. Not yet to safety, the girl turned back to save the pug just as a wall of long-horned beasts with flaring nostrils and fiery red eyes bore down on her. Tragedy was inevitable.

The dog fled, but the girl was done.

At that instant, a wild Indian on a tough little steed burst through the front wall of animals, jumped a step ahead, and in daring incomparable, reached toward the ground and snatched the girl up. When he swung her behind him, she could be seen clinging fiercely to his back. The arena fell to a hush; even the Indians ceased their gunfire. Then, the audience cheered madly.

Moments later, the Indian dropped the girl on the porch with Miss O'Connor, and the play continued. Finally, Buffalo Bill and his troop arrived, chasing the attackers off. The act over, the slain red men rose from the dead and hurried away with the other players.

One more turn was left to the day's performance. Producing a birch, Miss O'Connor drew the girl over her knee, lifted her dress revealing her blue pantaloons, and proceeded in front of the crowd to give her a thrashing, five swats on the backsides. Though she flinched at each stroke and tears could be seen, she never cried out. This too was applauded.

After the cowboy band played a passable "God Save the Queen," the show was concluded, but the audience seemed in no hurry to leave. It had been two hours of extraordinary sights and raw emotions. The Buffalo Billeriees had done their job well. All on horseback, they retreated from the field except a single Indian, the one who had saved the girl. He rode slowly toward the grandstand. He was a young man in a shocking state of undress, just hide leggings, moccasin boots, and a single feather dangling from his black hair. Three streaks of red decorated his bare chest and face.

Richmond, who was as yet collecting papers from his podium, announced that this was Wolf, the son of the great war chief Spotted Horse. Everyone waited to see what he would do.

At the railing, he leapt from his horse onto the grandstand, causing a few women to scream for he looked a fearsome creature to behold. He strode quickly up the tiered benches, scattering onlookers, and stopped at the Duke of Northampton's box. They rose to face him. Then a strange thing occurred. He took the duchess's outstretched hands, bowed, and placed them against his forehead. When he released her, she leaned over and kissed his cheek.

That the Duchess of Northampton should have an acquaintance with a wild aboriginal was the shock of the day.

CHAPTER SIXTEEN

Wild West Encampment, Earls Court London, May 9, 1887

As soon as *God Save the Queen* ended the show, Morgan took Glory by the arm, not letting go, back to the tent to get ready for the duke and duchess, who would arrive shortly. The girl fumed the entire way.

Once inside, Morgan ordered, "Put on your best dress, the one I laid out for you."

Quickly changing out of her own calico dress, shed put on a grey skirt and white blouse more presentable for a duchess, even one whom she'd once bathed naked with in a Montana river. On impulse, she switched to her beaded earrings, the ones Lame Deer had made for her more than a decade ago. Glancing in the mirror, she thought she still looked like the charwoman she'd once been.

When she placed herself just inside the tent flap to wait, an unfamiliar anxiety settled in the pit of her stomach. She kept smoothing her dress over and over. She glanced at Glory, who stood leaning against a chairback, wearing her homespun show dress and glaring at her.

"Why are you just standing there, Glory. Get dressed."

"I'm standing here because I can't sit down. My butt hurts."

"You had it coming," Morgan replied sharply, "You're still a child. That was the actions of a child."

"You won't let me be anything but a child," she wailed like an innocent prisoner found guilty. "I am twelve."

"That's a child. Hurry now, change. The duke and duchess will be here any minute."

Glory shot back, "I don't care. They're *your friends*. Not mine."

The look of hatred from her daughter shocked Morgan. She was about to order her to put on the other dress when the girl darted past her and out the tent, shouting again, "They're your friends!"

"Glory, come back here," Morgan called after her, but the girl kept running.

She sighed heavily. There was no time to go after her. Had she been too harsh? She knew that after the spanking, Glory was upset, though God knows she'd no right to be. She'd been in the wrong and deserved every swat. Her actions were reckless to the extreme. She could have died, and that thought brought Morgan to her knees. Her daughter's mad dash through the stampede still left her trembling. Will's death had been crushing. She could not bear to lose Glory too.

But perhaps she'd been too harsh, punishing Glory that way and doing it publicly. Yet, at the time, she couldn't have done anything else. She'd caught sight of her daughter helpless in the midst of a stampede about to be trampled to death. Screaming, she'd started for her just as Seamus burst out from the pack and scooped her up. Nearly losing her had brought a black terror into her heart that would have finished her. Family was all she had, the only thing that could break her. In the last hour, it almost had. Will's murder had done them all in. No ever felt worse, but the prospect of Glory under the beasts' hooves would have.

Her thoughts were interrupted by the sound of people approaching. Her friends were here. She smoothed her dress a last time, set a smile to her face, and stepped outside.

After the show, Julia's party made its way behind the arena to the Wild West encampment along with many in the audience come to see how the westerners lived. There, still in his Cheyenne garb, Seamus met them and guided them into the complex of white tents. As he led the way, Julia noticed Cousin Isobel's eyes following him like he was Lord Byron reincarnate. The girl was smitten. Oh, dear.

On seeing Morgan come through the tent flap, Julia grinned, rushed forward and embraced her old friend.

When they stepped back, she said, "Morgan, it is so good to see you again. You look much the same. Ranch life suits you."

She was lying. Her friend had aged. Though still pretty, lines crinkled around the eyes, and her face was weathered. Vanity told her that her own looks had fared much better. That gave her a momentary sense of victory, but it lasted less than a breath. It wasn't looks that made Morgan so formidable, and Julia wanted it to be so for the Duchess of Northampton as well.

"As do you, Julia" Morgan said. "Still Helen of Troy. I never thought I would see you again. Sorry. I should say Lady Becket or duchess."

"No, no, not at all," Julia said. "I like the sound of Julia. It will show how egalitarian we Americans are."

Edward took Morgan's hand and kissed it. "You've changed little, Mrs. Raines. Still lovely as ever."

"And you've become a smooth talker, sir."

He laughed. "A business necessity. I'd say call me Edward, but I have too many people who fear me that I wouldn't want to hear and take liberties. The title is an advantage."

"I understand, your grace."

After Julia introduced the rest of her family, Morgan led them into the tent. Inside was a garden of bright flowers, fur rugs on the floor, chairs and tables, and guns, lots of guns. Not far away was a rifle on a table with a couple cleaning rags. Inspired by Morgan, Julia had made herself a passable shot, which she hoped to display when

Morgan came up to the castle. Over the next hour, they drank tea and caught up on eleven years of life.

My anger at Mama burned like a prairie wildfire. She had done that in front of all those people. And I had to wonder if she loved me. How could you do that to someone you loved? Archie was with me. When I ran out of the tent, he was waiting for me. He was a smart dog. He'd skedaddled the moment Mama took the switch to me in the arena.

The tent city was crowded with people from the audience wandering about to see how we lived. Mostly, they were interested in the Indian village and most gathered there, peering into the tepees whether invited to or not. I'd wanted to see Shadow Horse but felt in no mood to see any of the audience who'd witnessed my shame. Instead, I wandered to the stable and brushed the mustang I rode. We had another show to do in less than two hours, and I'd have to ride him, despite my raw butt. As several of Cody's long-time players said *the show must go on.*

After an hour or so, I returned to the tent. The family of Mama's friends was still there sitting in camp chairs. Seamus was with them. Mama and a woman I assumed was the duchess were crying and fiercely holding hands till Mama abruptly disengaged and dabbed a handkerchief at her eyes. Then the tears were done. I wondered what that was about.

Standing nearby, a pudgy boy with curly hair was watching me. He wore a fancy suit like an adult, which he clearly was not. If it wasn't for his baby fat, he'd be a pretty boy. About my age, but I was a head taller. He stared for a moment till recognition came to him.

"Hey, I saw you in the arena," he said with a laugh. "You wear blue pantaloons on your bum."

I shot back, "You wear a donkey's ass on your face."

He recoiled, eyes wide. "You can't say that to me. I'm an earl."

"Nice to meet you, Earl. I'm Glory."

"No, no. My name's not Earl. I am an earl. My name is Toby."

"Toby the earl."

"Yes."

"Sounds like the name for a rocking horse. That what you ride?"

"Glory," a whiplash voice sounded from the front. Mama. "Come up here and meet the duke and duchess."

I rolled my eyes, went up front, and curtsied my way through introductions. Immediately, despite my current state of annoyance, I was transfixed by the duchess. Her smile was that of a princess. Almost from my birth, everyone said she was beautiful, but she was more than that. She was captivating.

"Your mother has told us all about you," the duchess said. "She said you're quite the spry one."

The duke asked, "Are you going to be a sharpshooter like your mother?"

"Don't think so, duke."

"Have you ever been to a ball?" the duchess asked.

"No, ma'am," I answered nervously. "A chivaree once after Dora got married. That's my aunt."

I thought her steady gaze reached inside my head and discerned all my secrets, so I stared down at the fur rug. People had also said she was as mean as a rattlesnake who got stepped on. Not Seamus, who loved her, but Mama said others did. I didn't see it. I saw an angel.

The duchess said, "Well, you and your brother will be coming up for several days with your mother to attend the Spring Ball at Becket Castle. Buffalo Bill has already agreed to it. You can be part of the first hour, even dance if you choose, then you may watch from the mezzanine as long as you can stay awake. How does that sound?"

"Sounds fine, ma'am," I muttered and wondered if I'd meet the queen at this ball but decided not to ask.

"On the following day, Saturday," the duchess went on, "we all will attend the Northampton Fair at the town's market square." The duchess's eyes gleamed with excitement. "You'll get to see dancing bears, jugglers, acrobats, fire breathers and all kinds of other amusements. Have you ever seen anything like that, Glory?"

"I've seen plenty of bear," I told her. "But they weren't dancing."

Outside, a few minutes later when the two women stood together saying their goodbyes, the duchess offered her condolences for Papa's death. So now I knew why they'd been crying.

Mama nodded then asked abruptly, "Do you know Clive Dunford?"

Auntie Julia—that was what she wanted to be called—answered, "Yes, I recently met the man. He's a close neighbor. Edward says he knows you, so I invited him to the ball. You'll see him there."

Mama's eyes turned that flinty gray they can get sometimes when she's got a bead on a rattlesnake by the barn. She said, "Oh, I intend to."

CHAPTER SEVENTEEN

New Bond Street, London, May 13, 1887

With Dunford living only a short distance from Becket Castle, Morgan's instinct was to be after him now. Put the son of a bitch down who murdered her husband. She could take the train to Northampton, hire a hackney to Wexham, and put a .44 caliber bullet into his chest. But she knew she must not. She was no longer Morgan O'Connor, the Captured Girl, her own law in a lawless land, but Morgan Raines with a dead husband and two children that needed her, despite what either might think.

And this was not Montana Territory. This was England with its bobbies on every street and detectives in every station. If she brought frontier justice to Dunford, she'd hang and leave her children without a parent. Being their mother was her vocation, her first job. So, she had decided she needed to push him into coming after her. If she killed him then, even British law couldn't touch her. She'd initiate her scheme to bring down the high and mighty Earl of Wexham at Julia's Spring Ball in front of all his upper-class friends including the Prince of Wales.

Only a few days off, the event had taken on legendary status, being compared favorably in publications to the famous Duchess of Richmond's ball before the battle of Waterloo. As soon as invitations had been sent out, society could talk of nothing else. When word spread that the Prince of Wales and his wife Princess Alexandra would attend, it became a matter of great prestige to be among the chosen. Invitations were like gold. People of all stripes tried to wrangle one, but Julia kept the lucky few to a modest three hundred.

Private trains were reserved for the short journey up from London. Hairdressers and dressmakers were brought over from Paris. All were kept busy throughout the long days leading up to the affair. Newspapers did not go a day without some story about it. Even the Prince of Wales quipped, "I was lucky the duchess is such a good friend, or I might not have made the list."

A week before the event, accompanied by her lady's maid the doughty Mrs. Hatch, Julia came down to London to shop with Morgan and Glory for their evening gowns, insisting she pay for them. When Morgan refused the offer, the duchess explained that it was just back pay for her time working for her family, even as miserable as she was at the job. This was true in both counts. She was no lady's maid, and while employed by Julia's parents, she'd found they were the cheapest people in New York, giving their servants wages that a ragman would find insulting.

"Besides," Julia added. "Edward needs you there decked out like a queen for business purposes. He's culminating some venture at the ball and needs us all to dazzle the partners."

Morgan didn't quite accept the explanation, but she needed the right clothes to attend, and Julia would provide them. She noticed, too, how giddy Glory was at the prospect and couldn't disappoint her. It might begin to thaw the wall of ice between them. The two of them would be fitted out in not just ball gowns but an assemblage of outfits for any occasion that weekend. It was clear Julia was enjoying herself shopping far more than Morgan.

Toward the end of that long day, the three of them, along with Lame Deer and the lady's maid Mrs. Gray, were in a private room of a dressmaker's shop on New Bond Street. The owner, a pretty French woman named Mrs. Abadie, asked Morgan to try on her ball gown so she could take it in at the waist.

"You have ze trim figure, milady," the dressmaker said in her heavy French accent. "No bustle, I must make ze alterations."

"Not milady. Just Morgan Raines," Morgan replied.

"Mais oui, Madam," Mrs. Abadie said. "But still ze bustle is tres élégante."

Julia said, "Burn them all, I say. Bustles are going out of fashion, Mrs. Abadie."

Wearing only her petticoat and black stockings, Morgan stepped into the ball gown and drew it up to her shoulders. It was a lovely thing, purple taffeta with a low bodice in front and back, short sleeved like all the ball gowns she'd seen. Elegant white gloves would be part of the outfit.

Julia clapped. "You look beautiful, Morgan."

"Not likely," she replied, frowning skeptically, but she was pleased.

Julia asked, "What do you think, Glory?"

The girl shrugged, her face a shroud of displeasure when it came to anything about her mother these days.

Lame Deer said in Cheyenne, "It's a long way from the Greasy Grass."

At that, Morgan gave an inelegant snort that raised Mrs. Abadie's eyebrows. Suddenly, the dressmaker squealed in horror and dropped her chalk and tape measure. "My God, look at that. What happened to you?"

She was staring at Morgan's right arm, her French accent completely gone. The purple scars of seven knife cuts were glaringly visible. Mrs. Hatch closed a hand over her mouth in shock. Morgan usually kept the wounds hidden, not because she was ashamed of them but to avoid such moments as these. How does one explain to people with no understanding of her past what happened so many years ago in a very different world? She had not thought about the Sun Dance for years, but now in an instant the entirety of it flooded back with all its physical and emotional pain. It was when she knew she loved Spotted Horse.

During the Moon When the Chokecherries were Ripe, just after Morgan's and Spotted Horse's exploration of the medicine circle, the band moved from the Bighorns to the Powder River country, and Running Hawk called for a Sun Dance. The buffalo were fewer and fewer and the herds that were found were small. It was time for the Cheyenne to renew their bond with the land and show respect to Heammawihio, the Wise One Above.

When he sent the crier about to proclaim the Sun Dance, Spotted Horse was one of four warriors who said they would participate in the Blood Sacrifice. Morgan was surprised at how much this upset her. She had never seen a Sun Dance but knew what happened on the last day. The affair was all about blood, but the final day was horrific. She asked Spotted Horse not to do it. He explained patiently he had sought a vision and was directed by the Wise One to sacrifice for the people.

Her temper flared and in English, she said sharply, "It's stupid and barbaric."

Not understanding the words, he stared at her for a few seconds. Clearly, he did understand the tone and turned abruptly, walking away. Spotted Horse never argued a thing, he always said what he thought or what he was going to do and left people to think or do as they wished, even her.

For the Sun Dance, everything was done with rituals and blessings much like one of the priests Morgan remembered from long ago as a child in Five Points. A cottonwood tree was selected, blessed, cut down, and trimmed of its branches. Then, the men carried it back to the place of the ceremony, hoisted it up into a deep hole and built an arbor around it. Someone created rawhide effigies of a buffalo and a man, both with massive sexual organs, and hung them from the pole.

Then, the dancing began. Without hesitation, Morgan joined the women as they circled the pole and the men. The men were adorned more elaborately than the women in body paint to match the four directions, black, red, yellow and white. As she danced, Morgan was caught up in the ululating cadence of their high-pitched wail, her voice blending in with the others, the rhythm of it racing up and down her body in primal ecstasy. For hours, they danced, only stopping when the sun went down.

Two more days were filled with rituals in which each member of the band took part, offering to the Wise One buckskin fragments, small bags of tobacco, and pieces of blue or red or yellow cloth. In the afternoon of the third day, mothers brought in their young children to have their ears pierced. A cacophony of wailing accompanied it.

Finally, the day Morgan dreaded came. The last day of the Sun Dance, the Blood Sacrifice. The morning began with the sky a perfect sapphire blue, already the heat drawing sweat. When the medicine men called for the participants, Spotted Horse along with the three other warriors came forward.

The medicine men then called for the wives and sisters and sweethearts of the Sun Dancers. Seven women entered the arbor, none of them for Spotted Horse. His mother was too old now and no other female relatives remained alive. Morgan saw him standing alone, his back straight, calm as always. After clutching the stone arrowhead on her necklace for a hesitant moment, she strode into the arbor. Everyone knew she was there for Spotted Horse.

She glanced at him, and he gave the barest hint of a nod, demonstrative for him. Uncertain what was coming—nothing good, she thought— she stood ready. Medicine men went to each woman in turn with a knife and slashed her upper arm, opening up a two inch gash and spilling blood. Doing this two, three or four times depending on how many the women could tolerate. No one more than four. Each cut brought glory to her warrior. Three of the women cried out but all withstood it. Morgan was last. When one of the medicine men came to her with his dripping knife, she was determined not to cry out or flinch.

Seven was a sacred number, and she thought this would give Spotted Horse strength for what he was about to do. She was aware of the excruciating pain about to come but his would be worse, far worse. The medicine man stepped up to her and cut across her arm.

Her jaw clinched. The pain exploded in her mind, terrible in its severity. She called for another and another, each time opening a cut that sent blood draining down her arm where it dripped in a steady flow onto the ground. Till he reached seven. When he finished, she retreated out the arbor where Owl Woman wrapped her arm in cloth to staunch the bleeding. Ignoring the searing pain, she sat with her and Lame Deer to watch the Blood Sacrifice.

It soon began.

Standing before each warrior in turn, the same medicine man who had cut her drew out a fold of skin from the breast, pierced the fold with a knife, then shoved a peg into the slot. This was done on both sides of the chest, and as they did it, a terrible intensity appeared on the warriors' faces, their chests heaving and glistening in sweat and blood. The peg ends were attached to rawhide strips and tied in long rope to the pole.

In a surge of strength, the men pulled back sharply, twisting and turning, trying to rip the pegs free from their skin. Agony was etched on their faces, even Spotted Horse's. A part of Morgan desperately wanted him to quit, to give up, but another part of her was proud of his courage and endurance. She did not know how anyone could withstand such pain, her own still felt like boiling water on her arm. She joined in with the other women offering encouragement by singing the praises of the warriors.

After an hour, one of the men passed out, and his friends rushed in, grabbing him by the waist, pulling him back hard and ripping the pegs from the skin. They carried him unconscious from the arbor and laid him out on the hillside on a bed of grass. Eventually, two others pulled themselves loose and staggered into the arms of relatives. Only Spotted Horse was left.

He was lean without great bulk and lacked the other men's weight, which Morgan realized made it more difficult for him. She could see the sun and heat draining his strength. The pain must be beyond endurance. After three hours, the medicine men wanted to cut him free, but he refused. Finally, gathering his strength for a last violent twist, he surged back against the ropes and, as blood spurted forth from his chest, wrenched himself free. Closing her eyes, Morgan sang a high-pitched song of his bravery.

Spotted Horse's father and several other men hurried in to help him, but he stood on his own, lifting his hands to the skies and offering a prayer to the Wise One. With his chest tangled swathes of skin and blood, he walked out of the arbor under his own power. Morgan could not have been prouder.

In the dressmaker's shop in London, the memory of the long-ago had flashed through her mind in just a few seconds. It had reminded her of the great love she'd felt for Spotted Horse and the terrible reason she ended up hating him. In her life, she'd loved two men with all her heart. One was murdered by Dunford. And the other? Just after her son Ho'nehe was born, she found Spotted Horse's sacred medicine bag and, curious, rummaged through it. Inside was a scalp lock. It was the long red hair of her sister Fiona.

The sound of Glory's voice brought her back to the present. Her daughter was telling Mrs. Abadie a story about a grizzly bear attacking her Mama and raking its claws on her arm. "Mama hit that big old grizz on the head with a shovel so hard it started singing 'Old MacDonald had a Farm.' That bear ran off so fast with Mama chasing it the birds laughed. I think she wanted to hit it again to see if it would sing 'Rock-a-Bye Baby.'"

Mrs. Abadie was frowning as Glory raised her right hand. "I swear, ma'am, every word the truth."

Lame Deer had a big grin, then Julia and Morgan began laughing and finally Mrs. Abadie couldn't help but smile. For just a moment, Morgan thought the rift between her and Glory had eased, but soon though, when Morgan wouldn't allow her the ball gown she wanted, her daughter became furious. The girl sucked in a breath, strode to the far side of the room and folded her arms over her chest, and scowled. That black, low back dress would look silly on a twelve-year-old girl, no matter how big she thought she was.

She heard her daughter's low mutter. "Thanks for ruining my life."

An hour later, they finished the fittings and rode the carriage back to the Wild West encampment where Julia caught her train home. Lame Deer, who would also be going up to Northampton to watch after Glory and meet the queen, which she was sure would be there no matter what everyone told her, had received a good dress for daytime but no ball gown.

CHAPTER EIGHTEEN

Train to Northampton, May 19, 1887

Charlie Acker was a big man, well over six feet with thick shoulders barely held within his brown frock coat. He had a boxer's face, battered in his youth into a nightmarish mask that caused both men and women to go dry in the mouth. Seven of his men sat in the crowded railway car as the northbound train rumbled through Bedfordshire. They were top-heavy men, ready for the mean business ahead, moving uncooperative tenants off Dunford's land before he attended his fancy ball. Cudgels in hand, they'd drive them out tonight one way or another.

Apparently, Dunford had the law on his side, and Henry Hobbs, the Scotland Yard Dick, had added Acker's men onto the police roles. Mutton shunters all now. It amused Acker. They were just going to do their civic duty and get paid for it.

He also found it strange that his old friend was now a bona fide earl. A pauper of one, but a nob, nonetheless. When Acker first met him, Dunford was on the street, his father having turned him out, living by the dodge and petty theft. He was quite good at them, taking people in with his smooth palaver. He might have been rich if he didn't spend the money faster than he made it. But then what was money for if not for gambling, drinking, and women?

They'd taken many a smuggling run from Portsmouth to the continent and once far afield down to Southern Africa, there to load up on ivory. They'd saved each other's lives more than once on that trip. Profitable as it was, Africa proved too dangerous. It was the European continent and moving ladies' clothes for them. That was before Dunford got a wild bug up his arse for the American cattle boom, and he was gone. So now, back together again, and the new earl owed him. Renewing their acquaintance might prove valuable.

With a stirring of desire, he suddenly noticed a pretty, Grey-eyed woman halfway down the carriage staring at him, then turning quickly away. Chuckling, he knew what kind of effect he had on women like her. Fear, utter fear, and that's how he liked them. For some, like this one, he intrigued them. Secretly wanted him. This one was small with a lady's bearing. The clothes bespoke wealth. A proud bitch in heat. Right now, he yearned to reach under her dress and grab her beef. Likely, she would protest at first but then give in and enjoy it. They all did.

With a low growl, he tried to catch her gaze, but she was talking with an old Hindi woman and didn't look his way again.

A few minutes later, his chance came. She rose and holding a young girl by the hand came down the aisle.

The train to Northampton rattled my head with its constant clankety clank. The day before the spring ball we took the early morning one. Girls my age could attend the dance for an hour to prepare for their season. I wasn't sure then what season they were talking about, but I didn't care for the Prince of Wales would be there. He'd ask me to dance. Me, Glory Raines from Lone Tree, Montana dancing with a real prince.

Seamus was going too, but he could stay for the whole thing, which didn't seem quite fair. He was over the moon about it though. Ever since Alice Olson told him he was too damn Indian to be sparked by, he'd been like a beaver that lost its tail. But now, he seemed in fine fettle, jaunty even. A jaunty Seamus was ridiculous. And he looked handsome as all get out in his new clothes, too, a regular Beau Brummell. The duke sent him to see his tailor and there you go. Catching me watching him, he seemed to read my mind and flipped his tie at me. No, it was called a cravat. Those English sure put on airs.

Across from me, Mama and Lame Deer were talking in Cheyenne, not realizing they'd slipped into it, which they did all the time. Lame Deer was telling a funny story about a rabbit and a fox that I'd heard before. Apparently, it was Mama's favorite as a girl when she first came to Running Hawk's band. According to Mama, Lame Deer was old even then.

For as long as I could remember, the Indian woman had been my companion. Not just me though, To Will, Jr and Lenora too before they died. She mourned them with Mama all night. I just cried in my bed. Sitting across from her on the train, I studied Lame Deer, that gray hair and wrinkled skin plain as your face. Old as Methuselah she was. I wondered if she could be over a hundred. A lot of people were older than a hundred in the Bible. Some said the Indians were a lost tribe of the Israelites. Maybe so.

When Lame Deer finished, Mama smiled even though she'd heard it a hundred times.

She wouldn't let me bring Archie. I was lucky she didn't make me get rid of him, and by rid of him she probably meant drowning him in a bucket. She was still angry with me for what I did in the arena, but I was angry right back at her. I didn't talk to her unless I had to. She had no business doing that to me in front of all those people, and forgiveness was not a quality I possessed in plentiful supply.

I've always known that my mother was a bit of hard leather, but even so, she'd never spanked a one of us until eleven days ago when she lit into me. Her eyes were flinting, sparking like a madwoman. It scared me. It still scared me. I used to think she loved me but couldn't be sure anymore because what I saw in her face was not love. I didn't know if I could be around her any longer but had to for now.

For some reason on this trip, she was carrying three weapons on her person, a pistol and knife under her dress and another pistol in her boot. She made me carry a knife. Most mothers gave their daughters necklaces or bracelets or other frilly things. My mother gave me a knife. Seamus carried more guns than usual as well. I didn't know what was going on, or if I should be worried. She also brought her rifle in its buckskin pouch, but maybe she was planning to put on a shooting display this weekend.

Suddenly, I remembered I had to pee. My insides were all water trying to burst out. We'd been on the train nearly an hour and still more to go. Mama asked if I could hold it till we get there, but I told her I couldn't. "If I wait any longer, I'm going to do my business on the floor."

"I take her," Lame Deer said.

Mama shook her head. "I might as well water the tracks too."

We were on the way up the aisle toward the necessary when a bullish man rose from his seat and blocked our way. He had a gargoyle grin on his face, and I was so scared of him I believed I would pee right there. Mama pushed me behind her. He doffed his bowler hat and said, "How do, madam? My name is Charlie Acker, well-known London businessman. Maybe you've heard of me. Perhaps, I can be of assistance."

A few men nearby snickered, but Mama wasn't buffaloed. I knew this about her: she could handle scary men. I'd long realized I'd never be like her in that way. Scary men scared me.

"I doubt it," she said. "My daughter needs to use the necessary… the loo. Allow us to pass, sir."

His eyes bugged out, pleased. "American. You're an American."

She didn't reply. When he next reached a hand for me, I flinched, and mama knocked it aside.

Acker shrugged as if wronged. "I just wanted to touch her hair, madam. It's so lovely. What's the harm in that?"

A cold edge entered Mama's voice. "Touch her, and you'll be taking your last breath."

His grin widened into a leer. "That's big talk for a tiny woman."

"I don't need much to get the bulge on a grass-bellied cow like you."

Anger flashed in his eyes as Mama slid her hand into her dress for the knife or pistol.

One of his men quipped, "Better be careful with this one, Charlie. She seems like a real fire eater." They all laughed, and Acker forced a grin. He stepped aside, gesturing down the aisle for us to proceed.

After the toilet, Mama and me returned to our seats. What a vile place that was! Next time I'd hold my water. I scooted in next to the window. The sky was sunny as you please, not a puff of cloud. The English countryside rolled by at a fair clip, all green with men carrying staffs and little dogs scurrying around sheep like they did back home. As I watched, I couldn't get that man's nasty face out of my mind. I glanced toward him, and he was grinning at me. I looked away quickly.

A half hour later when we reached Northampton, the duchess was waiting for us. Several servants jumped to when she ordered them to carry our luggage to her coach. She assured Mama that her groom will take good care of our horses and bring them to the stables. There was to be a fox hunt or a ride through the countryside this weekend and Buffalo Bill wanted us to bring our horses to show the aristocrats what kind of mounts we rode.

The coach was sure not a stagecoach. It was much, much more, something I could ride around in all day with its soft red seats and big windows and fancy pictures of flying lions on the doors. At first meeting back at camp, Mama and the duchess hugged each other like two porcupines, but now they're chatting non-stop like me and Shadow Horse always did.

Yet, there was something about Auntie Julia that was holding back. Like she's got to pass gas and she's afraid it's going to come out loud. I did that at school once. I never heard the last of it.

I'd always heard that she, the duchess, was a person everyone steered clear of because she was such a terror to be around, but she seemed friendly enough, and Seamus straight out doted on her. He was just sitting there staring at her like a puppy. Lame Deer had taken on the stone-faced Cheyenne pose she does around white people. Me, I decided I was going to sing a song but didn't because at that moment, I stuck my head out the window and gawked. There it was. Up came a fairytale castle.

CHAPTER NINETEEN

Becket Castle, Northamptonshire, May 20, 1887

On the morning of the ball, grey clouds scudded across the skies and a chill settled in the air as thirty men and women gathered for the fox hunt at Becket Castle. Astride their thoroughbred mounts, the men were decked out smartly in top hats, scarlet or black coats, white trousers, and knee length boots. The women all rode sidesaddle and wore long frocks that protected their modesty by reaching the tips of their boots. While footmen served glass flutes of champagne to the hunting party, the dogs swarmed the field around the Master of the Hounds. But for the dogs, all waited patiently for the hunt to begin.

Riding Bill's mustang, Morgan approached the group with Julia and Seamus. She was hardly dressed in proper foxhunting kit but instead moccasin boots, a calf-length Cheyenne skirt with designs ornately stitched by Lame Deer, a large red kerchief over her white blouse, and a floppy cowboy hat, the side brim flattened up. Her long auburn hair tumbled out in great rivulets.

This was the outfit she wore during the three sharpshooters' showpiece, and Bill had insisted she wear it. He dearly loved publicity among the hoity toity. She knew she stood out like a peacock in a party of squawking chickens. And she rode astride. Women just didn't ride astride. She received shocked glares but was indifferent to them.

However, Seamus had worked hard to appear like a young toff, including a bowler hat he'd shoved down on his head. He was nervous, his face taut as if he had lockjaw, concerned about how he would be received. He shouldn't be. He'd never be received by these people. They had their ways, and she, Seamus, and their kind had theirs. But he had to learn that for himself.

When they rode in among the hunters, Edward said, "Ah, here they are. This is our friend from the American West, Mrs. Raines. That outfit is from Buffalo Bill's Wild West Show." He turned to the others. "If you have not attended, I implore you to do so. It is a rousing affair, and she is spectacular in it."

He did not introduce Seamus.

Several people glanced pointedly between her and Seamus, confusion no doubt as to their relationship. He was dressed too well to be a servant so what was he? A servant? A foreign acquaintance? If they knew the truth of it, her son's coppery skin and Cheyenne features, so much like his father's, that would mark her for a far greater breach of society than riding astride or unsuitable attire for a fox hunt.

She was about to introduce him as her son, for he was better than all of them, but just then Edward addressed a handsome, sunburned man, "Sir John, if you would, please partner Mrs. Raines. Mrs. Raines, this is Sir John Coppersmith, a close friend of mine. He'll be able to guide you through the fox hunting."

As he moved his horse in next to her, Coppersmith gave off a self-assurance that reminded her of Will, not the Will she first met but the one who grew to manhood on the warring frontier. As for Coppersmith, there seemed a bit of the rake about him, a man who no doubt charmed the ladies.

After assigning Seamus to accompany Cousin Isobel and instructing him not to separate from the hunters, the duke left them to join another couple. Everyone was sitting their horses and waiting but for what Morgan couldn't guess.

"I hope there's more to fox hunting than this," she said to Coppersmith. "What are we waiting for?"

"The Prince of Wales," he answered. "The Master of Hounds wouldn't dare begin before his royal highness arrived." Coppersmith gave a half-smile. "Your outfit becomes you, Mrs. Raines. Not exactly fox hunting attire, but quite the sensation I should think. You have clearly shocked the natives."

She gave a short laugh that sounded to her too much like a snort. Her most unladylike feature was her terrible laugh. Fortunately, she didn't laugh much. "This is a costume for the show. I assure you I wear more practical gear at home."

"Where is home? America, I presume."

"Montana Territory." She glanced around taking in the chattering hunting party with her gaze. "I'd much rather be there now."

"Yes, I quite understand," he said. "I'm from the Cape Colony. When I'm not there, I miss it and long to be back. Do you know it?"

"I know where it is. Does your wife live there?" She couldn't believe she'd asked that like a trembling maiden looking for a husband. She didn't care, but the words had fallen out of their own accord. It felt like a betrayal to Will. "I'm sorry. I don't mean to pry into your personal life."

"No, that's all right. I've never married," he replied, "Haven't found the right mate. Too busy, I suppose. I spend most of the year in Africa contracting out to the duke's railroad interests while attempting to operate my own business."

"What business is that?"

"I'm a hunter and guide. I take parties of rich people into the bush after big game and try to get them out alive." He nodded toward the Master of Hounds sitting his horse a little separate from the party. "This sort of hunt drives me to drink. A little fox chased by so many. Doesn't seem sporting. We ought to try it with a cape buffalo. Now that would be a hunt worthy of the name. The duke tells me you are an expert markswoman. Have you ever hunted in the wilds of Montana?"

"Some."

At the talk of hunting, a memory jumped into her mind of her time among Running Hawk's band when she first became part of his family. She was already an accomplished hunter. It was Running Hawk who taught her how his people did it differently from the white man.

Each time the great chief took her into the hills after game, guilt shadowed her for her da had taught her before. It was time with him that she had cherished, and soon it was the same with Running Hawk. He was a kind and patient teacher. Though she thought she knew all there was about hunting, he taught her to think as animals think, to know the ways of deer, elk, buffalo, Bighorn sheep, antelope, black bear and grizzly. He even allowed her to shoot his prized Sharps carbine. He was not one for excited displays, but when he saw her first shot, a difficult one over two hundred yards at a grazing elk, he stood straight up from a squatting position and screamed, "Eeeyah!"

It was during the Hard Face Moon that they ran into the grizzly and she took on a special place among the tribe. The bear was huge with body fat, ready for his long sleep, yet not ready to pass up an easy meal. She was that meal.

Running Hawk was nearby, but she held the sharps. When it charged, she surprised herself with the calm that came over her. Like nothing mattered but the spot over the heart. She stood in its path, letting it close, unflinching, and killed it with one shot. When the beast fell not five feet from her, she stared at it coldly for two full breaths, then the fear came, and she took a staggering step back.

Running Hawk bragged on her prowess as a hunter around the campfires for two weeks. With a sense of pride, she added four of the grizzly's claws to her rawhide necklace, then draped it over her head and around her neck. Each piece of it had marked her passage to becoming a woman. The gold cross that her mother pressed into her hand before she died and the words accompanying that made her responsible for her family. The stone arrowhead from a people that lived long ago and passed from anyone's knowledge. It had marked her marriage with Spotted Horse.

The last was the bear claws that made her one of the People, a member of Running Hawk's band.

That night, though, she curled in her blankets against the cold and wind from a snowstorm, shame sweeping over her like the storm outside. She was Cheyenne now, and the Cheyenne had killed her family. Would they blame her for living, surviving, as best she could? Perhaps not, she thought. Running Hawk, Owl Woman, Lame Deer and the others were far different than Big Crow. If this was not the life she wanted, Morgan decided, it wasn't a bad one to have. From then on, she became Cheyenne.

Coppersmith leaned over the pommel of his saddle. "What's the most perilous animal you've hunted?"

Lost in her memory, the question caught her by surprise, and she answered without hesitation. "Man."

He seemed uncertain whether she was joking. "Indeed."

That's when five riders appeared coming out of a distant tree line and raced across the field toward them.

"The prince has arrived," someone called.

The hunt could begin.

To Morgan, fox hunting turned out nothing like the all-out roaring hunt the buffalo, the pounding thunder, danger and sometimes death. After a couple hours, it seemed little more than a Sunday jaunt over the countryside chasing dogs that were chasing the occasional fox they'd scared up. By noon, the hounds had found two in the the trees and thickets and run them down. Coppersmith explained that then they were "chopped."

At that moment, a hound bayed, and someone shouted, "It's Red Whiskers. By gad, it's Old Red Whiskers himself."

Almost in front of Morgan, a fox darted from the thicket out onto the field, pursued by the entire baying pack. The animal's lopped ear hung useless, and one eye had the look of the dead. He dodged his way through the horses, causing mayhem when the hounds bounded in after him, snapping at the little creature. He raced across the short grass to a large patch of forest tucked into a massive rock outcropping. A dead end. The fox couldn't escape.

Following the hounds, the riders charged into the trees.

"Shall we?" Coppersmith said.

With a shout, Morgan shot forward on her mustang. Hunting was in her blood, and her blood was up. Once in among the trees, the smaller, muscular horse, more nimble than the others, eventually weaved its way to the front and soon in among the dog pack. She saw what the fox could not possibly see. It was heading into a blind alley. It would soon be trapped against a wall of stone, and the hounds would tear it apart.

She had no particular sympathy for the fox. It took its chances in the wild like all other animals, even human ones. But this fox hunting did not fire her instincts. She hunted for food or to protect her livestock. The Brits could do what they wanted, yet she eased back on the reins.

She broke into the open just before the cliff face. Dashing about, the fox had nowhere to go, the hounds were almost on him. Ahead, up against the rock, was a well with a crank and bucket. Just out of reach of a large hunting dog's snapping jaws, Red Whiskers leapt up over the brick wall and plunged down into the well. A couple seconds later, Morgan heard the echo of a splash.

She dismounted among the baying dogs. Several stood with their paws propped on top of the well, wailing into the darkness below. She shoved them aside and peered down but could see nothing. She did hear the sound of splashing. The rest of the hunters arrived, and the Master of Hounds drew the dogs back. The prince, duke, and Coppersmith came up, several other men closing in behind them.

A jowl-faced man chuckled. "We can hardly call this treeing the beast, your highness. We welled him though."

"You sure he's in the well?" Edward asked Morgan.

"Yes, I saw him jump in."

When the Prince bent over to look, he nearly fell in, but the duke pulled him back. His top hat fell though and descended toward the water below. That gave Morgan an idea. She went to the crank and started lowering the bucket.

"What are you doing?" the prince asked.

"Red Whiskers is the Prince of Foxes, your highness," she said. "I'm seeing how smart he actually is."

In half a minute, she felt the rope slacken. Only a second later, she felt it go taut. Julia had taken up a position at the handle and both began cranking. After a few seconds, the prince took the handle from them. "We must not allow the ladies to best us, gentlemen."

Soon the bucket was up, and those at the well stared in shock.

Coppersmith said, "I don't believe it."

A drenched Red Whiskers sat in the bucket, his good eye staring at them quizzically. Not far away, the hounds began baying again. They had a kill to make. The fox leapt from the bucket over the stone wall and scrambled toward a nearby alder. Just ahead of the hounds, he climbed swiftly while the dogs circled below, baying in agony at not reaching their prey. Everyone watched as Red Whiskers crept out on a limb and leapt to a ledge on the rock face. In seconds, he made his way to the top of the outcropping and there turned to look back at them, then he was gone.

After a moment, the prince glanced at Morgan. "Well, you're the huntress here, Mrs.

Raines. What do you say to that?"

"Your highness, I'd say that was the Prince of Foxes saluting the Prince of Wales."

The prince broke into a loud guffaw. "Indeed. I'd have to agree. What do you say, folks? I believe that topped the day. Shall we retire now and make our preparations for the duchess's ball tonight? I believe it will be an unforgettable event."

With Dunford in mind, Morgan certainly hoped so.

CHAPTER TWENTY

Becket Castle, May 20, 1887,

The leather smell of books, that's what struck me when I snuck into the library, the one room in Becket Castle Duke Edward forbad children to go. I'd never seen so many books in my life, all containing an army of secrets. They filled the shelves. Any other day, I'd be on them in a second, seeing what was hidden within, except that was the furthest thing from my mind. I needed to hide. I scooted in behind a corner chair and slid to the floor, my knees bent, my shiny, black shoes tucked against my bottom.

I thought now I'm safe from Mama.

She'd just returned from fox hunting, and surely Toby had relayed to his own mother what I had done to him, and she would have told mine. And there lay the end of my chance to attend the ball and dance with a real prince. I knew Mama would be hollering mad and looking for me and maybe find another birch stick to swat me with. I'll not take that again. If I hide in the library for a few hours to let Mama cool off.

What happened was this: Earlier this morning Mama and Seamus took part in a fox hunt with a pack of people, a pack of dogs, and a few tiny foxes. I had been waiting outside the stable to see them off. Seamus rode out of the barn looking like a young toff, even wearing a silly bowler hat he'd shoved down on his ears. When I saw him, I burst out laughing, slapping my knees. "Look at you! Look at you! You're Little Lord Fauntleroy."

He'd shouted back angrily, "What do you know about it, Little Frog?"

Mama was furious. "Glory," she snapped, "say you're sorry to your brother right now. Go on. Do it now or you'll stay in your room tonight, and you can forget attending the ball."

It took me a few seconds before I muttered, "Sorry, Seamus, but who are you?"

"Glory," Mama warned.

"Yes, ma'am," I huffed for she was blaming me for things not my fault.

They rode off to the front of the house to join the other fox hunters.

That wasn't it though, only the preliminary because Toby and Tom Langham were standing nearby watching. The little gump grinned. "Your brother is quite the simpleminded dolt, isn't he?"

I said low and nasty, "You are the world's biggest ass, Toby. Toby the wooden headed rocking horse."

"Seamus is a fool!" he cried out, incensed, issuing spit from his mouth. "He looked like a pig in my papa's hunting kit." He started laughing like a cackling hen and wouldn't stop, blurting out, "It's so funny to see a darky like him getting above his station. Like dimwitted old Tom here going to Buckingham Palace to meet the Queen."

I knocked him into a pile of horse manure.

Both enraged and appearing maltreated at the same time, he shouted up at me, "You said the same thing about him!"

"Seamus is my brother. No one can say those things about him but me."

Then I ran back into the house to escape Tom, whom the little toad sent after me. Tom was no threat though. I could tell that. Once inside, I stopped and faced him. He waved me on. After a moment, I looked back, and he'd returned outside.

In the library, sitting on the floor behind the chair, I listened to the castle, the sound of a tall clock a few feet away ticking like Big Ben, the clomping of a horse just outside, and distant cowbells somewhere on the grounds.

Then, I started a list in my head of the things I hate about my mama. She's friendly about as often as Christmas comes around. She worked the ranch with Papa, Conor and Seamus more than doing the cooking and sewing, which Lame Deer and Aunt Dora did, and I had to help them. This was supposed to be practice to be a wife, which all women aspired to, and I had to admit I dreamed about sometime. I wanted to marry a prince but knew I wouldn't. That wasn't Mama's fault though.

She pretended not to like her reputation as the toughest wolf in the pack but actually did, so much so she had to be tough all the time to prove it. Including with me. That one made the list. She loved Seamus more than me. She'd never taken a birch to him. Maybe she didn't love me at all. That was just four. I needed more on the list.

I heard footsteps in the hall. I squeezed my arms around my knees tighter. When the door opened, I took a deep breath and held it. One person came in then another right behind, a woman then a man from the heavy boots. I eased out some air. Had to be Auntie Julia and Duke Edward. No one else would be here. She plopped down in the chair I was behind. She smelled like lilacs.

"The fox hunt went well," she said. "The prince was not bothered at all by Seamus's presence. I knew he wouldn't be."

"Of course not," Duke Edward said. I peek around the back to make sure. From the side and below, his face seemed to be frowning like he got a whiff of something smelly. "It's a different affair. The palace said there would be no problem with Seamus at the fox hunt, only the ball." He paused. "So, you haven't told Morgan. Julia, you promised. You need to keep your promises."

"I will"

"Then tell her."

"I know, I know, I know."

Tell Mama what? What were they talking about? It seemed a big deal to the duke. I leaned back against the wall and listened.

"I wish you'd not put stock in such things," Auntie Julia said.

The duke's sudden movement must have been something forceful for his chair scraped loudly on the floor. "Not put stock in such things." His voice was irate. "I want to preserve this estate and this title for our son and his son and generations after. Is that a crime? The inheritance taxes are crushing. I need to earn more and more money. And I need friends in high places to do so. No one higher than the prince. Insulting him will not do. It will not do at all."

"All right, Edward," Aunt Julia had a tremor in her voice. "I'll talk to Morgan."

The duke went on in a harsh voice as if she hadn't just agreed. "If Seamus attends, that will be an afront to the prince and the queen herself. The men from his household were very emphatic about that. I wish it wasn't so, Julia, but you must tell Morgan now. Seamus cannot attend the same social event as the Prince of Wales. He cannot attend the ball. Do you understand?"

"You know Seamus. He's hardly a savage."

"I know that. Do you understand, Julia?"

Silence lasted for several seconds, so much so that I thought somehow they'd left without making a sound. Then she said, "Yes, Edward, I understand."

"Good. Inform her now, this minute. Coming from you, it will be much better than from me. Afterward, come and tell me it's done. If you can't do it in the next hour, I'll do it myself."

His chair scraped back, and his boots struck the polished floor as he left the room. At that moment, I hated the duke.

Auntie Julia remained in the chair for several minutes. I wondered if I should speak up but decided not to. Eventually, with a loud sigh, she rose and hurriedly left.

I sat for a bit calming my excitements, which were boiling. It all stunned me. They're saying Seamus can't go to the ball because they say he's an Indian. At just sixteen, he was a better man than all of them, and he wanted to go to the ball as badly as I did. Now people wanted to say my brother is something bad.

My rage boiled over. I crawled out from behind the chair and ran after Julia. I knew where she was going, to Mama's room. I was going to tell her if Seamus can't go, then I'm not going to her damn ball either.

I rushed upstairs to Mama's room and burst in. Aunt Julia sat in one of the chairs, a taut expression on her face like she just sucked a lemon.

"There you are. I've been looking for you," Mama patted the sofa beside her. "Come over here and sit by me. We'll have to start getting ready for the ball soon. Women have a lot more preparation than men."

Mama, the society expert. But this meant Toby had kept his mouth shut about his plop in horse manure, and Auntie Julia hadn't said beans yet about Seamus outlawed from this evening.

"What are you two talking about?" I asked.

This made Julia blink like she was about to cry, or maybe she was just upset I'd said anything. Children were to be seen and not heard. That was a big saying in America but worse in England. I didn't think they wanted even to see their children in England at all.

Aunt Julia said, "Just remembrances about how your mother was my lady's maid. Did she ever tell you about that?"

"Yes, ma'am, she did," I said, tucking my hands under my dress. "She said you were quite the ornery one."

Julia laughed, enjoying the comment. "Oh, I'm still ornery. Did she tell you she saved my life?"

"Kind of."

Aunt Julia told how back then Edward's father, the then duke, and her own papa took a large hunting party north from Cheyenne into the wilds of Wyoming and Montana, right into the heart of the greatest Indian war ever in America. I already knew all this. The hunting party was after buffalo, which for the most part had already been killed off. With thousands and thousands of Indians around including Seamus's real papa Spotted Horse, it was like sticking your head down in a hornets' nest and hoping you're not going to get stung. Boy, did they get stung. It was Mama who guided Julia's family to safety.

Mama was more famous then than she was now, but they didn't know who she was. They did now.

Julia grew quiet. I figured both were thinking back on this time. Then Julia said, "I couldn't sleep that night. I stepped out of my tent and saw you leave with Seamus. I thought I'd never see you again. We were sitting ducks for the Indians, and you were gone from it. But at the time, I thought you were the fool. I thought we were safe. It was the reverse though. You and Seamus were safe. Then you came back to warn us the Indians were coming, put yourself back into certain peril. I always wondered why you did that. Why you came back for us."

"It wasn't me," Mama replied. "It was Seamus. I would have kept going, but when we saw all the Cheyenne and Sioux readying for battle, and you as you say sitting ducks, Seamus pleaded with me to go back." She hesitated a long time and neither woman said anything. Then Mama went on in a low, gentler voice. "It wasn't my instinct. I wanted to save him but knew he'd never forgive me if I abandoned you. He loved you. He thought of you as family." She shrugged. "So, I came back."

Their eyes staring into the past, they sat there a long time, them remembering on things that happened before I was born.

"Yes, well," Aunt Julia finally said, slapping her thighs and stands. I'm surprised to see her eyes glistening with tears. "I best go. There's much to do before the ball. You tell that son of yours to save me a dance."

So, she didn't say a word about Seamus's banishment. What will the duke say? What will the prince say?

CHAPTER TWENTY-ONE

Becket Castle, May 20, 1887

In the darkness, Northampton's great house loomed ahead, windows alight. Clive Dunford and his wife Lydia sat in their coach as it lumbered up the long driveway in line with hundreds of other conveyances. He knew he looked in his pomp. The coach had been repainted and polished, the footmen given new livery, and he himself decked out like Beau Brummell in black tie evening attire. And Lydia, wearing her red Paris gown, hair coiffured on top like a beehive, and bedecked in jewels rented in London, was the picture of a rich countess, though certainly not a beautiful one. They needed to project wealth. He couldn't bring off this game if he appeared a desperate pauper.

Tonight, he would be signing an agreement with the duke and his business partners including the Prince of Wales himself that would make Dunford a rich man. Three weeks ago, he sent Northampton paperwork written by a master forger with all the proper government stamps, reporting the mine was taking in a hundred thousand pounds annually with just picks and shovels. Ah, the masterful lie. Once that was believed, all else fell into place. Since the principals were scattered throughout Britain, the business partnership would be finalized during the ball.

He removed a small flask from his jacket pocket and sipped the brandy. His sigh of pleasure was from both the liquid's soothing bite and his own realization that this dodge could indeed bring him millions. The only fly in the ointment was the presence of Morgan Raines, but that too could be turned into a triumph. Until the meeting with the duke and prince, he would avoid her. Once the agreement was signed, he'd set upon her with pleasure, bringing up again and again his sorrow at the demise of his poor daughter till her heart visibly bled.

He took another quick nip of brandy, recapped the flask, and slipped it back into his coat pocket. A large crowd of five or six hundred people from nearby Northampton stood out on the front lawn, watching the grand coaches roll up and release the passengers. The crowd cheered each time as if they were favorite performers on stage. Dunford's coach stopped in front of the castle, and a liveried servant opened the door. As they stepped down, Lydia pulled her silk wrap tighter. "I do hope they've lit fires in the grates. It's positively chilly tonight."

It took him a moment to realize she'd spoken. "If they haven't, I'll request it, my dear," he said. Then, they walked up the steps into the light of the open double doors.

When Mama, Seamus and I trooped down the grand staircase, I was so nervous I felt like a calf wandering into a wolf den. My wolf den was a fancy English ball with a real prince, a duke, and a lot of the hoity toity. I wondered if the prince would think me beautiful or a frog? A minute ago in Mama's mirror, I saw me in this amazing dress, my hair done up to beat all, a dusting of makeup like a grown-up, so for the first time, I thought maybe I was.

Mama was strange. She was the only woman I knew who wore a necklace inside her dress and one outside. The one inside was her prize possession, something she treasured maybe more than me. It had the gold cross from my grandma, the claws from a bear she killed when she lived with Lame Deer and the Cheyenne, and stone arrow given to her from her first husband, Seamus's pa Spotted Horse. My ma would rip out the heart of anyone who tried to take that off her.

"Glory, wait, your sash," Mama said when we reach the bottom of the stairs. "It's coming undone."

Quickly, she tied it with a knot. She wasn't nervous like me. I'd actually never seen Mama nervous. She had got a heart harder than birchwood, so she didn't naturally feel the same things. Tonight though, something sure stuck in her craw. So preoccupied, she tensed as we reached the bottom and glanced about at the people arriving as if expecting one to charge us.

A footman led us into the entrance hall, which was decorated with rows of colorful flowers that flanked a crowded pathway to the duke's butler. When our turn came, Mama handed him a card with our names even though he knew who we were. Up ahead, there stood the prince himself and his princess alongside the duke and duchess. The royal heir was a short, portly man dressed to the nines, every inch a fairy tale prince to me.

In the lamplight, the two women glittered like Christmas trees, all decked out in diamonds, rubies, and other jewels. Once more, I went through my curtsy in my head. I'd practiced it all day. Don't shake hands with the royals unless they extend a hand first, and if they do, take your glove off. Don't speak unless spoken to.

I jumped when the butler announced, "A Mrs. Raines, a Miss Raines, and a, er, Mr. Spotted Horse."

Hearing that, the duke stiffened like he'd just seen Jesse James, who was dead. His eyes shot fire at Auntie Julia, but she ignored him, nodding for us to come. At her neck, I noticed she wore a diamond as big as an egg and sparkling like a star. And there was the prince, my first real prince, dazzling in his bearing. My nerves doubled, and I knew I was about to fall on my face.

The duke said to the prince, "Your highness, you know Mrs. Raines."

Mama made a fine curtsy, and the prince extended his hand. "Of course. So pleasant to see you again, Mrs. Raines, without either a horse or a gun."

As they all laughed, she removed her glove, and he kissed her hand. No cuts on this arm.

"It's a pleasure to see your highness again," she said as she rose.

Then he bent over me, which was kind of awkward since I was near tall as him. My curtsy was perfect. At least, I didn't fall over. When he stuck his hand out, I ripped my glove off, and he kissed my bare hand. My first kiss and it was from a prince. I was so excited I forgot you're not supposed to speak first. I waved my hand in front of my face as if it were a fan and blurted out, "Oh, my, I think I'm getting the vapors."

They laughed, even the prince, then I pushed my luck. "Sir, I come all the way from Montana Territory with one purpose in mind, one hope in my heart, and that's to dance with the Prince of Wales."

He laughed again delightedly. "We shall see."

He turned to Seamus, who bowed way deeper than he needed to like he was going to kiss his shoes.

From his stunned expression, I thought the prince was going to explode with anger or laughter, but instead he said, "Ah yes, Mr. Spotted Horse. I remember you from the performance Buffalo Bill was so kind to give for me. I'm just sorry I missed your derring-do on opening day. I've heard so much about it."

And so with that, we passed beyond onto the dance floor. Hundreds of men and women milled about in such finery you'd have thought all the hoity toity were in this ballroom. Right off, Seamus left us and made for Cousin Isobel. They huddled behind her open fan. Well, I'll be.

A few minutes later, after the prince and princess greeted everyone, the duke addressed the attendees. "Shall we begin. I would ask his royal highness, the Prince of Wales, to open the ball with the first dance."

I got excited, thinking he would pick me. He had to pick me. The prince took center stage, rubbing his beard like he was thinking on a serious problem, glances around the ballroom at all the fine ladies furiously whiffing their fans like their faces were on fire, then he did it.

He walked straight to me, extending his hand, which I took.

When he guided me onto the floor, the ballroom erupted with applause. It didn't matter that I couldn't dance anything but a reel. The music began, and he glided me into a waltz. I didn't know what my feet were doing, but I am flying, I am laughing, I think I am crying.

Slim in her blue, shoulder-baring gown, Morgan ranged through the ballroom, searching for Dunford. A few minutes before, she had sent a disappointed Glory off to bed, trooping out with three other young girls and Toby. Lame Deer had been waiting for her, but once upstairs, the girl snuck off and made her way to the mezzanine above the dance floor. She slumped down in a chair and watched. In moments, Lame Deer had scooted in beside her.

Within Morgan, rage had been her constant companion since Will's murder. Dunford was here. She was coming for him, and Hell was coming with her. Yet, with the presence of British law and her being a foreigner, she must proceed in a smarter way than sudden violence, which had been necessary on the frontier. She was yet unsure how to do that.

She searched the ball room. With so many people, the place had grown hot. Under the lighted chandeliers, rows and rows of dowagers sat fanning themselves as they watched their daughters dancing with young men. Nowhere was Dunford among them, nor the duke or the prince for that matter.

For a while she watched Seamus on the dance floor with Cousin Isobel. They seemed to have eyes for each other. He was too young for it, but so was she when she first married.

"Quite a remarkable sight, don't you think?" A middle-aged woman stood beside her, squinting out at the young couple. "How well he dances for a Hindi."

"You think so," Morgan said evenly.

At that moment, John Coppersmith approached and extended his hand. "It's another waltz. Shall we join them, Mrs. Raines?"

She took his hand, and he guided her out into an odd half embrace.

The waltz was far too intimate, men and women touching almost in a hug. Morgan felt Coppersmith's firm hand on the small of her back, sliding a bit lower and was angry with herself for liking it. But then she realized why. It reminded her of Will's hand, the only one he had, he always placed it there, which never failed to draw instant desire from her.

Coppersmith's blue eyes bore into her. With a diffident sigh, she put a hand on his chest. "I see the spark in your eyes, Mr. Coppersmith, and I am grateful for it. But it is wasted. There is no spark in mine."

He gave a seductive half-smile. "No? Are you not a little interested?"

"I love my husband."

"If you were my wife, I think I'd be here with you."

"I suppose he might if he had not been shot to death two months ago."

His dance step faltered. "I am sorry, Mrs. Raines. I feel like a fool. I did not mean to offend."

"You didn't. You could not have known." They fell silent as he guided her through a couple more hurried turns, then she asked, "Do you know a man named Clive Dunford. I understand he's now the Earl of Wexham."

"Of course. Is he a friend of yours?"

"No, he most certainly is not. He's supposed to be here, but I can't find him anywhere."

"He is here, but right this minute, he's in the library completing a business agreement with the duke, the prince, and their investment partners. It's a gold mine, literally, Dunford's gold mine in the Cape Colony. It appears quite the opportunity."

She halted abruptly, and they stood unmoving, holding to their dance pose, awkwardly staring at each other while other couples swept by.

Morgan said emphatically, "Then your friends will lose every penny of their investment, Mr. Coppersmith. Dunford is a thief and a sharper. If the duke is your friend, help me stop it."

In the Becket Castle library, Clive Dunford sat near the fire with the prince and the duke, sipping brandy in snifter glasses, satisfied at this day's work. It was done. All the signatures were on the documents on Northampton's desk. The stack of papers might as well be stacks of cash. Within the week, when the investors' money poured into his account, he, Clive Dunford, cast off son of the old Earl of Wexham, would become one of the richest men in the kingdom.

Winthrop and the textile man Wilson stood at the mantel, flanking the fire, listening to the conversation, smiling, even beaming, certain they'd just secured their futures. Over the next year, he'd feed them all reports of progress that seemed promising. With that, they'd keep the belief in their financial acumen right up till the final report in which the mine failed and their money was gone. Dunford would weep tears of regret so convincingly that they could not but believe he too had been brought down to penury.

Dunford would have to pay off Acker and Detective Superintendent Hobbs, but that would be worth it. Protection from both sides of the law. To succeed, he'd have to travel to the Transvaal and visit the mine. There, on paper, he'd purchase hydraulic machines, hire engineers that didn't exist, employ miners who'd never put a shovel in the ground. It was much like the abattoir in Montana Territory. It was the paperwork that made the dodge. None of it real. The money would go to fake companies, then moved into his banking account in Brussels. Now that the agreement was signed, his future was assured. He savored his brandy and chuckled at a silly joke the prince had made.

"Well, gentlemen," the duke said, rising. "I think we've kept the prince from the eager embraces of the ladies long enough, don't you? Shall we join them?"

That's when a loud knock filled the room. Surprised, the duke called, "Come."

Curious, Dunford watched as Coppersmith stepped in the room followed by a rather attractive woman in a bare shouldered gown. She looked familiar, a country friend of the duke's no doubt, perhaps even a mistress, but what possibly could they want?

Then, with horror, he recognized her, and a chill struck him, one so cold his heart froze.

He shot to his feet. "Do not believe a word this woman speaks!"

Morgan approached, fixed her eyes on Dunford. "Hello, Clive," she said in a low voice.

His dark eyes festered with hatred that matched her own. She could not quite believe she was this close to the bastard who murdered her husband. Her rage urged her to draw a gun and shoot him, but she knew she couldn't.

After Coppersmith spoke quietly to the duke, Edward glanced from him to Morgan with a grim expression, then said to the prince, "Mrs. Raines has information that may bear on our transaction. I think we should hear what she has to say."

Dunford stood erect, the affronted party. "I protest, your grace. This woman is from the gutter. She is a liar and known killer. I witnessed her hang four men the day I left Montana. She has been trying to destroy me for years. What can she possibly add to our business?"

The prince looked at Morgan startled. "You, *you*, hanged four men, madam?"

She blinked, not expecting this. "They had it coming," she replied simply and saw on the men's faces expressions of disgust. This wasn't a good start. She tried to explain, "Your highness, in Montana, , there is no law like here in Britain. We have to be our own law or be cut down like spring grass."

She saw she'd not convinced anyone. Even Edward was frowning, and the prince sighed. A vigilante hanging was too much for them. She would not apologize or explain herself further. Dunford sported a half-smile.

Still, the duke was on her side. "I think we should hear her out, your highness," he said. "It can't hurt to hear what she has to say. Go on, Mrs. Raines."

She met their eyes. "If you men have given this man money, consider that money lost. You will never see it again. Clive Dunford may be an earl now, but in Montana he was nothing more than a fraudster, a sharper. He stole from…"

"What rubbish," Dunford said. Abruptly, he strode to the desk. "The signing is complete. I intend to continue forward with our agreement."

When he reached for the papers, Morgan drove a bone-handled knife into them with such force that it pinned them to the desk. As if he'd touched fire, Dunford snatched back his hand, holding it as if she'd cut him.

He shouted, "You see, you see, the woman is mad."

Horrified, the men fell silent. This was not going at all as she'd planned. She doubted many ladies drew knives in English library rooms, but then she was not a lady and had no pretense to be. She could not escape her innate nature. She had been born in the criminal hellhole of Five Points, been raised on the Montana frontier, and grown up in the Indian villages of the Cheyenne. No, she was not a lady. And she only had to convince Dunford that she was a threat to him. If these men wanted to throw their money away, that was their choice.

Finally, the prince muttered, "Indeed, indeed." He was frowning, looking at the others.

Morgan decided just to go on as if she hadn't shocked them. She told how in Montana Territory Dunford had created one fraud after another. He brought in investors for a slaughterhouse that in the end proved to be only a design on paper, for a railroad line that had no rails, and countless stockholders in his ranch that proclaimed fifty thousand head of cattle but in fact never had more than five hundred. Banks failed, people went broke, and he got rich. Then he ran out on everyone."

"You can't prove any of this," Dunford stated flatly, then to the men, "I've offered you the opportunity of a lifetime. You will never forgive yourselves if you let it pass."

She interrupted him, addressing Duke Edward, "Do not invest in any of his schemes. He is a crook."

The men stared at her like an old-time jury of stern clerics, deliberating on her guilt as much as Dunford's.

After a short silence, the Earl of Wexham spoke, "As you men can see, it's just a hysterical woman, a violent one shouting out her claptrap." He waved his hand dismissively. "Nothing to it anyway. The papers are signed, so I intend to go forward as if this despicable woman had not interrupted our meeting. It will be as if the incident had not occurred."

The duke made the decision for them all. He withdrew the knife, handing it to Morgan. Then he calmly walked to the fireplace with the papers and dropped them in. They caught at once and roared up in flames.

Clinching his fists, Dunford was shaking with fury. "You cannot do that. It was signed."

The duke turned to the others. "I know this woman. I trust her with my life and the lives of my family. If she says something is true, it is true. I believe her. Despite knifing my desk."

A couple men chuckled, easing the tension. None of them contradicted him, even the prince. He nodded toward the Earl of Wexham. "Sir, our business is finished. You may leave my house."

Dunford gasped, then shot Morgan a glare of malevolence so intense it appeared to have physical force. With sudden insight, she realized she was looking into the eyes of madness. She thought he might attack her this very moment.

Instead, he spun about to face the men. "You sons of bitches, I'll..."

The prince blanched, and Dunford hesitated as if realizing what he'd just done. He'd insulted the heir to the English throne and in that instant put himself outside of society. He'd not be received anywhere. The door slammed, and he was gone.

This had been more than Morgan hoped for. The playing field was back in her realm. Now it would be frontier justice for both of them. Dunford was not a man to slink off. As she intended, he would now come for her. He had no other choice. But the man was now a wounded animal, and as she well knew, those were the most dangerous kind.

PART THREE
KIDNAPPED

CHAPTER TWENTY-TWO

Northamptonshire, May 20, 1887

When Dunford and his wife left Becket Castle in a rush, Lydia said nothing and remained quiet throughout the long, harried ride home. Clive was in a fury, and she knew it would do no good to ask him for particulars. For the entire journey, he managed but a few angry mumblings, *they'll see, they'll see, they will pay.*

On reaching Wexham Hall, her husband told her to pack her things. She would be leaving for New York the next day. The plan had failed. They were destitute. She had not known about any plan yet had long realized living with Clive was feast or famine, and she would endure whichever one came next. He told her he'd send for her when the time was right and then was off again in the coach.

By midnight, Dunford was huddled in a room above the Rose and Crown pub with Charlie Acker and Detective Superintendent Hobbs. The walls were dingy with ancient dirt, the beams and ceiling dry and warped, not an engaging place. Inside his coat pocket, Dunford gripped a pistol and planned to shoot both men if they attempted to exact retribution for this fiasco. It wasn't his fault. Morgan Raines had scuppered the dodge.

Acker was angry about it. He sat beside Dunford at a roughhewn table, glaring at nothing in particular, wrapping his fingers on the table over and over again. But he seemed still on Dunford's side. He couldn't be sure of Hobbs. The detective in his distinctive, ankle-high spats creaked the floorboards with his pacing like a poor actor strutting his part on the stage with exaggerated melodrama. A bushy mustache whose tips reached down to the edges of his chin gave pronouncement to his heavy grimace.

Hobbs had toiled decades with the London Metropolitan Police Force, long hours making little money as he saw it, even with the many bribes he exacted. Dunford's scheme had been his opportunity for wealth, to at last be among the beau monde, and he made no attempt to hide his rage that it had been scuttled.

Dunford saw the policeman had the heart of a weasel and trusted him no more than he trusted a petty thief.

"What happened?" the detective demanded. "It was set, and yet, somehow you buggered it."

"I did not bugger it, Hobbs. The contract was signed. Legal. Toasts were given. We had a fortune about to be made, then the woman showed up." He shook his head in dismay. "I just told you about her. She was..."

The detective cut in. "She was there. We understand that. But why? How did she know about our plans?"

Dunford shrugged. "Who knows? It hardly matters now."

Frustrated, Hobbs said, "It matters. How is it she knows you?"

Patiently, Dunford said, "From America. Then she showed up tonight in the duke's library of all places and accused me of every manner of crime. Northampton believed her and tossed the contract in the fire. At that point, there was nothing I could do but leave."

Hobbs looked disgusted. "Well, she's done us in good, and I for one would like to see her pay the piper."

"In time. In time," Dunford said emphatically. "You don't understand. Neither of you do. We just can't go willy nilly after her. This is no London housewife. Apparently, she's here with her daughter and halfbreed son working in that Wild West show in London. She's a markswoman, a rather famous one in America who's killed her share of men, and she wants to kill me. She's dangerous and won't hesitate to shoot any of us."

Hobbs said smugly, "But she doesn't know Charlie or me, does she? Just you."

Acker clapped Dunford on the back. "Don't worry, mate. Me boys will have her swimming in the Thames you just say the word."

He remembered the intense focus and even ferocity of Morgan Raines pursuit when she led the vigilantes after the cow thieves. They had not stood a chance. Hobbs's and Acker's dismissal of the threat she posed was a mistake that Dunford wouldn't make. He would get at the woman another way and in so doing still make his fortune.

"No, Charlie, not yet. We don't want her mucking up our plans," Dunford said.

Hobbs lifted his gaze with an air of disgust. "Plans! What plans?"

"There is yet a way we can take in the money we seek, and you, detective, will play the main part."

Hobbs sat abruptly in a chair across from him with a dubious expression. "Go on then."

"Gentlemen, I will not let this chance go abegging," Dunford sad. "This has been only the first act. I assure you the play is still on. There is yet the final act."

"Get to it, man," Hobbs said.

Dunford gave a humorless chuckle. "The duke has a son, doesn't he?"

The detective spread his hands in a halfhearted shrug. "Of course. So?"

"Then we will snatch him, but at the same time we must also take this woman's daughter. We must have some leverage on her, and the duke will pay a fortune to get his son back."

"And the woman's daughter?" Hobbs asked.

His voice cold, Dunford said, "She will not be going back."

Outskirts of Northampton, May 21, 1887

Lame Deer shifted with the gentle roll of the carriage. On the way to the Englander fair, she sat with Glory and the wasicus boy Toby.

Beside him, Big Hands Tom, the boy's shadow, was staring at Glory with the moon eyes of a calf. He fumbled his words badly around the girl. She'd noticed his ways and asked what was wrong with him, and Lame Deer had to explain it, calf love. Pleased with herself, Glory had given a silly girl laugh. Two men in the duke's red uniforms stood on a platform on the back of the carriage.

They were close to the city now, its buildings visible in the distance above the treetops. The sun burned hot on her face, something she was used to. Her life had been spent in the sun. So many days trekking on the plains, moving to a new camp, an endless circle of seasons. Those days returned to her, and she became lost in her dream wanderings. She remembered when she first saw the whites. She was a young girl, much younger than Glory, maybe four or five winters, and they came into her country, a strange tribe of white men, one black man, and an Indian woman, and her baby.

When her father learned of it from another warrior, he'd asked what they looked like. Strange people with hair on their faces, the man said. Did the Indian woman have hair on her face, Lame Deer asked, and they all laughed. Seen by some, they had come through the country before on a long journey to the great water far across the mountains. The wasicus were now returning to their own people who lay beyond the awakening sun.

Lame Deer's father became excited and took her up on his horse, and they rode off to see them. When they reached the big mud river, the wasicus were building canoes to float back to their home. There were so many men, rough looking, but their two chiefs treated Lame Deer's father with respect, especially the one with red hair. They exchanged gifts.

She was more interested in the Indian woman, indeed hardly more woman than she, sixteen or maybe seventeen winters, but with a baby in swaddle on her back. The men called her Bird Woman, and the red-haired chief once called her Janey. The little inquisitive boy, maybe a year old, was called Pompy and treated like a great warrior.

As Bird Woman worked gathering roots and berries, she used sign to tell a little of her journey with these men, of reaching the water that went beyond the far horizon. At her age, Lame Deer didn't understand much of it. Within that day, they left in their big canoes floating down river and out of sight.

That was long ago. Now she had become old, gray-haired, and wrinkly faced like a dried-up berry. And there were no clan warriors around but her and her daughter Crow Killer Morgan, who does not know where her steps should land, in the white world or the Cheyenne one.

Today like each day, Lame Deer's purpose was to protect Morgan's child, and she would do that with her life. She loved the girl as if she were her own, and indeed, she was. Hadn't she taught her the ways of the Tsis tsis'tas? This world of the wasicus could be a dangerous place. Lame Deer hoped she was not too old to keep the girl safe.

"Stop that, Toby," Glory called out, pulling Lame Deer reluctantly back to the present. "You're being a brat."

The boy had climbed onto his knees on the back of his seat and was using a long feather to tickle the nose of one of the uniformed men and giggling hysterically. Lame Deer reached across the carriage, placing a hand on his shoulder and yanked him back down in his seat.

"Hey, you can't do that," Toby wailed. "I'll tell my father. You're just a servant."

Her face warlike, Glory leaned toward him. "She's Cheyenne. She's no one's servant. You know what the Cheyenne women do to punish little boys like you?"

Toby squinted at her, uncertain. "No, I don't and don't care." After a second, he said, "What do they do?"

"They cut off a finger and sometimes a toe," she said. "Why, I've seen some Cheyenne boys walking around with no fingers and no toes at all. She carries a knife you know. So do I but I won't cut your fingers off. She will."

Toby glanced at Lame Deer, who kept her face as unmoving as

stone. He swallowed and sat back on the seat. Then said brightly, "I hear there's going to be a man who eats fire at the fair. You ever seen a man who eats fire?"

"Sure. Lots of times," Glory replied in a way that told the old Indian woman she had not.

Suddenly, Lame Deer regarded the countryside. Something did not feel right. She thought a terrible thing was about to happen. They were travelling along a path through scattered groves of trees. The birds had fallen silent. Nothing moved. Not a rabbit or a sage hen or the branches of the trees. The wind was holding its breath. The coach with the duchess and her three daughters should have been behind them, but Toby's sisters had been slow to rise and slow to dress. Those girls could not outrun a turtle. So the duchess told Toby's driver to start out for the fair, and she would catch up in the coach. They hadn't caught up and with those girls might not make the fair.

"Who are they?" Toby asked, pointing ahead to a group of five horsemen coming fast out of the trees.

"Pull up, driver," one of them, a big, broad man, called, drawing a pistol.

When he did, another man freed the horses from their traces and slapped their rumps, scattering them off at a gallop.

Lame Deer was already clambering out on the other side, pulling Glory with her. The girl tried to grab Toby, but he pulled his hand back. Everything then happened in snap bursts. A man jumped up into the carriage, and Tom punched him, knocking him to the ground. The big man rode up and shot Tom, the bullet snapping his head back, and he fell from the carriage.

The big man yanked a screaming Toby out and another man threw a sack over his head.

"Where's the girl?" the big man shouted. "Get the girl."

Bent over, Lame Deer and Glory disappeared into the tall grass. They scrambled another thirty yards and dashed into the trees. Behind them, the men were rushing about frantically searching for them. No one had seen them get away. It was not the first time she had to escape an attack by white men.

The old Indian woman pulled Glory down behind some underbrush surrounding several trees. In Cheyenne, she whispered, "We hide and wait. Someone come soon."

Glory nodded, the fright clear in her eyes, but she had control of it. She would not run off screaming like a wounded coyote chased by a bear.

Lame Deer sensed movement behind her and turning saw a man just above her on horseback swinging a club. It struck her head, and she was blinded by the sudden light exploding behind her eyes. She tried to rise to fight the man, but her legs had no strength.

"Quick. Grab the girl," the man called to someone.

In the swirling trees and the land flashing round her, Lame Deer saw Glory snatched up, screaming and her arms flailing at the attacker, a sack thrown over her head, spinning, spinning.

The old Cheyenne woman screamed her old war cry and lunged for the girl, but despair crushed her heart for Glory seemed farther away, unreachable. And that was when the blackness wrapped itself around her.

CHAPTER TWENTY-THREE

Field Outside Northampton, May 21, 1887

Detective Constable David Evans of the Northampton Police Department was alarmed. His day had gone from promise to imminent doom in the space of a few minutes. After six months as a detective, he'd been assigned his first major case, the kidnapping of the Duke of Northampton's son and another child. He looked forward to this evening when arrived home and told his new bride Arabella, about the confidence the superintendent had in him.

His initial excitement vanished when he learned he'd be working under the supervision of Detective Inspector Roger Bramley, who'd seemingly been around since old Bobby Peel. There couldn't have been a worse man for the job. He was not only a pompous ass but a dangerous fool. With his long unruly side whiskers, blue-veined nose, and breath that always stunk of stale beer and recent whiskey, he looked and acted like a bull on a rampage. He blustered his way from crime to crime causing havoc yet being praised and promoted by the high up nobs.

For DI Bramley indeed solved far more cases than anyone else in the department but did so by threatening and slapping around reluctant witnesses and beating confession from the first convenient suspect. Case closed. But Evans wondered how many of those cases had the right of it. Very few, he thought. With Bramley leading the charge on this one, those kidnapped children were as good as dead. And now, the man thought he'd already solved the case.

Earlier, riding in the police patrol wagon, the carriage driver had guided the two detectives and a squad of uniformed constables to the scene of the abduction. The carriage seemed odd standing on the path without horses. As the driver reported, the body of Tom Latham lay on the grass beside it.

"The footmen must have reached the duke by now, sir," Evans said. "The duke should be here. Should I send a man after him?"

"No, he'll be here soon enough," Bramley said.

The detective inspector ordered two men to carry the body to the wagon and sent the rest out to search the fields.

"What are they looking for, sir," Evans asked.

Bramley puffed himself up. "Suspicious signs, lad. Suspicious signs. They'll know them when they see them." He grinned showing yellow teeth. "Just watch and listen, Davy lad. You'll learn how it's done."

Moments later, two constables led a disheveled dark-skinned woman up to the detectives, her eyes vacant and blinking constantly. There was blood caked to the side of her head.

Bramley was writing something on a small notepad, using the patrol wagon for support. He looked over at them, then grinned with delight. "Now, who's this?"

"We found her wandering in the trees, sir," one of the constables answered.

"Was she running or hiding?"

"She seemed lost, sir," the man replied.

Bramley said, "Don't you worry, lads, I'll have her talking in no time."

She stared at him, confused. He leaned his face closer to hers and gave her an unpleasant grin. "Well now, we have the key to the case right here. Where are your accomplices, Miss Coolie Belle? Where are the little bairns? Tell me the truth, and it will go easier for you."

When she said nothing, he spoke louder, more sharply. "Mujee Batao."

Evans recognized it as butchered Hindi, and it garnered no

response. Bramley slapped the woman hard. Her eyes bulged in horror, and she began screaming, "Oonaha Keso! Glory!"

When she tried to get past the detective, he threw her back against the wagon.

"The woman is clearly daft, sir," Evans said. "I don't think…"

Bramley glared at him. "Shut your gob, Davy, and just watch. She knows something, and I'm the one that's sure as hell going to find out what."

Just then, a carriage rolled up to them. Bramley hesitated for inside was the Chief Constable Roger Pike, himself, the man who bossed them all, and beside him sat a figure he didn't recognize. When the two stepped out, the unknown man immediately took a pocket watch from his waistcoat and checked the time, then nodded to the chief. This new man was dressed almost like a dandy, especially with his fancy boots.

"Gentlemen," Chief Pike said. "This is Henry Hobbs, Detective Superintendent of Scotland Yard's Criminal Investigation Division. Lucky for us, he's visiting our fair city, and I asked him to consult on the incident. You don't mind, do you Detective Bramley?"

Bramley did. It was all over his face, but he said, "No, sir, but I think we have this one in hand. It was an inside job, and this here Coolie Belle knows a thing or two. I was just questioning her. When she answers up, I believe we'll have it all."

The chief looked to Hobbs, who said, "By all means, Detective. Continue."

Abruptly, Bramley thrust his forearm into the woman's throat and pressed her roughly against the wagon. "Now then, where were we? Yes, where did your people take the bairns? Speak up. You can save yourself years of prison time. Where are they?"

When she said nothing, he punched her belly, buckling her to her knees. Moments later, she rose, a knife suddenly in her hand, and plunged it at him. Bramley jumped back in time, the blade clipping off a button. The woman ran, but he tackled her to the ground.

When he lifted her forcibly to her feet, he held up the blade for the chief and Hobbs to see. "I guess this leaves no doubt as to her guilt. She'll spill it all soon enough. I just need a couple more hours with her."

The sound of horses coming hard caused him to turn and stare in the direction of Becket Castle. "Now what?" he blasted.

Evans saw seven riders in all, two far ahead of the others. It looked like a sprint they were approaching so fast. "It's the duke," he shouted.

But it wasn't the duke in front. A woman riding astride and wearing strange, gaudy clothing like a circus performer led them. Just behind came a boy, dark skinned like the Hindi woman but dressed like a toff. A hundred yards farther back, riding hard, came the duke and duchess with three other men. They'd be wanting answers for their missing boy, and Evans was glad he did not run this investigation for no one had any answers, certainly not Bramley.

Suddenly, terror gripped him when it became clear the front rider was not going to stop but crash into them all. He was about to jump aside just as the woman pulled up on the reins and lept from the horse before it had even came to a halt.

Irate, Bramley demanded, "What's the meaning of this? I am a police officer. I…"

He did not finish. A gun appeared in the woman's hand, and she swung it viciously, hitting him in the face. The sound of snapping bone could be heard just before Bramley's shriek. Blood spurted from his nose, and he stumbled back. She struck him twice more, bearing a look of animal ferocity that Evans had never seen on a woman. Bramley went down to one knee.

Mouths agape, everyone stood in a tableau of utter stupefaction. It was the Hindi woman who stopped the assault by rushing in to stay the next blow. The whole thing had lasted only a second or two. The other rider, the dark-skinned boy, stood by her side, a gun in his hand. It was pointed to the ground, but no one had any doubt as to his intention. His eyes said he was ready to kill, and none of doubted it. They themselves carried no guns.

Finally, with a deep breath, Chief Pike stepped forward. "Madam, you are under arrest for felony. You have just struck an officer of the Northampton Police Department in pursuit of his duty. Surrender your weapon at once."

"He's not dead," she said sharply, then turned to the boy, "See what the tracks tell you."

He hurried out to the field, intensely studying the ground as if searching for a tiny lost heirloom while the two women began speaking rapidly in that foreign tongue. Rushing them was the only logical course to follow, but no one seemed interested in that. The woman with the gun could shoot two or three of them. They were at an impasse.

Trying to stanch the bleeding with a handkerchief, Bramley wobbled to his feet and pointed a shaky finger at the woman. "I want her in handcuffs!" he screamed with a pronounced nasal tone. "She broke me nose. Do as the gaffer says, Evans. Arrest her now."

Drawing out their nightsticks, Evans and the two closest constables moved cautiously toward the women as the rest of the duke's party arrived in a thunder of hooves.

The duke jumped down. "Belay that order. Hold fast, the lot of you." He gestured to Bramley with a dismissive flick of the hand. "While my son is missing, you and your men blunder about, threatening these two women. Both are guests in my home and personal friends of the Prince of Wales himself. Chief Pike, I hope this isn't the manner in which you plan to conduct the rest of this investigation. At the moment, it's a shamble. My boy's life and that of this woman's daughter depend on you, and I am not reassured."

Pike sputtered then, but Bramley bellowed like a bull. "She attacked me, that's what she done, your grace. Look at me nose. She busted it. You see, I found out the kidnapping was an inside job. That Hindi woman there. I put it together with geometric police logic."

The London man Hobbs stepped up to Bramley. "Let's not pursue that thread, detective. I think we can take the duke's word for these two women, don't you?" He turned to Pike. "We're wasting time here, sir. I suggest we begin a pursuit now. The likely place they would take the children is Northampton, at least at first. They must get out of sight. We can all agree on that. I suggest we send men to the rail station and to every road out of the city to search every coach, every wagon. We must do this quickly, sir. They've had too much time as is."

"Who are you, sir?" the duke asked.

"Detective Superintendent HenryHobbs of Scotland Yard, your grace," he replied "I was here actually to visit the fair. The Chief asked me to assist. We arrived just before you."

Considering only a moment, Edward addressed Pike, "I'd prefer this man oversee the investigation, Chief. If you need help getting him assigned, I'll see to it. Are you willing, Detective Hobbs?"

The London man gave a sharp nod. "Certainly, your grace. I'll do what I can."

Upset, Bramley began to bluster, but the boy's voice from the field overrode him. "I've got the tracks, Mama," he called.

The woman and the boy rushed to their horses and shot off as if at Epsom Downs. Instantly, the duchess joined them. The three other men on horseback waited for the duke.

He indicated the Hindi woman and told Pike, "See that this woman reaches my home unharmed by anyone else. I'll hold you responsible." Then he climbed aboard his horse, and with his men, raced after his wife.

CHAPTER TWENTY-FOUR

Northampton, May 21, 1887

With Morgan and Seamus leading, the party made their way to a road crowded with wagons, carriages, and pedestrians heading toward Northampton and its fair. They lost the tracks among them but picked them up again in meadow just beyond. There, by a pair of trees, Morgan spotted the tracks of a wagon, now gone, that had been sitting there a long time.

Julia, her voice frayed, asked, "How do you know it's been here any time at all?"

Morgan could see her friend was barely maintaining her aristocratic composure. She herself was struggling to keep herself sane. Dread threatened to seize both women completely. Morgan couldn't allow that. She needed to keep fear and panic from her mind to have any chance of catching the kidnappers. If they got clear of Northampton, the children would be lost.

Calmly, she pointed out the deep wheeled impressions in the grass that even the youngest Cheyenne would spot. "But those tracks were made by a wagon at least a couple hours ago. The grass is already returning to how it was. The kidnappers must have come here, put Glory and Toby in it, and kept them hidden as they went into the city." She pointed to fresh wheel tracks. "That's them leaving with the children maybe a half hour ago."

"No, it was a coach," Julia said.

Morgan stared at her.

"They'd have to use a coach," Julia insisted. "No wagon, even one with a canvas top, is going to hide Toby. He'd be making all sorts of fuss. They couldn't control him in a wagon."

Morgan nodded. "True enough." She turned to the men. "They're going into the city. The tracks are fresh. Look for a coach."

They made for the crowded nearby road where the tracks quickly disappeared among the stream of people heading for the market fair. The coach could not be far ahead, but no tracker, not even Running Hawk or her first husband Spotted Horse, could follow it now. With the road so clogged, she led them over the fences and back into the fields again, keeping the road in sight and pushing hard for the city.

"There it is!" one of the men called, and indeed, far ahead, maybe half a mile, was a coach with a single man standing on the back in the footmen's post, not in any uniform. The vehicle squeezed onto a stone bridge with hundreds of people.

Morgan's heart leapt, and Julia screamed, "That's them." Tears were rolling down the duchess's cheeks.

They took to the road again, pushing into the melee, clattering up onto the stone bridge. Below them on the water, Morgan saw three of the oddest boats passing under the arches. They were long, thirty feet or so, and narrow, strikingly narrow, maybe six feet, and yet laden with canvas covered cargo.

The image was quickly lost when at the peak of the bridge, she saw the coach now no more than a quarter mile ahead, struggling to get through the people packed in between the row houses and businesses like cattle in a chute. A loud cacophony of horses, wagon wheels, and shouting reverberated from the mob. The duke's party rushed over the bridge and into the melee. Slowly, they worked their way ahead, foot by foot, never losing sight of the coach.

Then when they reached the market square, it was gone. Amid the crowd of thousands, amid the tents and stands and booths, there was no sign of the coach nor of the children. She searched frantically but just saw a mass of people. Hope was gone. Though she had held her desperation at bay, it swamped her now.

A hitch in his voice, Edward said, "Anyone see anything?"

No response. Then one of the men shouted, "There! There!"

Down a side street, Morgan saw the coach with the lone man clinging to the back. Instantly, she broke from the market, the rest of the party right behind, and closed on it. The coach pulled out from the city onto a sparce area with only one building, a three story tavern named the Crown and Flag. Several other vehicles and horses were tied up outside. The man jumped down from the rear platform and stared in shock as the party rode up to the coach. Two men and three women clambered out. The men were drunk, and though Morgan wasn't familiar with the breed, she recognized the women as ladies of the night. These were not the kidnappers.

For a few seconds, they stared bewildered at the threatening riders, then turned away and lurched drunkenly toward the oak door, arm in arm, laughing.

There could be no hiding from the fact they'd lost. The children were gone. Julia slid from her horse and fell to the ground, her chest heaving in great sobs. Quickly, Edward jumped down, knelt with his wife, and wrapped his arms around her.

In despair, Morgan galloped her horse to the edge of the cobblestones, where they became a dirt road that cut through a meadow of dry grass. Farther on were low hedges in which silent birds flitted between, and beyond stood a deep, shadowy wood. Accompanied by cannonades of thunder, massive black clouds were roiling in, flashing lightning, and bringing darkness to the day. Off to the right, she saw movement on the river that ran from behind the tavern, drifted gently alongside the field, and then curved through and behind the wood. The boats she'd spotted earlier were disappearing beyond the trees.

In a single, volcanic scream, Morgan split open the silence of the meadow, scattering birds squawking into the sky from a nearby hedgerow.

CHAPTER TWENTY-FIVE

London, May 27, 1887

Within a day, news of the Duke of Northampton's son being kidnapped had been cabled into the farthest corners of the realm. Every policeman in every city, town, and village was on watch for him and the girl who'd been with him. Also, the duke hired hundreds of men and sent them to scour the country. There was no trace. They seemed to have disappeared into the earth.

In the newspapers, he posted a reward of ten thousand pounds for information that led to their return, and that put the entire nation on alert. It was a staggering amount of money, more than most people earned in a lifetime. Hundreds of reports came in. The Northampton Police Department and the London Metropolitan Police, now fully involved, could not run down them all. More and more officers had to be added to the investigation.

Sharpers tried to claim the reward with sightings easily proved untrue. DS Hobbs was relentless in prosecuting them all to the fullest for false testimony. In the end, not a scrap of real evidence turned up.

As the days went by, Morgan and Julia sank deeper into a black despair, each in her own way. Remaining in her London townhouse, Julia often reverted to the young woman she'd been when she was known as the Dragon of Fifth Avenue. She snapped at servants for no reason, issued cutting remarks to her daughters' governess for her laziness and ignorance, and threatened to sack the butler and housekeeper for "monumental ineptitude."

The townhouse was where the duke conducted his operation, which kept him busy sixteen to twenty hours a day. He had no time to dwell in the misery that had affected his wife. Nor did he have much time to comfort her.

Morgan spent her days between the townhouse and the Wild West encampment. She did not return to performing, nor did Bill press her to, but Seamus did return.

"I can't sit about, Mama," he said. "I need to get on a horse."

She understood what he meant. For Morgan though, there was nothing she could do. She felt helpless. Despair and sorrow were old companions, battering her like a boxer with his opponent on the ropes. She had cried for Will, and now she cried for Glory. Morgan just couldn't see how they would get her daughter back. She had absolutely no trust in the police, even this man Hobbs, who seemed competent enough. Here in this country, there was law, and yet this law could not find her child.

Then, the break they'd all been praying for finally came. The kidnappers made contact. Through an intermediary, they would be presenting their demands to the families at police headquarters. In a hansom cab, Morgan rushed to the townhouse and arrived just as Edward and Julia were leaving. She climbed in the coach with them. As they rode in silence lost in their own turmoils, the possibilities swirled in her head like loose threads in the wind. She pushed aside the most dreaded one, that they were already dead. The other worry was that the kidnappers would ask for more money than she possessed.

For the duke, that wouldn't be a concern. She knew his wealth was vast, somewhere between ten and fifteen million pounds. Julia hadn't been sure of the exact amount. That meant sixty million or thereabouts in American, a number she could not fathom. He was wealthier now than Otto Kruger, his father-in-law. He could pay any amount. If the kidnappers wanted more than she had, she'd have to ask him for it. She'd never wanted to be beholden to anyone, but this was different. He would pay it, and she could not refuse.

As he himself explained, the problem for the kidnappers was moving large sums of cash without being noticed and caught. There were pound denominations of fifty, a hundred, five hundred, and a thousand, but using any of those would bring great scrutiny. Even a ten pound note would raise an eyebrow.

"Most people lived on less than fifty pounds a year," he'd said. "And did so comfortably enough at that income. Can you imagine paying for a tankard of ale with a hundred pound banknote. This Hobbs fellow would soon roll them all up."

Perhaps, people did live well enough on fifty pounds a year, but she'd observed as she passed through parts of London that the countless many at the bottom of that average did not. They struggled day to day. But they were not her concern. Glory was.

In small denominations, a few thousand pounds would need a wheelbarrow. A cheque drawn on a bank would have to be produced at that bank where presumably police would be waiting. She figured if pushed to it she could raise five hundred pounds and hoped that would be enough.

At Scotland Yard, a constable led them into DS Hobbs's office where at least fifteen mustachioed and bearded men stood in the small room talking in animated conversation. When the duke, his wife, and Morgan entered, they fell silent.

Hobbs was sitting at his desk talking to Bramley, the Northampton detective, who stood nodding obsequiously. A cloth bandage was wrapped around his head, and his nose was covered by a white strap contraption. They both turned to the three newcomers. That was when Morgan noticed Bramley's two black eyes from the swelling around them and from the glare directed at her within them. She wondered what the hell he was doing here.

"Good," Hobbs said. "Now we can commence."

He offered them seats and Julia and Morgan sat. Quickly, he

explained that these other men were detectives from all over England who'd joined the case. Morgan was grateful that Edward's wealth and fame warranted such influence. That Bramley was one of them though didn't give her much confidence.

The duke carried a black, silver-tipped walking cane and now tapped the floor with it loudly. "I don't have time for this, detective. Where is the intermediary? Let's hear from him."

Hobbs turned to a group of men behind the desk, and from the back, a man worked his way forward.

It was Clive Dunford.

Morgan shot to her feet. "What's he doing here?"

Dunford gave a helpless shrug. "The kidnappers came to me, Mrs. Raines. I had no choice. I could hardly refuse to help the duke or you in extremis."

Hobbs said, "Please, Mrs. Raines, let's see what he has to say."

Julia stood and put a hand on Morgan's forearm while the duke said, "Go on, then."

Hobbs nodded to Dunford. "Tell us what happened, milord. How did they contact you? Let's start there."

In minutes, Dunford told his story, how he himself had been abducted the night before. He'd just left his gentlemen's club in St. James Square when he was assaulted. One man clubbed him with a truncheon and the other threw a sack over his head. They tied his hands and led him away, presumably into an alley for he heard no more carriages or people. They walked nearly twenty minutes before entering a building and climbing stairs to a small room. He had a knot on the side of his head the size of an apple.

This didn't fit. Now, the earl was the individual she must trust to get her daughter back? Even so, Morgan would never forego her retribution.

By his expression, Duke Edward was becoming impatient. "Get on with it," he snapped.

"Did you see any of them?" Hobbs asked Dunford.

"No, I said they never removed the sack."

Suspicious, Morgan asked, "Why did they choose you to act as go-between?"

Dunford shrugged. "Who knows? The duke and I are neighbors. Perhaps that was enough for them. I think they assumed we were friends."

"Go on. Finish your story," Hobbs said.

"A man finally spoke from somewhere across the room. I'm sure I'd recognize it again if I heard it. He told me he had the two young ones. I didn't believe him at first, but another man thrust clothes into my hands and said they belonged to them."

One of the detectives brought Hobbs the clothes. Julia screamed and snatched the boy's coat from him. "This is Toby's." she looked at Edward. "It's his." Tears welled in her eyes.

Morgan saw the torn red cloth Hobbs held and recognized it as part of Glory's dress. She squeezed her eyes shut for just a second, then nodded to the detective.

"What happened next?" Hobbs asked Dunford.

Duke Edward cut in sharply, "Enough. What do they want for our children?"

Dunford glanced from the detectives to the duke, then said, "It's outrageous, your grace, but for your son, the man wants the Tudor Diamond."

There was a loud gasp in the room as Morgan did the quick calculations. The jewel was worth six hundred thousand pounds. That was nearly three million dollars. But the duke nodded quickly. "Done."

"What about my daughter?" Morgan demanded.

"For the girl, he said a thousand pounds in fifty pound notes."

"I haven't got that," she replied, nearly shouting.

"I'll pay it," the duke said.

"Edward," she whispered. "I don't know what to say."

The duke faced her. "We can never repay you for what you did all those years ago but let this be a start." He turned to Dunford. "When do you meet them again?"

"Tomorrow night, in St. James Square," he replied. "I'm to bring the diamond and the money then. They said if they see any police following me, they will kill the children."

Julia groaned.

"There will be no police," the duke said. "I give you my word. Tell them that. But you tell them also I want both children returned unharmed. If that doesn't happen, if any harm comes to them, then I will make sure that a one-million-pound reward be paid to anyone who brings me their heads. It will be posted everywhere in the world where there's a newspaper to print it or a printing press to issue notices. There will be no place they can hide. No one they can trust. No safe haven from being hunted down and executed. You tell them that also is my word."

"Yes, your grace," Dunford said. "I will see that they understand."

Hobbs had turned pale at the duke's words. To Morgan, that seemed odd. In fact, the entire meeting seemed off, but why it did, she couldn't grasp, the answer tantalizingly just beyond reach.

CHAPTER TWENTY-SIX

Scotland Yard, May 27, 1887

After the details of the ransom payment were worked out with Dunford, everyone left Hobbs's office. Outside on the front steps, the duke and duchess with the Raines woman caught up with, the two women's faces masks of distress and pain. He so appreciated that but hid it behind an expression of sympathy.

"I realize there's been a bit of a muddle between us, Lord Wexham," the duke said, the silver tip of his walking cane glittering in the sun, "but I want you to know that I appreciate your help in this matter, and I won't forget it."

Maintaining his concerned smile, Dunford seethed inside. The man had the effrontery to call his financial destruction by the Raines woman and the duke's betrayal a *muddle*.

The duchess reached out and clutched his hand. "Thank you, Lord Wexham."

He turned woeful eyes on her, then looked to Morgan. She gave a grudging half nod. In a sincere voice, he said, "Your graces, I am but a poor man trying to do what is right. Any man would do the same."

Both the duke and duchess nodded gratefully, but the Raines woman eyed him with the stare of a gorgon. He so much wanted to see the pain in those eyes when her daughter's body showed up on her doorstep. Then with a pickaxe and shovel, he'd dig a hole and put her toes up in the ground.

When they were gone, Dunford returned to Hobbs's office and shut the door. The detective sat tapping the desk lightly with a cudgel.

Dunford asked, "Well, what do you think? I'd say it went well."

Frowning, Hobbs shrugged. "I suppose. We'll soon have the diamond, which you will carry to Antwerp. There, it will be cut into manageable gems that we will sell for great profit. All the while, I'll continue to keep the pursuit away from Acker and our young guests. That much, indeed, went well. No potential obstacles with that." He tapped his palm with the cudgel. "And remember, Dunford, I have the full weight of the empire behind me. If you play the cross on us, more the fool you."

The ridiculous threat did not bother Dunford. "Don't upset yourself, Hobbs. I'm not a greedy man."

Both knew this was untrue and Hobbs scoffed. "Of course not. Not you." After a long pause, the detective added, "What Becket said can't be ignored."

"There's nothing he can do."

"Now you are a fool. His money has the power to do whatever he wants. If we dispose of those brats as we intended, he will come after us, and his influence will be great. There is no other way. We must return them unharmed." Hobbs held his hand up to halt Dunford's protest. "We have too many men involved in this. When he offers a million pounds for our capture, do you think any of those to whom we pay less than a hundred pounds will pass up millions? No, they'll run like rabbits to the nearest station house to turn us in and claim the money. We must keep the duke from offering that reward."

"I suppose you're right," Dunford said convincingly. He might give up the boy but never the girl.

"Of course, I'm right," Hobbs said. "So that means we cannot allow the bloody little sprogs to see anyone's face. If they do, everything changes. When they are returned, they can't know anything that would lead to an investigation of us."

"They've seen Danny Wilcox," Dunford said.

Hobbs slammed the cudgel on his desk, leaving a dent. "God's blood, which one is he?"

"The young lad who brings them their food. They get along with him."

"He'll have to be dispatched," Hobbs said. "I'll tell Acker to deal with it. I think I should pay our two little guests a visit to see what else they know."

"Is that wise?"

Hobbs chuckled. "It will be part of the investigation. After payment of the diamond, I'll be there to rescue them, you see. I'll be their savior, hero of the day. We'll be on our way to Fleet Street wealth."

Dunford didn't like the way the man had made himself the decision maker, but as the one leading the investigation, the DS had the say for now but only for now. Later, it would be different. At some point, he suspected there'd be a brawl to the death between them all, and he planned to be the victor. But that was for later.

Hobbs relaxed a bit. "Why do you so want the girl dead? That seems rather callous even for you."

When he answered, Dunford's mouth split open in a feral grin. "An eye for an eye."

CHAPTER TWENTY-SEVEN

Unknown Harbor, Late May 1887

Wherever we were, it was near the ocean. The smell of the sea was ever-present, and occasionally we heard the blast of ship horns. Blindfolded and bound up, terrified that we'd be killed any second, we'd been brought here from Northampton by boat. Almost the whole way, Toby sobbed and sniffled, while I kept my eyes squeezed shut despite the cloth blocking any way to see. I let my mind drift back to Montana when Papa was still alive. While we were hunting strays in the woods down by Lone Tree Creek, I asked him to teach me how to throw a knife. This pleased him, and he agreed.

"I only have one arm, Glory," he said, pulling out his old army blade, "but you only need one to throw a knife."

He chose a fat aspen as a target.

"Watch me," he said. Standing about fifteen feet away he poised himself and threw. The handle bounced off the tree. He tossed back his head and laughed. I joined in because Papa's laugh was so infectious you had to join in.

He retrieved the knife and gave it to me. "Now you try."

I did, and my throw bounced off as well. We laughed again. We were pretty bad at it.

We kept trying but accuracy with a knife, I learned, was overblown unless it was in your hand when it struck. I thought that was Papa's point. After twenty minutes of throwing, he got the steel end to stick about one in three times, me about one in ten because I missed about half the time.

But that was the best because we laughed hysterically with every clunk off the tree. Anyone who came along just then would have thought us madhouse escapees. It was such a wonderfully remembered time. I let it play in my head again and again till the kidnappers got us to where they were going.

Once on land, they stumbled us up five flights of stairs before removing our blindfolds and binds, then shoved us into a large room with a high, open ceiling, wood beams above. This was not exactly the Astor Hotel. Trash, dust and rat droppings covered the floor. Against the far wall stood a single bed with a grim, bare mattress. As if we had clothes to unpack, across the way stood a chest of drawers. And there above it were three shelves that contained a few food cans. It made me wonder if other kidnapped victims had been brought here.

I also noticed a small step ladder that had me momentarily hopeful but then we were five stories up and this was just four feet. In the far corner stood a bucket. I knew what that was for. Toby and I would have to unburden our bowels in full view of the other. I swallowed hard at spending time in this place.

He was still by the door, trying to open it, but it was locked. He pounded on it, screaming for them to let him out. From the next room, I heard muffled laughter. No one came.

I thought on what Mama would do. She would try to escape, that's what. Between the bed and chest of drawers, there was a dingy window you opened outward. I went and opened it. Fifteen feet away was the brick wall of another building. By its corner was a window with broken glass and a fire escape weaving its way back and forth down to the alley below. It was so tantalizingly close that I thought it might be a way to escape if we could just get across to it. But then I realized it was fifteen feet, and I couldn't jump that far with a running start.

I considered shouting for help, but the area seemed deserted. From what I could see, the building down the alley appeared abandoned, and nobody was about, if anyone ever came here at all. I dropped my gaze below and leaned out. It was a long way down, the height dizzying.

Toby's sudden scream caused me to jump out of my skin, and I nearly fell. When I scrambled back in and turned around, I screamed too. A large, furry rat the size of a big papa muskrat stared at us as if we were invading his territory. I stamped my foot and took a couple steps toward it, and it stood its ground a moment, then unhurried scuttled off through a hole in the wall. We spent the rest of that first day on the bed, our legs pulled up, fearful of a rat attack.

As daylight waned, two men came in, one carrying a tray with our supper. Not much older than us, he had a friendly smile and introduced himself as Danny Wilcox. He told us that no one would hurt us, which I didn't believe for a second. He presented the other man as Mr. Arlo Ives, Esquire and laughed like it was a joke. This Ives was lanky with greasy brown hair and beard. He wore a dirty blue jacket like something from a long-ago century. Possessing a face darkened by filth, he looked like the rat with a sharp nose and whiskers. All he did was leer at us and grin.

As we ate, we complained and begged them to let us go, but that got us nowhere. We told Danny there was only one bed and we only had a bucket to pee in and a giant rat was menacing us. Nothing seemed to move either of them to help.

I lowered my voice and tried to sound grownup. "Mr. Wilcox, as you can see this mattress is filthy. Also, it's still spring. Unless you've taken us to the Barbery Coast, the nights will be cold. I implore you, sir, to at least bring us some sheets and a blanket."

He nodded. "I'll see what I can do."

He said again no one would hurt us, picked up the tray, and both men left. Five minutes later, Wilcox came back with folded sheets and a wool blanket.

In the dark a couple hours later, Ives stumbled back in with a bottle of foul looking liquid in his hand. He was drunk. Not sleepy, we were sitting on the bed. Hovering over us, he just stood there, staring, saying nothing. Once or twice, he teetered like he might fall on us but didn't. Then, he finally fixed his evil eye on me. He was close enough I could see the black hole of his mouth hang open in a wide grin that revealed his rotting teeth. I didn't know exactly what he wanted, but I knew he wanted it from me.

They hadn't searched us, looking on us as kids, so they weren't aware I had a knife. I swore that if that man ever came at me, I would gut him. When he finally left and I could release the breath I'd been holding, a thought struck me and an icy shiver suddenly ran up my spine. We had seen their faces and they'd even told us their names. That meant they were either stupid, which I knew from cattle rustlers in Montana might be the case, or they had no intention of letting us live.

The last ordeal of that memorable first day was when we finally decided to try to sleep, and Toby ordered me to lay on the floor.

I threw up my hands, disbelieving. "What?"

"There's only one bed, and I'm an earl."

Despite our distress, I laughed. "We can share it, or we can fight for it. You choose since, after all, you're an earl."

We shared it. But all night, he complained that he didn't have enough room even though he was taking his half out of the middle.

For the next week, nothing changed. Wilcox brought us food by day and Ives staggered in drunk at night to stare at us. Once he even passed out and slept not ten feet away till morning when Wilcox came again and woke him up. This was not exactly the Jesse James gang, so I continued to think about getting out of there, fixing on the fire escape across the alley. There must be a way to get to it.

Despite Toby's protest, I used my knife to cut the sheet in strips, tied the ends together, and kept it under the blanket. But I still had no way to use it. From the window, it barely reached down to the third floor. We'd die in a fall from there or break all the bones in our bodies. I tried to lasso the fire escape but failed, and even if I did, I doubted it could hold our weight.

"You're hopeless," Toby said. "Papa will pay the ransom, and we'll go home."

"They'll never let us go," I said. "We can identify two of them. That will mean all of them will be caught."

"No, it doesn't," he protested.

"They are going to kill us unless we get out of here."

He waved that away, stalked over to the bed and sat with a petulant expression, but I could see his face had become pale. He wasn't so sure anymore.

Of course, we ended up doing our bucket business with the other in the room and immediately dumped the contents out the window. That was less than pleasant. When Toby asked me why my stuff stank more than his, my scream of fury shut him up instantly. Lucky him. One more word and I would have boxed his ears. It was one thing to endure so many days of terror in this room but quite another forced to do it with the most obnoxious boy in the world.

Late that night, another man came into our room. Toby was asleep, his soft wheeze of a snore making little noise, but I was wide awake, despairing over seeing no way out. And I needed to use the bucket. At first, as I pretended sleep, I thought it was Ives again, but it was another man. He stood back in the shadows. I could feel him staring at us. The room was pitch black, but for one area where a pitifully small moon cast vague shards of light across the floor next to our bed.

The shadowy figure stood for nearly ten minutes, then took three quick steps up to the bed and into the faint moonlight. His hands reached out, his fingers like claws opening and retracting over and over again. He teetered and almost fell over, then righted himself. He was drunk. Toby's wheezing snore stopped so I knew he was awake, but both of us lay there, feigning sleep.

Through the slits I made of my eyelids, I studied the man's clean-shaven face. He wore the coat and waistcoat of a dandy and a dark cloak draped over his shoulders, an incubus out of a bad dream. This had to be the leader, our chief tormentor. And I knew him.

It was Clive Dunford.

I'd seen him twice back in Montana and last week at Auntie Julia's ball. He took something from his pocket and held it out above us, nearly stumbling onto the bed. Toby flinched the man didn't see. He stood up straight and dangled the thing over us. Even in the darkness I could see it was a jewel of some kind, something big. The chain glittered gold in the moonlight, letting it swing back and forth like the pendulum in a grandfather clock. A little chuckle rumbled in his throat then he stuffed the jewel back in his coat pocket.

Next, he spun on his heels and strode from the room.

After a few moments, I said, "I think he's their leader."

Toby said, "He has the Tudor Diamond. It's Mama's. He must have stolen it. I know him."

"Yes, Clive Dunford."

The following night a policeman came and Dunford was with him. He brought in an oil lamp and wooden chair, sat and faced us on the bed while Dunford stood beside him, not hiding who he was. When the policeman set the lamp on the floor, it caused all our faces to look spooky. With a fixed smile, he told us his name was Henry Hobbs, Detective Superintendent at Scotland Yard, and showed us his badge and what he called a warrant card. He and the Earl of Wexham had come here to negotiate with the kidnappers and free us. That excited Toby and me, but I wondered how we were going to warn him about Dunford, who was one of the kidnappers.

"Can we go now then? Can we go now?" Toby blurted out.

"No, I'm afraid not yet, my lord," Hobbs said. "There are still points to be worked out. But your father has agreed to pay the ransom. We just wanted you to know that we'll have you out of here in no time." He leaned in, and whispered conspiratorially, "Have you seen any of their faces? Can you describe any of them?"

I told them about Wilcox and Ives.

"Anyone else?"

"No," I said quickly, afraid Toby would blurt out Dunford's name in front of him.

"Good, good," Dunford replied and placed a finger to his lips. "Tell no one. Keep that a secret till we all get you out of here."

Then Toby did a strange thing. He went to Dunford and hugged him, his head coming only to the man's stomach. Awkwardly, the earl patted Toby's back. "Yes, my boy, yes. Our duty, eh what."

"Thank you, thank you," Toby said, then returned quickly to the bed.

Hobbs asked a couple more questions then the two men left, taking the light with them.

I turned to Toby. "Why did you do that? Why did you give him that big old hug? You know he's a kidnapper."

He withdrew the diamond from his pocket. My eyes widened and I grinned. He laughed, pleased.

An hour later, carrying his lantern, the policeman returned without Dunford and now we could warn him about the earl's connivance. We sat on the bed across from him again as he told us the negotiations were complete, and we'd be going home soon.

Toby clapped.

I asked. "Is Mr. Dunford still here?"

"No, he left an hour ago. Why?"

Then it came to me, what bothered me about this man. His damn boots. I saw them in the lamplight and that scared me so badly I wanted to run to the bucket. Instead, I sat there frightened all to hell. Several days ago when I was snatched, a bag was thrown over my head and I was taken onto a man's saddle like a sack of potatoes. I was able to see only one thing, his boots, odd, fancy ones with white cloth fitted about the ankle with the imprint of a shield. They were called something like spits or spats, and only a few men wore them, even in America.

This man, this detective superintendent, was one of the kidnappers too.

Could it have been a coincidence? Not likely, not with that damn shield engraved on it. I looked with horror at Toby, moving my eyes, trying to warn him but too late. He jumped off the bed and thrust his chest out, his pudgy face burning with anger.

"Cause he's a liar," Toby screamed. "We saw him! He's one of that gang out there and my father's going to...going to..."

Instantly, the man's smile faded, replaced by an expression so cold it could freeze the night air. He looked in my eyes and knew the game was up.

He shook his head. "I wish you hadn't said that."

Abruptly, he rose and walked away, the circle of light from the lamp disappearing through the door with him, casting us back into darkness.

That did it. Now, we were in for it. The policeman knew we could identify him and Dunford as part of it. I should have been smarter. I gripped Toby's arm. "Listen to me. We need to escape and now."

CHAPTER TWENTY-EIGHT

East India Docks, London, May 28, 1887

In the dull lamplight of the next room, Hobbs went right past the men sitting at the table, saying only, "I'll return in half an hour. Do nothing till then."

He made his way from the complex of buildings into Blackwell and a telegraph office where he sent a cable to Dunford at the Savoy hotel. It said only: *Our two mice know all particulars. Suggest time for ending their stay. Await reply.*

Hobbs waited at the office insisting with his badge and threats that the operator stay open. It took two hours for him to receive a reply: *The prize is missing. Our guests may have it. Retrieve and terminate. Afterward, deliver female to mother.*

When Hobbs returned to the building, the five men stared expectantly at him for orders. For several seconds, he said nothing. He felt his life on a precipice about to fall, and he was not going to let it happen. The die had been cast and he was now in for both a penny and a pound. Yet considering it all, this might work out even better for him. If those two somehow had the diamond, he would take it off their bodies and claim he'd not found it.

He needed to blame Wilcox and Ives and gave them a look of frustration. "We were all set to make a pretty penny from this business. Five hundred pounds each at least, but now we may lose not only the money but perhaps our lives. Two of you are known to them, Wilcox and Ives. And from their descriptions, I can assure you, the police will track you both down, and then all of us will be arrested. I won't be able to stop it."

Ives said uneasily, "We was just feeding them, Guv."

Hobbs snapped angrily, "You should have bloody well covered your faces. We are sunk."

Shaken, all five men looked to him for an answer, and he gave them one. "Ives, you and Wilcox go in there now and snuff them. No blood. Strangle them. When it's done, I will examine them both. Then you will toss the boy's body in the drink. The girl's body will left for me. It's the only way to escape this with our lives. Is that understood?'

Ives gave a twisted grin. "Aye Guv. I'll do it right."

Hobbs glared at all of them, his voice cold. "Some of you might feel the urge to turn Queen's evidence, but you will meet Acker's knifemen that very day in or out of prison. He owns half the constables on the force. No one will be able to protect you, and your families will pay for it."

Some of the men blanched and all glanced around at each other. Three of them were actually policemen, his own men in fact, and they knew they had to do this right or give up the money and their lives.

Hobbs turned to Wilcox and Ives. "Go. Quickly now. I'll..."

A loud crash came from the next room. Hobbs rushed through the door, the men following. It was empty, and the window stood wide open.

He raced to it wondering how they could have escaped from this height. On the building across the alley, he saw a long ghostly strip of white hanging from the fire escape. That was impossible. Somehow, they'd reached it and gone down to the alley. He was the one undone.

"Bloody hell, the fire escape," he shouted and turned back. "We all hang if we don't catch them."

Within seconds, they'd rushed from the room, leaving silence behind. Then the rat pushed itself out of the hole, wandered out onto the middle of the floor and sniffed the air. Abruptly, it shot across to the other hole and disappeared inside.

CHAPTER TWENTY-NINE

Unknown Harbor, May 28, 1887

A full minute after the kidnappers left and the rat vacated the room, Toby and I squirmed out of the crawlspace along the eave. The first step in the escape plan had worked. A few moments before, I'd wrapped a tin can from the shelves in the strips of sheet and tossed it at the fire escape. The sheet unraveled on the way but made it, draping off the railing.

Then using the chest of drawers, the shelves and finally the step ladder, we clambered up to the cross beam. At first, this had appeared daunting but turned out to be no more difficult than climbing a tree. Toby handled it better than I'd expected. From the step ladder, I helped shove him up and into the crawlspace, then as I clung to the beam, I kicked the step ladder out from under me, clattering it noisily onto the floor. I was squeezing into the crawlspace when the men burst into the room. Unless we could sprout wings, we couldn't have gotten over to the fire escape. I crossed my fingers and prayed they wouldn't figure that out.

They didn't. In an almost funny pantomime, Hobbs threw his hands about like swatting flies, screaming we had escaped, and they were all going to hang for it. Then they ran like scared chickens from the room.

Now, step two. Flee the building.

Climbing down turned out to be harder than climbing up. I was a head taller than Toby, but the roly poly boy weighed decidedly more. When I lowered him close to the first shelf, the strain of it nearly pulled my arm out of its socket. From there, he scrambled the rest of the way down.

It was harder for me. Hanging from the beam, I had a three-foot drop to the shelf, and I should have realized that would prove impossible. When I hit, my knees bent and had nowhere to go, striking the wall and making me lose my balance. Going down, I scrabbled for purchase on the other shelves, found none, and hit the floor hard. Pain exploded in my right ankle, then an instant later, I slammed onto my butt.

I lay there for several seconds catching my breath and assessing my injuries. My hip hurt like hell, and my ankle felt busted all to pieces.

"Let's go," Toby shout-whispered, already running from the room.

Turning over, I pushed myself up, and limped after him, each step excruciating.

A minute later when I stumbled out of the building, I found Toby standing in the alley, uncertain which way to go. A strip of stars glittered above our heads and a sickle point of moon poked above one roof. Back home, we called it a stalking moon, light enough to stalk your prey but dark enough to hide. I liked that *hide* part right now.

But which way to go? One way might mean death, the other life. Or both ways death. Free for the moment, we stood there like two calves stunned by a blow to the head. I let my mother's voice rampage through my head. *Move! Don't stand about like an idiot. Get out of there!*

"This way," I said, grabbing his hand and turning to the left for no special reason.

As we ran, I gritted my teeth to the pain. The alley turned out to be one small part of a giant maze created by tall buildings everywhere. The tight passages seemed endless.

We kept running. Limping badly, I fell yards behind, and that was how we got caught.

At one intersection in these brick and wood canyons, a shadowy figure appeared carrying a lantern. "Help us," Toby shouted to him, running up to him and started blurting out our story. Truth was, so desperate was I, I'd have done the same. The man held the lantern up to Toby's face, then jammed the other hand around his throat.

He shouted, "I got one of them. Over here."

In Toby's struggling, the diamond had fallen from his pocket and clattered between them. The man's eyes bugged out. "Gol Damn," he muttered.

While Toby struggled, I snuck up, drawing my knife, and stuck his arm with two quick slashes. He screamed and dropped the lantern. "Bloody Hell!"

Toby scooped up the diamond, and we ran, escaping them once again. But when I looked back, my heart sank for a swarm of bobbing lanterns was chasing us still. So close they were, they'd catch us up soon enough.

For once, luck was with us. Appearing ahead through an arch was what looked like a drawbridge of all things, which several men were guiding a horse drawn wagon loaded with barrels through a giant open gate. We ran for it, me praying my leg would hold up just a little longer.

We burst from the maze, up onto the drawbridge as the wagon went in. Unseen, we ducked under it and squeezed inside.

CHAPTER THIRTY

East India Docks, May 28, 1887

From the rear of the chasing pack, Arlo Ives was sweating, gasping for breath, and lagging far back. He swore to himself he was not being paid enough for this shite. He wasn't a damn brown hare running around the Highlands. Ahead, he saw the two children scuttle into the ship and a few seconds later Hobbs and his three constables run up onto the gangway with Wilcox. Lang, one of them, was bleeding heavily from his arm. Stepping out from the wagon, several men from the ship blocked their way.

"Here now," the lead man said. "What do you think you're doing?"

Hobbs showed them his badge and warrant card. "We're pursuing runaway thieves."

The lead man shook his head. "Doesn't matter. You can't come on board this ship."

Over the rumble of the engines, they shouted at each other for nearly a minute till Hobbs drew his revolver and pointed it at the leadman. That settled it.

When Ives reached the gangway, the crewmen were raising their hands, and one of them said, "We saw no children come on this ship."

"But we did," Hobbs said angrily. "They're wanted fugitives."

The lead man pointed at Lang. "That man is injured."

"One of the little buggers cut him. It'll heal," Hobbs said. "Now step out of the way."

The crewmen did. Before he went in, Hobbs turned back to Ives. "You and Wilcox remain here and make sure they don't come back this way. If we don't get back, tell Dunford the little buggers have the prize. You got that? They have the prize."

"Aye, Guv." Ives tapped his head. "I've got it all up here."

The lead crewman grabbed Hobbs's arm. "This ship will be leaving port at exactly one minute after midnight whether you're off it or not, and nothing can stop it."

"We'll see about that," Hobbs said, wrenching his arm free. He rushed in, the other men following.

The crewman shouted after them, "This is a run for a speed record. Captain's not waiting for anyone. You're not off by midnight, coppers or not, you'll be on your way to Cape Town."

Ives knew the sea and its captains, and for a certainty, this one would not delay. On water, he was the law, and neither Hobbs nor his London constables could dispute that. Ives drew out his pocket watch, the one he'd copped from a nob last month while the mark was riding a Covent Garden nun. He held it to the light of the moon and made out fourteen minutes to midnight. This entire affair was going to hell, and he started thinking about getting himself out of it in one piece. What if the Guv didn't make it off the ship? Then it was every man for himself.

At ten minutes till midnight, the horses that had pulled the wagon onboard were taken off, and from the top, the door rolled down and slammed shut.

Ten more minutes, and at exactly one minute after midnight, the massive ship drifted away from the dock out into the Thames, blasting its horn. A couple minutes later it began its slow advance toward the sea.

Wilcox looked to Ives, his voice a frightened croak. "What now?"

"You go tell Acker what happened," Ives said. "Tell him the boy's got the biggest damn diamond in the world. Lang seen it. I'll stay here for the next turn."

When Wilcox stood there, looking at the ship steaming down the river, Ives smacked the side of his head hard. "Get moving, Danny boy, before I kick your arse. Go on now."

When Wilcox hurried off, Ives stuck his hands in his pockets and started walking down the dock intent on saving himself. He needed to take care of Arlo Ives. With the duke's heir and that other brat possibly free, a noose awaited them all. After all, what if the little buggers spilled all to the captain? What then? He gave a twist of a smile. Maybe, he can get himself out of this mess and make a little money to boot.

He hurried his pace toward the train station and the short hop back into London proper and salvation.

CHAPTER THIRTY-ONE

Earls Court London, May 31, 1887

Morgan found herself in a nightmarish landscape of lightning and rain crashing about her as she struggled to keep Glory from drowning in a rushing stream. Her hand slipping, a quicksand of terror engulfed her. A loud voice broke the nightmare, and she sat up in a sweat. It was before sunrise, and she'd just gotten to sleep. Lately, sleep had been a commodity hard to come by. A thick grogginess filled her head. Then memory slammed her back to the present.

The ransom of the fabulous jewel had been paid and neither Glory nor Toby had been returned. With each passing day, she'd been besieged by darkening gloom. Detective Superintendent Hobbs had disappeared, and Dunford himself was nowhere to be found. According to the new leader of the inquiry, that idiot Bramley, foul play was suspected in both cases. She doubted it. It was clear to her something was badly amiss in the entire investigation.

Since that puppet show in the superintendent's office in which Dunford claimed to be carrying a message from the kidnappers, she had begun to suspect him and trusted no one. She realized what troubled her about it. It sounded rehearsed, like a stage performer parsing out his practiced words quickly. When she told the duke, he at first dismissed it, but now, he had little choice but to consider that he'd been played the fool. And if that were so, he promised with barely controlled fury he'd wreak vengeance on them all.

Despite the bleak outlook, Morgan could not bring herself to believe Glory was dead. She couldn't accept never seeing her daughter again and bristled at anyone who suggested otherwise. She prayed, which she didn't do often, and at night, she buried her head on Lame Deer's shoulder and cried.

Now, from outside her tent, someone called for her again.

Beside her, Lame Deer said, "Maybe talk of Glory."

Morgan bounded up, threw on a robe, and hurried to the tent flap. It was Orville Gatewood standing nervously, his hat brim squeezed in his hands.

"Yes, Mr. Gatewood," she said abruptly. "What is it? Is it about my daughter?"

"No, ma'am. Sorry. Not that."

"Then what?" she snapped.

"It's Big Crow," Gatewood said. "He wants to see you, ma'am."

"You woke me for this?" she snapped, her disappointment fueling the anger. "I don't care a whit about what he wants."

He spoke quickly, "Ma'am, he's dying. Pneumonia doctor says. You must have heard. He won't make it to noon."

She hated the Indian more than any human save Dunford, and then she couldn't say which had her hatred most. Why would Gatewood think she would see the Cheyenne chief? Then she felt her darker angels change her mind. "I'll come. Of course, I'll come. I will gladly watch that man die."

Morgan dressed quickly, and they strode to Big Crow's teepee.

Gatewood touched her elbow to hold her up. "Something I wanted to say to you, Mrs. Raines, before we go in." He hemmed and hawed a moment.

"Get to it, sir," she demanded.

"You see, Ma'am, I'm an old man, but I ain't done in yet. I still got my wits about me. If you ever need me for anything, anything, you just say the word, and I'll come."

For a moment, he dark mood sputtered. "Thank you, Mr. Gatewood. I appreciate that more than you know. I'll keep that in mind." She patted his arm and went into the lodge.

Big Crow had shrunken to half his once massive size. Seeing him lying in his blankets, she knew she should feel pity but didn't. All she saw was his great axe falling on her little sister Fiona, him lifting her brilliant red hair to the sky and screaming his war cry as if he just struck down Crazy Horse. Fiona's little body lay at his feet. Then, she saw her brother Patrick and her da lying out near the corral, scalped and mutilated. Her mother was yet to die but soon would, scalped as well but living long enough to give her the crucifix that she she gripped now. So fierce and violent was her loathing for this man, she needed its solace of its touch to remind her she was strong, for it had long ago separated her from the frightened girl she'd been.

When he saw Morgan, his eyes squinted, and he spoke in Cheyenne, his voice a whisper, "Is my son well?"

He meant her brother Conor, whom Big Crow had raised for far longer than Morgan had been with the Cheyenne. "He is not your son," she said. "He has forgotten you."

Big Crow sighed. "He was to be a great warrior with many scalps, but then the People died. Soon I will see the buffalo again. I will see the lost ones and live again in the old ways and sit around the campfires at night."

Gatewood stood beside her with Big Crow's wife, whose brutality to her those many years ago Morgan remembered all too well. She hated this woman nearly as much as her husband.

The dying man coughed, and blood spewed from his lips. His wife rushed to his side, but he waved her away. "Before my spirit leaves for Seyan," he said, "I must tell some things to you. This is how I see it. I was the bravest man of my people, and I killed many enemy. We two were once at war; you and me, now we are at peace. It is good that there is peace between us."

Speech done, he now took a deep gasp of air then relaxed, his eyes on her, waiting for her response. She didn't know what this was.

Was he asking for forgiveness? No, Cheyenne didn't do that. Gloating more likely. His journey in this life done, he saw himself as great chief who had earned his way to the spirit world of his people.

Morgan said to Big Crow, "You were no great warrior. You were not brave. You were afraid to fight men. You made war on little girls and women. There is no peace between us. I have come here to watch you die."

The old Indian woman gasped, and Big Crow blinked several times. That's when Lame Deer stuck her head into the teepee and announced, "Duke says you come. Bad men talk now."

Morgan started from the teepee, stopped, and came back to Big Crow. She bent down and fixed her eyes on him. "There are no buffalo where you are going. No grass, no people."

Then she rushed from the lodge as his wife screamed at her.

When Morgan reached the townhouse, she learned another intermediary, one very different from Dunford, had made contact, a filthy street urchin of eight or nine years banging the door with its brass knocker. When the butler tried to slam it in his face, the boy darted by and into the house. A clamor went up, and other servants gave chase, but he dodged his way past and made it to the duke, who'd come out of his office to see what the clamor was.

"Here, sir," he shouted, holding out a message folded to a nub. "Take it."

When Edward read the message, he knew instantly it was legitimate. It called his son Toby, and no police report nor newspaper article mentioned that name. They always referred to him as the young Earl of Exeter or the Duke of Northampton's son. Never Toby or Tobias.

In barely readable English, the note said that the children were alive. To learn where they were, the duke must come to the Cock and Crown Tavern in the Billingsgate fish market at two this afternoon, bring a thousand pounds, and to come alone.

Edward gave the boy a couple shillings and sent him on his way.

That afternoon, chilly and overcast, the duke's small party made its way down Lower Thames Street into Billingsgate Market by the river. Several of Edward's men should already be inside the Cock and Crown, playing the part of patrons. Morgan, Seamus, and one other man accompanied him, the new head of the kidnap investigation Detective Inspector Bramley. Morgan railed against it, but Edward insisted he would be needed if the intermediary proved false. Neither she nor Bramley were happy about the other's presence, but the duke's social status and influence proved irresistible to authorities.

As they entered the market, the first thing that struck her was the evil smell of fish that grew stronger the farther into the crowded street they went. It was so heavy she thought she could grab a handful of it out of the foul air. She shoved her hands farther into her winter muff as if that would prevent the stink from clinging to them. The street itself was bursting with humanity, wagons plowing through the crush of people. Crowded fish shops and fish stalls lined both sides. The raucous din of fishmongers, buyers, and all manner of natives thundered as loud as a buffalo stampede.

The duke's party pushed its way to the corner where they saw the Cock and Crown Tavern, a shabby place that looked like it might collapse any second.

When they entered, the inhabitants appeared as murky figures in the gloom. The room fell silent, and Morgan felt as much as saw all eyes turned to them. A fancily adorned duke, a well-dressed woman clearly not of the soiled dove variety, a pudgy man wearing a bowler and a bandaged nose, and her dark-skinned son, appearing all Cheyenne even in workaday clothes. To the bar dwellers, it must have seemed like the circus had come to town.

A heavy-set woman approached. "Welcome to the Cock, your highnesses," she said with a cackle. "Follow me. He is waiting for you."

They were led to a small lamplit room in back where a lanky, bearded man sat at a table drinking a tankard of beer and eating a fish out of one hand. He wore a bib, but his blue jacket seemed already stained from countless previous meals. At their appearance, he shot to his feet, knocking over his chair.

He set the fish down, wiped his hand on his pants, and extended it to Edward. "Greeting to you, Duke. Name's Arlo Ives, at your service."

Edward ignored the hand. "Do you know where our children are?"

Ives patted his belly. burping. "I sure do. You was supposed to come alone."

"These are my financial advisors. Get to it. Where are the children?"

Morgan moved a few steps to her left forcing Ives to turn his head to see her, dismiss her as a threat, and look back at Edward. "Did you bring the money?"

"No, Mister Ives, I did not. I'm not bringing a thousand pounds into a Billingsgate pub."

With a pout, the man sat down and folded his arms over his chest. "I ain't lying. I know where them kids are. And if you want to know, you got to pay me my money."

"You'll get it, sir. That is my promise. However, if I think you're not telling me the truth I swear you will spend the rest of your life in Newgate prison." He nodded toward Bramley. "This man is Detective Inspector Bramley, who now leads the investigation. He will see that you are put in the darkest hole of that prison."

Bramley straightened, throwing back his shoulders as if posing for a picture.

Ives gritted his teeth and said, "No money, no talkie."

"First prove to me you know where my son and this woman's daughter are," the duke said and leaned over the table. "How, sir, do you know?"

After a moment, Ives gave a half smile. "I was one of them kidnappers."

This surprised Morgan. Edward said calmly, "Go on."

The man explained that he worked for Charlie Acker, the London crime lord, and he'd been sent up to Northampton with some other men to do a snatch job.

"It wasn't supposed to be no children," he said emphatically, slapping his hand on the table. "It was supposed to be the duke himself."

Edward gave no reaction and the man continued, "I never wanted to take them kids, but what else could I do?"

He told them how they took them by riverboat from Northampton to the sea, along the coast then up the Thames to the East India docks. There, they kept them in an abandoned building. "I was the one who fed them, helped them any way I could."

Morgan asked. "Was Clive Dunford involved?"

"He was, milady. Him and that detective Hobbs run the whole thing." He paused to let that fester in the room like the fish stink, then added, "You better hurry cause Dunford wanted that girl kilt all along. Your daughter, is it? Well now him and Hobbs want them both dead." He hesitated a second. "I figure I need another five hundred pounds to tell the rest."

At that, Morgan withdrew a pistol from her muff, and Seamus took out his colt. In a chorus of metal, they cocked their weapons and aimed them at Ives.

The man held his hands up in alarm. "Wait now. I told them they had to escape. I warned them. Me, Arlo Ives, and you know what? They did. Don't know how, but they did. Got clean away, and you see, I know where they are now. But so do Dunford and Hobbs. They're chasing them and if they catch them…" He drew his finger across his throat and gave a gargling sound. "They need them dead, see, so they won't turn Queen's evidence."

To Morgan, the man was lying, but perhaps not where it mattered. True or not, this was their only chance, and they had to follow it. She and Edward exchanged quick nods.

"All right, Mr. Ives," Edward said, "you've convinced me." He reached into his pocket, pulled out an envelope, and handed it to him.

"What's this?" the man asked.

"Open it. It's a cheque drawn on the Bank of England for a thousand pounds. Exactly the amount for which you asked. All you need to do is put your name on it, present it to the bank, and withdraw the money. You'll be a rich man. Now, where are the children?"

Ives stared at the cheque for several seconds, then he grinned. "They're on their way to the Cape Colony, steamed out of the East India docks three nights ago. The two bairns ran onto the ship to get away from Hobbs and his men. It left port with all of them onboard." He barked a laugh. "That ship ain't going to stop for nothing till it gets to Cape Town. Captain's trying to set a speed record like they all do."

"Cape Colony," Seamus muttered, running a hand through his thick hair.

Edward turned to Bramley. "Have you heard enough, detective?"

"Yes, your grace, I have. I'll arrest Dunford today. And Acker. But what about Hobbs and the children?"

Morgan saw a great weariness in Edward's eyes. "I'll worry about that," he said.

Bramley opened the door to the main room and left. Four rough looking men came in.

"Here now. What's this?" Ives swore, alarmed.

"Just a bit of insurance for you and for us," the duke said. "You have your money as promised, but it might be a while before you can access it. It seems we are going to the Cape Clony, Mr. Ives, and you're going with us. And God help you if any of this proves false."

Journal of the London Association of Engineers and Draughtsmen, May 1898

In 1884, Charles Algernon Parsons invented the turbine engine, but years would ensue before it was suitable for implementation in the naval fleet or the great steamship lines. However, when fit for use, the turbine proved a great advance in power and speed on the high seas, shortening, for example, the Liverpool to New York time from weeks to days. Before that could happen, much improvement had to be achieved.

In the late 1880s, experimental ships were constructed by several of Parsons's competitors to test their own turbines and new propeller designs. One of these was Oswald Browne, who was eventually determined to have infringed on Parson's patents. Browne's experimental ship, the Hermes, was small and sleek like a canal boat and on the sea had been pushed to over thirty knots per hour with only the occasional overheating engine. That velocity he attained was in an era when the top steamship speeds were fifteen to eighteen knots.

It was the Hermes that Clive Dunford, the Earl of Wexham, commandeered in the famous Northampton Affair for his mad dash to Cape Town.

CHAPTER THIRTY-TWO

RMS Trident at sea, June 6, 1887

Arthur McAuley sat at the desk in his first class cabin, going over design plans for the deep mining of gold. On a tight budget, he'd not wanted to pay the extra fifteen pounds for the step up in class, but his mother slipped him the money. She'd dreaded him sharing a loo with the inhabitants of second class or steerage. Now he had his own, if a pitiful one, with a tiny sink.

Buoyed by his recent engineering degree from the University of Edinburgh, he sought to make himself rich in the Witwatersrand gold fields using his superior knowledge of the newest mining processes. Once he achieved that wealth, he'd return to Edinburgh and wed his sweetheart, the beauteous Eugenie Colville, she of the dark, lovely curls. He carried a likeness of her in a framed photograph stored securely in his trunk.

McAuley had short-cropped, ginger hair and mustache. He'd been told by a professor that he possessed hungry eyes like a man who saw the world as a feast to be devoured. He was that ambitious and didn't mind saying it. He knew he would own many gold mines in the Rand someday and be talked about in the same breath as Cecil Rhodes.

Sipping his tea, he opened the tin of biscuits his mother had given him for the trip and blinked in surprise. This morning it had been nearly full but now was somehow down to three biscuits. Had the cabin boy helped himself when he cleaned the room? What else could it be? He took one, and as he bit into it, made a mental note to upbraid him for the theft.

He sat back and dreamed of a bright future with Eugenie at his side. It would all begin with Cecil Rhodes. The great man now controlled DeBeers diamond mining, and when gold was discovered in the Rand, he'd moved quickly to seize the lion's share of that as well. He would either be in Kimberley or the new town of Johannesburg, three hundred miles farther on. He had a slight connection with Rhodes, a letter of introduction from the man's cousin. McAuley's plan was to apply for a position with him, learn everything he could about the peculiarities of the southern African mining business, and then venture out on his own. He saw no reason why his future would not be assured.

The physical travel into the hinterland, he understood, could be hazardous. The train only went as far as Kimberley. If he wasn't there, Arthur would have to travel through wild country to reach Johannesburg, but then these days, the world being convulsed with gold fever, thousands upon thousands from all over were making that same journey. Johannesburg, it was said, was like the American Wild West.

He flinched when he heard movement behind him, but no one was there. For nearly thirty seconds, he sat still and silent, listening, then heard an angry, whispered voice. "I need more space, Toby. You're taking up all the room."

It emanated from the wardrobe where his newly bought clothes hung.

"It's you," came another hushed voice. "You have big feet. You have the biggest feet I've ever seen on a girl."

"I do not."

McAuley jumped up and flung open the wardrobe. Two adolescents stared up at him, wide-eyed and frightened. The girl was lanky and tall for that age, possessing a hint of beauty in the smudged face. Her reddish auburn hair would have been striking, except it badly needed a wash. The boy was a little cherub, like a round Christmas ornament. Surprisingly, their clothes appeared to be of merit but filthy and bedraggled. He was furious at being invaded by these two street urchins.

"Step out of there at once," he demanded.

Slowly, they did. The girl winced in pain when she stood.

"Are you hurt, lass?" he asked.

"My ankle is busted all to pieces," she said, not in a whine but a statement of fact.

She kept one hand in her pocket as if covering a disfigurement, but he suspected she was hiding something from him. On short evidence, she appeared to have an American accent.

"Can you walk?" he asked.

"If I have to."

"Good because I'm taking you to the captain," he said. "He will not be pleased with two stowaways onboard."

The boy became belligerent, standing to his full height, which wasn't much. "Sir, we cannot and will not go with you to the captain."

Swiftly, McAuley spun him around and clutched the scruff of his neck. "You have no choice in the matter, lad. Now, come, the both of you."

The girl stepped in front of him. "Let go of him," she demanded, wrenching his hand from the boy's neck. Neither fled as he would have expected but instead blocked the door.

The girl said, "Sir, if you take us to the captain, we'll be dead before nightfall."

He scoffed. "Don't be daft. The captain means you no harm."

"It's not the captain who frightens us."

McAuley was not practiced in detecting liars and more than once been fooled, mostly in the arts of love. Yet the girl seemed sincere. He hesitated, folded his arms over his chest. "All right. Speak up then. Why would anyone want to harm you? Let's hear it."

"We were kidnapped more than a week ago," she said, now breathlessly trying to get all the words out at once. "We escaped and they chased us onto this ship. We didn't even know it was a ship till we got on. They are here onboard and still after us."

"If that's true, the captain will protect you."

"No, he cannot. The kidnappers are policemen. Their boss is a man named Hobbs. He's a very important man among the police. He'll convince the captain to give us to him. Then they must kill us because we have seen them. Their big leader is a man called Clive Dunford."

"He's the Earl of Wexham," the boy chimed in. "A disgrace to the beau monde."

For several seconds, Arthur stared at them dumbfounded, trying to assess this fanciful story. Could it possibly be true? Finally, he decided *no*, it wasn't. It was much too wild. He smirked. "Quite the tale. You're both born storytellers."

Scowling, the boy put his hands on his hips. "I am Tobias Becket, Earl of Exeter and son of the Duke of Northampton. This is Glory Raines. Her mother is the leading lady of the Wild West in London. My father must have put out the hue and cry. Surely, you heard about us."

The girl quickly added, "Sir, you're the only one standing between us and certain death."

Shaken, Arthur took a half step back. He'd heard something about the kidnapping of a nobleman's son, but he was so busy preparing for this trip he'd paid little attention to it. There were other indications that suggested it was true. The clothes, filthy as they were, were of fine material and cut. The boy's manner was imperious, and the girl's accent was indeed American. He'd no time to attend the Wild West, but like everyone else, he'd heard of it. And here they were. This had to be them.

More importantly, he now knew the identity of the leaders. If he helped, he'd be in as much danger as they were. This was not how he wanted to arrive in Africa.

CHAPTER THIRTY-THREE

RMS Trident at sea, June 6, 1887

It was a risk trusting Arthur McAuley—that was his name—but we had no choice. The outlaw policemen were always searching the ship, and they'd nearly captured us hiding in one of the lifeboats yesterday. Toby and I agreed we'd likely be taken and tossed overboard if we didn't find help quickly. By circumstance, that became Arthur. Right away, I could tell he was one of those people who saw each of his decisions as monumental, pre-ordained by God, and that he had some great destiny to fulfil. This, I'd noticed, was a failing among Englishmen. Once he'd committed to a course of action, though, he pursued it with all the vigor and certainty of Crazy Horse, the great Lakota chief. We were lucky he agreed to help us.

And Arthur was true to his word. He tried to protect us for as long as he was alive, which, sadly, turned out not to be that long.

When we stood before him in front of his closet, the first thing he did was guide me over to the bed where he removed my unlaced boot and touched my ankle here and there to see if it was broken.

"I'm fairly certain it's sprained," he said. "You should be able to use it by the time we reach Cape Town." He gave a self-deprecating shrug. "I played rugby in school you see. Quite good, eh what. So, I've had experience with ankle injuries. Just stay off it for a few days."

"Right you are, sir," I replied, coming up with a smile for him.

"Both of you stay here. I'll be back in an hour," he said, then left.

We feared he might turn us in to the captain or to Hobbs and debated whether to try our luck elsewhere.

"No, this is it," Toby said with a heavy sigh. "If you didn't have that busted ankle, we could easily find a better place. I'm sure of it. But we're stuck here." He gave me a sour look. His unsaid words were *because of you*.

"You can go if you want," I said. "When they toss you in the ocean, maybe you can swim to the far shore like Robinson Crusoe before a whale eats you."

Arthur didn't return for four long nervous hours as twilight was turning to darkness and the ship's lights came on. He dumped an armful of boys' clothes beside me on the bed.

"There are no dresses," I said.

He ignored me. "Your policemen were indeed searching for you. They'd been doing so I was told since we left the Thames. One of them asked me if I'd seen two stowaway children and described you both to a tee. We must do something." Arthur paused a moment, "Both of you are memorable. Glory is a striking young girl with long, beautiful hair. People will remember seeing her."

My face flushed red. No one had ever said that about me.

"What about me?" Toby asked.

Arthur hesitated. "Well, you're memorable too."

"I know I am but how?" he persisted.

I grinned. "You're a fat rugby ball."

He scowled, about to retort, when Arthur held up his hands to silence us. "Can you two please restrain yourselves. The clothes are clean. I made sure of that. But you're not. I've reserved the bath for later this evening. You can lock the door. I'll sit outside as each of you takes a turn." He glanced over at me sitting on the bed. "But first, I'm going to cut your hair."

I loved my hair and cried in alarm, "What! Cut my hair?"

Arthur was clearly enjoying his new role now that he'd consented to help us. His tone was insistent. "Yes, we must disguise you as a boy, or I won't be able to get you off this ship."

In distress, my mouth moved but nothing came out of it.

He glanced about the room. "I wish I had a pair of scissors."

I knew he was right, so finally I took out my knife, its blade gleaming in the lamplight but for blood at the point. His eyes widened as he took it.

An hour later, cleaned up, my hair cut again even shorter by Arthur, I decided from a glance in a mirror that I could pass as a tolerable boy. When he left for the salon to eat his dinner, he promised to bring us back food and drink. In the future, he'd have the steward bring some of the meals to the cabin. As the door shut, I asked Toby if he still had it.

He knew what I meant. "Of course, I still have it." He withdrew the Tudor Diamond from his pocket and held it by the chain, sparkling like the morning star. We stared at it for a while.

"Can I put it on?" I asked.

"No, it's Mama's." He replaced it in his pocket. "It should be worn by a duchess, not a milkmaid like you. Besides, you look funny. Your hair is shorter than mine."

I wanted to punch him but that last hit hard. He was right. Instead, I buried my head under a pillow.

Days later when my ankle swelling went down enough, I ventured out with Arthur to test my disguise. Better find out now if it will pass muster before trying it when we disembark. Toby insisted he go with us, but I told him first he had to dress like a girl, which he refused to do.

I wore tweed pants and jacket, my own good boots, and a peaked cap. Instead of swinging my hips side to side like Auntie Julia sometimes did, I stuck my hands in my pockets and moved my shoulders side to side like the young men and boys I saw. Sort of like a rooster's strut without the bobbing head. No one seemed to take notice of me, just a boy on a walk with his dad or older brother more likely.

I studied the passengers, a few families, some couples but mostly single men, young to middle aged, all heading to the Rand like Arthur, to the biggest gold rush since California in 49. I heard countless different languages, I supposed from all over the globe, including strange English accents. In Montana, I knew something about gold fever, and these folks had it. That was all they could talk about.

On our second turn of the deck, I almost stumbled into Hobbs, who was talking with a couple sitting in deck chairs. He was using a hand at his shoulder to describe someone's height. That had to be me. I kept going, keeping my eyes out to sea at another ship on the horizon going in the opposite direction. He glanced at me as we passed but turned back to the couple.

Arthur's plan was simple. When we reached Cape Town, he and I would depart with the other passengers while Toby would be stuffed into the trunk that the porters would carry down to the dock. With his short stature and pot belly, he was much too recognizable to risk his appearance The conveyance looked like a pirate's treasure chest, just big enough for the brat to fit in. Air holes had to be punched in the sides.

"Do we have to punch holes?" I asked Arthur, and he laughed. Toby didn't.

Once in Cape Town, after we retrieved Toby, we'd go to the Government House where he'd turn us over to the appropriate British officials. The Governor of the Cape Colony was Sir Hercules Robinson, who, Arthur explained, ran a tight but fair ship. Though never actually meeting the man, he'd seen him speak in London on three separate occasions and swore by his righteousness. With him in charge, we'd be returned home to our families, and Arthur would be off for Kimberley on the train.

When we were three days out, I went up on deck in the early evening to get away from Toby's complaining as much as anything. One of the ship's officers stood at the rail, watching a distant vessel with binoculars.

It looked far away, yet even from this distance, I could see it was moving faster than us, in fact, much faster.

"What is that?" I asked.

He glanced down at me and handed me the binoculars. "Take a look, lad. A ship of some kind. I've never seen the like."

In the disappearing sunset, I saw the ship, its lights already on, and realized it was closer than I'd thought, just three or four miles out, but much smaller than us and ploughing up white water as it cut through the sea.

I gasped, "My God, sir, it's moving like a train."

PART FOUR
CAPE COLONY

CHAPTER THIRTY-FOUR

Cape Town, June 15, 1887

Our last night at sea before landing in Cape Town, sleeping was difficult due to the noisy clamor of porters handling the mailbags and luggage. And too, I worried about getting past Hobbs. To do that we needed to put Toby in the trunk. Arthur had instructed the porters to pick it up at 4:30 in the morning, and they did. But before they arrived, we had a time getting the boy in till Arthur gave him bread, a lump of cheese, and a canteen of water. When we stuffed him in, he scrunched his knees up to his chest and actually stuck his thumb in his mouth. Just before shuting and locking the lid, I pinched his bottom and giggled as he slapped my hand away.

I said, "It'll only be a couple of hours, Toby, then we'll get you out."

From inside the chest, his voice sounded tiny. "I don't like it in here."

Just then the porters came and took him away.

It was not till four hours later at 8:30 that the ship slid into its pier at Cape Town harbor. The moment it stopped Arthur went on deck carrying a leather case with all his private papers and a valise. Pulling my peak cap down, I hefted his knapsack onto my back and followed him out. Immediately, I was struck by a blast of icy wind straight from the South Pole. It was winter here and all I had on was the thin, tweed jacket. But then I knew cold and survived the Big Die-up, and this wasn't that.

The morning, though, was sunny. In the distance, a table top mountain loomed over the city. Passengers had formed a line on deck, waiting for the gangway to disembark, and we fell in with them. I searched for Hobbs and his men and saw them edging to the front of the line where they started checking faces. I glanced at Arthur.

"Bear up now, lass," he said, but his eyes were big as saucers.

I prayed, God, just let Arthur get us to the Government House. There, I felt sure we'd be safe. With no telegraph between Cape Town and London, a message back might take months, but if we could get passage on a ship bound for London and Mama, we'd have a chance. Surely, the duke's good name would see it done.

Down below on the wharf, people in the crowd were waving. I noticed among them sour men whose only quality was to break legs and punch faces. They stood out like Billy the Kid at a New York wedding. We had our share of rustlers, robbers, and killers in Montana, so I knew the breed well enough. The gangway finally in place, the passengers began making their way down. Slowly, we approached Hobbs, my throat like a dry well. I was sure he'd recognize me. We were ten feet from him, then five.

With a smile, Arthur put his arm over my shoulders and spoke across me with a frightened quake to an elderly woman. "Why, Mrs. Dandridge, I thought that was you. I don't mind admitting I will be much pleased to step on shore once again."

"Ah, Mr. McAuley," she said delighted. "This was a little jaunt compared to Australia. I can tell you we were so long on the seas then one thinks one may never see land again."

Arthur laughed in a freakish, high-pitched sound, and I did too.

Then Hobbs was upon us.

I looked at the old lady beside me as if she were my granny, and the policeman's eyes skipped right over me. It appeared the Dandridges and we were together, one big happy family. No stowaways in this party.

Halfway down the gangway, I got another shock. Clive Dunford himself was below, observing the passengers as they stepped onto the wharf. How did that man get here before us? God, they wanted us bad. Then I remembered the ship a few nights ago cutting across the waters with such speed. That had to be him.

I had no belief now my disguise would fool him and stepped in behind Mrs. Dandridge, hoping to slip by. We were almost down. The family just ahead of us stepped off the gangway, a couple with three children, one a girl maybe fourteen over whom I still had the advantage in height. She wore fine clothes, but what stuck out was the crazy hat, wide as a sombrero with frilly fluff on the brim and a great feather off some giant bird.

Dunford was giving her a long study, trying to see under the brim. As she stepped onto the wharf, she squealed and ran. It surprised him, and he gave chase with several other men. She ran to a man twenty yards onto the wharf and hugged him. That was our cue. We pushed past Mrs. Dandridge and hurried to the customs building down the dock.

Once inside, I hoped we'd be safe, but we had to wait an agonizing hour with about a hundred other passengers before an officious agent arrived and passed us all through without examination. Earlier, Hobbs had stepped in for a moment, glanced around, then left. Outside, we hired a carriage, strapped the trunk on the back, and ordered the driver to Government House.

"Toot sweet," Arthur told him, and that got him moving.

After a couple of blocks, we heard Toby's hollow voice yelling from the trunk. Beside a grove of trees, we stopped and unlocked the lid. Angrily, the boy stumbled out, ranting about being treated like a suit of clothes. Unable to stand, he fell to the road. When we helped him into the carriage and climbed in after him, the driver was staring at us. Then shrugging, he drove on.

When we reached the Cape Colony governor's mansion and pulled into the driveway, I sighed with relief and began composing my thank you speech to Arthur. Three men stood outside the great front door talking intently.

Arthur beamed. "That's Sir Hercules himself. He'll see to your safety now. God be praised."

As we neared, the three men turned our way, and I saw with horror it was Dunford and Hobbs with the governor.

I grabbed Arthur's arm. "It's them! It's them!"

Without hesitation, Arthur leaned forward to the driver. "Take us to the train station immediately. Double pay, sir."

"Right you are, Guv," the driver replied with a salute, then snapped the reins. The horse clopped on past at a trotter's gait and out the driveway.

I glanced back to see Dunford watching us.

When the dinner dishes were washed and dried, Lame Deer and Dora came into the living room to join the rest of us. Uncle Conor and Papa were sitting near the fire and talking ranch stuff. Mama was knitting a scarf for Papa. She was actually good with the needles though it was something she didn't do much because Lame Deer was better and enjoyed the work. Seamus being Seamus walked about the room woolgathering.

Standing in the middle of them, I watched them all. Papa was starlit. Everything about him was distinct. Tall and lanky, a far distance from the top of his glowing blond hair down his stretched out legs to the bottom of his wool socked feet. His face stood out in sharp focus. His high forehead was big enough to write a letter on. He had those clear blue eyes, the straight nose, and a brilliant, ready smile. It was a handsome face, a warm face, a father's face.

And he was dead.

I wanted to cry. I should warn him to stay by the wood stack when Dunford shoots at me. Seamus was beside me now, and I said to him, "This, you and me here. It's a dream." I glanced at Papa and my brother understood, nodding. Papa was dead.

"Should I tell him to stay by the wood stack?" I asked.

"What good would it do?" Seamus replied.

He was right. I went over to Papa and stood looking at him. He seemed so real. He noticed me and stood up. "What is it, Pumpkin? Are you all right?"

I burst into tears.

That was when I awoke to bright flashes of light. I felt tears on my cheeks and wiped them away. My cold truth had come back to slap me in the face. I was with Toby and Arthur in a crowded train car on our way to Kimberley, the diamond mine in the center of the world. There, Arthur could meet up with Cecil Rhodes, around these parts the biggest toad in the puddle.

Outside the window, the African sun burned down on an endless desert with low, empty hills in the far distance. There was not much vegetation, only patches of stunted grass, a few shrubs with dying yellow flowers, and an occasional scrawny tree. That mirrored my soul. What a place we'd come to. This Cape Colony, this Africa. In Montana, we have four seasons, but in Africa, they only have two, rainy and dry, and we were in the dry season. I wouldn't want to be stuck out there without water.

We had traveled through the night and into the next day. According to Arthur, we won't reach our destination till the following morning. What would happen to Toby and me then? Maybe we'd be on our own, Arthur finally casting us off. He'd be smart to do so. It was clear we'd have to get back to Cape Town somehow and sneak on another ship, one returning to England and Mama.

Suddenly, I gaped out the train window and saw the three largest birds in the world loping beside the tracks, easily keeping up. The long strides ate up the ground. But after a bit, they dropped away.

Arthur laughed. "Those are ostriches. Never seen them before?"

I frowned and shook my head. "In Montana, all our birds have sense enough to fly."

In a seat facing us, Toby had been snoozing and now woke up, stretching his arms with a yawn. "What are you two laughing about?"

I was not in a good mood, so I said, "You snoring. People thought it was the train whistle."

"Oh, haw, haw."

Arthur placed his hands on his knees and cleared his throat, which meant he was about to make a pronouncement. "This is what will do when we reach Kimberley. I'll put you two in a hotel, then I'll go see Mr. Rhodes. If anyone can see to your protection, he can. He'll get you back to your people."

He looked at us as if expecting applause. There was none. He went on, "If he's not in Kimberley, then we'll undertake a long trek, three weeks at least people say through wild country to Johannesburg. He'll surely be there."

Plenty of time for Dunford to catch up to us, I thought. I looked at Toby, who shrugged as if to say, what else are we going to do. Arthur was still smiling, waiting for a response, so I said, "Good idea."

The dry country flew past for another twenty minutes or so till the train chugged into a station barely larger than an outhouse. A few random buildings stood beyond, but no detectible street could be seen, not exactly a booming metropolis. A squad of British soldiers were waiting on the platform. Seeing them, I felt a stab of fear. Maybe someone had recognized us when we boarded in Cape Town. Had Dunford telegraphed ahead for these soldiers to arrest us?

They clambered onto the train and into our car. Most carried rifles but the last two had only pistols strapped to their waists. I figured they must be officers. They all wore dusty gray uniforms with what were called pith helmets. Finding seats wasn't easy, but they did by moving passengers whether there was room elsewhere or not.

I whispered to Toby, "Pretend you're asleep."

He did, lying down and closing his eyes as the two officers strode toward the rear where we were. The younger one appeared more boy than man with his round face and wispy try at a mustache. The other was short and looked mean as a badger. Thick eyebrows hung above black, scowling eyes. The nearness of the brows formed a kind of cross in the furrows of his forehead. His mustache dropped to sharp knife points below his chin. I pictured him with fangs. If he wasn't looking for us, maybe he'd order us to move.

Across the aisle, on the last facing seats, sat a family of Indians dressed as fancy as any of the fine folk in Cape Town. A husband, his wife, who was holding a baby, and three other young children. Not Cheyenne Indians but the British kind from India itself, and they shouldn't be here. Arthur had said that the moment he saw them. They'd be in trouble by just being in this car. The conductor tried to move them twice but gave up when the man refused to even respond, and no one else seemed to mind. Most, I figured, were intent on their own cares.

Evidently, there were special cars at the end of the train for Indians, kaffirs, and Hottentots, whoever they were. I was told those cars had no seats. None. That was crazy. How can a passenger train not have seats? So I went back and looked, and sure enough, no seats. The car was packed with people sitting about on the floor.

The badger-faced officer stopped beside them and scowled down as if he'd found his own stolen watch in the man's hands.

"You," his voice cracked like a shot, "get your filthy brood back where you belong."

The three older children seemed ready to cry. My temper boiled. Seeing that I was about to tell the officer that these people weren't causing any problems, not a whit, Arthur put a tight grip on my arm and drew me back sharply.

Across the aisle, the Indian man lifted his head higher and said nothing. Abruptly, the officer snatched the baby out of the woman's arms, strode to the door, and opened it. Good God, I thought he was going to toss the baby off the train and shouted, "No!"

But the woman was already screaming and running after him.

At that point, the Indian man shouted, "Wait!"

His head bowed, he followed with the rest of his children. At the door, the officer handed the baby back to the crying mother and pointed them into the next car.

"Well done, sir," the young officer said.

"Can't be too lenient with these kaffirs," the older man said as he sat and stretched his legs out on the far seat.

That night, when everyone was asleep, I snuck like Spotted Horse over to the officer and pilfered his gun, which I figured I might need. Though I wanted to, I didn't shoot him.

The next morning, we arrived in Kimberley.

Our luck held. We hurried from the train before the officer realized his gun was gone and no one was waiting for us. I thought perhaps no one saw us board the train in Cape Town. In that case, we might be safe for a while. Quickly, we hired a carriage and made our way through crowded streets to a modest two-story hotel. Arthur wanted Toby and me to wait there when he went to the DeBeer's building to meet Mr. Rhodes. Before that, he needed to wash the train ride off and deck himself out in his best suit.

"The most important element in a meeting such as this," Arthur explained to us, "is to look one's best."

This was, indeed, the most important meeting of his life, and he could not arrive looking like a vagabond. From his trunk, he withdrew his best suit, one his parents bought for him at Harrods in London for this journey. I could see by his nervous movements and constant chatter the unrest he felt at the prospect of meeting this Rhodes fellow, a man he hoped would be his mentor.

When Arthur lifted out the dark grey pants and jacket, the wide grin on his face drained away instantly. "They're wet. How did they get wet?" He clutched each garment. "They're all wet." Then he sniffed them. "They smell of urine." He looked at Toby.

The boy whined, "I had to pee. You kept me in the trunk half the day. I had to pee."

Arthur's face balled up into a horrifying expression of rage then bewilderment.

Quickly, I stepped up to him. "Give me the coat you're wearing." I took the worn, rumpled thing off him. "You go down to the bath, pass the rest of your clothes out to Toby, and I'll brush them off good. We'll have you fit as a fiddle and ready to meet Mr. Rhodes in a lick."

He did as he was told. It took us another hour to get him on his way to the DeBeers building. I had to admit the poor man looked like a vagabond.

Before he returned, we were running for our lives.

CHAPTER THIRTY-FIVE

From the *Tragic History of the Northampton Affair* by Rupert Owen, 1910, 1st ed.

Only a Goya painting could do justice to the forlorn catalogue of tragedies thrust upon so many innocents by the sinister triumvirate of the Earl of Wexham Clive Dunford, Chief Superintendent Henry Hobbs, and the potentate of London's vicious Black Alley Gang Charlie Acker. These were the men who conjured up and perpetrated the Northampton Affair. It was a theme so dreadful in its treachery that good people recoil from acquaintance with it. No one can learn of the dangers faced by the Duke of Northampton's young son and his companion Miss Glory Raines and of their ultimate fate without shuddering at such sorrow and madness.

On his arrival in the cape, Dunford made a Faustian bargain to ally himself with Moses Nyama, leader of the Fifty Tumblers, Cape Colony's most notorious criminal gang. Among their many victims, the Tumblers preyed upon lone miners on payday and city dwellers well into their cups. Riding into the wilds of the northwest cape was a new venture for them but the rewards were sizeable. With them, the fallen earl was able to put some forty men in the field, a formidable militia, and as it turned out, one without mercy.

Those who accompanied the Duke of Northampton into the breach were a much smaller contingent and formed the strangest army ever assembled.

The British: Edward Becket, the Duke of Northampton; John Coppersmith, big game hunter and Victoria Cross for action at Rorke's Drift; William Todd, hunter, Victoria Cross for Rorke's Drift; Thomas Adams, hunter, Victoria Cross for Rorke's Drift; Roger Bramley, British detective and leader of the official investigation; David Evans, British detective; Arlo Ives, informant, extortionist, kidnapper, murderer.

The Americans: Orville Gatewood, frontiersman, Seamus Spotted Horse, American aboriginal; Looks Behind, American aboriginal: Iron Chest, American aboriginal; Little Hawk, American aboriginal; Frank Bradford, Cowboy; Reece Potter, cowboy.

Three females accompanied the expedition: Julia Becket, Duchess of Northampton; Morgan Raines, mother of the kidnapped girl; and Lame Deer, American aboriginal.

Upon reaching Cape Town, the duke learned that his son had been observed on June 15 boarding the Kimberley train. He immediately cabled that town's mayor, Mr. J. Grewer, requesting any information concerning the children, then his party set out on the next train north, three days behind his son.

At each stop along the way, he availed himself of the opportunity to keep in constant telegraph contact with the mayor. It was in this manner that a melancholy scene took place in the rail car between him and Mrs. Raines, which was subsequently confirmed by many of those present. At one stop, Northampton explained to his flock that the latest cable reported his son had indeed been in Kimberley but stayed only a couple hours at the Union Hotel. He was traveling with an unknown boy and a young man named Arthur McAuley, who, according to the desk clerk, had gone at once in search of Cecil Rhodes. There upon, ten armed men stormed the hotel, searching for the two lads, finding their room empty and both gone.

The duke then handed Mrs. Raines the telegram and with a face of regret pointed to the mayor's last line. It read: It is my sad duty to inform you that no girl was traveling with them.

According to fellow passengers, Mrs. Raines appeared unaffected but what was going on within her mother's heart must have been terrible in the extreme.

By the time the Duke of Northampton's party arrived in the Kimberley of 1887, the people there had seen it all. For more than a decade, rush after rush of miners from around the world had come after diamonds. Then in '87, another bounty from the earth brought thousands through their streets, *the rush town being the last rail stop before the gold fields in the Transvaal. Yet, even so, the duke's odd menagerie of persons that disembarked that fine Monday garnered many a curious stare. How could they not?*

Kimberley, Cape Colony, June 20, 1887

As Morgan stepped off the train onto the platform with Lame Deer and Orville Gatewood, she squinted against the bright sun glaring from a cloudless sky. Crooked in her arm, she carried her Winchester 85 in a buckskin scabbard, wore a bandolier with .45-70 cartridges across her gray, woolen jacket, had a Colt .38 revolver strapped to her waist with her old bone handled knife, and saddlebags along with a canteen draped from her shoulder. There was a distinct chill in the air that she thought would last through the day, despite the sun. She couldn't quite grasp that it was June and yet winter here, part of her world being upside down.

Quickly, Morgan took in the town, a place foul with dust and flies. The streets were clogged with wagons, men on horseback, and pedestrians, all in a clamor, everyone dreaming of diamonds and gold no doubt.

"Reminds me of Alder Gulch," Gatewood said.

"It is good country," Lame Deer said.

Morgan didn't answer. She knew what the old woman was thinking and thought the same. England with its laws, police stations, and bobbies was eight thousand miles away. Kimberley was a frontier town, a boomtown, and the country beyond not much governed by laws, just by people's good will, and she had none. The shackles of so much civilization had crumbled to dust the moment she stepped onto the platform. Now, she would bring her law, and anyone who stood in her way, did so at their peril.

Close by, the two cowboys Bradford and Potter set their saddles onto the platform and waited for whatever came next. There, too, stood Arlo Ives and Detective Evans, who appeared a little befuddled and unsure of himself. The policeman's sole duty was to watch the criminal and to shoot him if he tried to run off. Morgan doubted he'd be capable of doing that.

A few steps away, the duke and Coppersmith were huddled together with the other two former soldiers in intense conversation. Morgan thought the soldiers were tough men and would do in a fight. They'd proven that at a place called Rorke's Drift, a Christian Mission, and the site of a battle in the Zulu War a few years back. According to Duke Edward, a hundred and fifty British soldiers held off four thousand Zulu warriors. Seventeen English were killed and nearly every man wounded. Coppersmith and his two friends received Victoria Crosses for bravery.

Of the African warriors, four hundred lost their lives and likely twice that number carried from the field wounded. The British had modern rifles, the Zulus jabbing spears. It was a slaughter, yet the warriors kept coming and nearly overran the mission station.

In America, little more than two years before Rorke's Drift, her husband Will took part in the Battle of the Red Fork, the last great fight of the Cheyenne Indians. Many died that day too, including her first husband Spotted Horse. The Cheyenne and the Zulu were nothing alike, and the two battles vastly different, yet Morgan couldn't help but feel deep in her bones a basic similarity. With far more pressing concerns on her mind, what that similarity was she couldn't puzzle out at the moment. It would wait for another day long into the future.

She sensed someone come up beside her and knew by the rancid cigar smell it was Bramley. His fat cheeks chomped down on a smoking cigar stub. She glanced at him, and their eyes met. Her hatred must have shown for he flinched and hurried over to the duke.

On the other side of the platform, Seamus in his stepfather's old cavalry jacket stood with Julia, neither saying a word. Since they'd left London, he'd been by her side ready to leap into the ocean for her should she ask. Since her temper could explode over the most insignificant trifle, his calm and adoring presence was the only thing that kept her rages in check. A little adoring went a long way with

Morgan's old friend. Clothed in an expensive riding habit, Julia was the only one in the company wearing any resemblance to fashion.

The last of the party to leave the train was the three Cheyenne warriors, elderly gray-haired men all, but they could still ride and, Morgan thought, fight. Caught also in Julia's orbit, they joined Seamus and her at the edge of the platform, saying nothing, staring impassively out at the town's crowded streets. After New York and London, they wouldn't be impressed.

Unlike the cowboys decked out in their gaudy show clothes, the Cheyenne wore a mishmash of parts, breechcloths with deerskin leggings, moccasin boots, reservation annuity shirts and suit jackets frayed to bare threads. Iron Chest even wore a top hat along with his old Spanish breastplate, which was pockmarked from so many bullet strikes. Hatless, Looks Behind sported a giant feather in his hair that he'd plucked from one of Julia's hats. She either didn't notice or didn't care. Armed with rifles, they made several passengers waiting to board other trains visibly nervous.

Quite the assemblage, Morgan thought, but figured they'd do in a tight spot, at least most of them, and she was comfortable with that.

Bramley's loud voice caught her attention. He was speaking to the duke. "Your grace, from this point on, it's men's work. The women will be in the way and slow us down. It might be best if they stay behind in Kimberley while we bring this business to a close."

Duke Edward turned to him. "You think that do you, Detective Bramley? Well, sir, Mrs. Raines goes when and where she chooses, and I suspect Lame Deer will go with her. As for my wife, if you would like to tell her she's to be left behind, go right ahead. But I'd advise you not to if you wish to leave this station alive."

Bramley glanced at Julia, slid his cigar to the other side of his mouth, and said nothing. Why he was with them at all Morgan couldn't fathom. Edward had said he was needed to deal with colonial police, but she saw him as far more of an anchor around their necks.

The duke called for everyone's attention. "Detective Bramley and I will meet with the mayor for anything further about Toby and

Glory. While we proceed to city hall, the rest of you please follow Captain Coppersmith to the stable where our horses should be waiting for us. We'll ride out immediately upon Detective Bramley's and my return."

As the two men set off in a hackney, the rest made their way through the crowded streets for the stable on foot while Julia and Seamus rode in the carriage that hauled the company's saddles and few pieces of luggage. With the three fierce looking Cheyenne at the front along with Coppersmith, appearing like they were stalking prey, people jumped quickly aside.

Ives called out, "Circus come to town. Just ten pennies for..."

Gatewood smacked his head. The criminal flinched and fell silent.

The company found Kimberly's vast market square a churning chaos of people, wagons, horses, and oxen teams. The Baggins Stable, their destination, was across to the far corner. When they arrived, Julia was standing in her carriage, stamping her foot, furious.

"He doesn't have our horses," Julia cried out. "We have no horses."

A wagon filled with supplies stood by the water trough, and Morgan was more surprised by it than Julia standing in a carriage and shouting. This was not going to be a Sunday picnic outing. They had no need for a supply wagon that would slow them to a crawl. This incensed her. She did see twelve horses, though they'd contracted twenty-four.

Nearby, Seamus stood talking with a small, bearded man, Baggins, the owner, Morgan presumed. When the man saw Coppersmith, he rushed to him and explained that all the horses had been requisitioned by an officer of her majesty's British forces.

"What could I do, Captain?" Baggins whined. "He is the British army. I told him they were spoken for, but he claimed them anyway. You must talk to him, sir. He'll be back soon."

As Morgan was helping Julia down from the carriage, Seamus pulled them quickly to Baggins and a frustrated Coppersmith. "Listen to this, Mama. This fellow said Toby and this McAuley hired a wagon from his stable, this very one. The other boy was with them."

"Is that so, Mr. Baggins?" Morgan asked.

The stableman pulled on his suspenders and nodded. "Yes, ma'am. I knew that little boy's description. It had been around for days you see. They hired themselves a wagon and one riding horse, then lit out in a hurry like the hounds of hell was after them."

"Thank god, he's a live," Julia sighed. "Did they have a girl with them?"

He shook his head. "Sorry, ma'am. No girl."

Morgan exhaled a long breath, but Seamus asked, "Could you see what color hair the tall boy had?

Baggins thought a moment, looked at Morgan whose auburn hair fell in a single ponytail from a flat crowned hat, "Well, kind of like yours, ma'am, maybe more red. Cut real short as I recall."

With a bark of a laugh, Seamus said, "I'll be damned."

Julia said, "#What? You think that is Glory?"

Morgan nodded. "It sure as hell is, and it's time for Seamus and me to go after them."

"Ma'am, I should tell you something else," Baggins said. "A few hours after they left, a great horde of men went riding after them."

"Why do you say that?" Julia asked, alarmed. "They could have been leaving for any reason."

Baggins shook his head. "Don't think so, ma'am. They weren't the only ones. Other men lit out after them too. People here abouts are in a hurry, but not that kind of hurry. Doesn't take a London banker to figure it, what with all the talk about two kids wandering lost in these parts with the queen's diamond."

Fear rose up crazed in Julia's eyes. "How do you know that? What diamond?"

"Why, Queen Bess's diamond. Richest in the world they say. Everyone knows how them kids stole it."

Coppersmith asked, "Mr. Baggins, did you recognize any of the chase party? Were any of them Englishmen?"

"That's just it. I did recognize them. That's why I mentioned it. Some forty, fifty men, some white, some kaffir, but English?" He shrugged. "I don't know, but it was Moses Nyama and his gang of cutthroats, that's for sure."

Coppersmith's face went pale. "Nyama. That just tears it. It puts us in a bad fix."

At once, Morgan told Seamus, "Get our saddles." Then to Coppersmith. "We're taking four horses and leaving."

He was shocked. "No, Mrs. Raines, I can't let you do that. With Moses Nyama, it's far too dangerous for a woman and boy alone. You must stay with the wagon."

"My daughter's out there. I'm leaving, Captain, and I'll kill any man who tries to stop me, including you."

Staring into her cold eyes, he took a half step back. "But…"

"Give her the horses, Captain," Julia ordered. "I'll deal with my husband."

After a moment, Coppersmith sighed. "Yes, your grace."

Lame Deer stood nearby, listening, and Morgan turned to her. She was a Cheyenne Indian and knew how to ride a horse but oddly had done very little of it. Most Indian women walked everywhere. The men did the riding. Morgan knew she would slow them down.

As always, Lame Deer read her thoughts. "I stay with duke," the woman said. "We find Glory, I see her no hurt."

Morgan squeezed the woman's forearm, then hurried to the horses. Seamus had two saddled already and leads on two more. They mounted and started from the stable, then Morgan turned back. "Captain Coppersmith, get rid of that wagon. It's not a damn Sunday outing. You need to ride hard after us. Mr. Gatewood and the Cheyenne can track us."

Gatewood gave her a casual salute. "Will do, ma'am."

Morgan leaned down and said to Julia in a whisper. "See they come fast and hard. And take care of Lame Deer. She's old and doesn't know it yet."

Julia nodded.

As Morgan swung her horse to go, Coppersmith called out, "Mrs. Raines, they'll likely stay on this side of the Vaal River going northeast, then they'll cross and go on to Johannesburg. We'll send word to you at the telegraph office. Leave any message for us there.

"Northeast?"

"Yes, they won't go north or west. That's the Kalahari, and no one wants to end up there."

Just then, staring out into the square, Baggins said, "Now we're in for it. Here comes them soldier boys."

Approaching the stable was a squad of British soldiers led by two officers, one young and boyish, the other small, strutting like a bantam rooster. He had a mustache that drooped below his chin, and his dark furrowed eyebrows created a cross between his eyes and wore his fury like a medal on his chest.

He drew his pistol on Seamus, "Halt, or I'll shoot you from that horse, boy."

Seamus pulled up as Morgan urged her horse in between them. She began shoving the officer back.

Shocked, he protested, "Stop this, madam. I am an officer of her majesty's 24th..."

Ignoring the protest, she herded him back. At first, he tried to stand his ground, then attempted to step aside, but each time she cut him off and pushed him farther and farther. With a last nudge, he splashed into the water trough, dropping his pistol. From behind her, she heard the sound of a hammer cocking. She glanced that way. The young officer was pointing his weapon at her, but from his horse, Seamus had his pressed against the man's head.

"Let's be calm about this, soldier boy," he said. "You shoot my mother, I'll give your head a good airing."

He leaned over, snatched the pistol, and tossed it to Morgan. She caught it and dropped it into the trough.

Beyond them, the squad of soldiers were holding their hands up in surrender, their weapons lying beside them. Gatewood and the three Cheyenne were aiming their rifles at them.

"This is outrageous," the captain shouted and started to rise from the water. "I shall have you arrested and shot, woman or no."

Morgan slammed her boot into his face and drove him back down into the trough. From the stable entrance came a shriek of laughter. It was Julia. "That's my lady's maid," she said.

Leading the spare horses, Morgan and Seamus galloped hard through the square. Behind her she heard the shrieks of Lame Deer and the Cheyenne men giving their war cries. She hoped it was meant as a sendoff for her and Seamus and not them scalping the soldiers.

CHAPTER THIRTY-SIX

Bechuanaland, June 22, 1887

We were not exactly lost. By the sun, I knew we'd been heading north for the last four days and according to Arthur's plan must soon head east to make our dash to Johannesburg. In this vast expanse of stillness, the land was both desolate and endless. Yet, the brown dry grass, red dirt with the giant hoof prints of monsters, and the faded yellow of half-chewed flowers wilting on the brush seemed to suggest life I couldn't see. Flat topped trees that Arthur kept exclaiming from the wagon to be acacias were few and stood like isolated sentinels. Several miles to the east, low hills rolled like sea waves. We hadn't seen a human in more than two days.

Fiercely lonely, every hour I wanted my family.

Our water was running low, so we'd have to find a source soon. This land did have its creeks and streams and water holes, many of them dried out this time of year. We could backtrack thirty miles to the last one, but I wanted to go on, sure we'd find water soon.

Arthur was laid up in the wagon, his head being stoved in when he hit it climbing down from the seat. That man was likely the clumsiest I'd ever seen in my life. Leaving Kimberley, he'd ridden the horse, but not much of a horseman, he fell off twice before he gave up and traded places with me. Toby just rode on the wagon seat, chattering like a scared magpie. But out here hellbent for nowhere, we were all scared.

No longer talking gibberish like he did that first day, Arthur was now burning with fever, sweat beading his face like he was roasting on a spit. I figured we needed to find somewhere to hold up and get him treatment before blood poisoning waggled his brains or killed him.

Over the last four days, we'd come across small herds of strange grazing animals feeding on the dry grass. And where they were, I was sure lions and leopards were lurking. These African terrors were big as buffalos, fast as lightning, and had teeth the size of Bowie knives. In Montana, I'd been close on with grizzlies and mountain lions before, but always with Mama, Papa, or Seamus. Those poor bears and cougars didn't stand a chance. Though scared then, it was nothing like the fear gnawing at my bones here on the African veldt. Those beasts plain scared the hell out of me, and me with just a pistol.

I wondered where Mama and Seamus were, and Lame Deer. Had they reached to South Africa yet? I knew they'd be coming. They would not quit till I was found, and that made me feel good for a bit till I realized they had no way of knowing where I was. That crushed any feeling good.

This is what happened in Kimberley. I'd seen Dunford among the men rushing across the street to our hotel, so it was easy to figure who they were after. Toby and I escaped by racing down the backstairs and into an alley. Before, I'd stuffed Arthur's leather case in the knapsack, so he'd have what he prized most in the world, that was except for Miss Eugenie Colville, his one true love. Since he'd gone to Debeers, we headed that way and ran into him.

"Rhodes is in Johannesburg," he announced when he saw us, then blinked, "What are you two doing out here? Someone might see you."

I replied, "It's good Mr. Rhodes is in Johannesburg because we can't stay here."

After Toby and I told him what happened, we hired the wagon and horses and raced out of there. A mile or two from town, I turned the wagon dead west into the hills. From there, we watched the road to see who would be pursuing us.

As it turned out, quite a few. Men in twos and threes came out right away, and I knew they were after us. No one ran horses that hard unless they were racing them, running from something, or chasing something, like perhaps two kids supposedly carrying the richest diamond in the world around like a cheap watch fob.

After two more hours, using Arthur's field glass, I saw a band of men, more like a cavalry regiment but unlike any cavalry regiment I ever saw. Seeing them clinging to their horses, I could tell they were not skilled riders. Yet, they beat hell out of those mounts to go faster. And there he was, the meanest bastard in the world, Dunford way out in front, looking back at them with fury and disgust. Of course, I couldn't see what he felt, but knowing him, that was what it seemed to me.

That's when Arthur came up with a new plan. We'd stay away from the treasure road and instead proceed due north till we reached a place called Rensburg and turn east for Johannesburg. It worked pretty well till he busted his head, and we ran out of water.

In that dry land, unable to wet my lips, I announced we were heading east before we and the horses died. That's when I caught movement behind an acacia just thirty yards ahead. I pulled up my horse and slipped my hand to the pistol in my jacket pocket.

"What is it?" Arthur asked, now on the wagon seat with Toby and handling the reins. His head bandage had a splotch of fresh red on it. His brow was drenched in sweat.

I gestured to the tree. "Something moving."

With a dismissive wave, Toby scoffed, "Pshaw, you're just seeing things. It's only the wind." Then his eyes doubled in size. "Oh, bloody hell!"

The monster had come out from behind the tree and stared curiously at us. It was the most extraordinary beast I'd ever seen. Tall as the tree itself. The name was hiding in my memory from school when Mrs. Braistworth talked African geography and animals. *Giraffe*, that was it. This one was so tall you'd think it could lick the sky. I knew right away it wasn't dangerous unless someone pushed it to be and that wouldn't be me.

Toby stood up on the wagon seat and shouted, "Halloo! Halloo!"

Grabbing the lead horse's halter, I started turning the wagon, and he almost fell off.

"Hey!" he shouted. His scowling face, once pale and round, was burned now and pealing like my own. I noticed too that he was not so round anymore, the baby fat draining away. A lack of food will do that.

Glancing back at the giraffe, I saw it decided to ignore us and return to the tree's leaves, which it took with its giant tongue.

"We need to find water," I explained, "and a place to put up. Arthur needs his head examined."

For a second, the Scotsman regarded me, then laughed. I laughed too. We were crazy. We were all crazy. He waved toward the eastern horizon. "Lead on, MacDuff."

I didn't know this MacDuff fellow, but I headed us east into the whirlwind.

Toward mid-afternoon, we came upon a farm, a big operation by the look of it. There were fields of barley and corn, trees planted likely for windbreaks, and about fifty head of cattle grazing nearby, fenced in by simple wire, no barbs. To the north were two hills. The one that was highest, maybe fifty feet, was steep

We eased onto a road that led to a large house on a slight rise. In this dry country, that house was a marvel with its terraced rose gardens and fruit trees. Somehow, the farmer was greening the land.

At a fence some thirty yards away, two men watched us approach, much like the giraffe no doubt determining if we were a threat. Despite the chill, both had their shirts off, one with a hammer in his hand and the other with a roll of wire. Trying to be friendly, I waved, and then so did Toby and Arthur. Sitting in the wagon seat, crazed with fever, Arthur had a ghoulish smile pasted to his lips.

After a moment, the two men dropped their tools. Each had a weapon at his waist but did not draw it yet. As Toby pulled the wagon to a stop, I nudged my horse up to them. "Hello, I'm Glory Raines, and those two are Toby Becket and Arthur McAuley. He's got a bad gash on his head and he's feverish. Is there a doctor here abouts?"

Muscular, blue eyed and blond, both men were versions of each other. Curls stuck to their foreheads from sweat. The younger one couldn't have been more than fifteen or sixteen and had about him an air of self-assurance. Desperate though I was, I found him as handsome as all get out.

"There's one in Rensburg," the older one said. "That's not far. I'm Joseph Bartlett and this is my little brother Aidan."

Aidan frowned at the word *little* but quickly his warm smile came back. He said to me, "You sure you can handle such a big horse like that, lad?"

That annoyed me. He couldn't have been more than three years my age. I boasted, "There's not a horse born I can't ride, *Lad*."

He gave a pleasant laugh. "All right. I believe you. You don't sound English or Boer. Where are you people from?"

"Montana for me. That's in America. Those two are English and Scottish." I addressed the older man. "Can you spare some water, sir?"

"You're welcome to the water," Joseph said, then gestured to Arthur with concern. "That fellow is about to fall out of the wagon. We better get him to the house."

When we got there, four women came out as the two men helped Arthur down. "He's got a wound on his head, Mum," Joseph said to the older woman, "Looks like fever too."

"Bring him in," she ordered. "We'll take a look at him."

Toby and I were ignored till Aidan glanced back and waved us in too. We sat on a couch in a huge living room with a big stone fireplace as the women rushed back and forth from the hallway, carrying towels and buckets of water. A couple of young children seemed to be in the way, but the women easily dodged them. More than once, the women glowered at us as if we'd stolen the family silver.

Toby said, "Do they think we hit him over the head?"

I shrugged.

A few minutes later, Aiden sat with us to explain that his mother and sisters-in-law were cleaning Arthur's wound. "He'll be fine, I'm sure," he said.

I wasn't.

Toby asked, "How many people on this place?"

Aiden explained he had five brothers who worked the farm with their father, three of them married. The youngest wife was pregnant while the other two had three kids between them, none over four. And the farm sold barley and maize, some fruit, but mostly wool.

Sheepherders, I thought derisively.

"How far are we from Johannesburg?" I asked.

He gave a shrug. "Three hundred thirty miles or so."

"What?" Toby and I bawled together.

"About that many miles. Why?"

Anguished, Toby said, "We're farther away from Johannesburg than we were in Kimberley."

I told Aiden, "Mr. Cecil Rhodes is there. Arthur kind of knows him, and we need to get there. Toby and I need his help."

He nodded. When he slapped his knees and got up, I blurted out, "What about lions and leopards? Don't they go after your sheep?"

"No, we don't fear them because there hasn't been any around here for years. Too many people, I guess. They're up north or over in the Kalahari."

I looked up at the wall where a lion's head hung, centered among those of horned animals, but I didn't ask about them.

Toby chimed in, "She's scared to death of lions."

"Well, who wouldn't be?" I said.

Aiden studied me several seconds. "Lions are indeed fearsome, but it's leopards you have to watch. They're cowards. They'll sneak up on you, but they'll run if you smack one with a good stick." He gave a gentlemanly bow. "Joseph and I need to go help Papa repair the dams. See you when I get back."

"Yeah, see you," I said.

It was only after he was gone did I realize Toby had called me, *she*. It didn't matter now though. "We have to tell them," I said. "We need to leave Arthur here and go on without him. We can't bring Dunford and all those men down on these people."

Reluctant at first, he finally nodded.

An hour later, the four women came out, staring disapprovingly at us. Mrs. Bartlett said, "Your friend is sleeping now. As soon as my husband and boys return, I'll send Joseph and Robert to Rensburg for the doctor."

"Will he be all right?" I asked.

Her face softened. "I don't know, lad. Let's wait for the doctor. Now, for the two of you. You're filthy and need a bath. We have a large tub for the both of you."

"What?" I muttered uneasily.

"Cleanliness is next to Godliness, my boy," she replied. "You'll need to share the bath. We can't spare the water."

In unison, Toby and I stood up. "No!"

Hands on hips like a nasty school marm, Mrs. Bartlett scowled. "And why not?"

I said in a shaky voice, "Cause I'm a girl."

While our clothes were being washed, Toby and I took separate baths but at the same time in the same building attached to the main house. It was divided by a short, wooden wall that didn't extend across the entire room and stood only five feet high. If it was Aiden on the other side, he'd easily be able to peer down at me. But it was short, plumpy Toby. I could hear him splashing around like he had boats.

In the warm water, I felt dirt and grit sliding off me. I had one of my legs propped on the side of the tub, soaping it, when I glanced over at the wall. There were Toby's two hands, nose and eyes. He was watching me.

I yipped in alarm and threw my soap at him. He laughed, and I heard his feet slapping on the floor as he raced back to his tub. Me, I had to get out and dash over for my soap in the cold.

Afterward, while my clothes were drying, I put on boy's clothes again. Aiden's. None of the women's would fit so all they had were old hand me downs of his. Normally, I wouldn't like wearing someone else's stuff, but putting on his shirt and trousers made me feel like he had an arm around me. I liked that.

Later, the family wanted to hear our story, the full version of it. After dinner, we all sat in the living room. No one had gone for the doctor. Mr. Bartlett and his sons hadn't returned till after dark, and since Arthur's death didn't appear forthcoming, it was decided that Joseph and Robert would set off for Rensburg the next morning.

In random turns, Toby and I told the story in detail, seeing their disbelief grow. We said nothing of the diamond. Where he was hiding it I didn't know. When we finished, they stared at us, silent for a long time.

Mr. Bartlett came out of his stupor first. "Now, how much of that is true?"

"Every spec," I said.

Balling his fist, Toby cried, "I *am* the Earl of Exeter, and my father *is* the Duke of Northampton."

Mrs. Bartlett folded her hands across her lap and said gently, "That's hard enough to believe, lad, but Glory's mother being some Old Testament avenger, that's a tough one to swallow."

Toby waved her concern away. "Oh, it's true. She's a fearsome thing to behold. I've seen her in Buffalo Bill's Wild West show in London." Then he laughed, slapping his knees. "Mrs. Raines lifted Glory's dress and whipped her in front of forty thousand people. She was crying loud enough to wake the dead. And she had on bright blue pantaloons that day."

So furious was I, I could have stuck him with my knife.

Bemused, Joseph said, "So, you're an earl. Are we to address you as Lord Exeter then?"

As Toby was thinking this over, I said, "No, he likes being called Lord Wee Wee."

They laughed, and it was Toby's turn to fume.

When everyone had quieted, I said, "What you must believe is that a lot of bad men are after us. We don't want to bring them down on you, so we'll leave in the morning with Joseph and Robert and make our way to Johannesburg."

"You most certainly will not," Mrs. Bartlett answered immediately. "We are not casting two children out into the wilderness. Robert and Joseph will fetch the doctor, your friend will heal, and then all three of you may be on your way, and not before then."

Mr. Bartlett added, "I can assure you, lass, my boys and I will handle any trouble."

The next morning at dawn, Joseph and Robert set out for Rensburg.

CHAPTER THIRTY-SEVEN

Cape Colony, June 23, 1887

Morgan smelled the smoke long before she saw the burned-out farmhouse. More than ten miles back, they'd caught the first acrid whiffs and knew what it was. Pushing their horses harder, they finally pulled up on a rise a quarter mile from the blackened ruin, curls of ashen haze lifting off the debris. A rock fireplace stood in the rubble as if the lone survivor. Morgan knew there'd be no human ones.

"It's not her, Mama," Seamus said.

Morgan gave a curt nod. "It's sure as hell them."

Iron Chest, the Cheyenne chief who'd caught up with them a day out from Kimberley, adjusted his tied down stovepipe hat, then quickly pointed. There was movement, five men walking among the blackened embers. One, a solid stump of a man, threw back his head and screamed in agony.

Morgan didn't believe they were part of Dunford's band, yet she decided to approach cautiously just the same. Nudging their horses down the rise, the three rode toward the burned-out house. When the men saw them, they unslung their rifles and stepped from the ruin.

As she kneed her horse closer, Morgan raised her hands. "We're no threat to you, sir. I'm Morgan Rains from America, and I'm sorry for what happened to your farm."

All five men eyed them with suspicion, going from her to Seamus and Iron Chest with heavy scowls. They did not lower their weapons. One, a boy no more than fifteen, was white as porcelain and appeared about to vomit. Fear bordering on panic shown in his eyes. If this turned bad, he would be the one to cause it.

"Not my farm. Belonged to the Hadleys," the man said.

Keeping one hand up, Seamus reached the other slowly into his saddle bag and pulled out a program from the Wild West show. He nudged his horse gently forward and handed it to the man, pointing out something on the cover, then indicating Morgan with his thumb, said. "That's her, that's us. We're all from the Wild West show."

He studied it, then gazed at Morgan and back to the cover. He gave a half smile, then said to the men, "Says here, Buffalo Bill's Wild West, Earls Court London, and down here Miss Morgan O'Connor, The Captured Girl, famous manslayer." He handed the program back to Seamus, then glanced over at Morgan. His eyes crinkled with a hint of mirth. "Oh, Lordy, so you're a manslayer?"

"I'm a rancher, sir, much like you. Mostly cattle."

He seemed to give another moment's thought then nodded for the men to lower their weapons. "My name's Ned Cobb," he said, "and these are my sons, except that one." He indicated the boy. "That's my nephew Lucas. He's been visiting. How is it an American girl iand her two companions are wandering around in our wilderness?"

Morgan's voice gentled. "I love my son and daughter more than anything in life. The men who did this to the Hadley's farm are pursuing my daughter. I plan to stop them." She indicated the farmhouse. "Is it still hot?"

Cobb handed the program back to Seamus. "Yes, ma'am, some, but we can bury the dead now before they attract jackals."

"What do you figure happened?"

Cobb glanced back over his shoulder at the ruins and spoke with vehemence, "Don't figure. I know. Brigands attacked the farmhouse and killed all the Hadleys. Allen, Agneta, and their two young sons. God knows why. They had nothing. Just meanness I suppose."

"You find their bodies?"

"Yes." His face anguished, he took several seconds before he went on. "They were killed out here and tossed into the fire. Maybe...maybe a couple still alive." He removed his hat and ran a hand through his thick black hair, shaking his head with incomprehension. "Sorry to be so blunt, ma'am."

There was a loud gagging sound, and the boy finally vomited, splattering the ground and grabbing his knees while man next to him placed a hand on his back. Everyone waited as he emptied his stomach, then gagged air. Finally, he rose, wiped his mouth with his sleeve, and said testily, "I'm fine."

Cobb turned back to Morgan. "Lucas saw it. That's how we know. He saw it all. He was riding over to visit the Hadley boys when he saw the attack. I keep telling him nothing he could have done but what he did do, and that was come get us. By the time we got here, the killers had gone. Their tracks said they were a big bunch. No chance the five of us could take them on."

"Were there any other bodies?" Morgan asked.

"Not that we found, ma'am. Your daughter wasn't among them." He gave her a hard look. "What's going on here? I got family to protect and neighbors to warn."

Morgan gave them a quick version, explaining that these raiders were after her daughter and a rich man's son for ransom. She said nothing about the diamond, not wanting to tempt anyone to the wrong side of the conflict. "The Cape governor and Kimberley's mayor should have telegraphed the authorities up here warning you about these men."

"We don't have telegraph, and there isn't much in the way of authorities. We take care of ourselves, ma'am. If you don't mind me asking, don't you think just three of you is a little light to take on fifty or so men?"

She leaned forward in her saddle, and her voice dropped an octave. "I'd say we got the number just about right." She glanced over at a milk cow that had had just emerged from the barn and started bawling. "Someone's got to milk that cow."

"Yes, ma'am, we'll see to it."

Her perpetual glower softened, and she said, "I'm sorry about these men coming into your country. You had no part in it. It's me and my daughter and the duke's son they want. He'll be along in a day or two. He's a good man. If you would, tell him we're still in pursuit. I bid you good day, sir. We have a lot of riding yet to do."

When they started to go, the man called out, "Wait. Can I ask a favor of you?"

"You can ask it?" Morgan replied.

He gestured to Lucas. "We were about to take my nephew back to his family in Whatley. That's forty miles north. Now, we best stay here in case that gang comes back. You're going that way. Can he accompany you? I'll send my son Albert along. He can use a rifle."

A dark-haired man standing next to Lucas lifted his head slightly at the name.

Morgan hesitated a moment, then said, "Get your horses, boys. If you can't keep up, I'll leave you behind."

Several hours later in the small town of Whatley, Morgan ran into Charlie Acker.

They'd just ridden in with the Cobb boys. The town was surrounded by trees and low hills. The main street was flanked by several sturdy buildings including General shops, a hotel, a windmill behind one building, and a tavern. Morgan's intention was to leave the boys at the hotel that Lucas's parents owned, then feed and water the horses, give them a couple hours' rest before setting out again.

The five of them were watering their horses at a trough when Lucas spoke in a quivering voice. "Mrs. Raines, look down the street. There's one of them."

When she did, she saw three men coming out of the tavern. The large, beefy man was limping noticeably and had to be helped onto his horse.

Breathing hard, Lucas said, "That giant dung beetle threw Lonnie into the fire. My friend was screaming."

He looked familiar to Morgan. You don't forget someone like him.

This was the man who confronted her on the train to Northampton all those weeks ago and tried to touch Glory. And now he was here in the Cape Colony. When the three men started out, the man's head lolled. Riding in the middle, his two men kept him upright. All were armed.

Morgan said to Lucas and Albert, "You two stay here and keep out of it."

They nodded, and she, Seamus, and Iron Chest mounted their horses, ambling them easily into the men's path. They stopped at five feet.

The beefy man gazed up, surprised.

"Acker, Charlie Acker, Dung Beetle," she said loudly as if speaking to the people now watching in doorways and on the street.

His head came up. "Who the hell are you? I don't know anyone in this Godforsaken country."

Morgan's voice could chill water. "That won't stop me from getting the bulge on a grass-bellied cow like you."

The words seemed to sting his eyes, and they blinked. Then they widened with recognition. "You!"

"You think you can threaten my daughter?" Morgan drew her colt and shot him in the chest. In shock, Acker gazed down at the smoking hole in his coat, then toppled to the ground. In the same instant, Seamus's colt fired, dropping the man in front of him, just as the third man's horse bucked in fright. Morgan snatched the horse's halter and got it quickly controlled. The man's hands were raised, his eyes bulging wider than the horse's as he stared at Iron Chest. So menacing was the Cheyenne, he hadn't even drawn a knife to subdue him.

Rushing up, Lucas and Albert stood only a few feet away, their weapons trained on the man. Morgan took his pistols from his belt, tossing them to the dirt. She saw in his eyes the fear of a trapped rabbit. He smelled like he'd just soiled his pants. When the townspeople recognized Lucas, he told them about the Hadley massacre. People started calling for a hanging. The man's rabbit eyes grew even larger, as he pleaded his innocence.

Morgan jammed her pistol into his chest. "Look at me. That's it. Tell me what I want to know, and I'll let you go. I give you my word."

When he hesitated, Seamus said, "Look around you, pard. It's the best offer you're going to get."

The man's words rushed out like the bullets of a Gatling gun. He told everything, that they hadn't caught Glory and Toby yet, that they had burned down three farmsteads, then tracked the runaways north but lost them in a sandstorm. At one of the farms, Acker had been wounded and left behind while the main group went on to Rensburg.

"I had nothing to do with any of it," he pleaded. "I wasn't one of the leaders. I'm just a bloke trying to earn a little money to feed his wife and kiddies. That's all."

"Then, you fell in with the wrong crowd," she said, "and you'll have to pay the piper for that."

When she, Seamus, and Iron Chest turned their horses away, several people yanked him down. He screamed at her, "You promised!"

No pity in her heart, Morgan shot back, "I keep my word. I have let you go, but I've got no say in what these people do."

Before sundown, the three of them rode out of Whatley with plans to ride all night. As they left, the man was hanging from a post. In unfamiliar brushland, it was too dangerous to continue once darkness fell. They camped after fifteen miles, set a fire, and waited for morning. No one could sleep. Under the vast spread of stars in an African sky, Iron Chest spoke of the old days in Cheyenne country, riding with Spotted Horse against their enemies. Seamus was entranced. Maybe they could have slept some, but he kept asking the old warrior for more and more stories.

When the first shards of gray light appeared in the east, Morgan roused them out of their blankets. Putting on his stovepipe hat, Iron Chest left camp to relieve himself, and when he didn't return, Morgan and Seamus went in search. The light was coming up and it was time to be riding. She would hector him for dawdling when important work had to be done, just like any squaw would. They found him not thirty feet from the camp sitting on a rock.

In alarm, Morgan asked, "What is it?"

With a shaky hand, he pointed to the ground. There was a snake, and both Morgan and Seamus jumped back, but it was dead, a knife stuck in its head. It was about a yard long and fat.

Morgan knelt beside the Cheyenne. "Where did it bite you?"

Iron Chest pointed to his calf. "I am such an old fool. This is not where I live. This is not my country. I stepped on it, and it bit me in the leg. What is snake to do? I don't feel so good. I think this is bad for me."

From the knee down, she cut his leggings away. Seamus gasped. The calf was swelling up already. "We have to get him back to Whatley."

They got Iron Chest on his horse and rode hard back. At Whatley the best they had was a veterinarian, a lanky man with a long black beard and a pipe in his mouth. He was about to protest caring for him when he seemed to realize this was the woman who'd just shot down the bandit and relented. As it turned out there was little the man could do. She and Seamus stayed by Iron Chest's bedside holding his hand. To Morgan, he was a connection to the old days when she had given herself over to the ways of the Cheyenne and was in love for the first time.

Towards evening, in a weak, raspy voice, Iron Chest sang his death song. Then said, "Don't bury me here. Not in this terrible place. Take me to Cheyenne country. Take me to the sweet grass and flowing waters. Take me home and let my heart lay at rest there."

"It will be done, father," Seamus said. It would be his dried heart that Seamus carried back to America with him.

Midmorning the next day Iron Chest died. He was left with the vet with instructions to prepare his heart and have it ready when they returned. Then, carrying fresh sadness, Morgan and Seamus set off north once again.

CHAPTER THIRTY-EIGHT

Rensburg, Cape Colony, June 23, 1887

In the early morning, Dunford sat along the stream bank writing a letter to his wife using a board propped against his knees. Last night, his ragged army reached Rensburg and camped on by the filthy little town. It would be a base of operation from which to send out patrols to find the brats, who were in the area, of that he was sure. Nyama's two vaunted trackers lost them forty miles back in a dust storm that wiped out their trail. These two men were Hottentots that Nyama claimed could follow a feather across rock. But they couldn't follow a damn wagon over the veldt. Furious at his men, Nyama castigated them in front of the company for the folly. Shamed, the trackers swore a blood oath to find the young ones and bring back their heads.

Dunford was satisfied with that. If he could present Morgan Raines with the head of her daughter, it would break her. Once again, he tried to focus on the letter. Ostensibly, he was traveling to his gold mine outside Johannesburg, his words to his wife a travelogue. Nothing of the farms burned and people killed, nothing of Nyama's army of thieves and murderers, and absolutely nothing of the two children they chased. He could not explain to his wife that he must kill the girl. He had no grudge against her, did not hate her like he did her mother. Did not loathe her very existence like he did her mother. It was the mother who must feel the pain of losing a child just as he had. No, his wife would understand none of that.

Nor did he reveal in the letter his utter frustration at the shambles this enterprise had become. A simple plan to exact money and revenge had disintegrated into a chaos of mishaps and slaughter. The killings had been regrettable. Soon, great forces would be assembled to pursue them. He must end this within days and flee this comedy of errors.

His frustrations had begun piling up outside Kimberley when they'd galloped hard after the two brats and the Scotsman till their horses started to flag. They should have come upon the slow-moving wagon by then but hadn't. Nor had any travelers seen them. Nyama sent out trackers and one found the ferry that took them across the Vaal River. They weren't traveling the treasure road northeast toward Johannesburg but for whatever reason headed straight north to God knows where. Though a good day behind, the chase was finally on.

North of the Vaal River, they'd come across a small farm that had sheltered them, a couple and their two sons. Dunford hadn't ordered the slaughter. From seeming calm, Nyama's men erupted into a spasm of violence, killing all four using jabbing spears instead of their rifles, then plundered the farm and burned it to the ground. Before reaching Rensburg, they looted two more farms, killing every inhabitant. It was at one of the farms that Each night in camp, the men got drunk and didn't continue the pursuit till late in the next morning.

"Someone coming," Hobbs called out. Standing outside his tent, he was shaving with a mirror.

Dunford glanced up and saw a lone man approaching, worn-out and about to topple from his horse. It was Arlo Ives. What was he doing in the Cape. Acker left him in England. Some of the men knew him and helped him from the saddle, giving him water. After a few minutes, he seemed revived.

When Dunford and Hobbs approached, he rose to his feet and saluted as if a proper soldier. "Arlo Ives, reporting for duty, sirs."

Hobbs still had the shaving hand towel draped from his shoulder and the razor in his hand. Astonished, he asked, "What in God's name are you doing here, Ives?"

The man shook his head. "Well, Guv, that's a long story, a long, long story."

With several men gathering, Ives spun a tale that had them all entranced and little of which Dunford believed. The rancid man explained that somehow the duke learned his boy was heading for the Cape Colony and he put together some men and hired a boat. "Now, I was thinking I could help my old mates by joining them and so I did. They been following you. When we got close, I decided I best get on my way and warn you. Left one of them dead when I made my escape."

"They're near?" Hobbs asked.

"Yes, sir. Maybe a day behind."

"How many men does the duke have?"

Ives counted in his head, then said, "I figure ten."

Several men laughed, and Hobbs sighed with relief. "Did you cross Acker coming here?"

"Acker's dead."

This silenced everyone.

"What? What happened?" Dunford demanded.

"That woman killed him," Ives answered. "Shot him dead in a place called Whatley yesterday. Gave him not a whit of a chance. Just up and shot him. She's here too looking for you with her kaffir son. I must have passed her today, but I don't quite see how."

Dunford ran his hand through his hair, and Hobbs asked, "Who's he talking about?"

"The girl's mother. You met her often enough."

"The American woman?"

Nyama had come up. He was a tall man with tan skin and dubious parentage. His flat brown eyes projected lethal menace. "You're not planning on running from ten men and a woman, are you, Dunford?"

Dunford scowled and said, "We'll find the brats first, then turn on the duke's army. That suit you?"

Nyama nodded. "As long as we get the diamond."

Dunford glanced at Ives. He had been lying for most of it and was just trying to land on the winning side. But soon, a violent split with Nyama was coming, and he needed men he on his side. He smiled, "Welcome back, Mr. Ives."

For the rest of the morning the trackers returned in twos and threes with nothing to report. No sign of the wagon or the brats or the girl for that matter.

Near mid-morning, another man caused an even bigger stir in the camp. Carver, the man the girl cut back in England, hurried from town at a hobbling gait, shouting, "I found them. I found them." Approaching Dunford, he exclaimed, breathlessly, "I was at the doctor's, and I found them." He stood as if waiting for congratulations.

Hobbs grabbed his arm. "The two runaways?"

"The duke's boy and that Scotsman. I was at the doctor's about the blisters on my feet. They're the size of…"

Hobbs gave his shoulder a jerk. "Get on with it."

"Right, right. Well, these two farm boys run in, and they want the doc to go to their farm. They got an injured man who showed up yesterday with two boys. One of the boys says he's an earl. Doc says he can't come right now cause he's got too many patients, and he does cause the whole room is filled with them, stomach complaints I think, oh yeah, so the farm boys say they'll come back at noon and take him out to their place." He postured, proud of himself. "I figure all we got to do is follow them back to that farm, and Bob's your uncle."

CHAPTER THIRTY-NINE

Bartlett Farm, Northern Cape, June 23, 1887

Being farmers, the family had eaten before dawn, then Joseph and Robert rode out for Rensburg. Mrs. Bartlett had found a fine day-dress for me to wear that belonged to one of her daughters-in-law. It was so pretty, I longed to put it on but instead wore Aidan's old clothes again. If Arthur was well enough to leave this morning, I'd feel safer traveling as a boy.

After breakfast when Mr. Bartlett and his other sons threw on their jackets and hats and started for the door, I burst out, "Wait."

When they turned with questioning looks, I pleaded that Dunford, the great depravity, was in the area and asked them to stay close.

"A farm doesn't run itself, lass," Bartlett replied. "There's work to be done. You know that yourself. Surely, you've been out before dawn."

"Yes, sir, many times, but Dunford's got fifty men. If he comes and if you're caught in the open, they will shoot you down. The house will be helpless. Sir, these men kill."

Before he could answer, Mrs. Bartlett said uneasily, "Colin, surely there's work to be done nearer the house."

"Aye, we've been putting off repairs to the granary. I suppose we can work there today."

I was relieved. This house might be a fortress, and these few might stand against Dunford's horde here. I wanted no one harmed on our account.

A few minutes later, Mrs. Bartlett gave me a tray of porridge to take in to Arthur. He was awake, and as reported, feeling better. Sitting up in bed, he was going over his drawings for mine equipment from his leather folder, the ones he planned to show to Rhodes when we found the great man.

He beamed at me when I came in. "Ah, breakfast and such a wonderful person to deliver it."

I set the tray in his lap. "It's just oatmeal with a little barley. You'll like the coffee though. How are you feeling, Arthur?"

"Better. I should be up and around tomorrow," he said. "We might be able to make our departure for Johannesburg day after."

Disappointed, I sat on the bed beside him, placing a hand on his forearm. "Arthur, I can feel Dunford close in my bones."

He frowned. "Perhaps. You think we should draw the scoundrels away then, don't you?"

"I do. We shouldn't have brought the Bartletts into it."

"We had no choice, lass. Be patient. I still have a fever and Mrs. Bartlett—I should say General Bartlett—won't let me up until it's back to normal, and she has my clothes. We shall be away tomorrow. I'll insist. How's that?" He grinned. "Is Toby all right? Staying out of trouble?"

Him being waited on hand and foot by four women, three of them young and attractive, might be a reason for not trying harder to leave today.

Frustrated, I sighed, then rolled my eyes. "He's Toby. We told them everything. They know I'm a girl and that Toby is an earl. He never lets them forget it."

As he laughed, there was a knock at the door, and Aiden stepped in. He was wearing a holstered gun at his waist. "Glory, Papa thinks you might like to see the irrigation system, you living on a ranch like you do. You willing?"

Thrilled to be alone with him, I jumped up off the bed. "Yes."

"Where are you two going?" Arthur asked in alarm.

"I'm showing her how we use the dams," he explained. "We won't go that far from the house."

"Then why do you need a gun?"

Aiden shrugged. "Always snakes, sir."

I didn't know why, but Arthur was upset and not about any threat of snakes. That had always been there. I thought maybe it was because he'd been called *sir*.

I said goodbye, then told Aiden, "Just a second. I want to get my gun, too."

I had to admit I was taken with this particular Bartlett boy and the thought of spending time alone with him had me more nervous than that first day at spring roundup when I was seven. Back then, I was handed a knife by Seamus, who was only eleven, and told to cut off a calf's tallywags. I was so nervous, but I did it. That had been a nose crunching experience, but this little jaunt with Aiden seemed far more promising.

Unfortunately, Toby ruined it. Not wanting to be left behind, he said he was coming too. I made faces at him, but he ignored me. So no romantic moment seemed likely unless I could shove Toby off a cliff, and there was one on top of the big hill. Aiden saddled his and Toby's horses while I saddled my own. We threw on canteens and saddle bags with sandwiches. It turned out that Aiden had planned a picnic for us while we were out.

As always, the sun was alone in a cloudless sky. When we rode toward the saddle back hills, I noticed the women and children were all outside too, tilling the garden. Everybody outside but Arthur.

We reached the first dam, called a catch-dam according to Aiden, logs, rocks, and sandbags backing up water in a canal. These dams, he explained, fed water to the entire farm. Ingenious and I didn't care a whit about it. I wanted Aiden to shut up and pay attention to me. Didn't he know this might be our one moment in time to be Romeo and Juliet? Yet, all he wanted to do was show me the farm dams. He appeared unaware of my growing irritation and embarrassment.

Maybe this was romance in this part of the world. A guy took his favorite girl to his yam patch, yanked one out of the ground, and presented it to her.

As we entered the canyon between the two hills, Toby rode up beside me and whispered in a mocking tone, "If you want him to notice you're a girl, stop wearing boy's clothing."

Disheartened, I muttered, "Oh, shut up."

At first, in my state, I took no notice of the change in landscape. When I did, I saw the place was green as mint leaves, a lush paradise of trees, flowered bushes and fat grass. Primrose and thick grass hung over the stream banks as water scuttled along at a goodly speed. Being the dry season, it was down four or five feet leaving steep walls of dirt on each side.

Two hundred yards into the canyon, Aiden pulled up. "I want to show you something. You can see all the way to Rensburg from up there." He indicated the largest hilltop.

"Let's race up!" I shouted and leaped from my horse. Hurriedly tying the reins to a tree, I ran for the summit.

With both of us laughing, Aiden sprinted past me and reached the top first. He was crouching a few feet from the cliff's edge when I came up and collapsed on his shoulder. "You win."

"Hush," he snapped, his focus on what was below.

Indeed, we could see all the way to the haze of buildings in Rensburg, but the entire Bartlett farmstead drew all our attention. Below Robert and Joseph were racing their horses up the long driveway, accompanying a man in a carriage who was lashing his single horse. A half mile back, Dunford's horde raced after them, a dust cloud rising in their wake.

I gasped and started to return down to the horses, but Aiden yanked me back. "No. Stay here."

We watched as his brothers and the third man, the doctor no doubt, rushed inside. The fifty men pulled up at the garden, looking every bit marauders ready to destroy all in its path. From around the corner of the house, several men were dragging Joseph's screaming wife.

When Toby finally made it up, he fell down beside us, gasping for breath. "What are you two doing?"

"Dunford," I said. "He's here and he has Joseph's wife."

He peeked up enough to see. "Now we're all in for it."

"You're out of it, you hear me?" Aiden said. "You can't be seen down there. If they think you're not with us, they may release Roberta and leave us alone." As if he thought me dense, he took my shoulders. "If you come down, you threaten us all. Go! Get away and don't come back. I'll leave you my horse. It's got provisions."

I shook myself free, hurt by his screaming again, "Don't come back."

"I heard you," I snapped.

His eyes seemed to blame me for all this, and it was true. Dunford's pursuit of Toby was just for money, but his pursuit of me was for blood vengeance against my mother. Aiden scrambled down the hill to his horse and rode off. A half minute later, we saw him emerge from the hills and dash for the house. No one fired at him. For that, I was thankful.

The men spread out with Roberta, a noose now around her neck in front of them. Dunford dismounted and took the end of the rope, tugging it till she was by his side.

"We only want the boy and the girl," he called out. "No one has to be hurt."

From the house, Mr. Bartlett's voice carried over the fields. "They are not here. That is God's truth. Give us our daughter back."

Dunford shouted, "I do not believe your God's truth. Send them out now. No harm will befall this woman nor Toby and Glory. We only want what's ours."

Beside me, Toby spit out, "Liar!"

Eventually, to our surprise, the person who came out was Arthur. Tucking his nightshirt into his pants, he snapped his suspenders onto his shoulders. Confident as you please, he strode up to Dunford and said something I couldn't make out.

Anguish in my voice, I muttered, "What are you doing, Arthur?"

"Being an Englishman," Toby answered me with a hint of pride.

Down below, the outlaw earl tossed the end of the rope to another man and began circling Arthur. The Scot had to turn his head to follow him while also watching the men with Roberta. From behind, Dunford shouted with sudden rage. "You have caused me much trouble, Mr. McAuley. I have had enough of your meddling."

Without warning, he drew his pistol and shot Arthur in the back of the head.

Both Toby and I screamed, a sound that carried, and several men turned to look up. Hurriedly, we ducked down and hugged the ground.

Toby groaned, "He shot him. He just shot him.

I fought back tears but gave up and let them go down my cheek. Arthur had been our friend. He gave everything for us, his fortune, his future, his life, and he didn't deserve the end he got.

Toby cut into my misery. "What are we going to do?"

"I don't know. Why do I always have to know?"

"They're going to kill all the Bartletts to find us. We have to do something."

He was right. We could not allow Arthur's fate to visit the Bartlett family. We had to do something. I jumped to my feet, drew my pistol, and fired a shot in the air. Toby joined me, and we began waving our arms, shouting, "Up here. We're up here."

Just as everyone turned to look up at us, we bolted for our horses. When we neared them, a man stepped out from between the two, holding the reins like a trophy. I couldn't have been more shocked. It was Arlo Ives, our tormentor when we were captives. He had a wide, black-toothed grin.

"Howdy do, you two," he said with a cackle of laughter.

Too late, we tried to pull up, but he dropped the reins and grabbed onto both of us.

"Bet you didn't think you'd ever see old Arlo Ives again," he said.

We struggled, but he was strong and held on, shouting to others somewhere back along the stream. "I got them. I got them."

We punched but with no leverage did little good. He laughed each time one of us struck him as if we were trying to tickle him.

Then from somewhere, Toby came up with a rock and smashed his face, breaking his nose and some teeth. That gave me the chance to fish for my gun but found my knife. When I plunged it into his shoulder just below the collarbone, he howled. Toby struck him again and I stabbed him. Wild animals, no better than jackals out for the kill. Again and again, we struck him and stuck him till he went down, and his open-eyed stare told me he was dead.

Immediately, Toby dropped his blood-stained rock and ran at the horses twenty feet away, screaming, "Whoa!"

"Stop!" I called out but too late. He'd spooked the horses, and they ran off, disappearing around the curve. With the clamor of Dunford's men coming from the other direction, we had seconds till they were upon us.

"Come on." I pulled Toby down with me onto the dry streambed near the water, hoping to squeeze in under the grass and primrose hanging down, but it was not enough room to be hidden. Then, I saw it. A few feet away, under the overhang, was a burrow that might have belonged to a jackal. We dashed for it and scrambled in just as we heard the men coming round the curve.

It wasn't very big, but I hadn't seen it from above and thought it would keep us hidden. We dare not move. We dare not make a sound as men shuffled above us. I went rigid, held my breath, and promised God I'd give up orneriness if he just saved us. In my terror, though, I felt a murderous rage and wondered what God thought of that. Was this what took hold of Mama when she rampaged in olden days?

Above, a man with an English accent declared, "God's blood, the little savages killed the bastard."

"Got Old Ives good," someone else added.

"Where the hell are they?" That was Dunford's polished, upper crust voice, and he sounded frustrated. "You men, see if they're in the brush and trees up there." Seconds later, I thought he found us for he spoke as if directly to me, "Glory, I will find you. Your mother owes me, and you, dear, will pay the bounty."

From the scuffing movement just above, some dirt dislodged and showered down. I heard the cock of a pistol and a barely audible whimper from Toby.

"What have you found?" Dunford asked someone.

"Their tracks," a man replied.

That's when something moved beside me. A snake poked its slender head out from the branches, its tongue flickering. Dread froze every muscle of my body. A trickle of pee eased out of me.

The snake rose higher, then slumped down to the ground between us, slithered over to me, and crawled up into my lap. I wanted to flick it off but knew that was suicidal. It was too big, nearly a yard long, and its bite would juice me up good. I was sure it would strike anything that moved. Seeing it, Toby's eyes grew wide as saucer plates.

"If you found their tracks," Dunford said, "where the hell are they?"

The creature lingered on my stomach. I feared it would curl up and make itself at home. *Get off me, get off me, get off me.*

Finally, it slid down between my legs and out of the burrow. I released a long sigh as a native man above spoke in broken English, "They step horse here. Horse go Rensburg."

"Johannesburg. They're heading for Johannesburg," the first Englishman insisted. "We might run them down if we can move now."

Dunford said, "Hobbs, stay at the farmhouse with five men. They might come back."

When they retreated toward the house, Toby and I scrambled out of the burrow and climbed up on the bank, then headed in the other direction. Beyond the next bend our luck finally changed. One of the horses, Aiden's, was trotting back toward the farmhouse but stopped instantly when he saw us.

I'm good with horses. Not as good as Seamus but good. I told Toby to stand still and shut up while I approached it. Moving sideways very slowly, agonizingly slowly, and looking down, I muttered soothing words and finally got the reins. Mounting quickly, I pulled Toby up behind me and we set off at a tot I hopped would not be too loud. On the other side of the hill, we rode part way for Rensburg, then splashed into the middle of the stream, turned about, and headed west. I thought Mama would be proud of my trickery. Soon the little waterway cut deep into a wide arroyo, and we followed that for miles, leaving no tracks anywhere.

After two hours, I thought we were safely away.

"Where are we going now?" Toby asked.

"Our plans have changed," I said. "They'd catch us out if we tried for Johannesburg."

I told Toby our new plan, to go back to Kimberley and on to Cape Town. Dunford's men were swarming east and south hunting us, so we would ride westward, turning gradually south in a wide arc. As long as we had the horse and water, I did not fear the open country. Respected all wild country, yes, but did not cower at its prospect. I was raised in wild country though not this strange kind.

I think it's called hubris. My hubris. I thought more of my wilderness skills than were warranted. It was the mistake of my life.

CHAPTER FORTY

From the *Tragic History of the Northampton Affair* by Rupert Owen, 1910, 1st ed.

The clash between Dunford's militia and the Duke of Northampton's pitiable little band was inevitable. By the time it occurred, the fallen earl's alliance with Nyama could call upon forty men while the duke had far fewer. Never much of a force to begin with, he'd suffered departures along the way till his small group was down to eleven men and two women including the duchess, ever a stalwart campaigner.

For days, the duke had been following his foes' passage of destruction through the wild country of the northern Cape while they were relentlessly pursuing his son and the American girl. The outlaw band believed the boy carried a queen's ransom, the Holy Grail of their dreams, but after the Bartlett farm where the two youngsters evaded them once again, their capture appeared ever more distant, and those dreams began rotting on the vine. By the end of June, they were aching for a fight. Like the Nile crocodile, these violent men were ready to strike out at anything, and here came the duke and his small party right into their path.

Locally it was called the Battle of Iron Springs, but had it not been for the exulted names of the combatants, it wouldn't have been known at all. The fight was brief and vicious. At the end, between both armed groups, more than twenty lay dead, another ten wounded, and the duke's force was no more.

Transvaal, June 25, 1887

Fear consumed Julia as she rode single file with her husband's troop through a dark wood. Above, thick, overhanging trees blotted out the sun. But for the clop of hooves, a pervading silence had settled on the world. No doubt numerous beasts skulked within the shadows, including Dunford's murderous rabble. Feeling them watching her, gooseflesh erupted over her body like crawling ants. No former soldier like Coppersmith, it didn't take a Pasha Gordan to realize they were in mortal peril.

"Duchee, this no good," Lame Deer said in a hushed voice from behind her.

"I know," Julia replied, impatiently.

The Indian woman harumphed. For the last hour, even before they'd entered the woods, she'd been going on that they were no longer the pursuers but the pursued. After crossing into the Transvaal, they'd found themselves closing on Dunford's horde, seeing them only a few miles ahead when they crested a high hill. Being so close was foolish, and she'd told her husband so, but it was Coppersmith who answered, insisting she had nothing to fear. Edward echoed his words, always relying on his friend in these matters.

The soldier gave her a reassuring smile. "Don't worry, Duchess. We have things well in hand. Besides, where they are, your son must be nearby."

"I know that, sir," she snapped, refraining from arguing. It would do no good.

Later, after crossing a stream, Dunford's tracks vanished on the far bank. Now, worry showed even on Coppersmith's face. With the Cheyenne Looks Behind, Gatewood set off to find them while the rest of their little band proceeded on to find someplace to make a stand. That jarred Julia. Making a stand didn't sound like things were well in hand.

The path broke out of the woods into a field of tall grass. Fifty yards away, the sun glittered off a small river. Now, in the open, they formed into a tight group in which she rode in the middle. Edward and Coppersmith led while Todd and Adams—Julia thought of them as the Rorke's Drift men—flanked on the right. In their wildly colorful garb, the two cowboys Bradford and Potter took the left. Potter worried her. A boy yet at seventeen, he'd fallen in love with her back in London. She knew the symptoms. For the baby-faced lad, it was like medieval courtly love. Nothing he wouldn't do for her, which he told her many times. Now, even in this extremis, he thought he was on a lark, an adventure. That was far from the truth.

The Northampton policemen Evans and Bramley rode at the rear. Their poor horsemanship, especially Bramley's, relegated them to that post. Since Kimberley, the fat detective struggled to maintain his seat on the horse while nightly complaining of his sore rump.

Lame Deer and Little Hawk rode on either side of Julia to protect her, which might prove difficult since the plan was to make a stand like this was Rorke's Drift or the Little Big Horn.

From beside her, Lame Deer muttered again. "This bad, very bad,"

Julia sighed, "I know."

At the sound of horses approaching, she snapped her head around to see Gatewood and Looks Behind galloping up next to her husband.

"They're coming!" the old scout shouted. "We need to find cover now!"

"We're looking," Coppersmith said lamely.

"Then pick up the pace, general" Gatewood responded. "We ain't got time to dawdle."

Lame Deer emitted a high-pitched cry. She was pointing ahead to something in the distance, but at first no one saw anything.

Then Todd called out, "I see it. It's on the other side of the river."

"It looks like an old church," Potter said. His horse danced about as if catching the scent of danger. "Maybe a quarter mile."

Finally, through the trees along the river, Julia saw a small white church with a toppled bell tower and stone courtyard walls.

"Too late," Potter said, gesturing to the woods. "The ball is about to commence."

Dunford's forty men moved out of the shadows into the light of the meadow, perhaps sixty yards away, but they just sat their horses, watching like lions after a herd of wildebeest.

'Move forward slowly," the duke said in a calm voice. "Make for the river as if we haven't a concern in the world."

"I got plenty of concerns, Guvnor," Bradford said.

The duke ignored him. "When they come at us, we go hell for leather to the church."

When they started forward at an easy walk, Dunford's men jeered and mocked them. They called out to Julia describing abominable things they would do to her when they had her. Their laughter echoed through the valley.

Edward called back to his wife, "Julia, come up here."

"I think I…"

He cut her off brusquely, "Don't argue. Do it now."

She did, kneeing her horse up between her husband and Coppersmith. Lame Deer and Little Hawk tucked in behind her, all protecting her like a crown jewel because she was a woman, a white woman, a duchess. To Englishmen and most American men, no creature on earth deserved protection more than her. And that was as it should be. But as frightened as she was, it rankled her that she was being pinned in as if led to the slaughter with little she could do to save herself.

Suddenly, a high-pitched screech emanated from the brigands. Turning, Julia saw a lone rider galloping toward them like a man caught in frenzy. Above his head, he was swinging a scimitar, its wide blade glittering in the sun, and he was coming straight for her husband.

Drawing his stone ax, Little Hawk bolted from the formation, racing toward the man. His war cry shook the valley. To Julia, it was crazy, astonishing, and wondrous, two men rushing at each other in single combat out of Homer. The man with the scimitar had the greater reach, but the determining factor turned out to be horsemanship.

As they shot past each other, Little Hawk slid effortlessly to the side of his horse, ducking the sweep of the blade. He rose up and swung his horse about, charging his opponent who was struggling to turn. Little Hawk caught him in the temple with his ax. The blow cleaved his head and reverberated like he'd struck a tree.

Exultant, the Cheyenne raised his bloody ax to the sky and pierced the air with his war cry. The world fell silent for a half second, then the horde unleashed a furious rifle volley, punching scores of killing wounds into his body.

With screams of rage, they charged.

Coppersmith's voice rang out, "To the river."

Moments later, Julia plunged her horse into the water and plowed quickly across to the other bank. The air around her was alive with bullets snapping past her head. Hell had erupted from beneath the earth.

As everyone clambered up the riverbank, Lame Deer's horse was shot from under her, and she fell into the water. Julia dashed to her as Edward shouted, "No! Leave her. Come."

She pulled the frail old woman up behind her and pounded back up the bank. She'd promised Morgan she'd look after the old goat, and she would. When she saw the two bodies floating face down in the river, she froze. Blood stained the water about them. The colorful clothing identified the stocky cowboy Bradford, and she felt glad it wasn't Potter. The other was a Rorke's Drift man, both caught in the current and being carried off like driftwood.

Lame Deer slapped her head. "Ride, Wasicus!"

She did, kicking the horse into a gallop. Once they made the church courtyard, both women dismounted, and Julia drew her pistol and took a place beside Edward on the wall.

"Go inside the church," Edward ordered. "It'll be safer."

She turned on him. "I will not cower in a church waiting for my executioners."

After a moment, he nodded. Her hands were shaking as she aimed at the rabble hurtling toward them like Mongol hordes.

Out on the field, Potter was sprinting his horse for the courtyard, his red shirt and blue kerchief gaudy in the sunlight. The front flap of his hat was pinned back by wind. He didn't head for the gate but instead came directly at the wall. In seconds, his horse flew over it, the cowboy screaming almost in joy.

"Where's Todd?" Coppersmith asked.

"Down at the river. He and Looks Behind won't be coming."

Jumping down, he looked at Julia who gave him the hint of a smile, then joined them on the wall. Edward, Coppersmith, Gatewood, Evans, Potter, and Lame Deer, not much to hold back the horde.

One more man remained out in the field, struggling to reach the church, Bramley. He was bouncing like a wooden Jack in the Box and frantically whacking his horse's neck with the reins, but it moved no faster. Thirty yards yet to go, the horse bucked him off and bolted away. His eyes bulging in panic, Bramley regained his feet. His mewling sounds reached the church.

Evans jumped on his horse and darted from the courtyard. When he reached the man, not forty yards from the charging horde, they grasped hands, and Bramley shocked them all by yanking his fellow policeman from the saddle. The execrable man scrambled onto the horse and in desperation got this one moving. It was the most detestable thing Julia had ever witnessed.

Within seconds, the horde rode over Evans. When Bramley reached the courtyard, both Edward and Coppersmith jerked him violently from the saddle and threw him to the ground.

Edward cursed, "You bloody coward. I've never seen such spineless behavior and treachery. When we make Johannesburg, rest assured I will see you in jail."

On his backsides, Bramley scooted away, his face white and his eyes seeing only horror. Without rising, he reached the church on his bottom then crawled in through the open door.

"They're coming, boys," Gatewood said. "Better get ready."

Julia wondered if she'd ever see Toby again.

When the horde came within twenty yards, Coppersmith yelled, "Fire!"

Their shots rang nearly as one, and several fell, yet they kept coming, narrowing and attempting to breach the courtyard gate. It was bloody business. The din of battle consumed all. Potter was hit. With blood pumping out of his neck, he sat down, trying to hold the flow back with both hands, then collapsed. Julia turned away, shaken, just as a head poked up from the other side of the wall. When the man saw her, he grinned. She shot him in the face.

Out of the corner of her eye, she caught movement. A few feet away, another man straddled the wall, aiming a pistol at her head. Before she could move, he fired.

Lame Deer saw the duchess go down and jammed her pistol into the man's ribs, pulling the trigger three times till he fell back.

"Duke," she cried. "Duchee hurt."

Not only the duke but Gatewood and Coppersmith converged on the duchess, everyone left. They kept up a barrage against those trying to breach the gate, but it was hopeless. Men were clambering over the walls now.

At that moment, Bramley burst from the church, a screeching madman. His shirt was off, and his bare belly hung over his belt. Before anyone could act, he shot past them, past the stunned men at the gate, and out into the melee of riders. There was a lull as the horde retreated a step or two, mesmerized or frightened by the bare-chested man screaming like a banshee. Then, they all fired.

"Get her into the church," Edward shouted.

He lifted her, and Coppersmith ran ahead, throwing the door open. Lame Deer followed while Gatewood covered them, shooting relentlessly from two pistols. He knelt by the church entrance and crossed himself.

"Orvill Gatewood," he shouted. "kilt this day by a pack of…"

Gunfire ripped through him.

Coppersmith tried to shut the door, but it wouldn't close all the way. Pistol drawn, he knelt by it. A few feet back by a toppled pew, the duchess was stretched out on the floor, perhaps dead. The duke gripped her hand, saying over and over, "Don't leave me, luv. Don't leave me."

No sounds were coming from outside. Lame Deer was sure that soon those men would come, and soon she would die. She'd lived a long life, longer than most. It had not always been a good life, but if it had come to an end, she was ready to meet her ancestors.

Kneeling beside the duchess, she saw the woman was breathing. The bullet had cut a deep gash across her cheek, the bone visible amid streams of blood. Then it had taken off the top of her ear. Her hair was messy with blood, and her face swelling up. The Cheyenne woman lifted the woman's skirt, and with her knife, cut strips from her white undergarments and bandaged the wounds. That was the best she could do. Duchee would live or die on her own.

A flat voice came from beyond the door. "Duke, I am Victor Nyama. Perhaps you have heard of me. We should speak. A truce. You see, you have bloodied us quite well. By my quick count, we have eleven men dead and four more not likely to make it through the day. That leaves just twenty-five of us and not all of them are in perfect health. You, however, are far worse off. You have no one left but Captain Coppersmith and an old woman."

Enraged, the duke shouted, "You shot my wife."

"I assure you that was not my intent. I gave strict orders she was not to be harmed, but alas, these things happen. Is she dead?"

"No, but she needs a doctor."

"We can arrange that. No one else needs to be hurt. I believe we can come to an agreement."

"I doubt that," the duke replied. "You are hardly trustworthy."

Nyama chortled. "Ah, my dear duke, you can trust my venality. Your son has led us a merry chase, and we have not the slightest idea where he and the girl are. The only possibility we have of achieving any financial gain is you. After all, you are a very rich man I am told. The way I see it, we will hold onto your wife and the others while you negotiate with Rhodes or whomever for a substantial loan, which you will then pass along to us. Let's call it a fee for helping you survive."

The duke and Coppersmith stared at each other a long moment, then the soldier shrugged.

The duke asked, "Will Dunford comply?"

"He has no choice."

"No harm must come to Coppersmith or the Indian woman."

"Of course."

After a moment, the duke nodded to Coppersmith, who stepped back from the door. "You have an agreement, sir. You may enter."

CHAPTER FORTY-ONE

Northern Cape Colony, June 25, 1887

To Morgan, it felt like they were getting close even though the African veldt seemingly spread endlessly in front of them. As she and Seamus pushed their horses as hard as they dared, noon came and went without her having a thought of stopping or eating in the saddle. They had nothing to eat anyway. They'd finished the last of the dried meat early yesterday, but they were not starving or desperate. There was enough game about. She just didn't want to take the time to hunt, skin, and cook. And besides, they had to be close now.

Temperatures had been freezing last night but had risen with the sun. Early on, Seamus had unfastened the brass buttons of Will's old cavalry jacket, and Morgan removed her coat and tied it behind her saddle.

An image of the burned-out farm they had stopped at with Iron Chest came to her and with it a surge of guilt once again for not acknowledging Seamus as her son. She'd introduced herself to the men there but not him or the old Cheyenne warrior. A small thing not meant as a slight. She simply didn't want to take the time to answer questions about it. But it had plagued her since. *Kaffir* was the term here, half-breed or Injun back home, and people took that as real, a part of the order of nature itself.

Her husband Will must be looking down on her with scorn. She could picture his face, a mild expression of disappointment that cut her to the quick. Oh, far worse even than her father's scoldings of which there'd been many. She would never fail to claim Seamus as hers again.

As they rode at an easy gallop, Morgan glanced at her son, at his drawn, determined face. He would not stop till Glory was back with them. This boy was the best of her family. Nothing could ruffle his feathers. He seemed incapable of a mean thought. He'd inherited his Cheyenne father's courage and her sand, but God knows where that even-tempered disposition came from. Only sixteen, he shouldered burdens even a grown man should not have to bear.

Seamus and Glory filled her heart. They were her life. That was the true nature of things. God sometimes put terrible hardships on people, she thought. With this relentless enterprise, she was likely to get her two remaining children killed. The Lord just couldn't put that one on her.

Impulsively, she asked Seamus, "You still sweet on that Olsen girl?"

Startled, he turned in the saddle. "What?"

"That Olsen girl. You still sweet on her?"

"Are you feeling all right, Mama?"

She chuckled awkwardly. "Sure. Can't a mother ask her son about the girls in his life?'

"No, she cannot," he replied. "Especially not in the African bush."

She held a hand up in surrender. "All right. I won't pry."

He shook his head as if trying to dispel an unwanted thought. They rode on in silence for a few more minutes till amid the drum of their horses' hooves Seamus said, "I'm kind of keen on Cousin Isobel."

"Cousin Isobel? You mean the duke's cousin?"

"Do you know another Cousin Isobel?"

"Well, she's better than that Lillian Smith," Morgan said. "There's no future in sniffing around a married woman."

Seamus chaffed. "I wasn't sniffing around her. She's just…forget it."

Morgan went on, "You know Cousin Isobel is part of an English noble family and…"

"...and I'm a half-breed. I know."

She looked hard at him. "You're my son. I gave birth to you, and I know this, boy, you're better than any of that British lot, and don't you ever forget it"

He laughed. "Calm down, Mama. Nothing to get upset about."

She sighed. "All I meant was Cousin Isobel's home is in England and you live in Montana."

He merely shrugged, and that ended their conversation. No more was said for the next half hour, not till they came to a creek and let the horses drink. Morgan gestured to the northeast. "The Bartlett farm should be up that way a few miles if that peddler fellow got the right of it."

Yesterday morning, they'd come across an itinerant peddler who'd told of Dunford's band raiding the farm a few days before but had no information about the children.

Seamus said. "Hope they're not burned out."

So did she since dead farmers could tell her nothing about where her daughter might be.

In another hour, they reached the Bartlett spread with fields of corn and barley and grazing sheep. A hundred yards from the house, they pulled up and sat their horses studying the fields, the outbuildings, and the hills to the north. Something was wrong.

"No one is out working," Seamus said.

"No farmer I know takes a nap in the afternoon." Then she added, "I'll take a look. Best you cover me from here."

His saddle creaked as he turned sharply to her. "Don't do that, Mama. You're not going to leave me back when things get rough. I go all the way with you and that's it."

She sighed. "All right. Let's see what this is."

Just as they started forward, two men stepped from an outbuilding followed by a third man leading a woman with a rope tied to her neck. Another one appeared on the roof with a rifle, his figure silhouetted against the pale blue sky. A fifth man hovered by the door. Morgan knew it was a show designed to be threatening and intimidating but not for them. They hadn't been spotted yet. Likely to those inside the house.

Several rifles poked from the house as an unarmed older man came out adjusting his suspenders. Proud in his bearing and stride, he walked right up to the two outlaws, not cowed by them or their menacing display. This was a Mexican standoff. When next one of the outlaws jabbed his finger into the old man's chest, a cry came from the outbuilding roof. The man there was pointing at Morgan and Seamus, and everyone turned toward them.

"I guess we just put a skunk in their barn," Seamus said.

He and Morgan ambled their horses up the driveway. She hoped no one would see a woman and a boy as a threat, no matter how well armed. Not yet at least. That hope vanished when she realized one of them was Henry Hobbs. He knew she was a sharpshooter with the Wild West, and that would put him on alert. But maybe not. She had a much different appearance from the last time he'd seen her in his Scotland Yard office. Now, she wore a flat-topped hat, had her hair tied in a long ponytail, and sported a workman's shirt.

As they drew near though, Morgan realized from his sudden grin he recognized her. When they dismounted and approached, she carried her rifle loosely, pointed harmlessly to the ground, and even forced a smile. "Superintendent Hobbs, what a surprise seeing you here."

He did not reply. Instead he took time to roll a cigarette as if he hadn't a care in the world. He licked the paper and stuck it in his mouth, then struck a match with his thumb and lit it, watching her the entire time over the sudden flame. He shook the match out and dropped it in the grass. As he did, she gave his outlaw partner next to him a quick glance. Blond hair perfectly combed and a trim beard like he was trying to maintain a well-bred appearance, yet his eyes were mad with fright or rage or both. His hands gripped tightly to a rifle as if he expected to use it.

"Ah, Mrs. Raines," Hobbs said, "your visit is quite unfortunate for you and your kafir."

"Why is that?" she said evenly.

He nodded toward the woman in the noose thirty yards away. "You see, that one we must keep saintly. Good faith in bargaining for the money the Bartletts have and we want. You? I doubt if you're saintly to begin with."

"Why are you even here, Hobbs? Why aren't you with Dunford?"

He cupped a hand over his cigarette, inhaled, then withdrew it from his mouth. "I don't know if you've noticed, but the earl is quite mad, and this whole thing is going to hell. He was never interested in the diamond, not really, just in your daughter. He wants to kill her to get at you. It even gives me the jimjams. The lads here and I are getting out of this damn country while we can. We're just trying to shake a little payment for our troubles out of these fine people. It only seems fair, don't you think?"

Morgan took in the other three men. Their attention was fixed on her. The man holding the noose stepped in behind the young woman, placed his hand on her hair, and jerked her head back. He gave Morgan a toothless grin.

She addressed the older man who'd come from the house. "Mr. Bartlett, I presume. Are there any more men here beyond these five?"

He gave her a curious squint. "No, ma'am."

Without warning, she raised her rifle and shot the man with the rope in the forehead. The crack of Seamus's gun erupted next to her as she fired at the man on the roof. He toppled to the ground with a dull whump. Lastly, she swung her aim to the man by the outbuilding door, and as he turned to run, shot him down, expending two bullets to do so. After that, everything was silent but for the screaming of the woman with the noose around her neck. She was running for the house, the rope trailing behind her, when a young man burst from the door and caught her up in his arms.

Morgan turned back to Hobbs, who was lying on the ground, his blond colleague dead beside him. Hobbs had a wound in his chest that was bubbling blood. Yet alive, he wouldn't last much longer.

Holstering his colt, Seamus stepped over to him and removed the pistol from the man's belt.

Morgan knew the dime novels written about her and others had the heroes giving the villains a fair shake in gunfights. That was comical. No one ever did that. She never did, and she'd taught Seamus that if the fight was to be deadly, he must shoot first. Exactly what he'd just done. Hobbs and the other man could not match her son's gun skills.

In a weak voice, the detective said, "He shot me."

"He did. He got you good," she replied and knelt beside him. "Where's my daughter?"

He coughed and spit blood over his cheeks. "We just wanted out."

Seamus said, "Well, pard, you're out right proper now."

Hobbs clutched Morgan's wrist. "Get me a doctor. I don't want to die here."

Morgan leaned over him so he could see her face clearly. "No doctor can help you now, Hobbs. In another minute, you're going to be negotiating with Saint Peter to keep you out of the fires of Hell. I'd get my speech ready. Help me and he might help you. Where's my daughter?"

His mouth opened and shut then he murmured, "She and the boy were headed for Johannesburg. That's all I know." He took several more breaths then chuckled, "Better hurry. Dunford's got fifty men and he was right behind them." He grimaced in pain. "I did some good work as a bobby. Do you think that will count with God?"

She said, "Nope."

He tried to reply but his eyes died out first.

She looked up and saw the entire Bartlett family had come outside and they were staring at her. Mr. Bartlett said, "You're Glory's mother, I presume. We did not think you real."

"I am real all right, and this is my boy Seamus, the best son a mother ever had."

The children laughed when Seamus rolled his eyes in embarrassment.

Morgan and Seamus didn't stay long. There were still a few hours of daylight left, and they could cover several miles in that time. They learned that Arthur McAuley was dead and buried on the farm and confirmed what Hobbs had said about the children headed east for Johannesburg, looking to find the big man in these parts, Cecil Rhodes. Aiden, the youngest boy, assured them they were riding a good horse and had some food and water to last a couple days.

Generously, Mr. Bartlett exchanged two of his best horses for their mounts, and the women packed their saddle bags with fresh provisions. Then they were off.

As they rode beside the stream in the direction of Rensburg, Morgan pulled up.

"What is it, Mama?" Seamus asked.

"What would your sister do?"

He gave a snort. "She's too ornery to do what anyone expects."

"That's what I was thinking. She could have gone anywhere. But Dunford was headed for Johannesburg. If I don't know where your sister is, I do know where he is. Kill Dunford and she should be safe. We're going to Johannesburg."

PART FIVE
THE KALAHARI

CHAPTER FORTY-TWO

Kalahari Desert, June 27, 1887

We'd come far into desert country, but I'd little choice. Men were following us, and I'd had to push the horse hard going directly west. With the moon up, we rode through much of the night, praying we didn't run into lions out hunting or anything else. In the morning the trackers were still back there. Had I swung south toward Kimberly as we intended, they'd have cut us off.

I'd first seen them two days ago from a hillock, just a haze of movement seven or eight miles back. I couldn't distinguish the shapes, but their advance was too steady to be anything but human. Later when they grew closer, I saw they were on foot, and they were relentless. That scared me. We had a horse, yet they gained on us. How could they do that? Now, they were less than three miles back and closing. And we were at their mercy, which I figured was in short supply.

The land was dry with brush, baked dirt, and the occasional stunted tree. So far though, we'd found enough water, or at least our horse had. I called him Horace. Horace the horse. A damn fine animal. Seemingly, he could sniff out water ten miles away. Giving him his head, he always found a hole or creek, few and far between as they were. I'd pat his neck and say, "Good boy, Horace. Quite the nose you have."

Toby missed a lot of this since he was always sleeping. Behind me in the saddle, he wrapped his arms tightly around my waist, rested his head against my back, and somehow slept without falling off. I was his bed and his pillow. I desperately wanted to sleep too but knew with certainty I'd fall off, bringing us both down and maybe losing Horace.

It was late afternoon, and I figured tonight those tracking us would catch us up. I settled into my head I'd have to use the pistol. Two of them, five bullets. Normally, that should be enough, but I suspected these were not men easy to kill.

Something else bothered me just as bad. Yesterday, I saw a big cat not a hundred yards away, loping along easy as you please, a small animal in its mouth. It wasn't a lion. I knew that. It was either a cheetah or a leopard. I remembered Aiden saying that all the lions and other killers were over here in the bush country. I hoped they would eat the men following us.

I woke Toby up with a shake of my shoulder. "Look."

"Blimey," he muttered. "I was safely back at Becket Castle, eating a big meat pie, then I wake up here with you."

"At least you slept. I've been awake for hours."

"Someone has to drive the horse."

I turned in the saddle. "You don't drive a horse."

"I know that. I was just joking. Where are we?"

"Who knows."

"Then where are we going?"

"There. That rock." I pointed to a rock mound a mile ahead. Maybe twenty or thirty feet high, it looked like God dropped a giant cow patty right here in the middle of the desert. "The men tracking us are closing. They'll catch up tonight. We can make our stand there. It's not much, but it might give us an edge."

"Our stand! We can't make a stand. We're just two kids. Why don't we just ask them for help? Did you ever think of that?"

"Damn it, Toby, keep up," I cursed. "They're here to kill us. If I go a little north, they follow. I go a little south, they still follow us. They want us and they want the diamond."

Disheartened, he replied, "Okay. Maybe you're right."

"You still have it?"

"Yes, it's in my underpants."

I snorted. "No woman will ever wear it now."

"Oh, haw, haw," he said, then added in alarm, "What is that?"

I stared ahead and saw something that shot spikes of terror through me. Far away, beyond the rock, a red cloud was rising out of the desert and coming fast. It stretched north and south as far as the eye could see and reached steadily toward the sky as it came on. I'd never seen the like of it, I had heard about dust storms on the prairie from Papa.

"Don't get caught out in one," he'd warned. "The dirt will tear the flesh right off your skin and fill your mouth. You'd be gone."

This one was red, all red like a wave of blood coming for us. I kicked the horse into a full on sprint for the rock mound. The storm blotted out the sun, and we rode into its great shadow. The wind picked up. So fast the cloud was, in seconds it touched the sky, a giant wall, and we were racing toward it. It seemed alive. Great swells and billows roiled up and down its surface. The thing kept coming and growing, about to roll over the mound. We weren't going to make it.

A hundred yards from the rocks, the storm had risen miles and miles high and howled like a thousand lions, its tendrils reaching out for us. As sand began stinging my face like needles, I banged my heels into the horse harder.

Just when the wall of furious sand rushed over the mound, we slid to a halt, jumped down and ducked into a little nook. I held fiercely to the reins. Day had turned to shadows. And there was the hard smell of iron. With the rock protecting us, dust swirled about but no worse than what a gust of wind might stir up. The roar was deafening, but the vast cyclone of sand was passing over our heads.

I pulled one of Aiden's shirts from the saddle bags and tied it around the horse's head, grabbed the blanket, then still holding tight to the reins, collapsed beside Toby.

He shouted over the din. "Do you think those men made it?"

"I hope not."

We pulled the blanket over us creating our own little cave and began the long wait for the storm to end.

That turned out to be all night and most of the next day. The storm was a monster. When sunlight finally returned and we stepped out of our little den, we saw the men who'd been tracking us, or what was left of them, and went out for a closer look. Fifty yards from safety was as far as they got. They were on their knees, huddled together arm in arm and covered in red sand. Their mouths, which were filled with the desert, stood agape in a rictus of horror.

"My God," I muttered.

"Come on," Toby said, pulling me away.

When we reached our nook, he said, "Let's not go anywhere today. It's almost dark, and our camp seems safe enough for the night."

I agreed, not wanting to venture on any more than he did. "We can head south tomorrow. We might even be in Kimberley in two or three days."

I gave the horse most of the canteen water, pouring it into a tin cup over and over as he lapped it up. I tied him about five yards off to a sturdy bush growing out of a crack in the rock.

"Sleep tight, Horace. You saved us all," I said, kissing his dirty cheek.

Toby and I had no food, and we drank the remaining water, a couple swallows each. Finding more the next day would be Horace's first task.

With the last of the sun, we snuggled into the nook's shadows. I had to admit Toby had been a good pard, as Seamus liked to say. An annoying one, yes, but he knew we were on the edge of never leaving this desert alive and yet did his part, that is if his part wasn't too demanding. I thought of telling him so but then he'd likely ruin it by saying something insufferable.

When darkness came, temperatures fell, and we pulled the blanket up over us. I put the pistol between us.

"Why are you doing that?" Toby asked.

"So you don't try anything, buster."

He paused a second then we both laughed, and I said, "It hurts to sleep on it, and if I need it, I have it right here."

While Toby fell fast asleep, I lay awake, seeing us riding around in circles in the next few days and never getting out of this damn place. Annoyingly, Toby was a turbulent sleeper, turning every whichaway and pulling the blanket off me each time. I yanked it back. I was all afret then, thinking how maybe Horace wouldn't find any water tomorrow and we'd die of thirst. Someone had to do the fretting.

Fortunately, those thoughts didn't come with me when I finally fell asleep. Instead, I dreamed of home and the sweet water of Lone Tree Creek. I saw myself picking berries along the banks with my brother Will Junior, who was long dead now of pneumonia, but not dead in my head. I felt comfortable, happy, warm, even loved, and never wanted to wake. I knew it was a dream but real to me because I saw Papa striding down the hill with a big grin and waving at us.

Then he was gone, and I was screaming.

A bear trap had clamped down on my shoulder. Enormous pain seared into me, and fierce yellow eyes glared at me just inches from my face. The beast's teeth had sunk deep in my shoulder, and it was dragging me off into the bush.

I tried to swing at it, but I had no leverage. Somewhere in my terror, I realized I was about to be eaten. My screaming echoed into the empty night.

Then I heard a gunshot, then another, and someone yelling. The beast flinched and dropped me. It growled, then dashed away after a third shot. A leopard. Aiden had said they were cowards, but who had come to save me?

And there was Toby standing above me with the pistol. He grabbed me and pulled me to my feet. "Come on."

We hurried back to the nook where awkwardly, he patted my back and told me it would be all right. Still caught within an unyielding terror, nothing hurt. I said through chattering teeth, "You saved my life."

Then, being Toby and mandated by God to say stupid things, he blurted out, "Did you have to scream so loud? Every lion within five miles is going to be on us."

A sharp retort flashed in my brain then was gone when pain so fierce came over me that my knees give out, and I hit the ground in a stupor. Vaguely, I was aware of Toby dragging me back to the blanket. Blood soaked my shirt. The leopard's teeth had opened several punctures in my shoulder and maybe broken my collarbone. Toby grabbed the canteen, saying he'd wash the wounds, but we had no water.

"Where's Horace?" I mumbled.

"The leopard scared him off," Toby said.

Then the horse was likely on his way back to the Bartlett ranch if he could make it. That put us in a bad way. I was sure I couldn't survive this. We were now stuck in a vast desert without a horse and no water. Soon, I would become feverish and then nothing could stop my slide into the afterlife. Who would I have married? Not Aiden, that was sure. How would my life have turned out? I've only been alive twelve years, not enough to live much, but not enough to have piled up too many wrongs. I guess I'd been nasty a few times, but God won't hold that against me, will he?

Toby stared at the canteen for a second, then said, "I still better clean your wounds as best I can."

He opened my blouse and using the shirt I'd put over the horse's head during the sandstorm, began washing the wounds with my own blood, which was flowing freely. His face was a twisted grimace of disgust. He didn't much like doctoring, and I chuckled. I thought he might faint.

"Don't look at my breasts," I said, hoping to distract him.

"What breasts? You haven't got any breasts."

"Well, I will someday."

"Yes, you will, and I'll say I was of speaking acquaintance with them when they were babies."

"Oh, you're such a rogue, Toby Becket."

Half smiling, he gave a snort.

After cleaning the wounds, he said he would stay up the rest of the night and keep guard with the gun and its last bullet. He had been right. Nothing attracts flesh eaters more than a scream.

By morning, I was on my way out of this world, and I was scared. It was cold, but I was sweating. My mouth felt like a dried up apple. My shoulder was on fire like someone dropped burning coals on it, and my stomach wanted to vomit up the nothing it had inside.

We started out walking anyway, Toby acting like the pack horse with our meager stuff but made no more than twenty yards before struggling back to the camp. I was done.

"Take the water and go, Toby," I said weakly. "You might run into someone."

He shook his head, gesturing to the great desert surrounding us. "We have no water, and in case you haven't figured it out yet, this isn't Fleet Street. I wouldn't make five miles."

So that was it. He sat beside me in silence, not upset, just resigned. He was twelve. He should have been railing against his fate. We spent the day lying in the shade and then that night snuggling under the blanket in the cold, the heat from my fever keeping him warm.

That final day, long before dawn and very cold, Toby and I remained huddled under the blanket. I was shivering. In my delirium, the sky was a starless black. Somewhere, a distant lion bellowed. Soon, a pinkish glow began to appear on the far horizon bringing dawn with it. Nearby, a porcupine that had been using a small cave in the rock, burrowed in to sleep for the day.

By daylight, I was gibbering, falling in and out of consciousness. During one of my waking moments, Toby jumped up and started shouting and waving his arms, "Hey! Over here! Over here! Help us!"

He was obviously crazy too. He picked up the pistol and fired the last bullet into the air. "Hey! Over here!"

I didn't know who he was yelling at. Finally, several half-naked men were hovering over me. There must have been a lot of insects around because I heard constant clicking. Reaching a hand up to them, I asked in Cheyenne, "Who are you?"

All the while, darkness was circling. It closed in and then dropped me into a vast nothingness.

CHAPTER FORTY-THREE

Transvaal, June 29, 1887

Swaddled in bandages, Julia's head throbbed like a horse was inside kicking her skull with its hind legs. The blue bandana Potter had given her covered her face. Her beauty had been her cachet, her weapon, but now she wanted no one to see the scarred, gnarled disfigurement of her face. Her jaw was so swollen, she could not eat. She could barely drink water, and talking was an effort of prodigious will. She supposed there would be many glad to see her silent.

After the battle when Julia had regained consciousness, she'd met the so-called doctor Nyama had promised, a man kidnapped for her and his own wounded men. He was a drunkard and not even a doctor, only a pharmacist from some small village, a man who lanced boils, gave enemas, and dispensed drugs for anyone who could pay. She would shoot him if he tried to give her an enema but prayed he had laudanum for the pain. He didn't.

When he poured whiskey over her wounds, she screamed loud enough to have the dead walking the earth again. Then he skewered her cheek with needle and thread, which had her moaning and in tears. Even Lame Deer, hardly her friend, tried to ease her agony. The quack left it to the old Indian woman to rebandage her. The duchess never wanted that man near her again.

Near sunrise, as she rested her head on her husband's shoulder, she stared at the odd arrangement of stars disappearing in the morning twilight. Both were wrapped in a blanket against the numbing cold. Coppersmith and Lame Deer huddled near the fire, all of them surrounded by vile men.

Julia observed with not a small level of disgust more and more men come out of their tents or sleeping blankets. This Nyama fellow had set his camp at the edge of a forest where a gentle stream flowed. Beyond that was an open field of shortgrass with another wood two hundred yards away. None of it suggested escape for them, and besides, she couldn't ride a horse at more than a walk without her head breaking apart. Riding in a wagon was also impossible because of all that jostling. Each day when the four of them were transported, she walked, fuming at the abomination of forcing a duchess to walk.

The four of them were listening to an argument among factions of Nyama's men, and it was becoming heated. A few wanted to continue after Toby and Glory because that's where the diamond was and a bloody fortune for all. That was Dunford. Most, though, saw this escapade of carnage doomed from the start and wanted to abandon it. Men had died, and those who remained had little to show for the effort. They wanted to exact money from Edward by ransoming the duchess, then scatter to the winds. Nyama's argument.

What lies! Dunford's purpose was to catch Glory, and that put Toby at dire risk. It was detestable, but that was Dunford in a word. *Detestable.* Once, Morgan had mentioned that she and the earl were bitter enemies over something to do with cattle and Indians, but Julia knew little more than that. All this because of that hatred.

Not listening to the argument anymore for what did it matter, she squeezed in closer to Edward. Coppersmith dropped more branches on the fire and sparks sputtered up. The flickering glow of the flames reflected off Lame Deer's leathery face. Squatting, she squeezed in closer, attempting to drive the chill from her old body. She wore a heavy coat Coppersmith had given her, saying he'd sleep by the fire that night and be warm enough. Typically good-hearted John.

Julia winced as a new barrage of pain banged through her head, and she groaned. Edward gave her a gentle squeeze with his arm.

She desperately wanted to throw back her head and wail but refused to give Dunford the satisfaction of seeing her in pain. Surprisingly, since the battle, the one who tended her was Lame Deer, changing her bandages, listening to her cursing, ignoring her complaining.

As Coppersmith stirred the fire with a stick, he spoke softly so as not to be overheard, "This Dunford Nyama alliance is about to bust asunder."

"We should be prepared to flee into the trees if the chance arises," Edward responded.

Coppersmith glanced at the old Indian woman. "Do you understand, Lame Deer?"

Her nose wrinkled as if sniffing a pungent odor, exaggerating the deep lines of her face. "Lame Deer understand your mother a goat."

Julia snickered. Then her shoulders tensed when she saw Dunford approach. Bundled in an extra coat and wearing a broad brimmed army hat, the man squatted at the fire and held his hands over it. "It's hard to believe we're in Africa and it's this damn cold."

"What do you want, Dunford?" Edward demanded.

"I want to give you a chance to stay alive," he replied, rubbing his hands together. "I'd kill for a pair of gloves." He cocked his head toward the duke. "Edward, you must know when Nyama gets what money he can, he will kill the lot of you."

Edward released Julia. "I am the Duke of Northampton, sir. I will answer to nothing else from you."

Dunford gave a short laugh. "He plans to kill all of you, uh, *duke*."

"We are aware of the possibility," Edward replied.

"Not a possibility. A certainty." Dunford gave Edward his most sincere expression. "At the snail's pace we're moving, we should finally reach Johannesburg day after tomorrow. My men and I can get all of you into the town before Nyama knows what's happening. You will be safe there."

The duke's answer to the proposal was cold as the morning air. "I wouldn't trust you, Dunford, if you were bearing a letter with the queen's seal."

At the distinct sound of a bird's call, a rapid, high-pitched trilling, Julia noticed Lame Deer's head snap around and her mouth lift in a thin smile. Julia didn't know what to make of that, but then the old Indian woman was an odd bird. She turned back to Dunford.

The man's thick brows knitted into an expression of infuriating smugness, the sincerity having vanished. "You should think it over. With the duchess's injuries, I don't think you have much choice."

She was the one who replied, the words struggling out slow but precise, "Bloody bastard. Go to hell."

Dunford rose. "I was sad to find that you'd been wounded in the face, duchess. Such a shame to have made grotesque that which had once been so beautiful."

Coppersmith shot to his feet, but the duke's voice was brusque. "Leave it, John." Then to Dunford, "Show yourself in England, I'll see you hang."

Tipping his hat to them, the earl strode back into the shadows. They were still staring after him when Nyama entered their firelight. "I take it, the earl has been his usual pleasant self."

"What do you want, Nyama?" Edward asked.

The highwayman held his hands out as if his purpose was obvious. "To barter for your lives."

Through the constant throbbing in her head, Julia tried to listen while her husband actually bargained with a man who was ready to end them if he couldn't get what he wanted. Eventually, the deal was set, but there was no shaking of hands. For Edward's life, the highwaymen would receive twenty thousand pounds. For Julia's, another twenty. For Coppersmith's, five thousand, and for Lame Deer's a farthing.

Nyama thought himself amusing, but Julia wondered what their true value was. In this place, in this situation, she'd come to realize Lame Deer's worth vastly exceeded her own. The Indian woman could sneak off and survive in the wild, but instead, she stuck by Julia and toiled to keep her alive. The duchess glanced at the wrinkled old termagant, at the countless lines in her face that told of strange and no doubt extraordinary experiences over a long life. She saw in the woman's face an earned confidence and an indifference to what others thought of her. For just a moment, the duchess envied her. Oddly, Lame Deer was smiling, and Julia doubted it was because the woman was being ransomed for a farthing.

Nyama was explaining that when they reached Johannesburg, Edward would enter the town accompanied by two of the outlaws. As the wealthy duke, he could easily raise the ransom in gold because that was what they had in abundance there. Edward agreed, the plan was set, and Nyama returned to his men.

When he was gone, Lame Deer leaned in and said in a low voice, "She has come."

"Who has come?" Coppersmith asked.

The Indian woman spit on the ground as if indicating he was a fool for not knowing. "Morgan. Morgan has come."

"Well, if she hasn't brought a platoon of fusiliers with her, she should ride on to Johannesburg for help."

The Indian woman hissed harshly, "Get up! The hunt start."

Coppersmith said, "What is the old bat blathering about?"

Edward stood, helping Julia to her feet. "If Morgan is near, we must be prepared to flee for surely something is about to happen."

Down at the stream, five men were taking care of their morning needs. One man had a towel draped over his shoulder and was kneeling, washing his face. A second was filling a coffee pot, another man a canteen. A little farther downriver two more men were peeing, not caring that women were nearby. The grass in the field bent in a light wind, and beyond, a flock of birds escaped the trees in the shadowy woods.

At that moment, Julia became aware of a profound silence. Everyone stopped what they were doing, and the birds ceased their morning songs. In the far wood, another flock of birds fluttered out of the treetops. One of the peeing men looked up. An instant later, blood, bone, and brain tissue exploded out the back of his head. Then came the sound of the distant shot.

Next, the man with the coffee pot was hit, the bullet bursting out his back. He tumbled backward and lay still. Again, the sound of the rifle followed an instant later. The rest of the men ran back for safety amid the trees. The second man relieving himself was not quick enough. Wetting his trousers in his haste, he took a single step, then a bullet impacted his back and debris exited his chest.

Chaos erupted in the camp, men seemingly dashing everywhere, ducking in behind trees, a few firing shots in the direction of the distant woods. When Edward and Coppersmith hurried Julia back into their little niche, the mad Indian woman gazed at them, her eyes alight. "Now you see. My daughter Crow Killer has come."

At that moment, Morgan and Seamus did an odd thing, stepping out of the distant woods into the clear, rifles in hand, and calmly walking several yards to a gnarled tree standing like a sentinel alone in the field. The two of them leaned back against it in a relaxed pose as if taking a break from a morning walk. They were daring Nyama and his men to come after them. It seemed foolish, but Julia knew that if these men did ride out, it would be a bloodbath.

Coppersmith said, "What is she doing? She'll get herself and the boy killed."

"I don't think so," Edward said. "No matter what happens, this is our chance. Take the canteens. When the shooting commences, our guards will be distracted, then we escape."

Twenty feet away, Nyama was looking through a spyglass. His voice rose. "Just two of them, a woman and a fakir. They must be decoys. There must be more in those woods."

Dunford came up on horseback, his saddle bags draped behind the saddle as if ready to ride out. "No, I assure you, there are just the two. That woman and her half-breed son. They are shootists, but we can easily ride them down. They'll run back for their woods like frightened rabbits anyway. If we do not deal with them now, they will be sniping at us all the way to Johannesburg."

Despite her pain, Julia cried out in fury, "You worthless bastard, Hell has come for you!"

He drew his pistol and rode directly toward her. Both Edward and Coppersmith stepped in front of her, but it was their two guards that stopped him, raising their rifles at Dunford. His eyes had darkened but not in anger. Julia saw that he was afraid. Dunford was afraid. Indeed, with Morgan about, he could not put himself out in the open without being shot.

Nyama's voice rang out. "Dunford, enough. Without her, we have no ransom."

For a moment, Julia thought the earl would shoot anyway, but instead his eyes bore into her like knives and his smile like that of a Bedlam inmate, one she knew she would remember for the rest of her life ut what he said would haunt her even more. "I will teach your child pain, Madam, then he will die with the girl."

Julia gasped as he swung his horse about and galloped off through the trees in the opposite direction from Morgan.

Nyama shouted after him. "Coward. Running from a woman!" Shaking his head in disgust, he turned to his men. "Don't stand there. Mount up. We can handle one woman and her fakir"

Nyama had left the wounded and the two guards, and that left fifteen men, last of the great Dunford Nyama raiding party. When they were ready and all sat their horses at the edge of the trees, they did not move. Julia understood. It was clear to them someone had made those long-distance shots and surely it was not either of the two standing out in the field.

As they waited, uncertain, Seamus appeared on his horse and rode thirty yards toward them, screaming insults that they were cowards who copulated with their horses and would only fight children. A couple shots were fired at him but missed. He turned his horse casually, rose up in the saddle, and slapped his hind parts. Then laughing, he rode back to his mother.

That did it. Screaming war cries, the highwaymen charged across the stream and onto the field, the pounding of hooves sounding like the rumbling of distant thunder.

Instead of fleeing, Julia, Edward, Lame Deer, and Coppersmith hurried to the edge of the creek to watch. They were followed by the guards and the wounded. In the morning sunlight, she watched the riders racing across the plain, shrieking like banshees, waving scimitars, firing their pistols and rifles.

Morgan and Seamus waited patiently by the tree.

"What are they doing?" Coppersmith muttered.

When the riders closed to within a hundred yards, Morgan and Seamus fired. Two men toppled from their horses, one on each flank. Eject the brass, lever a new cartridge, fire again. Two more fell. And then two more.

The return fire from Nyama's men was wild striking nowhere near the two. Even Julia knew it was difficult to aim atop a galloping horse. She was worried though that a stray bullet would find one of them, and that's what happened. Seamus went down, and she felt her throat constrict at the thought of losing the boy. Instantly Morgan went to him, but he struggled quickly to one knee, and this time using his pistol, continued to shoot.

By the time Nyama and his men came within fifty yards, there were only six of them left with riderless horses racing with them. Five of the men had had enough, turning off and riding away like the hounds of hell were after them.

Only Nyama kept on. Without hesitation, both Morgan and Seamus hurled a barrage at him, knocking him from the saddle like a floppy, rag doll. The morning was silent again. Gunshots echoed only in Julia's mind.

Beside her, Coppersmith exhaled loudly. "My God, it was the charge of the Light Brigade. They had no chance at all."

She heard horses' hooves and turned to see the guards and the wounded riding off. The Dunford Nyama militia of outlaws no longer existed.

Several minutes later, Morgan and Seamus rode up trailing six of the outlaws' horses behind them. She said something in Cheyenne to Lame Deer who shook her head.

"You're hurt," Julia exclaimed to Seamus.

His face was spotted with blood. "I'm fine, Auntie Julia" he said and explained a bullet had shattered the stock of his rifle and sent splinters into his cheek.

"Where's Dunford?" Morgan asked sharply.

"Halfway to Johannesburg by now," the duke said.

"Then that's where we'll go," Morgan said.

CHAPTER FORTY-FOUR

Kalahari Desert, January 21, 1888

I hated sleeping outdoors, but Toby often did when it was hot like last night. Just after dawn, I strapped on my knife and pulled on my boots, shaking them first for biters, then crawled out of our stick sleeping hut. After retrieving my gear for the hunt, including the bow and quiver of arrows hanging from a tree limb, I knelt on the slight rise above camp to wait. I was eager to go. Hunting made the hard daily grind to survive in this dry scrub land tolerable.

I watched the fifty or so people of the Juwasi band begin their day. Teshwa, the wife of Kwai, was gouging out a shallow cooking pit with her digging stick. Using a melon rind as a pot, she was preparing a breakfast of melon fruit, dried meat, and roots the women and I had brought back yesterday. Nearby, Kani was roasting a rabbit over a small fire. Not far from me, my friend Khoa sat cross-legged, sewing beads onto a leather loincloth. She glanced up and smiled at me, which I returned with a childish wave.

Juwasi women did not cover their breasts, but at nearly thirteen, I did, though Toby made fun of me for doing so. "It's not like you're running around with big melons."

"Oh, shut up," I said.

With my knife, I had cut a strip from my coat liner and strapped it on. Like everyone else, I wore a leather breech clout, but for modesty's sake, I hadn't gone completely native. I always had on my now dirty unmentionables that reached down to mid-thigh, and Toby did the same. The difference was mine didn't have a big, fat diamond stuffed inside. He wrapped that in cloth then bound it to his waist.

On days like today when we went out hunting, we put on white hoods fashioned out of Aiden's shirts that covered our heads and the back of our necks against the scorching sun. Even so, by now our skin was tanned to a burnished copper, but no one would mistake us for Bushmen. All these months, we'd stayed with the Juwasi because we didn't want to venture out on foot several hundred miles across a vast waterless plain, carrying nothing but a bit of dried meat and an ostrich egg of water.

I watched Kwai showing his four-year-old son how to use a bow. The child idolized his father but still occasionally shot looks toward a group of boys who had captured a turtle and were now tossing it around. Later, it would be cooked and eaten.

From the western horizon, mountainously high clouds advanced on us, casting patches of shadows that moved over the plain. Kwai had said there'd be no rain today, perhaps tomorrow, or the next. I didn't understand all his words but got the gist. He was tall for a Juwasi, well over five feet, nearly as tall as me. His hair was cut to a stubble and his jaw jutted forward like he was ready to fight you, but he was really a gentle, friendly man. Except hunting. He was renowned among the many Juwasi bands for his prowess in running down game. He'd once killed a charging ostrich, which are big and dangerous, by driving his spear into its heart.

There was a hunt planned for today but not until this afternoon during the hellish heat. That was when every smart lion would be beneath a shade tree sleeping. Too bad about the rain. It would cool things off. An hour after dawn, the temperature had to be a hundred and later out on the savannah would rise to a hundred and ten or twenty. Heat like that had physical presence. It felt as if you were walking through hot soup.

Among the Juwasi, women gathered and men hunted. I was not Juwasi, so I could do what I wanted. More than once, Toby and I had gone out with Kwai to hunt gemsboks or wildebeests. He taught us how to use their deadliest weapon, the bow, and we became pretty good at it.

Juwasi bows were nothing like Cheyenne ones. They were small, looking almost like children's toys, and didn't take much strength to pull back the animal gut-string. The arrow could not penetrate more than an inch or two, but the poison was always fatal. There was no antidote, no sucking out the venom if human, no surviving though it usually took all day to die. This poison came from beetle larvae and could even be lethal if touched. That was why men hung their quivers from nearby trees out of reach of curious children.

Today, we were hunting lion, a specific lion, a rogue that had been cast out by his own pride, likely for eating newborn cubs. Now, he had a taste for human flesh. Lost in the grip of madness, he'd spend his day bellowing endlessly at the sky and wind. One time, he stationed himself on this very rise and unleashed his anguished roar at us for hours. He did not attack; he just roared.

Eventually, Kwai approached him, waving his spear and shouting, "Why do you bother us? Go away."

Certain he'd be killed, I watched with Toby. That stick was no real threat to a beast like this and only anger him. An arrow would kill it, but that would take a day for the poison to do its work. Finally, though, for his own reasons, the lion abruptly turned and loped off.

"Perhaps Old Luke has a thorn in his paw," Toby suggested with an amused smile. He called him Old Luke for no particular reason, but it stuck, at least between us two.

Of course. most lions could take down a human if they chose, but the Juwasi and the pride of twenty or so that camped nearby had made a truce, almost like it had been negotiated. We stayed clear of them and they of us. We even used different waterholes.

Then, after Old Luke visited our camp, he killed a Juwasi woman.

It was yesterday when we women were returning from gathering roots and berries. The lion rushed out of the bush and attacked Old Nai, Khoa's grandmother, dragging her off. Some of us tried to drive him away with our shouts but couldn't. The beast stood over his kill and lashed out whenever we neared. By then, the old woman was dead, and we could do nothing for her so Khoi said we must return to camp. Tails between our legs, we hurried back. It was the worst thing I'd ever seen. Now lodged firmly in my brain, I'll never get it out.

With Toby along, the men went out to retrieve what was left of the body, which was being fed on by jackals. They brought poor Nai back and buried her.

In all the hubbub, seeing white men had slipped my mind, and I didn't tell Toby about it.

On the rise above camp, he approached and squatted beside me. "Come fix my breakfast."

Earlier, I had eaten a couple strips of dried gemsbok. "Fix your own breakfast," I said.

"Bollocks, you're a terrible wife."

I chuckled. I was. We did live together, which to the Juwasi meant we were married. On cold nights, we huddled as one, wrapped in each other's arms under our coats. We both knew what men and women did, but that was never a thought for either of us. We were brother and sister, both trying to stay alive another day.

"You're sure eager for the hunt," he said. "We won't leave for a few hours."

I shrugged. "I just want to be ready."

But in fact, he was right. I liked going out with the women to gather food from the ground, but I loved the hunt. When you came back from the hunt with a kill, people cheered like you were Buffalo Bill. No one did that when you brought back a yam.

Toby snorted. "My wife the hunter, home from the hills."

His voice had long since changed, not exactly base but no longer high and squeaky. I glanced at him and once again was struck by his transformation over the last seven months. That potbellied little boy was gone. He'd grown a head taller since the Juwasi rescued us, coming up to my chin, a lean specimen with ropey muscles like me.

The only remnant of that boy was his insistence that the Juwasi call him Earl though they had no grasp of what an earl was. I thought it funny because when they said it, it sounded like Oil.

Our time here had not been easy, but we adapted and made ourselves useful. Life teetered on a thin ledge in the Kalahari, so everyone must do his part for the People to survive. If we didn't, the Juwasi would have abandoned us, and I wouldn't have blamed them. I didn't know what they did to save my life, slapped some secret healing muck on my wounds, shook a rattle, or let them heal on their own, but after a week, my fever broke, and I began to get up and move about. It took three months for me to regain the full use of my left arm. Like Mama, my body will always have a nice set of scars, in my case a row of leopard teeth marks on my shoulder.

"Toby, I saw white men yesterday," I said. "I forgot to say anything with all that was going on."

He was alarmed. "Dunford?"

I shook my head and related the incident, telling him that we were gathering roots when we saw another band of Bushmen with men, women and children coming our way. They waved, and some of our women waved back. Apparently, they were expected. Suddenly, several armed horsemen rode in with wagons and swarmed around them. They herded the women and children into the wagons then hauled them all away with the men following on foot. Though the Bushmen had spears and bows, they didn't fight. How could they against guns?

Though we were not more than forty yards away, the slavers ignored us. All I could figure was we were only women and children. Two of the white men did stop to study us.

I said to Toby, "It seemed they were staring directly at me."

"They probably were. You stand out, Glory. Who were they?"

"Farmers according to Khoa. They live many days south, at least that's what I think she said. I can't be sure. I still don't understand all those clicks like you do. The farmers come here and take Bushmen back to work their farms. When the work's done, they let them go."

Toby's face was grim. "They took the women and children to keep the men from running."

I worried he might think I should have announced myself to them. "Toby, these weren't men I wanted to approach."

"No, I wouldn't think so," he said, hesitated a moment, then added, "We'll find a way home, Glory."

We fell silent then and watched the Juwasi for several minutes, our hosts, our saviors. It struck me they must have been living on the Kalahari a very long time. Changing little, living in stick huts, hunting with bows and poison arrows, gathering the same roots and berries. And surviving. How long? Years? Centuries? Longer?

"Toby, these people are old," I said. "They are really, really old."

He studied Khoa at her fire, then made a gruff sound of assent.

It was another three hours before we set out on the hunt.

That afternoon, the sun hammered down with unrelenting ferocity as we tramped across the savannah in single file. We carried our weapons and hunting bags that held digging sticks, fire sticks, and ostrich shells of water. Before we'd set out, we gorged ourselves with it, but after three hours, I felt dryness in my mouth. I knew better, though, than to start drinking now. Old Luke covered a wide territory, and we might be out for days.

Kwai led with Toby and me following and Gao at the rear where most attacks from dangerous animals would come. We spoke in hushed voices if we had to speak at all. Mostly, Kwai clicked or gestured if he saw some beast or herd in the distance.

I thought it an honor that he chose Toby and me for his hunting party, but when I told him so this morning, he looked at me baffled. I thought maybe I didn't get the words right, but Toby said he'd wanted me all along.

"You're good with a bow," he'd said. "Perhaps that comes from having a wild Indian for a brother."

That upset me because it sounded like he was insulting Seamus, but Toby was grinning, not a mean expression at all, so all I said was, "Don't be snooty, Oil."

Not long after we set out, Kwai led us on a path near the lions' water hole where I saw them all, the entire pride, about two hundred yards away under a tree, sleeping, all cozy-like in the shade. They looked like stacks and stacks of dead lions. I was glad when we put some distance between us.

Old Luke wasn't bellowing this day, so it took us most of the afternoon before we came across his sign. It had to be him for what self-respecting lion would be out in this heat. I could track, having been taught by my mother and Uncle Conor, but when Kwai followed the trail over rock, I couldn't spot a thing. A few minutes later, the Juwasi leader clicked, then pointed, and I saw him, Old Luke in short grass maybe three hundred yards distant. He was feeding on something, and I hoped it wasn't a human.

Toby and I glanced at each other, and I saw my fright reflected in his eyes. Not even a year ago, he'd been riding wooden horses and playing Knights of the Round Table with his friend Tom. Now he was stalking a mad lion in the Kalahari. We were downwind, so Kwai moved on Luke, us following, bending double through the grass, me trembling as we went. If he charged, we'd have to fend him off with our spears, not a reassuring thought.

Taking a zig zag course, we closed to within ten yards and stopped just as Old Luke raised his head and saw us. A great terror swallowed me up, but I did what Mama always taught me. Push your fear into the dark holes of your mind. Good thing too, otherwise I would have run, and Old Luke would have gotten me in two strides. He stared at us for several seconds, trying to make sense of us, made none, and went back to eating his catch. Thankfully, it was an eland.

Kwai clicked twice, and we all lifted our bows and shot. All four arrows stuck into the lion's side. Now he roared, a sound so loud it could be heard in Trafalgar Square. He tried to rid himself of the barbs by spinning in a frantic circle, but they stuck. Then, he rolled on his side and that broke them off, but the poison was in. Jumping up, he searched for his attackers and charged straight at me. His speed was remarkable, and he had me in seconds.

I leapt to the side and flat onto the grass as he skidded to a stop and turned on me. That's when Gao drove his spear into him. Toby was the second to stab, then Kwai.

Old Luke was stuck good but not at all done in. He swung out a claw and knocked Toby five yards back and opened his jaws to go at him. Then, Kwai would say later I must have been seized by madness sent from the gods for I sprang up screaming and leapt onto the lion's back. Astride, I plunged my knife into his neck again and again in a stabbing frenzy while Kwai and Gao jabbed, giving Toby time to scoot away.

The lion bellowed and spun, throwing me to the ground, but he was done. When the beast slumped to his belly, we took several steps back and watched. Soon he fell onto his side and went through his death agony. For a full minute, he lay there, his eyes blinking slowly, his breath coming out in whispers. Then the last heave of his great chest fell, and he was dead.

In relief, I exhaled and stared at the dead beast. I felt no sympathy for it. I remembered its jaws ripping flesh from Old Nai, a woman everyone liked because of her wisdom and toughness. She'd always reminded me of Lame Deer in that way.

Kwai removed an animal bone of about three inches. With his knife he notched another mark in it and slid it back into his pouch. I'd seen it before. It had about twenty marks on it. They were either a notation to commemorate a kill or perhaps even more fanciful marking the passage of days from one full moon to the next. He had several of them in his sleeping hut and once showed me one a little over two inches that was so old the bone was a deep brown. It had thirty notches. I once asked him what they were and he explained, but he spoke too quickly for me to understand.

At that moment, while flies gathered around the lion, I longed for Toby and me to be back in our little sleeping hut. Kwai, though, wanted to continue the hunt, this time for meat to bring back to camp. As late as it was, I knew we would be spending the night in the bush. I hated sleeping outdoors.

CHAPTER FORTY-FIVE

Johannesburg, February 9, 1888

Last night, Dunford had a dream filled with the screams of his enemies, the scimitars of his onetime army slashing flesh and splattering the earth red with their blood. So vivid was it that when he awoke, he wasn't sure which world was more real, the dreaming one or the waking one. Rubbing his face, he sat on the edge of his bed in the Royal Arms Hotel and tried to make sense of it. Did it mean anything? Were the two brats already dead? Was that it? Nothing had been reported of them for over seven months, and there were many still looking. After all, the rumor persisted that the boy carried the Tudor Diamond. But had they been roaming the countryside, surely they would have been spotted.

The dream stayed in his thoughts most of the morning, but near noon as he went into the post office inside a dry goods emporium, its images had fled though leaving him in a sour mood. How he hated Johannesburg. A dusty hellhole, it was hideous and detestable, no refinement, no dignity. A chaos of buffoons controlled the town's fabulous wealth, all of them Jews, Wesleyans, or Presbyterians. The town's only saving grace was the preponderance of gambling dens and bordellos.

When he went to the mail counter, the Postmaster's head bobbed up and down in an annoyingly toadying manner. "Good morning, Mr. Dudley," the man said to Dunford. "Looks like we're going to have a real gully washer today."

He was from America. His use of the Yank phrase didn't make Dunford pine for that distant country. He managed to say, "Yes, gulley washer. Have you any mail for me, Mason?"

Dunford was calling himself Charles Dudley these days since his lordship the Earl of Wexham was wanted for murder and mayhem throughout the Cape Colony. Fortunately, Johannesburg was in the Transvaal, the South African Republic, and no one was looking for him here. Since the Raines woman and the duke vacated the region and were now headquartered in Kimberley, still searching for their brats, it was the safest place for him. He wore a full beard and wire-rimmed glasses. His clothes, though serviceable, no longer gave him a Beau Brummel appearance but more like that of a solicitor.

"Mail? Oh sure, came in yesterday." The man went through a couple stacks and dug out a letter. "I knew I had one for you, Mr. Dudley, sir. Come all the way from New York City it has."

"May I have it?"

"Oh, yeah, sure, here you are, sir." He handed it to Dunford.

Addressed to Charles Dudley, the return address was C of W, 491 Fifth Avenue, New York City, America. C of W were initials for the Countess of Wexham. He'd written to her explaining that while bringing their gold mine into profitability, he had been pursued by brigands and needed to change his name temporarily, a totally ridiculous claim but she would not question it. He instructed her to use his new sobriquet for all mail. Lydia did but could not give up the noble title so easily and used the initials.

The Postmaster grinned. "Did you hear what Old Cecil Rhodes done?"

Turning away without response, Dunford left the store, stuffing the letter into his pocket. He'd look at it tonight. Her letters made him feel connected to the cultured world though reading them was tedious. They all said the same thing, how she missed him, then banging on endlessly about what she bought at the shops, whom she called on, and what she ate. The only good news came three months ago when she wrote that her father had died and left her a rattling amount of money. When this business was done and he made his way to New York, he'd finally be a truly wealthy man. Perhaps he would even father another child, make himself an heir.

He hurried across town toward De Haan's, a gambling establishment where he spent his afternoons. There, his skill in games of chance and his greater skill at producing the right card at the right moment paid his bills. When he turned onto Rissik Street, a blast of wind knocked him back a step. So preoccupied was he with his thoughts he'd not realized a storm had come. Massive black clouds were roiling overhead, and the temperature had dropped to a decided chill. In the churning dust, Dunford drew his coat tighter and dashed across the street, dodging a hurrying carriage.

"Mr. Dudley," someone called to him over the rumble of thunder. He turned and saw two men ahead on the boardwalk, their faces obscured in shadows.

He gripped to the pistol at his belt, not drawing it but ready.

One of the men held a hand up. "We mean you no harm, sir. In fact, we've come to offer you a service."

Not trusting them, Dunford demanded, "What do you want?"

At that moment, a flash of lightning forked down from the sky, the loud crack of thunder immediate. All three flinched. For a moment, the faces of the two men were illuminated. One was perfectly repulsive with a pockmarks, a hooked nose, and a patch over one eye. The other was thickly bearded and had dark, unrelenting eyes. It was this one who spoke, "This is Mr. Disraeli and I'm Mr. Gladstone. I believe, sir, it is about to rain. Shall we find a place where we can talk in a little bit more comfort?"

Not moving, Dunford asked, "What is this about?"

The same man answered, "A mate told us you were paying for information about two young runaways, a boy and a girl. Were we misinformed?"

Dunford hesitated. "It depends on what information you have."

The dark-eyed man pointed a finger at him. "And that depends on what you pay."

"Two hundred pounds sterling," Dunford answered. "If I deem the information worthy of such a sum."

"You will," Gladstone said. "We saw the girl near three weeks ago and learned later the boy was with her. Hotter than Hell where they're at. I can point it out exactly on a map."

Another crack of thunder exploded above, and the rain fell in a great deluge.

"Come," Dunford shouted over the storm and hurried down the boardwalk to De Haan's, the two men following.

Cape Town, February 13, 1888

Edward Becket, the Duke of Northampton, sat in Governor Hercules Robinson's office with three other men discussing the planned Kimberley to Johannesburg rail line. With the torment of missing his son and fearing he might be dead, the duke had immersed himself in work. It was where he felt most comfortable. In Kimberly with Julia, Morgan, and the Indian woman, it was constant torment, unbridled emotion and chasing after straws. For him not to work, he was sure, would lead to madness.

As usual, the Transvaal representative, a black bearded man named Retief, had not budged on where the track should be laid. In his country, he insisted, his people would determine where tracks were put down. That meant the Cape Colony rail line would have to be adjusted. Retief merely shrugged, and the meeting ended on that impasse.

As the men were gathering their papers, some scowling at Retief, Governor Robinson asked the duke if he'd heard any news of his son or young Miss Raines.

"No, governor, just rumors. Nothing that has proven useful."

Robinson gave him a sympathetic smile. "They are but children. God will protect them."

Edward's teeth grinded, but he subdued his impulse to snap at the man and merely muttered a *thank you*. He believed in God as much as anyone, but two children alone in the African wilderness would need the protection God gave Jonah. He didn't see that as likely.

As he was leaving the governor's mansion, Retief caught up with him. "A moment of your time, duke. I heard you speaking with the governor about those two lost children, one of them yours. Is that correct?"

Edward wanted to be away for despite his efforts, the melancholy was upon him. "Yes."

"I have something for you then," Retief said. "A rumor, yes, but I believe it has the ring of truth. A man who works with Hottentots in the Kalahari told me that two white children are living with Bushmen. That was all he knew and so that's all I know. It was only a moment in passing at a pub. I hope it's helpful."

"Thank you, Mr. Retief, I'm grateful," Edward replied, then climbed into his carriage. As it drove off, he sighed angrily. "Rumors, and rumors, and more rumors."

Kemberley, February 15, 1888

In mid-January, a police report had come in from Port Elizabeth on the Indian Ocean to the duke's large house in Kimberley. It read that two young people had been caught attempting to stow away on a ship. They were described as a boy and a girl of twelve or thirteen. Morgan, Seamus, and Coppersmith set out by train for the port city.

It had been nearly seven months since Nyama had been killed and the remnants of his band scattered to the winds. They and Dunford, who had escaped, were now hunted by the British army and the police of every municipality in the Cape Colony. Back then, Morgan had been sure her daughter and Toby would find their way to Johannesburg, but Cecil Rhodes had not seen them, nor had anyone else. In six weeks, searchers had not found a trace of them anywhere in the Transvaal. It was agreed the two had likely gone west or south, no one adding the words in the backs of their minds, *if they were still alive.* It was time to move elsewhere.

The duke set up his headquarters in Kimberley where they could reach most places in southern Africa more quickly. From there, he dispatched searchers throughout the colony while sending word by telegraph to every city, town and village in southern Africa that a two thousand pound reward awaited anyone with information that led to Toby's and Glory's rescue.

Since then, a flood of reports had come in, reminiscent of the England search in which most were shams or misidentifications. Still, Morgan and Seamus investigated as many as they could. They seldom went alone. On the most promising, Julia, Lame Deer, and Coppersmith accompanied them, and sometimes even the duke when he was in Kimberley. Port Elizabeth had been the latest of these. But Julia hadn't gone this time. She said she knew it wasn't Toby and Glory.

The duchess had become a mysterious figure in the town. On her few outings, she wore a large American bandana to hide her face that was said to be hideously scarred from a wound suffered in the famous Battle of Iron Springs. Often, people gathered across the street in hopes of spotting her with her old fakir woman leaving the house. Once when she did, she shouted at them, "Lay-abouts. Have you nothing better to do?"

It was held by all that once she had been a great beauty.

Lame Deer had not travelled to Port Elizabeth either. She said she would not spend days trapped in an iron lodge that moved for a wild goose chase. She flicked her hand dismissively. "Glory not in that place."

Morgan was relieved the aged woman would stay put. Her busy pace had slackened decidedly since they'd come to Kimberley, like the tick of a clock slowing down by the hour. Morgan was worried. A long trip south might wear her out.

"The old goat is right," Julia had said. "Toby would not stowaway on a ship. He'd march right into the nearest government office and declare himself to be the Earl of Exeter."

Morgan marveled that in the last few months a strange friendship had blossomed between Julia and Lame Deer. Throughout the day, they exchanged insults like two dogs growling over the same bone. Yet, they never seemed to be apart. They were still protecting one another like they had done at Iron Springs.

Morgan replied, "They stowed away once. Might do it again. We better make sure."

"Then by all means go," Julia said, waving her off.

So Morgan, Seamus, and Coppersmith set off for Port Elizabeth where it took weeks to run down the two children. They turned out to be part of an urchin gang that plagued the city and had only snuck aboard in order to plunder the ship. Glory and Toby, they were not. Once again, Morgan's disappointment was like an endless parade of wolves gutting her.

When she returned to Kimberley, she was immediately shocked by the change in Lame Deer, after only a month. In the faded, yellow glow of the drawing room lamps, her Cheyenne mother's face was hollowed out and had a sick grayish tint. Her body sagged in the rocking chair by the unlit fireplace, looking like a rag doll that had been tossed there.

Morgan wanted to run to her but knew the old woman wouldn't like that. Instead, she asked in Cheyenne. "How are you feeling, mother?"

Lame Deer replied in English. "Chipper."

At the British word, Morgan glanced at Julia, who shrugged. Perhaps the change had been too gradual for the duchess to notice, while Morgan herself had been too preoccupied. Something, though, was terribly wrong. It felt like an anvil suddenly pressed down on her heart.

The next morning, when Lame Deer said she would walk in the sun today, Morgan took her to the Public Gardens where they wandered among the trees and green bushes and bright flowers. Along the paths, they passed others but were barely aware of them. They remained silent for nearly half an hour. What was there to say except this one thing, that Morgan loved this woman.

Eventually, Lame Deer stopped and turned to her. "You stubborn like bear. You keep me here all day to get from me what you already know. We all die, Daughter. The wasicus doctor says I live maybe weeks, maybe months, but this body, it dies."

Words Morgan longed to say choked in her throat.

The Cheyenne woman held up her hand. "No need to say what we know in hearts. We go back now. I want rocking chair."

The doctor said she had weeks, perhaps months, but Lame Deer died that night.

She passed just after midnight. Morgan, Seamus, and Julia gathered in the bedroom with her, Morgan holding her shriveled hand. Masked in the blue bandana, Julia was sitting beside Morgan, staring down at the small woman in shock.

Seamus stood in the corner, his eyes shut, tears sliding down his cheek. He didn't bother to wipe them away. When the doctor arrived with Coppersmith, he barely examined her, telling them her time had come, and there was nothing anyone could do but make her comfortable.

In a harsh tone, Morgan said, "Then get out."

As he hurried from the room, a small cuckoo clock on the nightstand sounded midnight with a bird popping out again and again emitting a pitiful squeak. It was a gift from Julia and Lame Deer's one prized possession. Often during the day just before the hour, she would rush into her bedroom to watch it come out. Now as she lay on the bed, Morgan thought she saw the hint of a smile but couldn't be sure in the muted light.

Abruptly, Lame Deer's head lifted, and her eyes opened. They were alight. "Neho'eehe," she called out, then fell back. Her body slackened like it had been emptied out. Morgan thought she saw the soul lift from her. Lame Deer had died.

She took the woman's tiny medicine bag and placed it on her chest.

Above the bandana, Julia's eyes had filled with tears. "I can't believe how much I loved her." Then in a barely audible voice, asked, "What did she say?"

After a long moment, Morgan answered, "Father." Then in a whisper, "She saw her father."

CHAPTER FORTY-SIX

Kalahari Desert, February 17, 1888

Sometime today, we, the Juwasi, would begin a long journey across the savannah to a different campsite where forage would be more plentiful. We'd emptied out this area. While we were gone, it would replenish and be ripe for the digging when we came back next year or the year after. I wondered if Toby and I would still be with them then. I loved them but wanted to go home to my family.

Also, part of our change of camp was due to the local lion pride becoming more threatening. It was strange in the extreme but killing Old Luke, even though he was an outcast among them, broke our fragile, age-old truce of avoidance. A pack of them tracked one of our hunting parties, which Kwai said they'd never done before, closing till the men had to drive them off with spears and threats. Another pair of females—it was always the female lion doing the hunting—followed a party of our women digging up roots. They hadn't attacked, but at some point, they would realize they had killing superiority, and then we'd be fighting for our lives. The Juwasi had such a perilous balance of survival we could not afford losses.

We would not be leaving on the trek until the heat of the day. Kwai said it would rain today, and that would cool things off for us. That morning, Toby and I were eating antelope jerky when Khoi approached us at our hut, her year old baby boy on her hip. She was a short stocky woman with strong arms and legs.

She motioned to me. "Come, Tall One. We fill water for long walk."

I retrieved my animal hide cape. All the women wore them, folding them into carrying pouches when needed. That was what I did. Slinging it from my shoulder, I stuck in three empty ostrich eggs. I wondered if there would be any men accompanying us but saw none, just ten women waiting at the edge of camp. Despite my having ridden a big African cat like a bucking bull not long ago, I had no desire to truck with them alone if they were about.

Toby seemed to read my thoughts. "I'll come," he said, getting to his feet but running off into the bush. He called back with a laugh. "I just have to wee wee first."

"Thanks." I shouted sarcastically. "Catch up."

Before leaving, I snatched my bow and quiver from a tree limb and set off with the women. An arrow wouldn't kill a lion right off, but it might slow it down if I hit it in the snout.

To get to the waterhole a half mile away, we walked single file through a wood of spread-out trees with tall yellow grass everywhere. In the middle stood a temple of dirt twice as tall as me, a giant anthill that gave me the willies. The little beasties weren't actually dangerous, but it hurt like hell when one bit you. I sure wouldn't want to pitch a tent beside them.

When we came upon the water beneath a ledge, I was among the first to fill my containers, then I climbed up atop the rock. Only ten, fifteen feet high, but from there, you could almost see into tomorrow. Hundreds of miles it seemed. To the east were distant mountains, to the north our encampment and beyond the dry bushland where the Juwasi and the animals of the Kalahari lived. To the west, the same land of trees and grass. Turning to the four winds, I finally faced south where the flat desert pan stretched out forever in endless rising waves of heat.

My body jerked erect, and I cupped my hands over my eyes. Distorted in a plume of heat not a half mile away sat a lone figure atop a horse. His white shirt billowed in the wind. The glint of sunlight reflected off what had to be a spyglass. At once, he slid it into a saddlebag and drew his rifle from the scabbard. It was Dunford.

I screamed, "Run!"

Dunford took aim. At this distance, he knew he couldn't hope to hit anything, but he could scare the little monkeys and show them what they were facing. The one on top of the rock was surely the girl, tall and much lighter skinned. Finally, he had her. She leapt to the ground and jumped up and down, waving her arms shouting and hurrying the bush women away. He fired. One of them went down. He fired again, but this time hit nothing but dirt. The downed woman was helped to her feet, and all of them scattered beyond the rock ledge.

Dunford trotted his horse to the waterhole and let him drink. In no hurry now, he filled his canteen, then with his rifle clambered to the top of the rock. In the distance, he could see the Bushmen's camp and the women rushing into it, heard their frantic shouts. The girl was nowhere to be seen, nor did he spot the boy earl. Dunford would have to end his life too. Likely, he no longer had the diamond, but perhaps he hid it somewhere and under the correct persuasion would reveal the location.

At that instant, something forceful struck him just below the left shoulder and he took a step back. His eyes widened in shock when he realized it was a small arrow, and it had penetrated his body about an inch, no more. It had not hurt but surely it would in time. Shouting in rage, he yanked it out, tossing it dismissively aside.

Dunford called out, "You think you can worry me with your toy bow and arrow, girl? It's nothing."

Then he saw her beside an acacia tree twenty yards away, standing waist high in the surrounding yellow grass.

"The arrow is poison," she said. "You're dead, Mr. Dunford."

His voice took on a forced calm. "I don't think so, girl. I think you are lying."

Yet, he had a niggling memory of one of the two men who'd guided him to within a few miles of this place saying that, indeed, Bushmen used poison-tipped arrows.

"It is always deadly, Mr. Dunford. There is no antidote even if you reach a doctor. If you found someone to suck out the blood, it would do no good." She was irritatingly didactic like explaining a school lesson to a child too stupid to understand. "You won't feel it right away. You have time yet, maybe a full day. You'll just start walking funny, and that will be the first sign. Then you'll go fast. I'd say…"

He raised his rifle and shot at that smug face. As she ducked back behind the tree, he sprinted to it only to find her gone. Frantically, he glanced about, saw movement, and fired off another shot. She wasn't there either, just the furnace hot breeze stirring the grass. Unbidden, his laugh erupted out of him, sounding like the cackle of a hyena to his own ears. He was letting the girl's threat of poison get to her. He must gather himself. He was all right. She was lying.

"I'll find you," he called out then swung about, heading back for his horse, then stopped abruptly. It was gone. In the distance, he saw the boy riding away. Lifting his rifle, Dunford paused to take careful aim and felt the thud of another arrow plunge into his back. Flailing, he reached around and pulled it out. Again, it had barely penetrated his flesh. He'd be all right. Just wash the wounds when he had the chance after dispatching these two brats.

He looked about but could no longer see the boy, nor her. Furious, he decided to go after the bushman encampment and started for it. That was when he saw her in the high grass only fifty or sixty yards away, running toward the far distant Korannaberg Mountains. He snapped off a hurried shot but missed. Fast like a springbok, she cut through the grass. He kept pace, not letting that head of reddish hair out of his sight. She would not get away. Yet always, when he got close, she disappeared. After he picked up her movement again, and he always did, she was once more a good sixty yards ahead.

This cat and mouse game went on for hours till he began to wonder which he was, the cat or the mouse. He was not stupid. He'd known all along the play was to draw him away from the Bushmen. But now the game was over. His breath was coming in shallow gulps, and he'd worn himself out in this brutal heat. At moments, he even felt a bit dizzy.

Sliding the canteen from his shoulder, he drank till it was empty and screwed the cap back on. Time to return to the water hole, refill, and find his damn horse. The girl had no place to go. He'd eventually catch her but needed to see to his own survival first.

Getting back to the waterhole turned out to be difficult. He did not know exactly where he was, and it didn't help that the world began to spin like a carousel. If he stopped and sat amid the grass for a while, it would pass, and he could move on. Then he hit upon the idea to keep the distant mountains behind him over his left shoulder. That way he should get back to the waterhole. He walked on and on.

With his world spinning about him more and more, Dunford knew he was flagging and desperately needed somewhere to rest, certainly a place in the shade. He came to a giant dirt mound that cast a long shadow across the field. In that shade, he sat and leaned back, giving a sigh of relief. Near the waterhole now, he'd just rest here a minute or two then fill his canteen.

Consciousness came and went while his breathing grew more difficult. A sudden shuffling caused his eyes to fly open in alarm, but it was only those damn guttersnipes standing a few feet off. The boy held the reins of the horse, the girl his rifle. They just stared at him.

Finally, she said, "That's an anthill, Mr. Dunford. You might want to move."

The boy said, "They won't eat you like people think, but a lot will crawl over you and their bites really sting."

"Where is your army?" the girl asked.

Dunford laughed and waved his hand disdainfully. "Gone. Dead, the fools. Your Mama killed them. I tried to warn them, but they wouldn't listen. The real game was yet to be played, and I have won it for here you are." He coughed violently and wiped bloody spittle from his mouth with the back of his hand. "You have led me a merry chase, but I have you now."

Wobbling, he attempted to gain his feet but fell back against the dirt mound. Soon, the ants were crawling all over him. He felt their bites and frantically tried to brush them off.

He reached out a hand to the kids. "Come here. Help me up."

They did not move. Finally, he called on the last of his strength and rose up. Still swiping at the ants, he stumbled through the grass to a nearby tree and fell below its branches. He told himself all he needed was rest.

When Dunford looked up, the brats were gone. Again, he closed his eyes. He couldn't say how long he stayed that way, minutes or hours. The image of his wife came to him. Pudgy, little Lydia, who loved him dearly. The only person in his life to give her heart over completely to him. When he got to New York and her money, he would be the nabob, a prince of them all. He saw the cool water running from the fountains of Central Park. He felt the tingle of the cool autumn breeze on his skin. He saw himself and Lydia in a large coach with the horses clomping down Fifth Avenue while everyone stared with envy. Then the image shifted to London, the same coach, his wife at his side, riding through Piccadilly. It was all for him to claim.

A noise broke his dream thought, the brats returning to torment him. He'd have them soon enough. His eyes opened; they were not there. Instead, three massive lions hovered so close he could feel their hot breath and see into their gaping mouths.

CHAPTER FORTY-SEVEN

Kalahari Desert, February 17, 1888

At the waterhole, Toby and I filled Dunford's canteen and two ostrich eggs each, then with our white sun veils on, set off to the southeast on the horse for Kimberley and civilization. Both of us were sad to leave the friends who protected us, taught us, and, yes, loved us for seven months. We were able to say goodbye to them before we all started our treks to new destinations. Kwai presented me a tiny bone notched with knife marks, one that was a calendar of a single month long, long ago. I was touched by the gesture. It had much value. I gave him my knife. He told us their new camp was several days' walk, but the land there would have fresh forage and plentiful game to hunt.

"And not so many lions," I said.

He grinned, saying something with a lot of clicks that I didn't understand but nodded anyway. When I tried to tell him, his wife, Khoi and the others how much I'd miss them, I choked up and couldn't get the words out. Toby raised his hand and said in English, "Goodbye, Old Chums." And then we were gone, riding away.

When I glanced back, I saw them, fifty or so men, women, and children moving across the veldt in single file. I knew I'd never see any of them again.

A few hours after sunrise on that first day, I felt a wet drop on my face and looked to the sky for rain. Not a single cloud could be seen. I wiped the drop from my face and realized it was blood. Stopping,

I dismounted to check the horse. He had been laboring since we began. I saw what I feared. His nose and mouth were covered with blood. This was a quarter horse, bred for speed yet she doubted I doubted he'd ever reach a full gallop again.

I patted his neck. "Poor fellow."

"What's wrong?" Toby asked.

"The poor thing is done," I replied. "Dunford must have ridden him into the ground."

Toby threw back his head and gave a silent scream. After another moment, he stared at me. "Now what do we do? We can't walk to Kimberley."

Patting the beast's neck again, I said, "We have to ride him till he gives out."

With the remaining sunlight, our courageous horse carried us another fifteen twenty miles before we camped by a set of trees. I tied him to one and gave him a little water but not much for he would die soon.

Though a campfire burned throughout the night, and one of us was always on guard with the rifle, I just couldn't sleep under the stars. I imagined lions and leopards coming at me out of the darkness and dragging me off. When it was my turn to watch, I sat there for the rest of the night while Toby snored beside me. Several pairs of yellow eyes peered at me from the shadows. It was a long night, and I knew there'd be many more long nights ahead.

The next two days, we travelled southeast on a faltering horse in a direction I thought vaguely would take us to Kimberley. Once there we would sell Dunford's belongings for enough money to purchase train tickets for Cape Town where we'd contact the governor. This time no one would stop us. Wherever Mama, Seamus, and Lame Deer were, they'd find us there.

At night, we did not camp by water because that was when flesh eaters came to drink. Instead, if we found water, we'd draw back and wait till midday to refill our canteens and ostrich eggs when the dangerous predators were sleeping. Avoiding the worst of the heat ourselves, we'd set off again as the sun slid closer to the horizon. We were always on the lookout for beasts of prey, us being the prey, seeing their sign often and hearing their distant roars, growls, and laughs at night. Some like leopards and jackals usually gave us a wide birth. If one didn't, I shot it. The rest darted away then.

We lost the horse on the fourth day.

By then, he'd slowed down considerably, each step taken as if a vague memory of his purpose in life. Perhaps lions sensed a weakened animal for they began to appear lte in the evening with twilight just beginning. For a while, they kept pace some thirty yards off, females since females were the hunters.

Then more, a half dozen at least. They seemed in no hurry to come at us, which I thought odd, and guessed maybe they were uncertain what we were and a little hesitant. They only knew we were wounded. I drew the rifle and shook my shoulder to wake Toby.

Groggily, he began, "Why did you…oh my God."

Turning my head from side to side, I tried to keep track of the lions. Sure I was going to be taken by them, panic threatened to undo me. Ahead a half mile was a river, maybe twenty yards wide, a couple large creatures floating within. I thought if we could make the river, the lions wouldn't follow. After all, house cats weren't supposed to like water. Maybe lions felt the same. I just hoped the horse could make it there.

Toby put the canteen strap around his neck, drew Dunford's pistol and fired a shot at the beasts, hitting the ground near one. They all froze for a second, then kept on. The shot woke the horse out of its stupor. Sniffing the air, he caught the scent of the lions, shrieked, and broke into an agonizingly slow run. The lions were on us in a lightning tick. In panic, our horse shot forward nearly toppled Toby. With a screech of desperation, he righted himself.

I was so scared I thought I could probably run as fast. The lions fell behind, though still loped after us. If the horse gave out, they'd be on us, and I knew Toby and I couldn't kill them all with our firearms. At full speed, we splashed into the river as one of the monstrous floating things came after us. It was like a giant headed cow with a mouth that could clomp down on a bear. As big as it was, it was also fast in the water. Several lions made the river just behind us, but more of those beasts arriving chased them away.

Our magnificent horse made it to the far bank and up, then ran on for another mile till it died in mid stride and went down.

Kalahari Desert, February 19, 1888

Morgan found Dunford's body in a grassy field where the Juwasi had said it would be. Since breaking camp beside them hours before, she and the five riders had travelled through the arid country back to the Bushmen's previous encampment. The riders now sat their horses in a half circle staring down at the man. His remains had been picked clean by scavengers.

Seeing Dunford's broken skeleton with scraps of clothing still attached, Morgan's rage swelled up at what this man had put her child through, put them all through. She edged her horse forward, drew a pistol, and fired a shot into the white, sun-polished skull. Julia joined her and the two women sent shot after shot into it until their guns clicked on empty and the head lay in pieces. When they turned around, the duke and Coppersmith were staring at them, mouths slightly agape.

Coppersmith said, "Fear the lioness with her cubs."

Glancing toward the south, Julia glowered. "What forlorn and dreary plains. Sun scorched. My God, fit for nothing but snakes and lizards. Will it never end?"

Kabo, the wizened Tswana guide, replied, "Oh yes, Miss. You walk long time, bantsi bantsi. Thousand miles, Englanders say. Kalahari no more."

Even on the road, Julia wore the blue bandana but had a black veil that draped down over it from her small-brimmed hat. She harrumphed. "Thank you, Mr. Kabo. What I meant to say was, what now? Our children are still out there and only God knows where."

"We will locate them, Duchess. I promise you," Coppersmith said. "First thing now, we must find their tracks."

The guide shook his head. "No tracks here, boss. Rain come two days past. Banti, banti long walk maybe find tracks."

Morgan addressed her words to the duke, "Best we split up. We can cover more ground. Head back toward Kimberley. Seamus and I will take the eastern trail, you the western."

"You think they are going to Kimberley?" the duke asked.

She gave a shrug of her shoulder. "That'd be my guess."

Coppersmith said skeptically, "If they even knew where they were and then where Kimberley was, why would they choose to go that way?"

"Glory knows where it is. It's not that hard to figure," Morgan said, keeping her voice even though impatient to get moving. "They went toward Kimberley because that's where the nearest towns are."

"My God," Julia exclaimed. "We might have come within a few miles of them on our way here."

"It's likely," Morgan said.

Her horse suddenly bounding beneath her, Julia stared at her husband. "I'm going with Morgan and Seamus."

When surprise appeared on the duke's face, she added quickly, "Another pair of eyes for them, and you'll have Kabo."

Morgan knew that despite the harpy tendencies of his wife, Edward Becket loved her deeply and would not want her out of his sight while in this country. He'd almost lost her at Iron Springs. Now, she wanted to separate from him. Weariness in his eyes, he stared at Morgan for several seconds till she gave him a barely perceptible nod.

"Fine then," he said. "Kuruman is two hundred miles southeast. We'll meet there in five days., and may God protect our children."

A few minutes later at the waterhole, they allowed the horses to drink and filled their canteens. Morgan knew that if they wanted to survive, finding water would be their most important task. In desert country, they did not dare go beyond forty-eight hours without water or risk losing the horses. During her time with the Cheyenne, the people had often travelled a long way without seeing water, but every warrior knew where it was and could find it when needed. She came to know the wide reach of Cheyenne country as well, but this frying pan landscape was as foreign to her as the surface of the moon.

Only Kabo knew where the waterholes were, and he'd be with the duke and Coppersmith. With a sense of enormous pride, she told herself that Glory and Toby had managed to survive all this time. They just needed to do it a little longer.

On the afternoon of the third day, Morgan, Seamus, and Julia entered into a country of rolling terrain with sparce hills and arroyos. With the sun blazing alone in an empty sky, they peeled down to their blouses and shirts and drew their hats low to shield their eyes. As they rode, Morgan and Seamus studied the ground for tracks, finding only lion spore. All the while, Julia stared straight ahead, cursing the dreary landscape. She swore that when she found Toby she'd take a switch to him for what he'd put her through.

Abruptly, she pointed east and shouted, "Look."

Morgan followed the direction and spotted the specks circling in the sky several miles away. "Vultures," she said with a shiver. *Oh God no!* What were they flying over? The words flashed through her brain, but she would not voice them.

"Ride," she ordered, and they set off at a hard gallop.

Ten minutes later, they drew up and cautiously approached to within a hundred yards of the killing scene. It was too dangerous to ride in closer. Scavengers in a hierarchy of terror were feasting on something or some things. In a feeding frenzy, hyenas ripped at the carcass. So numerous were they, the dead animal or animals were unseen. Several feet away, jackals, much smaller than the hyenas, drifted about, impatient for their turn. Vultures and other giant birds sat nearby waiting for what would be left. A few of them still circled above.

Morgan knew that approaching the melee to identify the dead animal would tempt fate. According to Coppersmith, Hyenas hunted in packs so large they were better termed clans. Nearly a hundred and fifty pounds with bone-crushing jaws, they were as deadly or more deadly than lions. Because of their numbers, a lion facing them alone would retreat from a kill instead of contesting it. They scared Coppersmith and so they scared Morgan.

She dared not let herself consider the worst possibility of what they were feeding on, but still, she needed to know for a certainty. She drew her rifle from its scabbard and from a hundred yards, took aim and fired. An instant later, one hyena went down, and the others jumped back. At the sound, the birds took to the air and the hyenas gazed about, then went back at the carcass. Morgan shot another and the beasts drifted back, confused, long enough for her to see the fleshless remains of a horse, saddle still attached. From the debris of broken ostrich eggs, she knew this was clearly what Glory and Toby had been riding.

And there were no other bodies. Her heart leapt with relief.

With a release of tension, Seamus voiced just that. "There are no more bodies, Mama. They're still out there somewhere."

Barely audible, Julia said, "Thank God."

To avoid the scavengers, they rode wide and then swung back around to cross Glory's and Toby's trail. They did, quickly, spotting a pair of boot prints led unsteadily across a sandy coulee, then on for another hour to a set of hills glaring white in noon sun like porcelain mounds. Morgan knew the children would be miles ahead, yet she pushed the horses at a quick trot, relentlessly chewing up the miles hour after hour. With the sun about to go down, she knew they'd have to camp soon.

Even at speed, the trail had been easy to follow for Morgan and Seamus had no reason to hide it. The boot marks, a scuff here and there, now skirted a low hill and entered into a sandy, undulating valley of brush and occasional trees. Animal prints were plentiful. Up ahead several hundred yards, more vultures were circling something dead or dying. Instantly, Morgan kicked her horse's flanks into a full-on sprint despite its lungs laboring, Seamus and Julia close behind.

With their big wing spans, the birds were circling lower and lower, and three bold ones had landed, sitting in the sand and short grass, staring fixedly at an acacia tree.

And so, Morgan and Julia found their children.

They were lying in shade, either dead or asleep. The two women jumped from their horses and ran to them. Seamus, with forced calmness, tied the reins on a prickly branch, then stood behind his mother, who was kneeling over the body of his sister. She did not seem to be breathing. Tears began welling in his eyes.

"Glory," he muttered softly.

Morgan clasped her daughter's hand and was relieved to feel the warmth within it and whispered her name several times to wake her as she had done when the child was younger.

Glory's eyes opened and she appeared confused. She gazed at her mother several seconds then said, "Mama." She bolted into a sitting position embracing Morgan. "I knew you'd come." Her eyes filled with tears. "I knew you'd come. I knew you'd come."

After several seconds, she saw her brother. "I knew you'd come too."

Jumping up, she threw herself into his arms.

Morgan rose and with both hands wiped her eyes. She glanced over at Julia, who held Toby. His head was on her shoulder. He was a little boy again.

"Where's Papa?" he asked.

"Not far. We divided into two groups," Julia explained "Your father will be so happy to see you, Toby, my dearest boy. We'll meet him in Kuruman."

Glory asked, "Where's Lame Deer? Is she with the other group?"

Morgan's mouth went dry. She couldn't answer. So many times, she'd faced the worst life threw in her path, knew what to do and did it, but this instance made her a coward. She couldn't hurt her daughter again, not after what she'd been through. There'd be time for it.

But the decision was taken from her. Seamus, with a strained expression, said, "Glory, she was so old."

For a half second, the girl was confused then understood. Her face went pale and her eyes teared up.

Morgan found her voice. "In her heart, she knew you were safe, so she could go." Then softly she shared the one moment of comfort. "She saw her father and went to him."

Next morning, they rode on and made Kuruman by nightfall. Made up of missionaries and their native converts, the town welcomed the five strange refugees that stumbled in just before darkness. The clergymen and their wives stared at them as if they'd just risen from the ground. Strange, indeed, they were, a boy and girl dressed like savages, and as it turned out a real duchess. They were fed, allowed baths, and provided with clean clothes.

Later they were parceled out to two separate homes for the night, the duchess and Toby in the main house while Morgan and Glory would sleep in a neighbor's cottage. When the chief clergyman assigned Seamus to the servant's quarters, Morgan said forcefully, "No, he stays with us. He's my son."

At that, an expression of disdain appeared on the clergyman's wife's face. She was about to speak when Julia added, "And my godson."

In the end, he was given a small accommodation in the cottage, one recently vacated by a young missionary from England. That night, in the darkness of their room, Morgan pulled Glory into her arms and held her as the girl lay her head on her mother's shoulder. Moonlight spread through the room and the thin, lace curtains shifted in a cooling breeze.

Morgan waited, and after a while Glory told her what happened, told all of it including the demise of Arlo Ives, the escape from thr trackers out on the Kalahari, her being dragged off by a leopard, their rescue by the Juwasi, her killing the lion and later Dunford.

"He kept chasing me," she whispered. "That's what I wanted so he would not harm my people. I think that killed him faster." She fell silent so long Morgan wondered if she'd fallen asleep. Eventually, she spoke again. "He was an evil man, Mama. It seems like some men are bad because it's just easier to be that way. But I think something in Mr. Dunford made him want to do the things he did."

"You're safe now, honey," she said. "I know you've proven you can take care of yourself, but I'm going take a mother's pride in doing that job for as long as I can."

The next day, the duke arrived with his small party and was reunited with his son. They met outside the chief clergyman's home under trees that shaded the porch. Edward hugged his son then with both hands on the boy's shoulders held him back so he could gaze upon him. The father's face shined with pride. His eyes watered. "By gad, Toby, you have grown into a young man."

He hugged his son again.

They stayed another two days then that last night before leaving for Kimberley and on to Cape Town, the missionary leaders threw the duke and his party a dinner with the entire missionary community attending.

Before going over to the main house, Glory sat in her shift at the vanity table as her mother combed her hair. She had washed it three times since they'd been in Kuruman, and it needed at least a hundred strokes to get under control. Her mother worked on it patiently with far more satisfaction than even when she cleaned her guns.

Finally, Morgan set the brush down on the table and placed both hands on her daughter's shoulders. "I have something for you."

A moment later, Morgan was dropping something down over her head onto her neck. It was her bear claw necklace with the stone arrowhead and gold cross. Of all her mother's possessions, it meant the most because it represented so much about her life. It carried a power of sorts, like a talisman. It was the only adornment she ever wore and most often when she did, it was beneath her clothing.

"You don't have to wear it," Morgan said. "But I want you to have it. I had intended to wait till you were older, but, well, clearly, now is the time."

Overwhelmed, Glory felt something swell in her chest. Her eyes watering, she glanced up and said, "Mom."

At dinner, it seemed to Morgan as if they were back in England. With all of the missionaries and their wives being from there, they believed in the hierarchy of English society almost as much as their religion. They insisted the duke sit at one end of the long table and the duchess at the other. Those two were not dressed in fancy attire, but the rough clothing they rode in wearing, washed and cleaned, yet hardly up to standards of the long-ago spring ball.

Around her neck, the duchess wore the famous Tudor Diamond, which sparkled in the lamplight. With the blue bandana covering her face, she was still the woman of mystery, the one on whom the missionaries and especially their wives fixated.

Toby and Glory were wearing borrowed clothes, she in a dress for the first time in months. But for their sun darkened skin, they appeared the proper young boy and girl, not the young savages they'd appeared to be days before. Morgan saw that her daughter was wearing the necklace she had given her outside her clothing. Another piece had been added, an old, animal bone, tarnished by the years with several notches on it. Occasionally Glory and Toby shared a knowing glance, an amused smile or burst of laughter for no discernable reason that the others could see. To Morgan, they clearly knew what the other was thinking.

Though they spoke little at the dinner party, their tale having been told many times in the last few days, toward the end of the evening, Glory clinked her glass with her spoon for attention. When the room fell silent, she addressed the duchess, "Tante Julia, you told me that you would do anything I ever asked of you."

Her eyes above the bandana suddenly wary, Julia said, "Yes?"

"You've seen the scars I bear," Glory said. "I would like to see yours. Would you remove the bandana for me?"

Though the room was already silent, the request shot tension through it like a charge of heat lightning. Her friend Julia was a formidable woman so Glory's request had taken courage.

Scowling for several seconds, the duchess stared, never blinking once. Then slowly she pulled down the bandana. She flinched at the audible gasp like a slap. Over the duchess's right cheekbone ran an ugly scar, furrowed and purple. It disappeared behind her blond hair. Her face was chiseled stone, but her eyes blazed in fury.

Glory put her hands to her own cheeks in astonishment. "My goodness, Tante Julia, only you can be shot in the face and look even more beautiful."

Amazingly, Morgan saw that it was true. Julia still maintained her otherworldly beauty, but now it was one of character, substance, and a riveting fierceness.

Her husband said, "I told you, dearest. It's indeed true."

At that, everyone broke into applause as if they'd witnessed a miracle. Morgan watched her daughter. While Julia respectfully accepted the applause, Glory turned to Toby, gave a barely perceptible nod, and he returned it. Morgan knew somewhere in God's realm Will was looking down on his daughter with a father's love and pride.

When the room finally grew silent, the duchess gave a hint of a smile. She addressed the chief reverend, "Sir, shall we finish the wine? I know you've saved the best for last."

Made in the USA
Middletown, DE
03 November 2024

63326708R00205